At that moment there was an angry call from the doorway of the room they had just left. *Ouma* Viljoen was standing in the doorway, hands on hips, the face looking out from beneath the stiffly starched Cape bonnet red and angry.

'Come in here this minute, girl. What are you thinking of, standing out here in the dark passageway with a young man – a *Retallick* at that. Haven't we had problems enough with that family? Come in here this minute, I say.'

'Yes, Ouma.' Johanna's reply was all that might have been expected from a dutiful grand-daughter, but as Johanna turned to go, she said, 'Will you come to see us again, Nat? When this war is over? When you come to visit Adam, perhaps?'

'Yes . . . But first I need to find out what's happening to Adam . . .'

'Things might be different when the war is over. Perhaps I might even be able to forgive you for fighting on the side of the *khakis*. I'll try.'

Then Johanna was gone and the door of the room in which the Viljoen family were gathered was very firmly closed.

Stricken Land

E.V. THOMPSON

sphere

SPHERE

First published in Great Britain by Macmillan London Limited in 1986
First published in paperback by Pan Books Ltd in 1988
This edition published in 1999 by Warner Bros
Reprinted 2001
Reprinted by Time Warner Books in 2005
Reissued by Sphere in 2011

A CIP catalogue record for this book
is available from the British Library.

ISBN 978-0-7515-4517-3

Printed and bound in Great Britain by
CPI Mackays, Chatham ME5 8TD

Papers used by Sphere are natural, renewable and
recyclable products sourced from well-managed forests and certified
in accordance with the rules of the Forest Stewardship Council.

Mixed Sources
Product group from well-managed
forests and other controlled sources
www.fsc.org Cert no. SGS-COC-004081
© 1996 Forest Stewardship Council

FSC

Sphere
An imprint of
Little, Brown Book Group
100 Victoria Embankment
London EC4Y 0DY

An Hachette UK Company
www.hachette.co.uk

www.littlebrown.co.uk

Dedicated to the memory of
Nelson 'Jack' Burton

GLOSSARY

The meaning of some Afrikaans words has changed to a lesser or greater extent over the last hundred years. I have attempted to give the translation most generally accepted. When in doubt, wherever possible I have sought a contemporary source.

biltong	spiced, dried meat
burgher	citizen
impi	Zulu fighting unit
inkosi	Matabele term of respect
kaross	animal-skin rug
kopje	small hill
kraal	settlement
laager	defensive camp
mombies	cattle
Oom	Uncle
Ouma	Grandmother
Oupa	Grandfather
Predikant	Preacher of Dutch Reformed Church
rinderpest	infectious cattle disease
sjambok	heavy leather whip
spruit	small stream
stoep	veranda
takhaarlen	word used to describe the 'wild' Boers from the frontier regions of N.E. Transvaal
uitlander	foreigner
veld	grassland
voortrekker	pioneer
vrou	woman

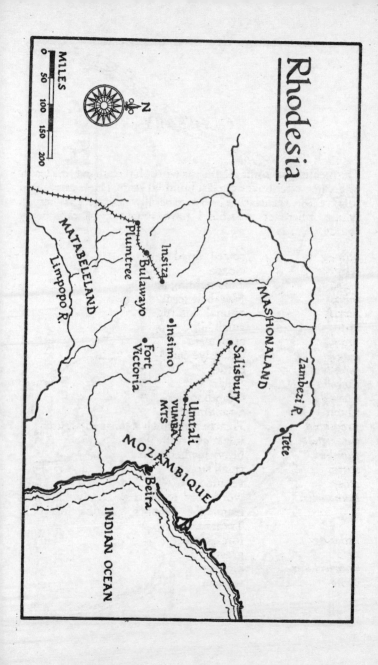

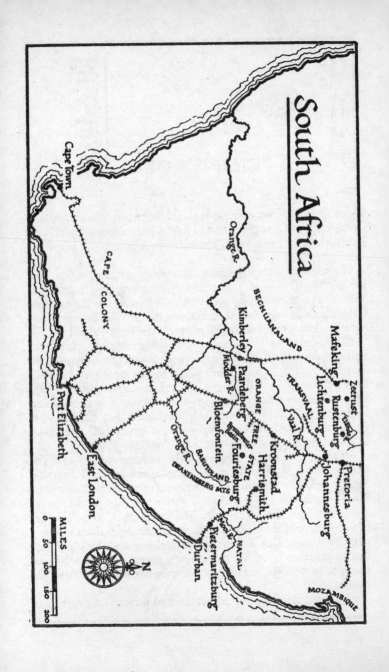

CHAPTER ONE

News that the simmering quarrel between the two Boer republics and Great Britain had flared into war reached Elvira Retallick forty-eight hours before it was forced upon her eldest son.

The message was brought to the remote Insimo valley by a British South Africa Company policeman, sent from Fort Victoria, more than fifty miles away. He rode for the last few miles through a torrential rainstorm, the first in Matabeleland for two years, and was lucky to reach the house alive.

At the entrance to the valley was a river bed. Rock-strewn and dry, water had not flowed here for as long as anyone could remember, but only seconds after the company policeman reached the far, crumbling bank a flash-flood roared down from the nearby hills. The awesome torrent of water carried with it hundreds of tons of mud and boulders, carving new gullies and straightening the ancient course of the river, devastating all before it on its route to the lowveld.

Battered and blinded by rain, the sodden rider found the Insimo farmhouse more by chance than any sense of direction and he needed to hammer at the door for a full minute before his desperate efforts were heard above the fury of the storm.

Helped into the kitchen by Elvira Retallick and Ben, her fifteen-year-old youngest son, the protesting policeman was rapidly stripped of his dripping clothing and, while Elvira fetched clothes from her eldest son's room, a servant braved the rain to lead the exhausted horse to the stables behind the house.

Not until the unexpected visitor had downed a tumbler of

brandy and stopped shaking did Elvira allow him to tell why he had defied the storm to reach Insimo.

'It's war, Mrs Retallick . . .' The shaking began again, but it owed much to excitement now. 'We received the news on the telegraph. Great Britain has been at war with the Boer republics since five o'clock last night.'

Elvira saw the excitement mirrored on her son's face and it frightened her. 'News of war should be greeted with sorrow, not rejoicing. Men will die. Good men . . . on both sides.'

The policeman looked at her with unfeigned surprise. Sadly, Elvira realised it shocked him to know not everyone welcomed the outbreak of war between Great Britain and the Boers. For many years it had seemed that war was inevitable, but the two sides had been quarrelling for so long Elvira had begun to hope it would never develop into anything more. She should have known better. Cecil Rhodes had always been possessed of a burning ambition to unite all of southern Africa under the flag of Great Britain. He was not a man to rest until he realised his ambitions – or until they killed him.

'We didn't start the war, Mrs Retallick – it was the Boers.' The young policeman spoke defensively.

'In thousands of Boer homes they'll be saying, "It isn't us who started the war, but the British." What does it matter *who* begins a war? Whoever it is, you can be quite certain they are not the ones who will need to fight it.'

Elvira Retallick had been brought to the Insimo valley from the neighbouring Portuguese province of Mozambique as a bride thirty years before, yet she still spoke with a Portuguese accent. There was a great bitterness in her voice as she said to Ben. 'Your father and your eldest brother were both killed in a war that was not of *their* making. In fact, your father did more than any man to try to *prevent* it happening. That was six years ago . . . Six long years . . .'

For a few moments Elvira lost herself in reminiscing, but she did not miss the apologetic look that passed from Ben to the other man. Suddenly brusque, she said to the policeman, 'You didn't ride all this way to listen to my views on war, or to tell us what is happening in the world. What *is* your business at Insimo?'

The company policeman looked suddenly ill-at-ease. 'I have a message for Mr Retallick . . . Nat Retallick.'

'Nat is my eldest son . . . the eldest *surviving* son. What is your business with him?'

'My message is for *him*, Mrs Retallick. From Colonel Plumer.'

'Nat is not at home. Either you tell me, or your soaking will have been for nothing. What business has this Colonel Plumer with Nat? Does he wish to buy cattle?'

'No. Er . . . when will Mr Retallick return?'

'Who can say? A week. Two weeks. A month . . .'

The policeman came to a rapid decision. 'Colonel Plumer is raising a force to protect our border with Transvaal. Mr Retallick knows the country better than anyone else. Colonel Plumer would like him to join his force, as a scout.'

'Would he, indeed? Nat runs a farm – a farm of two hundred square miles. He has no time to play at being one of this Colonel Plumer's soldiers. You can tell him so.'

'If it's all the same to you I would rather hear it from Mr Retallick himself, ma'am. This is war. His country needs him . . .'

'*His* country? *Matabeleland* is his country. Not England. Not even Rhodesia. *Matabeleland*. Nat was born here when the land was ruled by King Lobengula of the Matabele tribe. The valley was given to Nat's father by the king. Not even that robber Rhodes dared try to take it from him – although he took everything else. *Insimo* is the Retallicks' land. *Our* country. Nat is needed *here*.'

'I'll go with Colonel Plumer, Ma. I know the country as well as Nat. I'll go and scout in his place . . .'

Ben's enthusiastic outburst ceased abruptly as his mother turned her gaze upon him.

'You are barely fifteen. If you want to behave as a man go out and check the animals and outbuildings. The rain is easing off now.'

The clouds had split wide open above Insimo. Rain still fell on the house, but farther along the valley sunshine sliced to the ground, its heat raising steam from the sodden earth. Beyond the valley, where the land dropped away to the lowveld, the rain had washed the undulating hills sparkling clean and they displayed all the colours that only Africa can produce.

Elvira walked to the window and looked out. It was a view she had first seen as a young woman, standing here with her

3

husband's arms about her. In this house she had given Daniel four fine sons and the valley had prospered. When Daniel and their eldest son, Wyatt, had died at the hands of Matabele tribesmen during the war of 1893, she had raised the three surviving sons, Nat, Adam and Ben, and the valley had continued to flourish. Further native risings had not touched them. While settlers and tribesmen died in the land that stretched between the Zambezi and Limpopo rivers — now named 'Rhodesia', in honour of Cecil Rhodes — Insimo remained at peace.

Now there was another war. A war between white men whose quarrel was about lands beyond the borders of this infant country. Yet Elvira feared this conflagration threatened life at Insimo more than anything that had gone before.

'Where is Mr Retallick, ma'am? I was told to deliver my message to him personally. Is there some place where I might look for him?'

Elvira turned from the window. She had been lost in her thoughts for far longer than was polite. 'Not unless you're prepared to ride all the way to Mafeking. Nat and his brother Adam have taken five hundred head of cattle there. To Colonel Baden-Powell. He bought them, unseen, when he and Nat met in Bulawayo a month or so ago . . . Why, what's the matter?'

Elvira was suddenly concerned by the expression of consternation on the face of the young company policeman.

'To Colonel Baden-Powell, at Mafeking . . .? We had a message from Mafeking during the night. Just before the lines were cut. The Boers have attacked Baden-Powell. Mafeking is under siege . . .'

CHAPTER TWO

For two days the train carrying five hundred head of cattle from the Insimo valley coughed its way southwards through Bechuanaland, along the railway line that linked Rhodesia with the Cape Colony. It was an uncomfortable journey for man and beast alike as the line flirted with the Kalahari desert for much of the five hundred miles between Bulawayo and Mafeking. Although heavy thunderclouds were gathering in the east and would soon fill the sky, it was oppressively hot.

Crowded together in high-sided, open trucks, the cattle suffered noisily, bellowing their discomfort to an uncaring world, until heat and dust reduced them to silence. It was a hard journey for them. Nat had expected to be able to stop at night and put the cows out to graze, but there was a serious outbreak of *rinderpest* in Bechuanaland and he could not risk infecting the herd. All that could be done was to water the animals whenever the train stopped.

Perched precariously on the sides of the trucks, the Matabele herdsmen called excitedly to each other for every mile of the way. Used to calling from hilltop to hilltop, across the wide valleys of Matabeleland, their voices carried easily above the complaints of the cattle and the noise of the train.

At the rear of the train, travelling in a roofed truck that had many windows but no glass, Nat rode with two other white men and the guard. The heat was oppressive in here, but at least they had some shelter from the fierce October sun.

'How much longer do we have to put up with this?' The peevish question came from Adam Retallick. Sixteen years of age, he was almost four years younger than Nat, and not the

5

most patient of young men.

He had asked a similar question at least a dozen times during the past few hours. Nat, sitting on the floor of the jolting guard's van with his eyes closed and his head resting against the side, made no answer.

'Another three or four hours and we should be in sight of Mafeking. By the look of that sky you'll be cursing the rain by then.'

The speaker was the grizzle-bearded Jaconus Van Eyck. He was seated on the floor beside Nat, a grease-stained, soft-brimmed leather hat tilted forward, hiding his eyes, and he spoke past a pipe clenched tightly between his teeth.

Jaconus Van Eyck had been around the Insimo valley for as long as the Retallick boys could remember. A friend of their father, he had been a witness to Daniel and Wyatt's murders by Matabele tribesmen. To him had gone the sad task of bringing in the bodies of father and son and burying them at Insimo, where Jaconus's own son was buried.

Jaconus Van Eyck was an Afrikaner. A Boer. In his younger days he had been a true *voortrekker*, a man to whom all artificial frontiers were anathema and settled communities places to be avoided. During the course of his life he had fought and killed natives in half-a-dozen tribal wars. He had also fought and killed white men, both English and Afrikaner. Jaconus Van Eyck was the product of a violent age, raised on the veld, where death was as constant a companion as a man's own shadow. In spite of this, the bearded Boer was a soft-spoken man, his manner deceptively gentle. His loyalty to his friends was beyond question. When Daniel Retallick was killed Jaconus Van Eyck had taken on the burden of running the Insimo valley. Gradually, over the years, the burden had passed to Nat, but Jaconus Van Eyck stayed on in the valley, a loved and trusted friend and adviser to the Retallick family.

'You been to Mafeking before, Jaconus?'

It was the first time Nat had spoken for more than an hour.

'Not for some years.' Jaconus Van Eyck removed his pipe and knocked ash out of the nearest window. 'It's just a collection of tin-roofed houses. Knee-deep in mud when it rains. Dust enough to choke you when it's dry. Not the sort of place a man needs to see more than once.'

6

Nat grinned. Jaconus Van Eyck would have been no more enthusiastic about Cape Town, or even London. Jaconus would always remain a *voortrekker* at heart. The sight of more than two houses placed close together pained him.

Not so Adam. Having lived in the lonely Insimo valley for the whole of his young life, there was a magical quality about even the smallest of towns. He was about to reply heatedly to Jaconus Van Eyck's derogatory remark when the occupants of the guard's van were suddenly thrown off balance as the engine driver applied his brakes violently. Truck slammed against truck as the heavy chains joining them together sagged.

Cursing the engine-driver's unexpected action, the guard dived upon the huge wheel mounted on a drive shaft at the back of the van and began turning it with some difficulty. The wheels beneath the floor of the guard's van squealed in protest as the heavy leather pads of the brakes began to bite.

'What the hell's going on?'

Nat struggled to his feet, bracing himself against the violent movement of the train. Clinging to the edge of the window, he peered ahead, beyond the curving length of the train.

'There's someone waving us down.'

A hundred yards ahead of the engine a horseman sat waving a dark-coloured cloak, at the same time trying to control his horse. The animal became more unmanageable with every yard that the hissing, squealing locomotive skidded along the tracks towards it. Finally the horseman was forced to drop the cloak and use both hands to bring his prancing horse under control. But his signalling had served its purpose. The train juddered to a halt when there were still a dozen yards of clear track between train and rider.

From the rear of the train, passengers and guard could see the train-driver and the mounted man in animated conversation, while the African fireman took advantage of the welcome respite to squat wearily on the footplate. As they spoke, the horseman frequently pointed ahead to where the tracks disappeared beyond a slight rise in the hazy distance.

'It seems something's happened at Mafeking. We'd better go and find out what it is.' Jaconus Van Eyck dropped from the guard's van to the ground and started towards the locomotive. Nat, Adam and the guard followed suit.

By the time the men reached the locomotive there was already a crowd of inquisitive Matabele herdsmen around the horseman.

'What's happening?' Nat called out the question as he reached the circle of herdsmen and pushed his way through them.

'War's started between the Boers and the British. The Boers have torn up the track and put Mafeking under siege.' The engine driver could hardly contain his excitement. 'Had we carried on we'd have gone clear off the end of the track and ended up dead – or maybe prisoners of the Boers.'

'Is this true?'

The horseman was not certain whether he needed to repeat his information to the young man standing before him. Dressed for herding cattle, and with a bandolier of Mauser cartridges slung across one shoulder, Nat looked no different from the hordes of Boer horsemen who had swooped upon Mafeking from across the Transvaal border, only a few miles away.

'My name's Retallick.' Nat could see the man's reluctance to speak. 'These are my cattle in the trucks. I'm taking them to Colonel Baden-Powell.'

All doubt left the mounted man's face. 'I'm Trooper Ducket, of Nesbitt's Horse . . .' The speaker hesitated. When speaking to the engine-driver he had exaggerated the dangers of the situation. Now he thought the occasion demanded the full truth. 'The line *is* cut, about seven miles on – and Mafeking *is* besieged, but the only Boers I've seen on the way here were in the distance, heading south. They appeared to be going *around* Mafeking. When the war started we were waiting for a train to reach us from the Cape, bringing guns and ammunition. Rumour has it that General De la Rey intends capturing it for the Boers. He'll get a shock if he tries. The train is armoured, with British troops on board . . .'

'De la Rey? I wonder if that's Koos De la Rey?'

'I don't know. All I know is he's a Boer general.' The horseman looked at Jaconus Van Eyck suspiciously. 'Do you know him?'

Jaconus Van Eyck met the other man's eyes. 'I know him well. Koos De la Rey is one of the finest men I've ever met – British or Boer. I also know he's always been against this war. If he's finally chosen to fight then the British have a fight on their hands,

8

by God – and God is the only one who Koos De la Rey fears.'

'Is there going to be fighting? Are we going to see a battle between the Boers and the English?' Adam asked the question eagerly.

'Not if I can help it. We will deliver the cattle and then clear out for home.'

Nat spoke to the horseman again. 'How far is it to Mafeking from the spot where the rail is cut?'

The soldier shrugged his shoulders. 'Four miles. Five, maybe.'

'And no Boers to talk of . . .' Nat was thinking. He looked at the bank of black storm-clouds towering high in the sky to the east of the railway line and turned to Jaconus Van Eyck. 'When do you think that storm will break?'

The bearded Boer looked up at the bank of dark cloud, his finger absent-mindedly tamping tobacco in the large bowl of his thornwood pipe. 'Hour or two, maybe. But it won't be much. Might even miss us altogether.'

'We'll take that chance.' Nat made up his mind. Returning his attentions to the mounted man, he said, 'I'll take the cattle as far as the line goes, then try to run them into Mafeking. Will you act as our guide?'

The soldier looked startled. 'You'll never succeed. One man on a horse . . . perhaps. A herd of cattle and half a tribe of natives . . .? No chance. Besides, my orders are to ride north-wards until I meet up with Colonel Plumer's men and report on what's happening in Mafeking.'

Dismissing the uncooperative horseman from his scheme, Nat appealed to the engine-driver. 'Will you go on towards Mafeking?'

'I'll go as far as there's track to run on – but one of you will need to sit up on top of the engine and give me plenty of warning when we're nearing the end of the line.'

'I'll do that,' Adam volunteered eagerly. After a moment's hesitation, Nat nodded.

Ten minutes later the train moved off slowly and cautiously. Adam was balanced precariously on a small platform at the front, his arm crooked about the handrail which ran the full length of the engine. He was smarting because Nat had refused to allow him to carry his rifle. Nat was taking no chances with

9

his impetuous younger brother. A Boer marksman was likely to shoot an armed man and query his age afterwards.

They had been travelling for an hour when Adam suddenly shouted and pointed ahead of the slow moving train. The engine driver tugged at the great brake handle, and with locked wheels screeching in protest the cattle train came to a sliding, rattling halt.

Fifty yards further on the railway line came to an abrupt end and only the heavy wooden sleepers showed the direction the railway line had once taken. The rails had been unbolted and moved away. Some of the lines lay nearby on the veld. Others had been dragged far away and buried.

The dark storm-clouds had lowered now and visibility to the south was no more than a half-mile, but the rain had not yet arrived. Neither had the Boers, and Nat decided to go ahead with his plan, such as it was. He intended driving the cattle along the line to Mafeking. If they met up with any Boers along the way he would stampede the cattle and hope to escape in the ensuing confusion. However, Nat hoped the rain would arrive before then and drive any Boers in the vicinity to shelter.

At first Nat's plan went smoothly as the rain moved in a mighty wall of water towards them. All three men had water-proof coats in their bags and they donned them just before the rainstorm reached them.

The first heavy drops gave the riders warning to pull their hats down low over their faces before the main belt of rain struck them with brutal force. For about ten minutes they rode on blindly. Then, as suddenly as the rain had begun, there was a lull as a break appeared in the clouds overhead.

To Nat's alarm he discovered they were not alone on the veld. About twenty mounted men were riding towards them. Heavily bearded, they wore crossed ammunition bandoliers over their coats and each man carried a rifle. Nat did not need to be told he was looking at a Boer commando.

The commando changed direction and headed for Jaconus Van Eyck, who was riding on the right flank of the scattered cattle.

Nat's heart sank. It was the sheerest bad luck. Another few minutes and they would have passed the commando unnoticed in the noise and darkness of the storm.

The Boer commando gathered about Jaconus Van Eyck and Nat turned his horse towards them. He wondered what the Boers would do with the men from Insimo. They would confiscate the cattle, certainly. They might also make the three Insimo men their prisoners.

As Nat neared the group one of the Boers said something to Jaconus Van Eyck and pointed to the south-east, away from the line of the rails. Then, with a cheery wave in Nat's direction, the Boer turned his horse and led his men away, riding hunched in the saddle, his head turned away from the rain which was moving in once more.

Nat kneed his horse forward to Jaconus Van Eyck's side. 'What's happening? I thought we'd lost the cattle, at least.' Nat needed to shout as the wind snatched at his words.

'I said we were delivering these *mombies* to Koos De la Rey. They told me he was farther to the east.'

There was a twinkle of amusement in Jaconus Van Eyck's eyes, but when he spoke it was with great seriousness. 'We were lucky, Nat. *Very* lucky. If it hadn't been for the rain they wouldn't have been in such a hurry to move on. As it is, they're likely to run across the train and guess the truth. We'd better get into Mafeking as quickly as we can.'

Nat nodded – rain was coming down hard again now. 'Keep them moving . . . I'll tell Adam . . .'

Most of his words were snatched away by the wind, but detailed instructions were unnecessary. Jaconus Van Eyck knew what needed to be done.

It was not easy to keep the cattle together in the storm, but they managed somehow, and quite suddenly the three men and the herd from Insimo rode out of the rain into brilliant sunshine. The veld was not even damp here. It was a phenomenon all three men had experienced before on the vast plains of Africa.

'Keep them moving.' Jaconus Van Eyck shouted the words as the cattle began to slow. He pointed to the horizon, to one side of the dark cliff of rain. A couple of miles away a long file of horsemen was cantering towards them. From the way they rode it was apparent they were armed burghers, citizens of the nearby Boer republic of Transvaal.

But the cattle drive was almost over. Close as were the

Boers, Mafeking was closer. An untidy, dusty cluster of tin-roofed houses, it looked as though it had suddenly sprung, mushroom-fashion, from the ground on which it stood. There was a network of railway lines to one side of the town, silent evidence that this had once been an important railway centre.

Between the Insimo men and the town were a great many African huts, loosely grouped into two untidy villages. Nat drove the cattle towards the gap between the villages, forcing the reluctant animals to a trot.

He had scant time to notice the consternation in the villages. He could hear a new sound above the drumming of the hooves now, as though someone was firing at them — but the sound seemed to be coming from Mafeking! This belief was confirmed when Nat saw a couple of the leading cattle pitch to the ground, the remaining animals forking past their bodies.

Then they were among houses and men were waving and gesticulating in front of the tiring cattle. The stampede came to an end as cattle turned back upon cattle, and minutes later the whole herd was milling about in bemused confusion.

'We did it!' Nat shouted his delight, but his jubilation was short-lived. Even as he swung down from his horse and removed his waterproof coat, a thick-set, red-faced man in a khaki uniform, with the insignia of a captain on his sleeve, ran past, a number of soldiers carrying rifles close behind him.

The soldiers dropped to one knee in the gap between the huts and began firing at the Boer horsemen who had stopped about a half-mile away. Declining to return the fire, the Boers rode off without suffering any casualties and the uniformed captain hurried back to the men from Insimo.

Puffing heavily, he stopped before Jaconus Van Eyck. 'Are you in charge of . . . of *these*?'

The captain raised an arm in the direction of the cattle and Nat glimpsed a wide stain of damp perspiration spreading out from his armpit.

'The cattle are mine. I've just brought them from the Insimo valley, in Matabeleland.'

Nat might have said the cattle had been shifted from adjacent grazing-land for all the impact his words made on the perspiring captain.

'Do you realise you've just driven your cattle through a

minefield? It took us three days to lay those mines and map the area. Three wasted days! Not to mention the gap you've created in the town's defences.'

'I think that what the captain is trying to say is, "Thank you for bringing your cattle more than five hundred miles by rail, then running them through the lines of a besieging army, in order that Mafeking might hold out for another week or two." Isn't this what you're trying to say?' Adam looked angrily at the British officer.

'It doesn't matter, Adam. See if you can find some water for the cattle.'

Turning back to the red-faced British captain, Nat said, 'Perhaps you'll get word to Colonel Baden-Powell that Nat Retallick has delivered his order. When we've got a receipt we'll see about going home again.'·

His anger seeping away, the British army captain watched Nat walk away and his mind recalled what had been said. 'Nat Retallick . . . from Matabeleland?'

'That's right, Captain. Too far away to be involved in your little war down here. As Nat said, we'll leave you to it just as soon as we've handed over responsibility for five hundred head of prime cattle — and we're including those shot by your sharpshooters,' said Adam.

Colonel Robert Stephenson Smyth Baden-Powell called the three men from Insimo to his headquarters later that evening. A dapper, military-looking man, Baden-Powell sported a heavy black moustache that was immaculately trimmed. No more enthusiastic than his captain, he casually thanked the three men for delivering the cattle to him. He might have been a city householder accepting a delivery from a butcher's boy.

The attitude of the military commander of Mafeking incensed Adam in particular. He was particularly indignant that no one had expressed a word of gratitude for their resourcefulness in running cattle through the Boer lines to a 'starving' and beleaguered township.

Jaconus Van Eyck was more philosophical. 'At least the colonel didn't make us pay for the mines we exploded on the way in.'

A hotel room had been allocated to the three men by Baden-

Powell's adjutant, who also informed them they were to eat in the officers' mess that evening. Unfortunately Colonel Baden-Powell would not be there. He always dined privately in another hotel with a few of his staff officers. Among these were Major Lord Edward Cecil and Captain Gordon Wilson – whose wife, Lady Sarah, one of the Churchill family, had been ordered from Mafeking immediately before the siege had commenced.

Nat was astonished at the size of the meal set before him in the officers' mess and served by uniformed African waiters. There was no hint of a food shortage, neither was there any attempt at economy. It was a sumptuous and varied meal such as none of the three had eaten for a very long time, and was washed down with wine or champagne, depending upon the whim of the diner.

When Nat commented on the apparent abundance of food, one of the British officers explained that Colonel Baden-Powell had anticipated the siege. He had stocked the town's warehouses with everything the town might need to sustain them during the weeks ahead.

'So I needn't have bothered to bring my cattle into Mafeking? I might as well have taken them back to Insimo?'

'I wouldn't say that, old chap,' said an officer of the Mafeking Town Guard, waving for an African servant to refill his glass. 'We'd have found ourselves damn short of fresh meat had you not brought them in. Mind you, I doubt if Captain Nelley will ever forgive you for showing up the weakness of his precious minefield. It was his boast that it would kill the whole Boer army if they tried to take Mafeking!'

Walking back to the hotel with Jaconus Van Eyck and Adam after the meal, Nat repeated what he had said to the Mafeking Town Guard officer. 'We'd have been better taking our cattle home again as soon as we learned the line was cut. Baden-Powell doesn't need them. We took too many risks for nothing. Now we have to try to return home having stirred up the Boers.'

'Mafeking *will* need those *mombies*, you mark my words. Everyone here is talking as though Koos De la Rey's burghers will pack up and go home in a week or two. That's not going to happen. Koos and his men will stay until they're driven off –

and whoever tries that will have one hell of a fight on his hands. All the same, don't expect Colonel Baden-Powell to acknowledge that Insimo cattle might have tipped the scales in his favour. He's sending out reports filled with stories of how he and his brave men are holding out against a strong enemy that has him trapped inside Mafeking. He'd look pretty foolish if word got out that three men drove a herd of five hundred cattle into Mafeking without a shot being fired – by the Boers, that is.'

'As far as I'm concerned they can play at war as much as they like. Tomorrow we head back to Insimo and forget about both sides. I only hope the driver is holding that train. If it's gone we're going to have a long ride.'

The next morning the three men were awakened by the sound of rifle fire from somewhere just outside the town. The shooting went on for some time, punctuated at intervals by the more persistent stutter of a Maxim gun.

Nat dressed hurriedly and went outside accompanied by Adam. Many of the town's residents were already on the dusty street, together with Mafeking's motley array of defenders. Word quickly went around that Colonel Baden-Powell had sent out a raiding-party to attack a Boer fort being constructed close to the town.

The firing continued for about an hour before the small raiding-party straggled back to Mafeking, carrying dead and wounded with them. Among them Nat recognised a young officer with whom he had been talking the previous evening. Recognition was not easy. A soft-nosed bullet from a Boer Mauser had shattered the cheekbone on the left side of the officer's face. Bloody and loose-jawed, he was supported by a soldier on either side. Legs dragging in the dust, he was mercifully unconscious. At this moment war lost its sense of unreality for Nat Retallick.

He turned to follow the progress of the wounded and disfigured officer and caught a glimpse of the unguarded expression on the face of Adam. Nat was shaken to see a fierce pleasure there.

As the eyes of the two brothers met, Adam's chin came up in aggressive defiance. 'Perhaps this has taught the British a lesson. Now they might stay earthed up in their holes and keep their hands off a country that doesn't belong to them.'

'You're talking about British soldiers, Adam. *Our* people.'

'They're not *my* people – nor yours. We were born in Matabeleland long before Rhodes came to claim the country for Britain. The British would have taken our valley too if Pa hadn't been too clever for them. You know it's the truth.'

'You're forgetting Pa was British.'

'*No!*' Adam spoke fiercely. 'Pa was the same as us. The British treated him as an *uitlander* . . .' Adam deliberately used the Afrikaans word for 'foreigner'. '. . . We owe *nothing* to the British – unless it's the death of Wyatt and Pa.'

'We're just as much *uitlanders* to the burghers of South Africa, and will be no matter how hard we might try. Just keep such thoughts to yourself while we're in Mafeking.'

Neither brother had seen Jaconus Van Eyck's approach. He had heard Adam's indiscreet outburst and now said, 'The best thing we can do is get out of Mafeking as quickly as possible. There are dead and wounded here now and anti-Boer feeling is running high. If any of the townsmen hear Adam talk like that, he'll be lynched.'

But leaving Mafeking was not to be as simple as Nat had hoped. Baden-Powell's foray against his besiegers stirred the burghers to angry retaliation. Snipers ensconced in the surrounding countryside fired at anything that moved in the straight, wide streets of Mafeking.

Nat was told there could be no question of his party leaving that day. They would have to wait until the following day. It would be Sunday and it was believed the deeply religious Boers were unlikely to continue fighting on the Sabbath.

Nat was anxious to reach the train as quickly as possible, but he reluctantly agreed that any attempt to leave Mafeking in the present climate might well prove fatal for them all. They would remain for another day.

That night the Boers brought one of their big guns into action against the tiny town. It was a 75mm Creusot, purchased from France when the Boers realised war with Great Britain was likely. Manned by German-trained artillerymen, the gun was sited some three miles from the vulnerable township and lobbed shells with frightening accuracy amongst the tin-roofed houses.

The first shell crashed into the open street not fifty yards from where Nat, Adam and Jaconus Van Eyck were seated inside their hotel room. Glass shattered everywhere and all the movable objects in the room crashed to the floor as a wave of hot air and dust swept in through the broken window.

Outside, the residents of Mafeking ran for cover in the underground shelters prepared weeks before by order of Colonel Baden-Powell. By the time the second shell landed the three men from Insimo were the only white men above ground, sharing the dubious honour with a few hundred terrified Bantu servants.

The bombardment marked the end of Nat's patience with the difficult situation in which he and the others found themselves. When the third shell landed, farther away this time, Nat began stuffing his few possessions into a saddle-bag, angrily telling the others to do the same.

'Where we going, Nat? We going to find ourselves a shelter?'

'We're going home. I've had enough of being caught in the middle of a war that's none of our making. We're going back where we belong. To Insimo.'

Chewing on the end of his pipe, Jaconus Van Eyck said, 'I can't help thinking you're over-simplifying things – but I'm not arguing. I never have enjoyed being in a town, and this one has less to recommend it than most I've known. Do you have a plan?'

'Only that as soon as it's completely dark we'll ride out of Mafeking, heading north.'

'How about Captain Nelley's mines?'

'They've only been laid *between* the African compounds. We'll go straight to a compound and out the other side – the same way the Boers will come in, when they want to. All we have to do then is find the railway line and follow it until we reach the train.'

'Like I said before, it's all *too* easy. But let's get to the stables and find our horses before I can think up a reason for staying.'

CHAPTER THREE

An hour later the three Insimo men were leading their horses away from the European houses of Mafeking in the darkness, heading for one of the compounds occupied by the Africans who worked in and about the town.

There had been no shelling for twenty minutes and the occupants of Mafeking were beginning to emerge from their shelters. Calling to each other in the darkness, their voices expressed both relief and elation at having survived the enemy's first bombardment.

A picquet of the Mafeking Town Guard was positioned on the outskirts of the town, close to the compound, but no attempt was made to stop the three men, whispered good wishes following them into the night.

Carefully skirting the low burning cooking-fires, Nat led his companions into the darkness beyond, still leading the horses.

There was no moon yet, and few stars. Rain had missed Mafeking so far, but storm-clouds still curtained much of the sky and the night was as black as Nat could have wished. It took the men only a short while to find the railway line, and once there the going was easier.

They had been walking for forty minutes when Nat pulled his horse to a sudden halt. He had heard a sound from somewhere ahead. Behind him, the others demanded to know what was happening. After a whispered conversation Nat handed the reins of his horse to Jaconus Van Eyck and crept forward slowly and cautiously.

Nat's caution was fully justified. The track curved gently around a hillside and he had not gone far when he saw the twinkling of camp-fires in a hollow only a couple of hundred yards from where he had left the others. Then from somewhere much closer Nat heard a man coughing. The sound was accompanied by a shower of sparks as a pipe was carelessly knocked out against a steel railway line, the sound ringing for a hundred yards in each direction.

'Hendrik! What the hell you doing, man? You ringing a bloody supper gong for them *khakis* to come running?' The questions were in Afrikaans, the language of the Boers. '*Khakis*' was the name given to the British soldiers, a reference to the uniforms with which they had been issued for this war.

'If you gave up smoking that pipe you wouldn't need to beat hell out of the railway line every half-hour. What you smoking in it, anyway? It smells like kaffir cow-dung.'

'How would you know, eh? You Johannesburg boys have lived in a town so long you wouldn't know a kaffir cow from an elephant . . .'

Nat backed away from the Boer sentries. He had learned all he wanted to know. There was a large Boer encampment astride the railway line. He would need to lead the others on a detour.

Re-tracing their footsteps in the darkness, Nat and his companions left the railway line at a point where there was a shallow valley which they hoped might eventually take them to the opposite side of the hill from the Boers.

The hill was barely discernible in the darkness and they had hardly begun to skirt its lower slopes when they felt the first drops of rain from yet another of the localised storms that swept the highveld during the rainy season.

Struggling to don his waterproof coat in the darkness, Adam said grumpily, 'They were complaining in Mafeking about having no rain. They should move the town a mile or two this way.'

'Be grateful,' replied Nat. 'The rain helped us to give the Boers the slip before. Hopefully it will do the same for us tonight. Just keep together and don't get lost.'

The three men mounted their horses now, allowing the animals to pick their own way around the hill in the darkness.

They began the detour with the wind and rain at their backs and it made travelling far easier. However, when they had been riding for about an hour and the wind was still blowing them on their way, Nat became uneasy.

Waiting for the others to catch up, he said, 'I think we've made a mistake. We should be rounding the hill if we're to find the railway line again.'

'I agree.' Jaconus Van Eyck sat hunched in the saddle, rain pouring from the limp brim of his felt hat, a pipe clenched upside down between his teeth. 'We'll need to swing to the north-east pretty soon.'

'I think we should find somewhere to shelter until it's light.' Adam was wet and irritable. Rain had seeped beneath his oilskin and he was sitting a wet and uncomfortable saddle.

'Time enough to think of resting when we've found the train,' said Nat unsympathetically. 'Unless you want to be taken by the Boers?'

He swung his horse away and Adam's disgruntled reply was lost in the wind-swept darkness.

Putting their horses to the hill, the three Insimo men began travelling with the wind beating against the side of their faces. Nat had hoped they might be able to follow a gentle slope around the hill, but the going became steeper as they climbed higher and eventually he was forced to dismount, the others following suit.

They had been climbing steadily through increasingly rocky terrain when the rain suddenly ceased, and now the three men heard a new sound. It was the noise of fiercely running water. Minutes later they encountered a fast-flowing river which cut the hillside in front of them. It was too dark to see how wide or how deep the river was, but the noise made by the water left them in no doubt of the dangers of attempting a crossing.

'We'll have to climb the *kopje* and hope we can get beyond the source of the river,' said Jaconus Van Eyck. 'Although at the rate this water's flowing it might prove to be quite a climb.'

'We won't be able to go much higher. It's becoming too steep for the horses. Besides, if it's as high as I believe it to be we're likely to find a Boer look-out at the top.'

'So we go down again . . .?' There was the brief flicker of a flame as Jaconus Van Eyck crouched in the shelter of a pile of tumbled boulders and lit his pipe.

Nat nodded reluctantly. 'We go down.'

'I don't see why we can't go straight along the railway line and tell the burghers where we're going,' protested Adam irritably. 'They're not at war with *us*.'

'Matabeleland is part of Rhodesia now. Administered by Rhodes's Chartered Company on behalf of the British Crown. That makes us British as far as the Boers are concerned. Not only that, we've just given Mafeking the means to hold out against them for another week or two. They're hardly likely to give us a pat on the back and send us on our way with a warning to be good boys in future. No, we'll keep well clear of them.'

The wet and despondent men followed the river to the valley whence they had come, only to find it joined by another river too wide and deep to ford. They were forced to follow the river for another two hours before a change in the sound of the fast-running water told them of shallows. Tentatively, Nat edged his way across, discovering to his relief that the water seldom rose higher than his horse's belly.

When they were all across, Jaconus Van Eyck commented, 'That's a man-made crossing. The chances are there's a farm hereabouts.'

'Then we'd better find it and learn where we are,' declared Nat. 'We're hopelessly lost. For all I know we might have doubled back on ourselves.'

Half an hour later the sky had lightened sufficiently for them to find wagon tracks on the veld, and soon they saw a farmhouse in the distance. Half-hidden by trees, the farm was little more than a stone shack with a wood roof, surrounded by an assortment of mud and stone outhouses, some larger than the farmhouse itself.

Jaconus Van Eyck dismounted and went to the door while the others stood back. The chances were that a farm so far removed from civilisation would be occupied by a Boer family, one of many who had trekked northwards with the founders of the Orange Free State – and kept on trekking in order to escape from all forms of governmental interference. Similar homesteads were to be found loosely dotted across the vast veld of southern Africa.

It was early, but the door of the homestead was standing open. The day began at dawn and ended at dusk on such farms. The *voortrekkers* and their descendants lived simple, frugal lives. Candles were for emergencies and it was doubtful whether the family possessed a lamp.

Jaconus Van Eyck knocked on the door and it was answered by a tall, thin woman. She held a grubby, naked baby in her arms and two more clung to the skirts of her drab, rough-spun, brown dress. She was probably not yet twenty-five years of age, but the woman's face already had the lined, washed-out appearance of a *vrou* who had been exposed to too much harsh, highveld weather and had known too many years of annual child-bearing.

Doffing his hat as though he might have been addressing the mistress of the smartest town-house, Jaconus Van Eyck asked the woman if she could direct him to the railway line that ran northwards, to Rhodesia.

After a moment's hesitation, the woman shook her head. 'I cannot help you.'

Jaconus Van Eyck did not believe her. She was being deliberately unhelpful. 'We got ourselves lost during the night. Which direction is Mafeking? How far?'

Looking past Jaconus Van Eyck to where Nat and Adam stood with the horses, the Boer woman shook her head.

'We are also hungry, wet and cold. Would you have food – and fodder for the horses?'

The woman shifted her gaze back to Jaconus Van Eyck. Tipping her head very slightly in the direction of Nat and Adam, she asked a one-word question. '*Uitlanders?*'

The word meant 'foreigners'. It was used by the Boers to describe anyone whose mother tongue was not Afrikaans, the language of those who could claim descent from the early Dutch, Huguenot and German settlers.

'We're from Matabeleland,' Jaconus Van Eyck persisted. 'We're trying to get back there. The railway . . .'

The woman's glance shifted again and suddenly her expression of sullen ignorance became one of triumph.

Swinging around, Nat was dismayed to see a number of bearded men emerging from the large, stone-walled barn. Each man wore at least one bandolier of cartridges, most had two. They also carried rifles and the guns were pointing at the men from Insimo. Nat and his companions had been unfortunate enough to find an isolated farmhouse where a Boer commando had sought shelter from the rains of the night.

The rifles were removed from the Insimo men's horses and they were ordered to mount. Protest was useless. The corporal in charge of the Boer commando was dour and uncommunicative. Nat, Adam and Jaconus Van Eyck were prisoners – and this was all they needed to know.

Surrounded by men of the Boer commando, the three men were escorted from the remote farm. As they passed the house door the woman, still surrounded by her young family, glared malevolently at Jaconus Van Eyck and spat out a single word.

The word was . . . 'Traitor'.

CHAPTER FOUR

The three men from Insimo were taken to the large Boer encampment Nat had seen the previous evening. After riding all night they were still no more than four miles from Mafeking.

News of their capture was shouted ahead of them by the escort and all the encamped burghers came out to see the prisoners.

A great deal of vilification was directed at Jaconus Van Eyck. His heavy beard and mode of dress marked him as a Boer and his arrest in the company of two *uitlanders* branded him an unforgivable traitor. Jaconus seemed unperturbed at the anger of his fellow countrymen. He had been allowed to keep his pipe and with this gently smoking in his mouth he rode easily, hunched in the saddle in the manner of a man who had spent much of his life there.

Although the camp had not been here when Nat and his companions brought their cattle from Rhodesia, it was apparently intended that it should remain for the duration of the siege. Many makeshift dwellings had been constructed from blankets and sticks and there were a number of tents and many canvas-topped, high-wheeled wagons.

Nat was surprised to see many women about the camp. Wearing long, shapeless, home-made dresses of wool or nankeen together with full-length pinafores and bonnets shading their faces, the women gave the camp the air of a picnic outing. But the rifles carried by the men, or stacked close to their camp-fires, provided a constant reminder that this camp was occupied by men who were at war.

If any further reminder was needed, it was provided later the same morning. Guarded by four boys, the oldest of whom was only Adam's age, the three prisoners sat beside a fire in the centre of the camp while a council was held to decide their future.

As they waited, one of the Boers with a wagon sent them coffee to drink. It was carried to the prisoners by the man's daughter, and beneath the bonnet Nat glimpsed a young face with dark, alert eyes. She must have been no more than fifteen years of age.

Taking the coffee, he said, 'Please thank your father. We have had nothing to eat or drink since yesterday.'

'Johanna! I said you could take coffee, not talk to them. Come here at once, girl.'

Without a word the girl hurried away. When she reached her family's wagon she began an animated conversation with her father and mother. After a while the man nodded his head and walked away. The two women then busied themselves over the cooking-fire. Fifteen minutes later the girl returned to the prisoners carrying a dish on which was re-heated mutton, bread and hot mealie meal.

'Bless you, Johanna. You're an angel.' Nat took the dish from her eagerly, suddenly aware of how hungry he was.

If the girl was taken aback by Nat's use of her name she did not allow it to show. 'It's nothing. I wouldn't allow even a captive animal to starve.'

Jaconus Van Eyck choked on the piece of bread he had taken to his mouth, 'I reckon that puts you firmly in your place . . . Knowing you mean as much to that young lady as some captive animal.'

'You should be *grateful* to her, not making fun.'

Adam's admiring glance had been following Johanna as she walked away, and he spoke so fiercely that Nat looked at his younger brother in surprise. The expression on Adam's face made Nat bite back a flippant reply.

There were no young girls at Insimo and the distances involved meant the Retallicks rarely paid a visit to any of Rhodesia's towns. Adam had met very few white girls of his own age and it was evident that this young Afrikaner girl had bowled him over completely.

'You're right, Adam. She's a nice girl. I *am* grateful to her.'

Jaconus Van Eyck had listened to the exchange with equal sympathy and he smiled over Adam's head at Nat. Adam never noticed. His eyes were on Johanna as she busied herself around her father's wagon.

Nat felt sorry for his younger brother. Adam had chosen the daughter of one of his captors to be his first love.

He was given little time to ponder the problem. The three prisoners were still eating when their captors returned, and the Boers wasted little time on niceties.

'On your feet. You're to be taken before Field-Cornet Lemmer.'

The Insimo men put up no argument. Nat was anxious to have the matter of their arrest cleared up as quickly as possible. There was work to be done at Insimo. Work that young Ben could not undertake alone.

Nat expected the Boers to ask awkward questions and persuading them to accept his answers might take time. Nevertheless, he did not doubt for one moment that the Boers *would* eventually accept his explanation. Baden-Powell had bought his cattle and had paid for them. Nat had been under an obligation to deliver them, as promised.

'You . . . and you,' Field-Cornet Ignatius Lemmer's short, stubby forefinger jabbed first at Nat, then at Adam. 'Why aren't you wearing uniform?'

'Uniform?' Nat was puzzled. 'What uniform?'

'Don't play games with me. Army uniform. *British* army uniform. Without it you can be shot on sight . . . but you know this, of course?'

'I am not a British soldier and never have been. My name is Nat Retallick and I farm the Insimo valley in Matabeleland. This is my brother Adam. I demand you release us to go our own way. There's work to be carried out on a farm at this time of year, as you may know . . .'

'You *demand*? You are accused of spying yet you *demand*?'

Suddenly Field-Cornet Lemmer turned his full attention upon Adam. 'You . . . What *are* you doing here?'

'We brought some cattle down to Mafeking for Colonel Baden-Powell . . .'

Adam was tired and had been caught off-guard, but Nat

winced at his brother's imprudence.

Field-Cornet Lemmer looked triumphant. 'As it happens, we know all about you and your cattle. We also know that one of you –' he rounded on Jaconus Van Eyck – 'it must have been you – told my men the cattle were for Commandant De la Rey. You lied. You're an Afrikaner, Van Eyck. But you're working with the British against your own people. Delivering beef to help British soldiers – the *khakis* – while we are fighting for our very existence. You're a traitor, Van Eyck. We shoot traitors . . .'

'Jaconus Van Eyck takes his orders from *me* – and we are from Matabeleland. None of us has anything to do with this war. We didn't even know there *was* a war until we reached the broken railway line.'

Field-Cornet Lemmer ignored Nat's outburst. 'You've heard what I've said to you, Van Eyck. Is there anything you wish to say before I have you taken away and shot?'

The sharp intake of breath from the listening burghers told Nat more clearly than any words that Field-Cornet Ignatius Lemmer was in deadly earnest. The bad dream had suddenly become a nightmare.

'You can't . . .' Nat began, but Jaconus Van Eyck was already speaking.

'Before you do anything we'll both regret, I suggest you speak to Koos De la Rey. He might not agree with you.'

There was a stir of interest from the assembled burghers that the Field-Cornet could not ignore. 'You know General De la Rey?'

'I've fought kaffirs with him a time or two – and with *Oom* Paul too.'

'*Oom* Paul' was the affectionate name given by the Transvaalers to their president, Paul Kruger. As Jaconus Van Eyck had anticipated, the mention of the Transvaal president's name shook Field-Cornet Lemmer's confidence.

Before the war Ignatius Lemmer had lived a very humdrum life. Most of the men in his commando were farmers, but Lemmer owned a general store. Like every other burgher between the ages of sixteen and sixty, he was obliged to belong to a commando. He had been elected to the post of field-cornet for no other reason than that he could read, write and keep records. He was also an unmarried man, able to devote time to the organisation demanded of someone in such a responsible post. When the order for mobilisation had been received from the Transvaal government, Lemmer had ridden from farm to farm, personally notifying each man in his commando.

Being a field-cornet was not an easy task, especially for Lemmer, who was not a natural leader. Each man under his command retained the right to question every order he was given, and the last few days had not been good ones for Ignatius Lemmer. He had seen his authority steadily eroded from every quarter. The burghers were beginning to carry out their duties as they saw fit, without even consulting their field-cornet. Lemmer believed that the execution of a traitor on *his* orders would restore his waning authority and assure him of new respect in the community to which he would one day return.

'I doubt if either *Oom* Paul or Commandant De la Rey would care to be reminded that they once knew you . . .'

'Shut it, Iggy.' The interruption came from Johanna's father. 'Send someone to ask Koos what you should do. Until you have the answer *I'll* look after Van Eyck and the others.'

Turning his back on the field-cornet, he motioned for Nat and his two companions to follow him.

'Not so fast, Cornelius. *I'm* in charge of this commando . . .'

'Right. So it's for you to do what's needed. Send word to Koos and wait for his answer. Jaconus Van Eyck won't be going anywhere before then.'

Cornelius Viljoen walked away from the thwarted field-cornet, heading for his wagon, and Nat, Adam and Jaconus Van Eyck went with him.

When Nat tried to thank the burgher for what he had just done for them, the big, bearded Boer brushed the words aside.

'Every burgher in this army is a free man, with the right to speak his mind and act as his conscience dictates. That's what this war is about . . . The right to live *our* lives, *our* way. I didn't like what Iggy Lemmer wanted to do, so I said so and did something about it. Anyway, most of the commando agrees with me.'

'What would have happened had they *not* agreed with you?' Adam asked the question.

'Your friend would have been shot. You too, probably.'

Smiling at the startled expression on Adam's face, their rescuer rested a hand on his shoulder. 'Don't worry. No one will harm you while you're with Cornelius Viljoen. My daughter didn't fatten you up for a killing.'

If Johanna Viljoen was pleased to have the Retallick brothers at her family's cooking-fire she was careful not to allow her pleasure to show. She busied herself about the wagon, occasionally coming to the fire to help her mother prepare the midday meal. More than once a girl of Johanna's own age would wander from another part of the camp and stop to talk to her. It did not take Nat long to realise that the presence of the prisoners had made Johanna the most popular young hostess in the Boer camp.

As Jaconus Van Eyck and Cornelius Viljoen sat together talking of mutual friends and acquaintances, Nat saw Johanna and her mother take a large, empty barrel from their wagon to the fast-moving stream that formed the southern limit of the camp. Nudging Adam, he said, 'Come on, here's a chance for you to earn your keep.'

At the stream the water barrel was relinquished to the two brothers and Johanna's mother said, 'I hope you two boys help your own mother this way when you're home.'

Sophia Viljoen's accent was that of the *voortrekker*, the pioneers who had remained one step ahead of civilisation for so long they had begun to speak in what was almost a new language, one that was almost unintelligible to those who lived in the towns and cities of the Cape Colony. Nat and Adam were quite at home with the accent. Most of the Boers they met in Matabeleland had been *voortrekkers*.

Looking at the woman, Nat saw that Johanna had inherited her dark eyes from her mother, but a demanding life spent in the harsh environment of the highveld had exacted a heavy toll on the beauty that had once been the older woman's.

'We should be at home helping Ma now,' said Adam. 'But why are *you* here? Your men are fighting a war.'

'Our farm is in the Lichtenburg area, not very far away but pa and my brother Lucas are here with the commando. We might as well be here as there.'

After a brief silence, Johanna asked, 'Do you have any

brothers or sisters?' She was looking at Nat, but he realised she was hoping for an answer from Adam, and Nat let him speak for them.

'We have a younger brother, Ben. There *was* another . . . older than Nat. He and Pa were killed by the Matabele, six years ago.'

Sophia Viljoen erupted in angry sympathy. 'You don't need to tell *me* about such happenings. When I first met Cornelius I was grieving for a father and *two* brothers, all killed by Zulus. Cornelius had also lost a brother in the same troubles. That's why this war is so . . . so *stupid*! Englishman and Boer should be standing side by side fighting the kaffirs instead of warring with each other. Together they could drive the Zulu and the Matabele right out of our countries. Until they do we'll always be fighting them somewhere. I've said so many times, so has Cornelius.'

'We're obliged to your husband,' said Nat. 'But for his intervention we'd be in serious trouble now.'

'He's a good man,' agreed Sophia Viljoen. Her expression softened for a moment as she looked to where her husband sat with Jaconus Van Eyck. '. . . But so too are most of the burghers here. This war is not of their making. For years they've fought and worked hard to make a life for their families – as did their fathers and grandfathers before them. There's not an Afrikaner family in the land who can't name loved ones who have died for this land of ours. We *can't* give it up now. The British have become used to grabbing whatever they want, but this time they're trying to take a country from *white* men – men armed with guns. Not ignorant savages with spears in their hands.'

'*I'd* fight if I were a Boer,' said Adam fiercely. 'I'd fight for you anyway, given the chance . . .'

Nat took the barrel from his brother and swung it to the wooden ledge on the side of the Viljoen wagon, holding it in place while Johanna secured it with a short length of rope.

'We Retallicks have fought our war with the tribes in Matabeleland. This one is between the British and the Boers. We'll leave them to do the fighting and not get mixed up in something that has nothing to do with us.'

Sophia Viljoen looked at Nat and shook her head sadly.

'You're part of southern Africa, Nat Retallick. Part of Cecil Rhodes' empire. You won't be *allowed* to stay out of this war.'

'The Insimo valley is run by the Retallicks, not by Rhodes. We were living at Insimo before he ever set foot in Africa. When Rhodes moved into Matabeleland he signed a special agreement with my pa. That agreement says that the valley and everything there belong to us – not to Rhodes, or his company. We manage our own affairs and leave others to run theirs.'

'You're a proud man. Far too proud to allow a war to shape the countries about you and do nothing about it.' There was respect in Sophia Viljoen's voice. 'I hope for your sake – and for ours – that you choose the right side.'

'All this stupid talk of war. He's right. We should all go about our own business and leave war to those who have nothing better to do than fight.' Johanna spoke vehemently.

'I'm not sure that's quite what I said.' Nat was disturbed by the passion in Johanna's voice. Men and women at nearby fires had stopped what they were doing and were looking across towards the Viljoen fire. The last thing Nat wanted was to start a general argument about the rights and wrongs of the war. '. . . But no doubt it's close enough. Still, I'm surprised to see so many families here. It's more like a social gathering than a siege.'

'Tell that to the families of the men killed by Colonel Baden-Powell's soldiers yesterday . . .' Field-Cornet Lemmer had come up unnoticed while Nat was talking. He waved a piece of paper in Sophia Viljoen's face. '. . . I've got a list of casualties here. Young Pieter Scheepers is among those killed.'

'Oh no!' Sophia Viljoen's hands flew to her face.

'Oh *yes*. Your neighbour's son. The boy of seventeen who grew up with your daughter.' Field-Cornet Lemmer was triumphant.

'I must go to Ella . . . her poor boy . . .' Sophia Viljoen hurried away. Johanna stood silently gazing after her for a few moments, then moved towards her family's wagon, tears filling her eyes.

'It seems you're not as popular as you were,' said Field-Cornet Lemmer maliciously. 'Stay around here long enough and I'll have you all shot yet.'

CHAPTER FIVE

General Jacobus Herculaas 'Koos' De la Rey rode into the camp in the heat of the afternoon, when most men were taking advantage of whatever shade they could find to escape from the sun. He arrived unaccompanied and unannounced, but within seconds men were running to meet him. By the time he stepped down from his horse he was surrounded by the excited burghers under his command.

Koos De la Rey stood head and shoulders above most of the men about him and he would have been conspicuous in any gathering. Well over six feet tall, De la Rey wore the garb of a farmer, the clothes hanging on his great frame as though carelessly thrown there by someone in a hurry. But it was De la Rey's face that attracted immediate attention. A hawk-like nose protruded from a massive, bushy, square-cut beard, while beneath shaggy eyebrows his expressive eyes missed very little of the world about him.

The Boer general presented the appearance of a genial, engaging personality, and his first words, booming out across the camp, fuelled this impression.

'Jaconus! It *is* Jaconus Van Eyck. I told the messenger there had to be some mistake. That the Jaconus Van Eyck I once knew had been dead for many years. It's a great delight to be proven wrong, my friend.'

Shaking Jaconus Van Eyck warmly by the hand, the giant of a man stepped back and held him at arm's length. 'Let me look at you . . . Agh! God has been good to you, Jaconus. Only your beard has changed – and grey is a colour that gives you authority.'

'*You're* the one with authority, Koos. A man for others to follow.'

Koos De la Rey released his friend. 'I am not proud to be leading men to war, Jaconus. I worked very hard for a just peace . . . but it was not to be.' Koos De la Rey looked deeply and expressively unhappy.

'How is your family, Koos? Your son Adaan . . . he is well?'

'Adaan. Ah, there is a good boy. A *fine* boy. He serves in my commando with his brother, young Koos. One day they will both help to lead their country. I pray it might be in peace and not in war . . . but enough of me. What of you? I was given a message that you and your friends had been arrested by Field-Cornet Lemmer – for spying!'

'I'm no spy, Koos. Neither are the Retallick boys.'

'Retallick? Are they sons of *Daniel* Retallick?'

Jaconus Van Eyck nodded. 'I was with Daniel when he was killed. So too was Nat. I help him run the family farm in the Insimo valley, in Matabeleland. We've brought some cattle here.'

'So I have heard. Let me speak to this Nat Retallick.'

Nat was tall, but Koos De la Rey towered above him when the Boer general shook hands gravely.

'So you are the English spy, eh?' Koos De la Rey's voice was as big as the man.

'No, I'm a farmer. I came here to deliver cattle, that's all.'

'You bring cattle to a garrison we are trying to starve into submission and you say "that's all"? I hope you never come here to do something you believe matters.'

'I delivered the cattle because Colonel Baden-Powell had *paid* me for them. I'd have done the same had I sold them to you, or your men.'

Koos De la Rey looked at Nat silently for a few moments before nodding his head. 'I believe you. Your father would have done the same. I met him many years ago, when he was visiting Transvaal. You are like him.'

Hiding the pleasure Koos De la Rey's words gave him, Nat said, 'I don't think my cattle will make very much difference. There doesn't seem to be any shortage of food in Mafeking.'

'No doubt you're right. Colonel Baden-Powell has been filling the Mafeking warehouses for many weeks. We should have attacked the town in strength when the war began. However, General Cronje is in command of this area. He thought otherwise. It's too late now.'

Nat shrugged. This was not his war. 'So . . . what happens to us now?'

'You are free to go home. But I would rather you did not bring any more of your cattle to Mafeking. At least, not until it belongs to *us*.'

Nat's grin was the only outward sign of the great relief he felt. He had been deeply concerned about Jaconus Van Eyck.

'I'll tell Ignatius Lemmer to give you a pass to take you safely on your way – just in case you meet with the burgher to whom you told the story that the cattle were for me. I doubt if he would believe you again.'

'Thank you, General De la Rey. When this war is over – however it ends – you'll always be a welcome guest at Insimo.'

'There are many battles to be fought yet, but the war *will* be won by our republics, because God is on our side. But I believe He will sorely try our faith before the end comes. I wish you a safe journey, young man. Now I must speak with Ignatius Lemmer before I go. I have an army to lead and only *British* generals expect the events of war to await their arrival.'

Nat and the others did not remain long in the Boer camp after General Koos De la Rey rode off. They had been away from Insimo for too long. Nat knew that if news of the war reached his mother she would worry about her sons.

While Nat and Jaconus Van Eyck went to catch the horses, Adam returned to the Viljoen wagon to collect their saddles and belongings. Johanna was tidying up after the meal.

'So you are going home to Rhodesia?'

'That's what they call it now. I still think of it as Matabeleland.'

'Is it good land there?'

'The Insimo valley has the best grazing in the whole of the country. It's a fine place. From the house the valley drops away to the lowveld and on a clear day you can see for more than forty miles.'

'It sounds like the mountains of the Drakensbergs. I went there once, on a visit.'

'How far is your farm from here?'

'Only about forty miles across the border. Koos De la Rey farms there too. Pa says most of the commando will be moving off to join Koos in a day or two. We'll be going home again then.'

'Perhaps I'll visit you there one day.'

'I would like that,' Johanna said quietly, and Adam was suddenly lost for words.

Coming up with the horses, Nat saw the two together, and he frowned. Adam was young and impetuous and his sympathies lay with the Boers. It was a good thing they were returning home.

Nat had discussed with Jaconus Van Eyck the likelihood of the train still being at the end of the line from Rhodesia and they both agreed it was highly unlikely. Even had the train driver been able to escape detection he would have heard the sound of the Boer guns bombarding Mafeking. No doubt he had made the decision to return to Rhodesia.

Nat's fears were realised when they reached the place where the cattle had been off-loaded. The track curved gently away towards the hills to the north. Distance and a heat-haze distorted the symmetry of the dully gleaming twin rails, but there was no train here.

Then, as Nat reined in to discuss their next move with his companions, a figure rose, seemingly out of the ground itself. It was one of the Matabele herdsmen. His body had been so smeared with mud and dirt as to render him almost totally invisible on the scrub-covered veld.

Complimenting the herdsman on the effectiveness of his disguise, Nat asked what had happened to the train.

Grinning his pleasure, the herdsman said, 'The Matabele are of the earth. We can become as one. The white man and his train cannot. They went to hide in the hills. I stayed here to wait for you.'

With the herdsman trotting ahead of them, the horsemen rode for about seven miles before they found the train. The driver had stopped it in a curved cutting that sliced through the heart of a low hill. It was visible only to someone following the line.

The train driver had not wasted time while he was

waiting for the Insimo men to return. The herdsmen had been out scouring the countryside for wood and the three cattle trucks nearest to the locomotive were filled with fuel for the furnace.

'All we'll need along the way is water,' explained the driver. 'If we've still got track to roll on I'll have us back in Bulawayo by nightfall tomorrow – or as close to it as will make no difference. You get some sleep now. You look as though you could do with it.'

The three men from Insimo had not slept for thirty-six hours, and in spite of Nat's protestations that he would not rest until they crossed the border into Rhodesia he was asleep as soon as he settled down on a blanket in the guard's van. Neither a storm flickering and grumbling on the horizon to the east, nor the monotonous booming of the Boers' Creusot gun bombarding the beleaguered town of Mafeking disturbed his sleep.

With two herdsmen sitting on the roof of the guard's van looking out for damage to the rails, the train headed northwards at full throttle. More than once during that day and the next they sighted horsemen, but they were always too far away for identification. Then, on the second day, with the sun not yet touching the horizon, the train steamed into the border town of Plumtree with whistle blowing triumphantly, bringing townsfolk and soldiers running to the station. It was the only train to reach Plumtree from the south in more than a week.

The first man to board the train was a British army officer who introduced himself to Nat as Captain Carey Hamilton of the Hussars. He had been sent out from Britain some weeks before to raise a volunteer force to defend Rhodesia's borders against Boer attack. He had arrived in the border town only two days before and knew nothing of Nat's journey southwards.

'Where have you men come from? We thought the line to the south had been torn up.'

'So it has. Our cattle had to run the last few miles into Mafeking.'

'You've been to Mafeking . . .? The town is under siege. Are you trying to make a fool of me?'

Nat told him their story but the British officer still looked at the three men uncertainly. Then Nat pulled a piece of paper from his pocket and handed it to the soldier. It was a receipt for five hundred head of cattle. Signed by Colonel Baden-Powell's adjutant, it was date-stamped 'Mafeking. October 14th 1899'.

The British officer looked at Nat with new respect. 'I'd like you to remain here until Colonel Plumer's return, Mr Retallick. He'll be most interested in all you can tell him of Mafeking.'

Nat shook his head. 'I've been away from my farm for too long already. If Colonel Plumer wants me he'll find me in the Insimo valley. You won't mind if I take the train on to the railhead, beyond Bulawayo? It's as close as I can get to Insimo.'

'Of course not, but you'll dine with me first. I want to hear about Mafeking – and Colonel Baden-Powell. He's set to become a great hero if only he can hold out against the Boers for a week or two more, until help arrives.'

'He should find little difficulty in holding out for as long as he needs to,' commented Jaconus Van Eyck. 'He's got food enough for months, and the burghers aren't keen to storm the town.'

'Koos De la Rey could take Mafeking if he wanted to,' Adam blurted out heatedly. 'Baden-Powell wouldn't be able to keep *him* out.'

'General De la Rey?' Captain Carey Hamilton raised an eyebrow at the outburst and looked to Nat for an explanation.

'General De la Rey refused to allow us to be put on trial. Instead he gave us a pass to return here. He made quite an impression on my brother. On me too, if I'm strictly honest.'

'I believe a great many of the Boers are sincere, well-meaning men,' agreed Captain Hamilton. 'Unfortunately, we are at war with each other. However, the next best thing to a gallant ally is a brave and gallant foe.'

'The Boers don't look upon war as some game played to predetermined rules, Captain,' said Jaconus Van Eyck bitterly. 'The burghers are fighting for their country and the future of their families – and they are convinced that God is on their side. It's a combination that won't be easily beaten.'

'But beat them we will, Mr Van Eyck. The sooner the Boers

accept this, the sooner the war will end. It could save very many lives.'

'Most of President Kruger's burghers are poor men, Captain. They have nothing to give their country but their skill with a rifle – and their lives. Under-estimating the value of either will cost your country dear.'

'I am a soldier, Mr Van Eyck, paid to fight and not to think too deeply. But come and have a drink with me now. I intend inviting some of my fellow officers to dine with us. I am certain that what you have to say will prove of immense interest to them . . .'

Dinner that evening was a lively affair. Nat shared Jaconus Van Eyck's view that the British regarded war as a game, and it quickly became evident that few of the officers present shared Captain Hamilton's regard for the Boer as a fighting-man. Most thought the British government had over-reacted to the situation and committed far too many troops to South Africa. They were of the opinion that the war would be over in a matter of weeks, anticipating that the Boers would capitulate as soon as some 'real' fighting began.

Nat kept most of his opinions to himself. So too did Jaconus Van Eyck. The only major disagreement with the British officers came in a brief outburst from Adam. He declared that the British were in for a shock when they met up with Koos De la Rey and his commando.

Adam's assertion caused a few raised eyebrows among the military diners, but Adam's obvious youth, and Captain Hamilton's explanation that General De la Rey had saved the Insimo trio from a spy trial, restored good humour to the company. Nevertheless, Nat breathed a sigh of relief when Adam made the excuse that he was tired and left the room.

CHAPTER SIX

Life at Insimo quickly settled back to normal. Fifteen-year-old Ben was envious of his brothers' adventures at Mafeking, but soon everything except Adam's hero-worship of Koos De la Rey, and his praise of Johanna, was no more than a memory. The war was being fought a long way from the peaceful valley, and now the rains had arrived in earnest much needed to be done.

Occasionally, news filtered through to Insimo of British setbacks in their war with the Boer forces. The mightiest army in the world, unaccustomed to defeat, was reeling before a motley collection of farmers who possessed little military training, and no discipline worth the mention. Each member of a Boer commando was a rugged individualist. Most shared with his companions only a common language, faith in his own ability – and an unshakable belief that God's might was behind the Boer cause.

Once in a while thoughts of Koos De la Rey and the Viljoen family passed through Nat's mind and he vaguely wondered how the progress of the war was affecting them all, but he wasted few thoughts on the war itself. Even Adam's unquenchable enthusiasm for the Boer cause failed to move him. There was far too much to occupy his mind at Insimo.

Captain Carey Hamilton came to the Insimo valley during the second week of November, 1899, bringing with him a mounted escort of thirty men of the Rhodesian Defence Force. The captain had grim news of the British campaign in South Africa. At Ladysmith a thousand British soldiers had surrendered to a Boer force inferior in numbers. British morale in

Africa had fallen to a new low ebb.

All this was told to Nat as he led the young British officer into the whitewashed house and introduced him to his mother. Elvira Retallick commiserated with Carey Hamilton at the British setbacks before leaving the house to busy herself arranging quarters for the officer's escort among the many outbuildings that had sprung up at Insimo over the years.

Pouring a drink for Carey Hamilton, Nat said, 'You're not going to tell me you've ridden all this way just to give me the latest news of the war?'

'No.' Carey Hamilton accepted the glass from Nat's hand and carried it to the window. From here he could see for miles along the green valley. Two miles away the younger Retallick boys were moving a huge herd of cattle, aided by Matabele herdsmen. 'Is Van Eyck not here with you?'

Nat joined Carey Hamilton at the window and pointed out a small cottage, almost completely hidden by trees, a half-mile away. 'That's Jaconus's place, but he's off hunting. He keeps the valley in meat.'

Suspecting more in the British officer's question than a casual interest in the Boer hunter's whereabouts, Nat added, 'Jaconus has lived in this valley for very many years.'

Moving to a wide window, Nat pointed out a small plot of fenced land on the hillside. 'His son is buried there, murdered by two Boers who thought they were above the law. Jaconus hunted them down and killed them both. As far as I know there's still a murder warrant outstanding against him in the Transvaal. So you can forget the idea that he's working for anyone but me.'

'I believe you. Anyway, I'm here to buy cattle to feed the troops we're expecting to reach Bulawayo soon. How many can you let me have?'

Nat shrugged. 'As many as you want. I've got cattle enough up in the hills to feed the whole British army. Where are all these troops coming from?'

'From Beira, in Portuguese East Africa. They're coming by sea from the Cape, and then by rail to Salisbury before marching down here. It's a long journey.'

Nat nodded. The journey from Beira involved about three hundred and fifty miles by rail, and then three hundred more across rough country on indifferent roads. It was Cecil Rhodes's intention to have every major town in Rhodesia linked by rail. The war had set back his ambitions ... but Carey Hamilton was still talking.

'This brings me to my second reason for coming to Insimo. I'm on my way to Fort Victoria to take over the garrison there.'

'Good. We should see more of you once you're settled in. Fort Victoria is no more than a half-day's ride away.'

Carey Hamilton grimaced. 'I doubt if I'll have much time for socialising. I'm to raise and train two companies of volunteers. When they're ready my brother-in-law will be arriving to take command. He's at present at Beira.'

'I can think of healthier places to be at this time of year. Beira is surrounded by swampland. When they were building the railway there only one in three white men survived.'

'Then it's even more urgent that my *sister* should be brought out of there. She's with her husband. He has telegraphed that he wants to send her to stay with me at Fort Victoria, to await his arrival.'

'She's coming via Salisbury and Bulawayo? That's no journey for a woman.'

'It's the route our troops take. Is there a quicker way?'

Nat nodded. 'There *is*. Fort Victoria is no more than a hundred and fifty miles in a straight line from Umtali, where the railway enters Rhodesia, but I doubt if you'll find many who've made the journey and I doubt if you'd get a wagon through at this time of year.'

'Have you made the journey?'

'Yes. My mother's family home is in the Portuguese territory. Her father was governor for a while. Pa would occasionally take us there on a visit.'

Carey Hamilton looked embarrassed. 'To be honest ... I'd heard as much already. That's the main reason I'm here, really. I could have bought cattle anywhere — but I couldn't find another man capable of bringing my sister to Fort Victoria from Umtali. Certainly not a man who knew the country *and* whom I could trust.'

'You want *me* to bring your sister across country from Umtali to Fort Victoria?' Nat suddenly realised the trap he had dug for himself.

'You've said yourself that Beira is no place for a woman, and if she travels along the army route the journey will take at least a month. Even the fast coach from Salisbury to Bulawayo takes eight days – and once there she'd need to await an escort to bring her on to Fort Victoria. There are also disturbing rumours that our setbacks in South Africa might give the Matabele an incentive to stage another uprising. I can't risk allowing her to make the coach journey.'

'You're asking me to leave Insimo when there's the possibility of a Matabele uprising? Do you realise that all my workers are Matabele? If you include their wives and families I've more than a thousand Matabele in just one village in the north end of the valley – not to mention all those in the compound, not half a mile from this house.'

'I know all this. I also know that neither of the last two Matabele uprisings has troubled you here. Your father was friend and adviser to Lobengula. Because of this the Matabele would go to war *for* you, but never *against* you.'

'In that small graveyard over there lying beside Jaconus Van Eyck's son you'll find the graves of my pa and my brother Wyatt. Both were killed by Matabele spears. If it hadn't been for Jaconus I'd be lying there with them. Do you still think we're protected by the memory of a king who died six years ago?'

Carey Hamilton looked suitably abashed. 'You're right of course. I had no right to come here and ask for your help. Please forget everything I've said.'

Nat frowned irritably. 'This sister of yours . . . can she ride a horse?'

'Of course. She's a fine horsewoman. But . . . why do you ask?'

Further discussion was brought to a close by the return to the house of Elvira Retallick. The soldiers had been accommodated in the outbuildings and Elvira had returned to enjoy a role she rarely fulfilled in the lonely Insimo valley. That of a hostess.

Gradually the remainder of the family and their friends who lived in the valley drifted to the house. Jaconus Van Eyck arrived with a freshly killed buck slung across his horse as a present for Elvira. In return he accepted an invitation to stay for dinner.

Another guest was Victoria Speke. Victoria lived in a house not far from Jaconus Van Eyck. Now in her fifties she had lived an exciting and adventurous life. The daughter of a Herero tribeswoman and a shipwrecked British sailor, Victoria had experienced a great many things that would have shocked most women. A childhood friend of Nat's father, their ways had parted when he met Elvira and Victoria became the mistress of Mozambique's most notorious bandit. When he was killed she had graduated to the mining camps of South Africa. After saving the lives of Daniel and his bride, Victoria had returned to the valley with a young daughter. That had been in 1870. The daughter had married a Portuguese army officer and was now settled in Mozambique, but Victoria had remained at Insimo. Looking at her now it was difficult to believe she had once ridden with bandits and shot more than one man to death. However, her past was known to the Matabele and they treated her with a great deal of respect.

Victoria had finally settled at Insimo with the brother of her first love. He too was buried in the small Insimo graveyard and there was only an occasional flash of fire to enable a stranger to glimpse the woman she had once been.

Carey Hamilton had no knowledge of her past and he treated her with an old-world courtesy that endeared him to her from the beginning of their acquaintance.

The meal was almost over before Carey Hamilton mentioned his sister again. When the two women heard she was in Beira they were both aghast, insisting he bring her to Rhodesia as soon as possible.

Not wishing to embarrass Nat, Captain Hamilton murmured that it was hoped she would be travelling to Rhodesia with a British regiment in the very near future.

'She intends going to Salisbury first?' Victoria was incredulous. 'It will take her *weeks*. She should come south from Umtali. Travelling through the Vumba mountains, past the hot springs, she'd be in Fort Victoria in no time. Why, I once did the journey in six days – and I carried a young baby too.'

'You've done the journey?'

Victoria looked at those about her at the table. 'We *all* have at one time or another. You speak to Nat, he's the clever one. He'll draw you a map.'

'There will be no need of a map.' Nat reached across the table and filled the British officer's glass. Without looking up, he said, 'I'll be going to Umtali to bring his sister back to Fort Victoria.'

CHAPTER SEVEN

Nat travelled alone from the Insimo valley on his journey to Umtali, the small town on the Rhodesian side of the border with Mozambique. It was a journey he had made on a number of occasions, but the awesome grandeur of the country along the way never failed to impress him, especially when he reached the mountains close to his destination. Here the rocky granite hills of the lowveld gave way to high, misty mountains with wooded slopes, tumbling waterfalls and distant, purple horizons.

Once Matabeleland was behind him, Nat avoided the native villages whenever possible. The Retallicks were known and respected in the land once ruled by the Matabele king Lobengula, but this became a disadvantage outside Matabeleland. Lobengula had held the surrounding tribes in subjugation for many years. His warriors had ranged far and wide, arrogantly asserting their superiority and dealing out summary justice to those who were slow to pay homage to the Matabele king.

The arrival of Cecil Rhodes's chartered company, the defeat and death of Lobengula, and the joining of the tribal lands between the Zambezi and Limpopo rivers into one single country had changed everything.

Backed by Great Britain, the chartered company had crushed the might of the Matabele nation, and the lesser tribes were now eager to avenge the wrongs they had suffered at their hands. Their wrath was directed at anyone who had found favour with the Matabele king -- especially if he happened to venture into their lands.

Nat had made excellent time, but while he was skirting the foothills of the Vumba mountains, luck deserted him.

Rain-clouds had been building up over the mountain tops since dawn and they now began billowing down the slopes as the faint track he followed rose to meet them. Nat knew he was going to be caught in a storm -- and storms in these mountains could be brutally violent.

Two miles back Nat had skirted a grass-hutted village. Turning his horse he shook out the reins and set off at a gallop, hoping the tribal chief would prove to be friendly. The villages around here belonged to the 'Manica' tribe and they were far enough from Matabeleland not to have attracted the attentions of Lobengula's ruthless *impis*. In any case, Nat had little choice. He needed to find shelter from the storm, and find it quickly.

Already the rumble of thunder was echoing across the mountains and it was accompanied by a sinister hissing that grew rapidly louder, heralding the advance of the rain.

Nat gained the Manica village only minutes before the storm and slipped his rifle from its saddle-holster as an eager Manica boy took his horse from him. As Nat was shown inside a large, wattle-walled hut, heavy raindrops began to beat an erratic tattoo against the thatch of the roof.

The hut was occupied by a Manica chieftain named Tandi and the chief's greeting told Nat that he had been seen riding past the village earlier.

'You do not wish for the company of my people, white man, yet our huts are preferable to the violence of a storm.'

Chief Tandi spoke in the Mashona dialect and Nathan replied in the same language.

'I am in a hurry to reach Umtali, Chief Tandi, but only a fool would defy such weather.'

Even as Nat spoke a squall of wind and rain struck the hut, shaking it as though it were caught in the throes of an earthquake and beating the smoke from a small fire back inside the hut.

Chief Tandi nodded his acceptance of Nat's words, 'You and I have not met before?'

'It is possible we met when I was a small boy and travelled with my father. He was a trader until he was killed by the Matabele.'

'Ah!' The chief's sigh was echoed by some of the men who sat about the low fire in the centre of the room, their faces indistinct in the gloom. 'The warriors of Lobengula left many widows and fatherless children to mourn their passing. Where is your home now, white man?'

Chief Tandi was asking more questions than was polite. A gust of wind suddenly coaxed a flame from the dull fire and in its uncertain light Nat saw a number of men huddled inside the hut. Those nearest to Chief Tandi bore tribal scars on their cheeks, but they were not those of the Manica tribes. They were the scars inflicted soon after birth on the faces of boys in neighbouring Mozambique. Nat had stumbled upon a meeting between the tribes – and the knowledge made him uneasy. He hoped the weather would improve quickly, so he could go on his way.

'I live in the Insimo valley. Beyond the great house of the chiefs.'

Again there was the sound of a concerted sigh from the men in the gloomy hut. The 'great house of the chiefs' was a huge, stone-built ruin, reminiscent of a medieval European castle. It stood alone and mysterious, only a few miles from Fort Victoria. To the Mashona tribes it had always been a holy place, home of their great spirit, Chiminuka. One day Lobengula had come along and slaughtered the medium through whom Chiminuka was in the habit of speaking to his people, together with the medium's entire retinue. Since that time the 'great house of the chiefs' had been occupied only by ghosts and was a place to be avoided. But there was not one man of the tribes who did not know of its existence.

'You have come far, and alone! When other white men pass through here they come many together and travel with their homes on wheels and drawn by many oxen.'

In spite of the misgivings he had about his present situation, Nat smiled at the chief's description of the trekkers and their ox-wagons. 'A man travelling with his home must travel slowly, Chief Tandi. I am in a hurry to reach Umtali.'

Nat needed to raise his voice to make himself heard above the din of the storm. Thunder rumbled all about the mountain-side village now and rain lashed down on the thatched roof,

47

trickling in beneath the wattle door and tracing rivulets of mud on the earth floor.

'Do you speak Portuguese, white man?'

The question came from one of the unseen men sitting beyond the red ashes of the fire, where swirling smoke trapped inside the hut by the wind added to the gloom.

Nat hesitated, but only for a moment. His mother was Portuguese and she had brought up her sons fluent in her native tongue – but the Manica village was close to the Portuguese border. Before the coming of Rhodes these people had been subjected to the heavy-handed administration of the Portuguese authorities. He did not want to have to explain his command of the language.

'No.' The lie came easily in the darkness.

'Do you fight in the war against the bearded white men who live beyond the Limpopo river?'

Nat was surprised that these men in this remote Manica village had heard of the month-old Anglo-Boer war.

'I am a farmer. I am too busy fighting *rinderpest* and lion and locusts to join in the wars of other men.'

As the questioning continued, the unseen men in the hut began talking quietly among themselves. They were speaking in Portuguese, and from the snatches of conversation he overheard Nat realised the talk was of some heavy fighting that had taken place.

At first he thought they were discussing the Boer war, but then realised this comprised only part of their conversation. They were also talking of *another* war, one being fought between the tribes and the Portuguese.

Yet there seemed to be some tie-up between the two wars. With a thrill of horror, Nat realised the men in Chief Tandi's hut were discussing tribesmen on both sides of the Mozambique border joining forces! They expected to inflict a defeat on the Portuguese army and to return with their combined tribes to attack the whites in Rhodesia, ousting them from the country while the soldiers from Great Britain were being defeated by the Boers.

The storm had subsided a little now and, rising to his feet, Nat declared his intention of resuming his journey to Umtali. His words brought an immediate chorus of protest.

'You are in a great hurry to leave us, white man. Is our hospitality so poor? But of course . . . where are the women? Bring the white man food. Bring him beer.'

There was movement towards the rear of the hut and some half-stifled giggling. A woman came from the shadows and placed a bowl before Nat. It contained native beer, a substance with the consistency of thin porridge which exuded a pungent, sour-sweet aroma. Another woman pulled meat from the fire. Impaled on wooden skewers, it had been wrapped in leaves and laid on hot stones. There was a large cauldron on the fire and another woman reached inside with her hand and pulled out a handful of thick corn-meal paste. This she placed in a bowl with the meat.

Nat accepted both meal and drink, murmuring his thanks to Chief Tandi. 'The generosity of the Manica is well known to all who travel these lands – but I am expected in Umtali.'

'Even without rain it would be impossible to reach Umtali tonight, you will remain here. You were hoping to share your *kaross* with a woman in Umtali, perhaps? This too you shall have. Nanda, come here.'

There was another stir at the rear of the hut and more giggling. An African woman came to the fireside. In her late twenties, Nanda was overweight in a fashionable, native way. When she smiled, Nat had an impression of white teeth with a wide gap between the two in the front of her mouth.

'She was my own nephew's wife. He was killed by a buffalo a year ago. She has not had a man since. She will be happy to make you forget the rains and the journey you are so anxious to make. She might even persuade you to remain here and become a Manica.'

'Such beauty is indeed a great temptation,' lied Nat. 'But I have responsibilities to my own family. I will sleep alone and make an early start on my journey.'

The smile disappeared and Nanda stepped back to be lost in the darkness once more.

'The white men here are not like those of our land.' The quietly spoken words were in Portuguese. 'Our women need to flee when the white men come to our village.'

'What will you do with the white man, Chief Tandi?'

'He poses no threat to our plans.'

'He is a white man. He must not be allowed to leave alive.'

'We will talk of this when he has been taken to his hut.'

The low-voiced conversations were carried on in Portuguese, but the hatred in the voices needed no interpretation.

'Nanda will show you to your hut, white man. If you should change your mind . . .'

'I am grateful to the chief of the Manica.'

It had stopped raining now and the skies were clearing. Although it was almost dark there was enough light for Nat to see the sidelong glances the Manica girl was giving him as she walked beside him.

'Nanda, where is my horse? I need some things from the saddle-bags.' In truth, Nat wanted to know where the horse was being kept.

The Manica girl changed direction without a word. At the edge of the village was a wooden-walled stockade, topped with branches cut from long-thorned bushes. Here were kept the village cattle to protect them from the predators of the night. A smaller stockade beside it held Nat's horse. It had not been unsaddled and Nat made a great show of removing a blanket-roll from the animal.

Nanda took the blanket from him and led him to a hut not far from the chief's own. As they walked together in the darkness her body kept bumping against his, and once more he was aware of her sidelong glances.

Inside the hut she spread the blanket on the floor and gave him a look that reinforced the chief's invitation. As though weakening, Nat said, 'Stay and talk with me for a while, Nanda. Tell me about the village and the mountains . . . about your people.'

Nat received the full force of her smile now as, squatting before him on the floor of the hut, she began to tell him about life in the Manica village.

Gradually the village sounds died away outside the hut and Nanda's voice began to falter. Judging the time to be right, Nat said, 'I *would* like you to stay with me tonight, Nanda. Get undressed, and wait here for me. I have a present in my saddle-bag . . .'

It was very dark outside, and because of the recent rains there were no cooking-fires burning. As Nat made his way through the ankle-deep mud towards the stockade where his horse was kept, he saw a gleam of light from Chief Tandi's hut and the glint of metal as someone came out through the door. He knew then he was right to be making his escape.

He made his way to the animal stockade – and here he came face-to-face with a guard. Both men were taken by surprise, but Nat recovered first. Raising his rifle, he brought the brass reinforced butt down on the other man's head. The Manica tribesman fell to the ground without so much as a grunt and Nat slipped inside the smaller of the two pens.

Swinging to the saddle, Nat rode quietly and cautiously away from the village. There were a few stars sprinkled in the sky above him now, but it would be at least another hour before the moon rose and he would be able to move with any speed. He had hoped his escape would not be discovered for a while, at least, but he was no more than two hundred yards from the village when he heard the crackle of musket fire and a sudden blaze of light lit up the night sky as the thatched roof of a hut went up in flames.

As Nat put his horse to a canter he heard many voices shouting in jubilation. It was a matter of minutes only before the sound changed to howls of anger. Nat guessed that Chief Tandi and his men had poured shot into the hut where they believed him to be sleeping. Either deliberately, or more likely by accident, they had set fire to the thatch inside the hut and in its light found they had been shooting at Nanda.

He felt a twinge of conscience over the fate of the amorous Nanda, but there was little time for mourning. By now they would have checked the pen and discovered his horse had gone. The chase was on.

Nat urged his horse forward, hoping it would not step in a hole, or stumble over a rock in the darkness. If it did he would have no chance of out-running his Manica pursuers.

For a full hour Nat kept the horse going at a pace that seemed agonisingly slow, and more than once he thought he heard the sound of pursuit. Any moment he was expecting shots to be aimed at him from the darkness.

But none came, and when eventually the moon rose above the mountains to the east like a giant, candle-lit pumpkin, Nat forced his horse on faster.

Before long Nat came to a swollen mountain river. He swam the horse across, holding fast to the animal's tail. The water was cold and chilled him to the bone, but once on the far side he knew he was safe from further pursuit by Chief Tandi's men. There would be other dangers in the African night ahead of him, but with a bright moon above and a good Insimo horse beneath him, he was confident he would reach Umtali by morning.

CHAPTER EIGHT

Nat rode his tired horse into the Umtali valley as sunshine spilled from the mountain peaks. The newly laid-out town provided a welcome sight. During the night he had survived a frightening fall, both horse and rider sliding fifty yards from a mountainside track rendered treacherous by rain. Then he had been stalked for two hair-raising miles by an unusually bold and cunning leopard.

Approaching the town, Nat saw the twin silver rails of the narrow gauge railway threading its way through the Mozambique mountains to the east. Westwards, the wider gauge of the Rhodesian railway system crossed the plain and disappeared in the hills. The two railroads met here and passengers were forced to sample the few and simple pleasures of Umtali as they changed from one to the other.

The railway was the sole reason for Umtali's presence in this place. Some years before the town had been ten miles away, on the far side of the hill. When it was found to be impossible to bring the railway to the town, Cecil Rhodes had brought Umtali to the railway, building an identical town where the two railway systems met and moving all the residents from old town to new.

There was a large tented army camp close to the railway station and two long lines of picketed horses indicated that many of the soldiers were cavalrymen. Some would undoubtedly be the escort arranged by Carey Hamilton for his sister. Nat wanted to speak to their commanding officer, but no one would be about at this time of the morning and first he needed a rest, a bath and a good meal. Then he would be ready to face the world.

Umtali's only hotel was an untidy, sprawling, single-storey building with a red-painted corrugated iron roof. A young Indian night porter was on duty at the reception desk, but when Nat said he wanted a room, the porter explained that he would need to speak to the owner.

The hotel's owner, Henry Brown, came from the kitchen scowling and wiping his hands on a dirty piece of cloth that might once have been an apron. Unshaven and unkempt, he looked more like a miner than a hotelier.

'Bloody kaffirs!' Brown's voice rasped out. 'Can't trust 'em to so much as place a pan of water on the stove without putting the fire out. Have to get up and do the job for myself. God only knows how they existed before the white man got here . . . But you're not up this early to hear me talk about my useless staff. What can I do for you?'

'I've been in the saddle for twenty-four hours. I'd like a room so I can sleep for a couple of hours. Then a bath and breakfast should set me up to face the world once more.'

Henry Brown shrugged. 'I can fix you up with breakfast. I can probably organise a bath. But a room . . .! All mine are full – most with army officers. There's even a waiting list of army men willing to pay double rates for a room, just to get away from those tents across by the railway line.' Then he grinned. 'Don't reckon they're used to Rhodesian rain. The first camp they made was down by the *spruit*. When the rain came they found themselves under two feet of water. They're learning now, but it'll be a while before it's safe to turn 'em loose on the veld.'

Henry Brown looked at Nat's clothes which had only half-dried on him. Then he stepped closer and peered into Nat's face. 'Been riding through the night you say? Trying to beat the rains yourself?'

'No, I was outrunning a bunch of Manicas. They didn't like me travelling through their country.'

'We should shove the whole lot over the border into Mozambique, I say. Manicas are nearly as bad as the Matabele. Where have you come from?'

Nat managed a smile. 'Matabeleland. I'm here to meet a Thomasina Vincent and guide her and an escort to Fort Victoria.'

'Mrs Vincent? She's been expecting you. Been expecting you for a week – and her temper hasn't improved with the waiting. I'll be glad to see the back of that one, I don't mind telling you.'

Nat was taken aback. Carey Hamilton had said nothing of his sister's character. But the hotel proprietor was looking at Nat with a new respect, tinged with sympathy. 'You'll certainly need sleep before tangling with her. Tell you what I'll do. I can't give you a room, but I can offer you a bed. Belongs to an engineer on the railway. He was called to a derailment, part of the track washed away. Said he'll be back at nine this morning. That'll give you three hours. Here, take a drink up with you – a large whisky. I'll have a meal ready for you when you wake. You'll be in a better state to face her ladyship by then – but don't expect any help from me. I've kept out of her way these last couple of days, and life's been easier for that.'

In the railway engineer's room Nat sat on the bed. Easing off his tall riding-boots he lay back and was asleep within a minute.

He was awoken by a storm outside. At least, he thought it was a storm until other sounds broke in upon his consciousness. Voices . . .

'Mr Retallick, will you come out, or must I come in there?'

It was a woman's voice. But it was not his mother . . . Nat opened his eyes and moved his head. Nothing was familiar. Then his glance fell upon a brass travelling-clock. It showed the time as half-past eleven.

Suddenly Nat remembered. He was in an engineer's room in Umtali's hotel – and the engineer should have returned at nine a.m.

'Mr Retallick! I know you can hear me perfectly well. I am coming in.'

Nat swung his feet to the floor and reached a hand to his head just as the door opened and a young woman stood in the doorway glowering across the room at him. She took in his untidy state, the rumpled bed and his unshaven, unwashed face. Her expression became one of acute distaste as her glance fell upon the untouched drink at his bedside.

'I thought so. You've been drinking! I was told when I woke that you were here, in the hotel. I've been waiting for three hours for you to come to my room and discuss my journey to meet my brother. I suppose you arrived yesterday evening and spent half the night pouring cheap alcohol down your throat?

55

Well, you can nurse your sore head on the way to Fort Victoria. My brother has employed you as a guide and that's what you are going to be – intoxicated or sober. I've spent a whole week in this dreadful hotel. I don't intend being here for one more night. I'll be ready in an hour. Inform Lieutenant Inch and his escort to have the horses in front of the hotel at twelve-thirty.'

Before Nat's confused mind could even begin to think of a reply, Thomasina Vincent turned and strode from the room. On the way out into the passage she brushed aside the crowd of interested onlookers who had gathered outside the door.

Henry Brown stepped inside the room looking sheepish. He was still clutching the filthy apron, and still wiping his hands.

'I'm sorry, Mr Retallick. My reception clerk told her you were here. He'll get an earful from me . . .'

'I thought the railway engineer needed his room by nine o'clock?'

'He's been sent further along the line towards Beira. They've got more trouble. He won't be back until tomorrow. I looked in to tell you, but you were dead to the world and I let you sleep.' The hand-wiping ceased and the dirty piece of cloth was looped around the hotelier's belt. 'You want me to tell the lieutenant to get his escort here?'

Nat stood up and moved his arms to ease the stiff muscles across his back. He ached in every joint. 'I want you to get a tub filled with piping hot water so I can have a bath. When I come out I want a good big meal. Steak, eggs, bacon, fried bread – whatever you can find. While I'm eating send someone to fix an appointment for me to see whoever's in command of the troops camping by the railway.'

The hotel proprietor boggled in disbelief. 'But . . . what about Mrs Vincent?'

Nat began stripping off his clothes. 'She'll just have to go and stamp her feet somewhere else.'

Bathing at Henry Brown's hotel was more in the nature of a ceremony than a necessary ablution. The bath itself was a huge, galvanised affair. Long and coffin-narrow, it rose in a high curve at one end, the metal flared to allow an occupant to lean back and rest his arms on the sides. The bath stood in solitary splendour in the centre of a stone-floored hut. Water for it was provided by a number of Mashona servants who ran between an outside boiler and the bathroom, bearing steaming buckets.

Nat stepped in the water and sat down gingerly. The water was hot enough to be painful, but as he leaned back with a sigh that was half pain, half contentment, he felt his knotted muscles begin to relax.

He took a long, leisurely bath, the water being frequently topped up by two Mashona attendants, in order to compensate for a slight leak. As he bathed Nat was shaved by another attendant.

When he eventually stepped out of the bath-house dressed in clean clothes, Nat felt and looked a new man. Walking through the hotel reception hall on his way to the dining room he passed Thomasina Vincent. Dressed in riding apparel she was standing impatiently by the porter's desk. It was not until he was some paces past her that she realised who he was.

'Mr Retallick! Are you ready? Where are the horses?'

'*My* horse is in the stables and needs to stay there for another day at least . . .' Henry Brown was standing nervously in the dining-room doorway and Nat nodded to him, calling back to Thomasina Vincent, 'I'm going in for a good, solid meal. You're welcome to join me, if you wish.'

Thomasina stared after him in disbelief.

Inside the dining room, Henry Brown said nervously, 'I hope you haven't upset her ladyship unduly . . .'

'I invited her to eat with me. Where am I sitting?'

The dining room was well patronised. As Henry Brown led the way between crowded tables, he said, 'You wanted to meet Major Gurney, commanding officer of the troops in the camp. He's eating here and says you're welcome to share his table.'

Major Gurney was dining with three of his officers at a large corner table. He nodded Nat to a vacant seat, at the same time introducing the two officers who sat with him. 'Mr Retallick . . . Captain Forbes, and Lieutenant Inch.'

The three men nodded to each other and Nat sat down. The soldiers were taking a light midday meal and gazed in astonishment at the high-piled plate placed before Nat.

Observing their surprise, he said, 'You'll need to excuse my greed. I haven't had a good meal in a while.'

'I understand you wish to speak to me, Mr Retallick?' The British army major put the question.

Cutting off a piece of steak, Nat conveyed it to his mouth and nodded. Suddenly the three officers put down their eating utensils and rose to their feet, the three chairs scraping noisily on the rough, wooden floor.

Looking up, Nat saw Thomasina Vincent bearing down upon the table, her face flushed and angry.

'Major Gurney! I demand to know why you are encouraging this . . . this *man* to waste time – and my brother's money too, I have no doubt. He has been engaged to act as a guide to take me to Fort Victoria and I have been waiting a *week* for his arrival. I have no intention of spending another week in this dreadful hotel while he is wined and dined by the army . . .'

'I think you'd better sit down, Mrs Vincent. We're not going *anywhere* today. In fact, unless Major Gurney is in agreement with what I have to ask, you'll be travelling to Fort Victoria via Salisbury and Bulawayo – and so will I.'

Thomasina Vincent was uncertain whether she was angry, indignant – or both. She was much younger than Nat had imagined the wife of a British army colonel would be. Not more than twenty-five years of age, she was attractive in a cold, haughty way – although the African sun had raised a crop of freckles on her nose that no make-up could hide.

'I'd like to make another thing perfectly clear. Your brother is *not* employing me. Carey asked if I would come to Umtali and guide you to Fort Victoria across country. He asked me because I've made the journey before. The only reason I agreed was because I didn't like to think of a woman suffering the discomforts of the veld for more than a month when I could shorten the journey to six or seven days. I trust I'm not going to regret my decision.'

Pulling out a chair beside him, Nat said, 'Sit down, Mrs Vincent . . . Henry! A drink, if you please.'

Thoroughly bemused, Thomasina Vincent sat down heavily and Henry Brown, a look of sheer joy on his face, eased the chair closer to the table before hurrying away.

'It *is* possible I owe you an apology, Mr Retallick. Nevertheless, I do believe . . .'

Nat held up his hand. 'If you don't mind, *I'll* do the talking for a moment. I have something of importance to say to Major Gurney.'

For a few seconds Nat waited for the fury he saw in Thomasina Vincent's eyes to erupt. Instead, her mouth closed tightly, and she stared down at the faded tablecloth in front of her, saying nothing.

Major Gurney looked at Nat with new respect. Very much younger than Colonel Digby Vincent, Thomasina had become the pampered darling of her husband's regiment. Since her arrival in Umtali she had made Major Gurney's life miserable, blatantly using her husband's senior rank as a lever to get her own way when her beauty proved inadequate. He had been forced to provide large escorts to accompany her on daily rides through the surrounding countryside; arrange for a hunt; organise a race meeting — and even throw a disastrous ball.

'You have travelled to Umtali *alone*, Mr Retallick?' asked Major Gurney.

Nat nodded. 'I travelled the route with my father many times. There aren't usually too many problems along the way. Unfortunately, last night I had to seek shelter from a bad storm in the village of Chief Tandi, up in the Vumba mountains. It seems I caught him at a bad time. He had a whole lot of Mozambique chiefs staying with him and from the questions he asked me I'd say they've been cooking something up between themselves.'

'What sort of "something"?'

Nat took another mouthful of food before replying. 'As you probably know, the tribes are in a state of rebellion against the Portuguese in Mozambique — especially in the north-west region of the country, and these chiefs were from that area. I recognised their tribal markings. I believe the Manicas are considering some sort of a pact with their neighbours across the border. The Manicas will join in their fight against the Portuguese, if the Mozambique tribes come here to help in a Manica rising against the British. The timing of all this depends on how badly you fare in your war with the Boers.'

'Then it could be at any time now, Mr Retallick. The news from South Africa is bad. But how certain are you of all this?'

'Certain enough for Chief Tandi to want me killed. He tried last night but I escaped and rode through the night, reaching Umtali soon after dawn.'

Thomasina Vincent was looking hard at Nat and he knew she was remembering her earlier remarks about his being intoxicated the previous evening.

'I think this must rule out any possibility of Mrs Vincent taking the short route to Fort Victoria . . . But what do you suggest I can do about this situation? I can't declare war on the whole Manica tribe. I have no authority for such a course of action – even if there were sufficient troops in Rhodesia to ensure a quick victory. My duties are to establish a staging-post and speed troops along the route to Bulawayo. Mafeking is under siege and we need to organise relief columns as quickly as troops become available.'

'You have a chance to nip the Manica rising in the bud if you act now, Major. Mafeking can wait. I was there recently. They have food enough to survive a siege of many months.'

'You were in Mafeking? *Before* the siege began, of course?'

Nat shook his head. 'Colonel Baden-Powell bought five hundred head of cattle from me. I took them to Mafeking by rail to deliver them . . .' Aware that the youngest officer at the table was gazing at him with an expression akin to awe, Nat added quickly, 'The line was cut but the siege hadn't been on for more than a day or two and the Boers hadn't got the place properly sewn-up. I wouldn't like to try it now.'

'Mr Retallick.' There was deference in Thomasina Vincent's voice now, but a degree of belligerence too. 'Are you saying I must take the long route to Fort Victoria? Travel with the army to Salisbury and Bulawayo?'

'Not necessarily. It depends entirely upon Major Gurney.'

'Please go on, Mr Retallick. What do you suggest I can do?'

'You have a large number of cavalrymen here at the moment, I believe?'

Major Gurney inclined his head. 'A squadron of lancers, recently arrived from India – plus Lieutenant Inch's half-troop of hussars, of course.'

'That should be sufficient. Most African tribesmen still hold horses in awe. Trained cavalrymen could make a lasting impression on them. One that might last longer than any battle. Chief Tandi's village is no more than a comfortable half-day's ride from here. If we left in the morning the Lancers could put on a display of riding for the Manicas and return to Umtali the same day, knowing they had made an important contribution to the peace of this country. Meanwhile I would be riding on to Fort Victoria in perfect safety with Mrs Vincent and Lieutenant Inch's hussars.'

Both the lancer captain and Lieutenant Inch were highly enthusiastic about Nat's idea, but Major Gurney was turning over in his mind the many things that might go wrong with such a plan.

'I don't know. I'm thinking of Mrs Vincent . . .'

'I am perfectly capable of making my own decisions, thank you, Major Gurney. Mr Retallick has suggested a bold and tactical plan. I believe you should act upon it. On occasions such as this, Digby is fond of quoting from the speech made by the French revolutionary, Georges Danton, to the French Assembly: "*De l'audace, encore de l'audace, et toujours de L'audace*" . . . "Boldness, more boldness, and always boldness".'

'Colonel Vincent will never forgive me should anything happen to you . . .'

I will never forgive you if you force me to travel with your army for a month. I will telegraph Digby and insist that *you* accompany me to Fort Victoria, if necessary.'

Thomasina Vincent turned to Nat. 'I *do* owe you an apology, Mr Retallick. I have been *abominably* rude. Please forgive me, and I trust we might be good friends now. Tell me, how is my brother? When did you last see him . . .?'

Before Nat could reply, Major Gurney coughed to attract his attention.

'I have thought very carefully about what you have told me, Mr Retallick. I believe the peace and security of Rhodesia must take precedence over every other consideration in the present circumstances – especially as it will only mean committing my mounted troops for a day. Captain Forbes will issue the necessary orders this afternoon and will lead the lancers. Lieutenant Inch's hussars' sole duty will be to protect Mrs Vincent. They will go no closer to this native village than is necessary to remain in touch with events. Mrs Vincent, I trust you will do nothing foolish to make me regret my decision?'

'I have no doubt your prompt action will ensure many lives are saved, Major, and I assure you that Digby will be fully acquainted with my view.'

'Thank you, Mrs Vincent. Now, if you will both excuse us, I think we soldiers are in for a busy afternoon. It has been a pleasure meeting you, Mr Retallick. Just one thing . . . I will be grateful for a written report on your experiences and observations before you leave. It might prove useful should my actions be questioned, you understand . . .?'

The three soldiers left the table and collected a number of fellow officers as they passed through the dining room. Nat watched them go and turned back to find Thomasina Vincent studying him. Suddenly she smiled and there was unexpected warmth in her expression.

'You can't know how utterly bored I have been this last week, Mr Retallick. Major Gurney has fussed over me for all the world like a mother hen. He's a very kind man, but . . . oh, so pompous! He's terrified to do anything that might affect his promotion chances.'

Nat smiled in return, but said nothing. He doubted very much whether Major Gurney had been any match for the wilful, arrogant and tempestuous young wife of his superior officer.

Much of Nat's lunch had grown cold while he talked and Thomasina looked at him sympathetically as he pushed a cold egg across the plate away from him. 'I am afraid I have spoiled your lunch, Mr Retallick. Perhaps you will dine here with me tonight and allow me to make amends. Besides, I want to hear *all* about Carey. We were very close as children, but I haven't seen him for almost three years . . .'

Nat spent much of the afternoon with the local Native Commissioner, discussing what he had learned at Chief Tandi's village. The commissioner had heard rumours of the Manica tribe's links with its neighbours across the Mozambique border, and he gave full approval to Nat's plan to impress the Manica and Portuguese chiefs. He promised to accompany Nat as far as Tandi's village, escorted by a troop of the British South Africa Company's mounted police to augment the two hundred and fifty horsemen of the lancers and hussars. Together they would make an impressive sight – one to make the Manica and Portuguese chiefs think very seriously before rising against the Rhodesian authorities.

Nat's dinner with Thomasina Vincent proved to be a very pleasant occasion. The hotel restaurant was unusually quiet. All the cavalry officers were at their railside camp, making final checks on their troops in readiness for the events of the next day.

Much of Thomasina's talk was of her brother and of their days together in the Cotswold hills, as children. Nat told Thomasina what he could about her brother, and gradually she steered the conversation towards his life at Insimo.

'You mentioned delivering cattle to Mafeking, Mr Retallick. Do you have many on your farm?'

'Quite a few,' replied Nat vaguely.

'We also had cattle in the Cotswolds – and sheep. My family own a large estate there. More than three thousand acres.'

If Thomasina had expected Nat to be impressed, she was disappointed.

'How large is this farm of yours – Insimo, is it called?'

Nat nodded. 'It's pretty large.'

'How many acres?' Thomasina persisted, her curiosity aroused by his reticence.

'The boundaries have never been accurately fixed, but when the valley was surveyed by the chartered company, they estimated Insimo contained about a hundred and thirty thousand acres.'

Thomasina was stunned. 'That's not a farm ... It's an *empire*! How was Cecil Rhodes persuaded to grant your family so much land?'

'Rhodes had no say in the matter. My father was given the valley by King Lobengula of the Matabele long before Rhodes set foot in Africa, and the Retallicks have fought both Boer and African to keep it. Rhodes may be a very powerful man, but he'll never take Insimo from the Retallicks.'

CHAPTER NINE

When the mounted party left Umtali the following morning most of the townspeople turned out to watch them go. Soldiers sent from Britain to fight in the Boer war had been issued with the new 'khaki' uniforms, but the lancers had arrived direct from India complete with their full dress uniforms and they wore them today. Led by Captain Forbes, they were resplendent in red uniforms faced with blue; black, plumed helmets; and gold braid and buttons that reflected the sun. As they rode, a light breeze sprang up to ruffle the red and white pennons fluttering at the ends of two hundred lances.

Behind the lancers were fifty hussars and their packhorses, led by Lieutenant Inch. More soberly dressed than the lancers, they were still an impressive troop and they carried rifles in addition to their swords. Behind the hussars Nat rode with Thomasina and Native Commissioner Ronald Nesbitt.

Last of all, but refusing to allow themselves to be overshadowed by their military companions, rode a hundred policemen. Green uniformed, they too carried lances bearing pennons of red and white, but in a saddle holster each man also had the more workmanlike, bolt action, breech-loading ·303 Lee-Enfield rifle.

Riding two abreast, the colourful column extended for half a mile.

Although heavy cloud clung to the peaks of the Vumba mountains it had not rained for twenty-four hours and the *spruits* and rivers along the way posed no problems to the riders, six hours of fairly easy riding bringing them to within sight of Chief Tandi's hillside village.

Here the horsemen formed extended lines of fifty abreast, Lieutenant Inch's hussars falling back with the indignant Thomasina in their midst. She felt she should have been at the head of the troops with Nat, the Native Commissioner and Captain Forbes.

Unnoticed until they were within a mile of the village, the cavalrymen caused a panic among the Manica tribesmen and women. Nat had brought the soldiers and police from the gentle slope above the village, and looking down he thought the scene resembled a disturbed ants' nest with figures scurrying to and fro.

When the horsemen were still a couple of hundred yards from the mud and straw huts, a party of Manica elders came to meet them led by Chief Tandi.

The Manica chief faltered momentarily when he recognised Nat but, recovering quickly, he advanced to greet Commissioner Nesbitt.

'*Inkosi!* Father of the Manica people. You are welcome to my village. Why did you not send a messenger ahead to tell me you were coming? I would have prepared a proper welcome.' As he spoke, Chief Tandi's glance moved nervously from the Native Commissioner to Nat, and on to the ranks of horsemen. 'You come with many armed men. I greet you in peace, with only my elders about me.'

'We are here as friends, Chief Tandi. Indeed, we have ridden all the way from Umtali to put on a special entertainment for you – and for your guests.'

Chief Tandi's glance flicked to Nat once more, and as quickly moved away. 'I have no guests. Only my family and my people.'

'Have the chiefs from across the border left so soon, Chief Tandi?' Nat put the question in fluent Portuguese and the Manica chief's face registered dismay. '. . . And what of Nanda, the widow of your nephew? I do not see her standing with the other villagers. Have her brought here. I would speak with her.'

It was a few moments before Chief Tandi replied. Not looking at Nat, he said, 'She is no longer here. There was an accident . . .'

'It is well I did not remain in your village, Chief Tandi. I too might have had an unfortunate accident. I suggest you bring your friends from Mozambique out here to watch the entertainment. Or should the Commissioner send in his police to find them?'

A most unhappy man now, Chief Tandi spoke rapidly to one of the younger sub-chiefs in his party and the man hurried away to the village.

Native Commissioner Nesbitt knew enough Portuguese to have followed much of Nat's conversation with Chief Tandi, and he asked, 'What was all that about?'

'It was about a killing. It was meant to be mine, but you'd never collect enough evidence against Tandi to charge him. However, I think you'll meet his friends from Mozambique now.'

Some minutes later Chief Tandi's messenger returned to the gathering accompanied by between twenty and thirty men. Most were from Portuguese Mozambique – and many carried guns.

The sight of the guns brought an immediate and angry reaction from Native Commissioner Nesbitt. 'Chief Tandi, order those natives to throw down their guns immediately. Any who refuse will be shot. I don't give a damn whether they're Rhodesian subjects, or Portuguese. No kaffir carries a gun in *my* territory.'

His words provoked a bitter argument among the tribal chiefs from Mozambique, and Nat explained quickly that they were calling the authority of the Native Commissioner into question.

Without more ado, Nesbitt snapped an order to the captain of the police.

The mounted policemen kneed their mounts forward to form a line between the lancers and the angry tribesmen. As they drew their rifles free of the holsters a cartridge was levered into the breech of each gun. At a shouted command they brought the weapons to their shoulders, a hundred men taking aim at the gun-carrying chiefs from Mozambique. Without further argument, the natives from Mozambique dropped their guns to the ground as though they had suddenly become red hot.

When the weapons were gathered up by a detail of the police

troopers, the rifles lined up on the chiefs were lowered and the mounted policemen filed back to take up position behind the lancers once more.

Native Commissioner Nesbitt now ordered the villagers forward. They were to sit on the ground about their chief and witness the demonstration of horsemanship planned for them.

The villagers were as eager as the chiefs were surly, and they quickly surrounded their tribal elders and the guests of the tribe. The children in particular were as excited as children anywhere who were about to witness a spectacular. Seeing so many horsemen gathered together was in itself quite exceptional. The fact that they were actually going to put on a display for them brought the excitement to fever pitch.

The lancers began with an exhibition of ordinary parade-ground drill, wheeling, turning and manoeuvring in unison, their precision bringing gasps of appreciation from the watching villagers.

Next, the soldiers showed off their skills on the open ground in front of the watching crowd, and the response from the crowd grew in proportion to the difficulty of the feat. Spearing rings on the gallop, bowling over man-size targets and, finally, spearing oranges brought from Umtali and strewn on the ground ahead of them.

Not to be outdone, the policemen also performed this last trick. There was a brief moment of drama when the police captain's horse stumbled, throwing its rider to the ground, but the alarm of the watching natives turned to spontaneous applause when one of the charging police troopers checked his horse and reached down. The dismounted captain was carried to safety with one foot secured in his rescuer's stirrup. But the police ingenuity was not exhausted yet. When the lance-bearing policemen were a hundred yards beyond their inoffensive targets they turned. Then, leaping from their horses with drawn rifles, they shot the remaining oranges to pulp with well aimed bullets.

While the watching villagers were still chattering noisily about the skill of the policemen, lancers and police horsemen combined to form a single line about a half-mile distant.

Obeying the strident commands of a bugle, the long, colourful line began to walk towards the assembled villagers, each red and white pennon reaching out towards the next horseman's lance in a fresh cross-wind.

Another bugle call and the horses began to trot. As the horsemen gathered speed, the long line buckled slightly, but quickly recovered. Another bugle command and the trot became a canter, the steel tips of the lances still pointing to the sky. Then the lone bugler sounded a new command, the very urgency of the call requiring no interpretation. The gleaming steel tips of three hundred lances dipped in awesome unison and the pounding of hooves caused Nat's stomach to contract in fear ... and he was not in the path of the charging horsemen.

Squatting in the path of the hooves and steel-tipped lances of the wildly shrieking cavalrymen, the Manica villagers were convinced they had been lured to their own slaughter. As the ground trembled about them they scrambled to their feet, stumbling over each other in their haste to escape from imminent death.

Then, just as the crescendo of screams of the terrified villagers had reached a pitch greater than the shouts of the horsemen, the lance points were raised and the horses slithered to a halt only an arm's length from where the front rank of Manica villagers had been squatting.

It was some moments before the panic-stricken Manicas realised the charge was over. As the headlong flight faltered and came to an end, men and women looked at each other, grinning sheepishly. Then a young girl laughed nervously. The sound was quickly taken up and the tribe purged its mortification in over-loud laughter. Gradually, as it was realised that Tandi and the Mozambique chiefs had been in the van of the undignified flight, the tribal laughter was directed at them. Chiefs and headmen stood huddled together in a dejected group, burning with humiliation.

As the Manica villagers drifted back to stand grinning up at the men who had struck such terror in them only minutes before, Nat and District Commissioner Nesbitt dismounted and strode to where the small group of chiefs stood together.

Native Commissioner Nesbitt singled out the Manica chief for his immediate attention. Speaking in the Shona dialect used by the Manica, he said, 'These soldiers and police are here today as a warning. This is only a very small part of the army belonging to my country. Many more soldiers who ride horses will be coming through Umtali during the coming months. They will be on their way to win the war being fought against the bearded men of the south – and they *will* win, because their numbers are without end. If I hear any more rumours that you are making rebellious talk with the chiefs from across the border I will bring these soldiers back to find you. If I do the day will not end in laughter for your people. The soldiers will destroy your villages and hunt down your men until there are no Manicas left in these mountains. This is my promise to you.'

The Manica chief maintained a sullen silence while the Native Commissioner was talking, but now Nesbitt turned his attention to the Mozambique chiefs. 'As for you . . . I would be within my rights to order your arrest and execution for trying to stir up rebellion amongst the Manicas.'

His words caused immediate consternation among the visiting chiefs and he held up a hand for silence. 'I am not going to have you killed . . . this time. Instead you will return to your own country and tell your people what you have seen today. The British queen has a greater army than any that has ever been known. If you ever interfere in Rhodesian affairs again I will personally bring that army to Mozambique and destroy your villages in the same manner as I have promised to deal with the people of Chief Tandi. You will give your names to the captain of the police now, and return to Mozambique immediately. If any of you is ever found in this country again you will be shot on the spot. Is this understood?'

The Mozambique chiefs nodded their heads vigorously, anxious to be on their way. They did not doubt Native Commissioner Nesbitt's authority any longer and knew they were fortunate to be leaving Manicaland with their lives. They wanted to leave quickly in case Nesbitt changed his mind.

'I thought that went rather well,' said Nat with some satisfaction, as they walked back to where the soldiers' and police grazed their animals surrounded by inquisitive Manica children.

'I'm grateful to you for your information,' replied the Native Commissioner. 'If this hadn't been nipped in the bud I would have had very serious trouble on my hands.'

Nat nodded to where the soldiers were talking to the children. 'Not while you have such expert horsemen to call upon. That last charge put the fear of God in *me*. I never thought they'd stop in time.'

'Unfortunately we'll not have the lancers – or any other troops – with us for long. Things are going from bad to worse in South Africa and they need reinforcements urgently. We've suffered heavy defeats on every front with generals throwing away men like farmers scattering corn. We'll win the war eventually, of course, but the cost is going to be high. Far too damned high.'

'I'm glad I'm not involved,' said Nat complacently. 'I've too much to do at Insimo to get involved in other men's wars.'

'It isn't as simple as that,' declared Nesbitt grimly. 'War has a nasty habit of reaching out and ensnaring many men who would rather be doing something else. That includes most of the Boers. I hope for your sake you *are* able to stand back from the conflict – but I doubt it very much.'

The two men shook hands warmly, and the Native Commissioner went off with some of the policemen to search for guns in Chief Tandi's village.

Nat made his way to where Thomasina stood with Lieutenant Inch and his hussars. She was still filled with excitement over the spectacle she had just witnessed and Nat saw her for the first time as a lively young woman, not merely the dignified wife of a senior army officer.

'Such *superb* horsemanship,' she bubbled to Nat. 'It couldn't fail to impress anyone who was watching.'

'The Manicas were impressed all right,' agreed Nat. 'But by the time the police have finished searching their village they'll be resentful too. I want to put a few miles between us before then.'

That night Nat brought the party down from the Vumba mountains and they made camp by a steaming hot spring. With Nat and Lieutenant Inch standing guard, Thomasina was able to enjoy a dip in the hot water. Enriched by mineral salts, the spring water was believed by the Manicas to possess healing powers bordering on the magical.

After her dip Thomasina swore she felt fitter than she could ever remember. She certainly looked the picture of health when she emerged from her small tent later that evening. The sun was setting beyond the lowveld in a blaze of tropical colours, although a few dark storm-clouds still embraced the mountain peaks. The troopers were enjoying the hot springs now, while at the camp a large hartebeest shot by Nat, not two hours before, was spit-roasting over a crackling fire tended by two cooks who cast many envious glances in the direction of the springs.

'It's time I brought the men back to camp,' said Lieutenant Inch. 'I don't want them wandering all over the African countryside once it gets dark.'

'Have a dip yourself while you're there,' suggested Nat. He had bathed while Lieutenant Inch escorted Thomasina back to the camp. 'It won't be dangerously dark for another forty minutes.'

'I might do that,' agreed the young lieutenant gratefully. It was much hotter here on the lowveld than it had been in the mountains and the soldier's khaki shirt was stained with perspiration.

When the lieutenant had gone Thomasina offered Nat a drink of brandy. This was the heart of Africa, but Colonel Digby Vincent had ensured that his wife would enjoy as many of the pleasures of civilisation as possible. Nat's insistence that they use packhorses and not wagons had meant leaving the bulkier comforts behind at Umtali, but her tent and the brandy were considered 'necessities'.

'This is a beautiful country, Nat. It's easy to understand people falling in love with it. I think I would too, if I were a man.'

'Beautiful, yes. But the veld has to be treated with respect. You can never take Africa for granted.'

'It sounds like a woman. Perhaps that is why I have this very strong feeling of it being a man's country.'

'Probably. It's inclined to deal harshly with women.'

'Do you know many women?' It might have been a coy question, but it was not.

'My ma and Victoria are the only women who live at Insimo. Victoria has a daughter, Elvira, but she's eleven years older than me and married to a Portuguese army officer. She comes back on a visit occasionally.'

'How about girls of your own age? There must be some, surely?'

Nat shook his head. 'Years ago an occasional *voortrekker* might find his way to Insimo. His family usually included a daughter or two, but *voortrekkers* don't cross the Limpopo river these days.'

'What will you do when you decide to take a wife? You *will* want to marry one day?'

Nat shrugged. 'It seems to worry Ma more than it does me. I've thought about it . . . Not often though. There's too much to do at Insimo.'

Thomasina hoped Nat's mother would be around when he met up with the girl who decided she wanted to marry *him*. His lack of experience with the opposite sex, combined with his vast land-holdings, made Nat a prime target for the wrong type of woman. He was also a very good-looking young man . . . As she looked at him, Thomasina reminded herself that Nat Retallick's future was not *her* concern.

'I'd like to see this valley of yours some time.'

'Why not? Ask Carey to bring you to stay for a few days. You'll love it, I'm sure.' Putting down his drink, he said, 'I'll go and see what's happening at the cooking-fire. I doubt if the soldiers have ever cooked a hartebeest before.'

'Neither have I . . . but I'm willing to try.'

At the fire Nat suggested to the two perspiring soldiers that they should join their colleagues for a dip in the hot springs before darkness came down. When Thomasina added her weight to the suggestion, the two reluctant cooks needed no more persuading.

When Lieutenant Inch returned from his dip a short time afterwards he saw Nat and Thomasina crouched over a cut portion of the hartebeest. She had skewered a piece of meat with Nat's skinning-knife and was gnawing at the cooked flesh. With grease on her flushed cheeks and with shreds of lank hair hanging out of place, she looked less like the Colonel's lady, and more like a camp-follower. Enjoyably surprised at the taste of the meat she rested her hand on Nat's arm in a quick, affectionate gesture. At that moment Lieutenant Inch was glad that Thomasina Vincent was not *his* wife.

The night camp at the hot springs was one of those rare, magic occasions for every one of those who was there.

Thomasina, Nat and the hussars sat around the aromatic wood fire that crackled and sizzled with fat falling from the cooking hartebeest. As the colours in the western sky faded and died, a plump moon floated into view in a silver-dusted velour sky and frogs in the surrounding pools puffed out their throats and ground out their unmusical songs.

Singing of a far more musical nature was brought to the lowveld after the hartebeest had been reduced to charred bones that quickly disintegrated among the ashes of the fire. Most of the soldiers had been recruited in Ireland and now they began to sing of the virtues of the land they had left behind, and of the charms of the women who dwelled there.

Cocooned in the warmth of an African night, the soldiers dreamed of home. For an hour or two, thousands of miles away, Ireland became the dream island of their songs, and not the troubled land of reality.

73

CHAPTER TEN

When morning came Thomasina Vincent was the Colonel's lady once more. Her morning tea was too cold, the water provided for her ablutions too hot. The orderly was 'slovenly', the men too noisy – and her horse had not been groomed to her liking.

Her bad mood remained with her until the party was no more than a day from Fort Victoria. They had left the lowveld behind once more and were now in the foothills of the highveld that extended throughout the whole of central Rhodesia.

Ordering a camp to be made earlier in the day than usual, Nat suggested to Thomasina that she might like to go hunting and provide supper for the party. In view of her mood of the past few days, he expected a curt refusal. Instead, she accepted with an alacrity that took him by surprise.

Lieutenant Inch wanted to send an escort with them, but Nat refused to have the soldiers with him. The accoutrements of a hussar were not designed for stalking game. One British cavalryman made more noise than a whole Boer commando. Unlikely to meet up with any Boers in this remote part of the country, Nat and Thomasina would hunt without an escort.

The cavalry lieutenant conceded the truth of Nat's argument, but not without many misgivings. His unease increased as he watched Nat and Thomasina ride out of the camp together, but his fears had nothing to do with any dangers they were likely to encounter. Thomasina was smiling for the first time in days, and the young lieutenant remembered how she had looked at Nat when they made camp on their first night out of Umtali.

The two riders did not need to go far to find wild animals. Less than a mile from the camp they came upon a pride of lions. One of the lionesses had made a kill earlier in the day and the tawny-maned leader of the pride had gorged himself until he could hardly move. While the others fought over his leavings, he lay on his side, his tail twitching spasmodically, a growl rumbling in his throat whenever one of the lionesses disturbed his repose.

Thomasina wanted to shoot the lion, but Nat stopped her.

'Shoot him and you'll frighten all the game for miles. If you want to shoot lions I'll take you on a lion hunt when you visit Insimo. They use our cattle pen as a larder, so we have to keep their numbers down.'

'Do you entertain many guests at Insimo?'

Nat shook his head. 'We're too far from anywhere. Ma would enjoy more company, and both Adam and Ben wish we were closer to a town, but I like things just the way they are.'

They rode together for another couple of miles and Nat talked about Insimo, prompted occasionally by his companion. Then, after a brief period of silence, Nat leaned across and touched Thomasina's arm, signalling her to bring her horse to a halt.

Thomasina looked startled, but Nat held a finger to his lips before pointing towards a clump of straggling msasa trees nearby.

Seeing nothing, Thomasina looked at him inquiringly.

In a whisper, Nat explained, 'Buffalo . . . see? In the shade of the largest tree.'

The colouring of the buffalo blended perfectly with the deep shade and it was some minutes before the animal betrayed its presence with a twitch of its long, black-tipped tail.

'It's huge!' whispered Thomasina excitedly. 'Can I shoot it? Surely it's good meat . . .?'

Nat nodded. 'Close in slowly – but don't fire until I've made certain there isn't a cantankerous old bull out of sight just a few yards away. When you *do* fire, make certain of killing it with one bullet. A wounded buffalo is the most dangerous animal in Africa.'

Thomasina nodded, but she was already unsheathing her rifle, her gaze not leaving the buffalo.

Nat circled well wide of the animal, keeping a careful look-out for other buffalo. They were gregarious beasts and usually grazed in large herds. When he saw no other buffalo nearby, he realised something was wrong. Even old bulls deposed from authority by younger, stronger animals remained with the herd until old age or injury left them prey for the veld's many predators.

Tangled trees and undergrowth intervened between Nat and Thomasina when he turned his horse. It was his intention to check on the animal and learn why it was alone. But even as he slipped his heavy Mauser rifle from its saddle-holster there was the report of a rifle of a much smaller calibre than his own.

Digging his heels hard into the flanks of his horse, Nat charged through the thick undergrowth, disregarding all caution. He emerged just in time to see both horse and rider go down as Thomasina's animal slipped whilst trying to execute an impossible turn to escape the charge of the buffalo.

Thomasina was a keen shot, but she had learned her skill on her father's safe Oxfordshire estate and she had never shot at an animal larger than a fox before today. The thought of writing and telling her father she had actually killed a *buffalo* was uppermost in her mind as she moved slowly towards the animal.

The buffalo was watching her too. She knew this from the way it stood unmoving in the shadows. She half-expected the animal to charge, but when it finally made a move it was surprisingly slow – and it moved *away* from her, heading for the thick tangle of bushes beyond the tree's shade.

Seeing her intended quarry about to disappear, Thomasina raised the light Remington rifle she carried and fired off a quickly aimed shot. The bullet hit its target – she heard the 'thwack' as it struck the tough hide of the buffalo – but instead of falling the animal lurched forward and the undergrowth closed about it, hiding the great beast from view.

Disappointment took precedence over common sense and, forgetting Nat's warning, Thomasina spurred her horse forward, hoping to get in another shot and finish off the wounded buffalo.

She had almost reached the spot where the buffalo had been standing when it suddenly emerged from the thicket with a speed that took her by surprise, and startled her horse.

Thomasina brought her gun up to snap off a second shot, but the action proved her undoing. As she brought the weapon to the aim, her horse side-stepped – and slipped. She was unable to keep her balance, and both horse and rider crashed heavily to the ground, the gun falling from Thomasina's hands.

The angry buffalo caught the flailing horse a side-swipe with its heavy, curved horns, knocking it back to the ground as it tried to rise. Then it was Thomasina's turn. She saw the blood on the buffalo's neck where her bullet had struck home, and then the beast lowered its head and came at her as she lay upon the ground.

Thomasina was never aware of her scream, only of a desperate scramble to remove herself from the wounded beast's path. She succeeded – just – but there was no time for self-congratulation. More than half-a-ton of buffalo skidded to a clumsy halt, wheeled, and repeated its charge.

This time there was no escape. Her previous effort had landed her against the base of a tall ant-hill, preventing her from rolling away. She could only watch helplessly as the animal charged towards her. Then the wounded buffalo expelled its breath in a great grunt, as though of surprise, and its front legs buckled. As the animal's nose dropped and the curved horns carved a double furrow in the soft earth, Thomasina heard the delayed report of the rifle-shot that had brought the life of the buffalo to an end.

It was probably the best shot Nat had ever made. Five hundred yards away when the buffalo turned for a second charge, he had aimed and fired in a split second. The gun Nat carried was a powerful, large-bore rifle designed by Peter Paul Mauser, the brilliant German inventor. Heavier than the weapon issued by the Boer government to its commandos, it was capable of killing at a range of two thousand yards.

By the time Nat reached her, Thomasina was on her feet gazing down at the buffalo. When Nat jumped from his horse she shifted her gaze to him. All her arrogance had fallen away, and her expression was that of a shocked young girl who had just been through a terrifying experience.

'I thought it was going to kill me. It *would* have killed me . . .' The words came out in a frightened whisper and she began to shake.

'It's over now.' Nat put an arm about her shoulders and she clung to him, trembling violently.

'It's all right, Thomasina . . .' Nat could think of nothing else to say. 'It's all right . . .'

Gradually Thomasina regained control of herself. Her breathing, although still deep and uneven, became easier. Looking down at her, Nat knew a feeling he had never before experienced and his hand came up and touched her hair.

Thomasina looked up at him. She was dry-eyed, but her face was pale and drawn. She knew how close she had come to death. So too did Nat, and the knowledge affected him strangely. His arms tightened about her and, bringing his face down to hers, he kissed her with ferocious inexperience.

For a wild moment, Thomasina responded, her mouth moving beneath his, her body meeting every demand of his own. But the madness ended as suddenly as it had begun. Her mouth moved away from his and she whispered, 'No, Nat. No . . . please!'

She pushed him away then, and for some moments he stood awkwardly before her. 'I'm sorry, Thomasina . . .'

Her finger cut off the apology. 'Don't say anything more. If you do I shall have to apologise too. I was as much to blame as you.'

She looked up at him with a strange expression on her face, and in that moment Nat wished he had more experience with women. He might have had some inkling of her thoughts.

'The best thing . . . for both of us will be to forget what just happened,' she said.

'I'm not sure I can. I'm not at all sure I *want* to.'

Thomasina's chin came up and Nat realised she was once more in total command of herself. 'That would be a great pity, Nat. I hope to see you again after we reach Fort Victoria. I have been looking forward to visiting this valley you love so much. I can do neither if one foolish moment is allowed to remain between us. You would always be hoping for far more than I can ever give. Eventually there would be so much bitterness in you that you would begin to hate me. This would make me very unhappy . . .'

Suddenly Nat felt very much younger than Thomasina. Far younger than the few years between them.

'I'll catch your horse and we'll go . . .'

'Not before we take what we need from the buffalo. The animal came damned close to killing me. The least I can do is ensure it's eaten.'

Thomasina's horse had been thoroughly frightened and it took both time and patience to catch it. When Nat finally brought the animal back to her, a cursory examination disclosed a gash on its flank, caused by the buffalo's horns but although the horse was trembling, it seemed otherwise unhurt.

The problem of cutting up and carrying meat from the buffalo was solved when a party of ten hussars unexpectedly put in an appearance. The misgivings of Lieutenant Inch had won. He had sent the troopers after the two hunters and they had been guided to the spot by the shots. If Thomasina was relieved the troopers had not arrived some minutes earlier, she did not allow her feelings to show.

When Nat looked more closely at the buffalo, he saw Thomasina's shot had been a good one. The beast would have been killed immediately had the calibre of the rifle been larger. As it was, the buffalo would have died anyway, but such was its strength that it was still able to make a last, near-fatal charge.

Nat also discovered why the buffalo had not been able to keep up with the herd. It had evidently been a target for other hunters and had the metal head of a spear embedded in a rear leg, close to the knee-joint. The normal movement of walking must have brought great pain to the animal. Its charge was the final, determined act of a courageous creature.

Nat, Thomasina and the hussars dined well on this, the last night of their journey together across Rhodesia. By the time the buffalo horns were presented to Thomasina in a brief, informal ceremony, the party had regained much of the camaraderie achieved on their first night together. Thomasina was the light-hearted centre of attraction, complimenting the hussars on the quality of their singing and behaving as the wife of a commanding officer should.

To Nat the evening was an ordeal. It came as a relief to wrap his blankets about him and try to put the confusing events of the day into some order.

*　　*　　*

The entry of Thomasina Vincent to Fort Victoria with her escort of hussars was in the nature of a triumphal procession.

Long before they reached the small town, lookouts in the tower of the police fort were reporting their coming. Women stood in the doorways of mud and timber houses, and small children spilled from the school, temporarily released to witness the arrival of the cavalrymen.

The presence of the soldiers came as a great relief to the residents of this small pioneer town. Most of the garrison had been called away to carry out duties on the border with Transvaal, amidst rumours that an irregular Boer commando had crossed into Matabeleland. Outlying farmsteads and communities were in a state of nervous apprehension as rumour followed fast upon rumour.

Now, with so many heavily armed and experienced soldiers to swell the garrison, the residents of Fort Victoria could breathe easily again. A Boer commando was unlikely to attack such a well defended town.

Captain Carey Hamilton was waiting outside the fort to greet his sister, and the affection between them was immediately apparent. Not wishing to intrude upon the happy family reunion, Nat was already walking his horse away when Carey Hamilton called after him.

Clasping Nat's hand, the officer said, 'I can't tell you how grateful I am to you. Thomasina didn't leave Beira a moment too soon. I've had a telegraph from her husband. More than half his men have gone down with fever. He's calling for every available doctor to be sent to him there.'

'Beira is no place for an Englishman,' Nat agreed. He looked towards Thomasina and she waved to him. 'Bring Thomasina to Insimo when she's bored with Fort Victoria. My mother will enjoy having her as a guest.'

Nat was about to go on his way when Carey Hamilton called to him again, and something in the officer's voice brought Nat to an abrupt halt.

'Nat . . . Jaconus Van Eyck was here a week ago. He left word for you to return to Insimo as soon as you could.'

'Why? Has something happened? My mother . . .?'

'No, it's your brother Adam. He's gone south to join the Boer army.'

CHAPTER ELEVEN

When Nat rode away from the valley to Umtali, Adam was left in nominal charge of Insimo. In fact, the arrangement was merely a sop to the youthful pride of the middle Retallick brother. If a family decision was required it would come from Elvira Retallick. Even the supervision of the Matabele farm-hands and herdsmen would not weigh too heavily upon Adam. It was a task for which Benjamin was better suited, and the Matabele always looked to him for their orders.

Hot-headed to the point of rashness, and painfully jealous of his older brother, Adam was a skilful and natural hunter, happiest when on horseback on the veld, a gun in his hands.

Adam had been looking forward to Nat's absence, anticipating that he would be able to go after an elephant herd that had been reported on the Lundi river, no more than twenty miles from the valley. Adam had a yen for a pair of fine ivory tusks to adorn the wall of his room.

Much to Adam's disgust, Jaconus Van Eyck announced that *he* was going hunting, to procure meat for the wives of the Matabele workers to cure and dry. In order to find game in sufficient numbers he needed to go out of the valley. It meant that Adam must remain at Insimo, at least until Jaconus Van Eyck's return. Nat had ordered that either Jaconus or the oldest Retallick should remain in the valley while he was away.

When Adam objected to Jaconus Van Eyck going on a hunt, Elvira Retallick entered the argument on the side of the ageing but still tough Boer hunter. Adam would remain in the valley.

Adam stomped off in a huff, unaware that Jaconus Van Eyck's departure had nothing to do with hunting. Rumours of a Matabele rising coincided to take advantage of the Boer war were in the air. Jaconus Van Eyck was going to visit a few of the Matabele villages to gauge the mood of the tribesmen.

While Adam was still smarting at the blow to his plans and his authority, a friend of Jaconus Van Eyck, called at Insimo, en route from Bulawayo to Fort Victoria.

Jaconus Van Eyck had left by this time, but the friend stayed overnight and during dinner he painted a vivid account to the Retallick family of the set-backs suffered by the British in their war with the Boer republics of the Orange Free State and Transvaal.

The next morning Adam was gone. The note he left behind for his mother spoke of the frustration he felt at being a younger son, expected to devote his life to Insimo without regard to the things *he* wanted to do. Adam complained that he possessed no more authority than a hired hand. He believed the time had come for him to choose his own path in life. A path that would take him away from Insimo and the growing British influence in the country about them. He was going to make his way among a people he both liked and admired. Adam Retallick was on his way to join the Boer army.

Distracted with worry, Elvira sent farm-hands off in all directions seeking the help of the Matabele headmen to find her fifteen-year-old son before he reached the Limpopo river, border between Rhodesia and the independent Boer Republic of Transvaal.

The Matabele headmen and their villagers had known the Retallick family since before Daniel Retallick had moved to the valley with his Portuguese wife thirty years before, and they sent out trackers to find Adam. But these very trackers had taught their skills to Adam – and he had learned well. They failed to find him.

When Jaconus Van Eyck returned to Insimo from his 'hunting trip', he also set off in search of Adam. But by now the trail was cold, and when he reached the Limpopo river Jaconus Van Eyck was forced to acknowledge defeat. Across the river was the Zoutpansberg, an area beyond the fringe of the Transvaal's most primitive settlements. The Boers who dwelled here were the *takhaaren* – 'the wild ones'. Primitive, no-madic hunters, they lived lives of rugged, biblical simplicity.

Their unwritten laws were dictated on a daily basis by expediency and maintained with the aid of a seldom wasted bullet.

When Adam left Insimo he rode hard, knowing his mother would instigate a search immediately it was discovered he had gone. He would have no difficulty out-distancing the Matabele — or even Ben, should he be allowed to come after him. Jaconus Van Eyck was another matter. If his mother could find the old hunter in time there was a faint chance that Adam might be prevented from crossing the river to Transvaal. But such a possibility was remote. The border was a hundred and fifty miles from Insimo, and Adam could take any one of a hundred routes.

Adam rode sixty miles that first day and made a fireless camp beside a fast-flowing stream. Towering above him was a mountain that the Matabele believed sometimes spat flame and grumbled as though angry with the world. Consequently, none of them would venture close. Adam knew he was as safe here as anywhere. He dined on water and *biltong*, the highly spiced dried meat carried in the saddle-bags of every hunting man in this part of the world.

Leaving home remained an exciting adventure for Adam until the moment the sun finally set over the mountain, but then loneliness and darkness closed in about him. He had been hunting on many occasions without his brothers or Jaconus Van Eyck accompanying him, but there had always been Matabele hunters hunched around a shadow-chasing fire when night fell. Exchanging tales of past hunts in their loud voices, they helped to keep the night at bay.

Tonight Adam had only his close-tethered horse and the cold comfort of his rifle on the blanket beside him for company. As he looked up at the sky, liberally sprinkled with stars, Adam thought of his mother at home in Insimo. She would be in bed now, or perhaps kneeling in front of the cloth-covered cabinet in a corner of her room. On the cabinet stood a crucifix, a candle, and an exquisite statuette of the Madonna bearing a small child in her arms.

His mother had spent many nights kneeling before her personal altar after Adam's father and eldest brother had been killed. He had heard her begging the Virgin Mother to give her the strength to live through another twenty-four hours. Elvira Retallick's prayers had been answered then and on many other occasions when life threatened to overwhelm her.

Once, when Adam was a small boy, he had contracted a fever and for four days and nights alternated between delirium and unconsciousness. His mother had nursed him constantly for all this time. One night he woke to find the fever gone. Weak, but with the strength of childhood, he had left his bed and gone in search of his mother. He found her in her room asleep before the altar, the crucifix clutched in her hands, her bowed head resting on the small cabinet.

The memory brought a lump to Adam's throat, and for many moments his resolution to begin a new life wavered. For a few weak minutes he even contemplated returning to Insimo and all that was familiar. Then Adam remembered the note he had written in the heat of jealous anger. If the note had not been written he might have gone back. But it was done. There would be no return. He had to go on.

In spite of such unhappy thoughts, Adam slept until the night was at its darkest. He was woken by his horse. Able to move only in a short circle on its rope tether, the animal was snatching at the rope and snorting in fear.

Reaching for his rifle, Adam knew immediately what was frightening the horse. He could smell the rank, odoriferous scent of a hyena — and then he saw its yellow eyes. The sloping-backed beast had been circling the camp growing bolder with each uneventful circuit. Soon the animal would have made a sudden rush and clamped shut its amazingly strong jaws on a foot, or a leg . . . It was a fate that had overtaken many unwary sleepers on the veld.

Slowly and carefully, Adam eased the bolt of his rifle home and raised the weapon. He caught another glimpse of the eerie yellow eyes and squeezed the trigger. The loud report startled the horse and it squealed and tried to rear away from the gunsmoke, but the horse's terror was lost in the din that erupted from the darkness nearby.

The hyena was screaming in pain and anger, gyrating in a tight circle, snarling and snapping in vain at the pain that burned through its stomach. It fell and rolled over and over in a frantic attempt to dislodge the unseen pain-maker.

Jumping to his feet, Adam jerked the empty cartridge case free and levered another bullet into the breech. He stood over the snarling, biting, writhing shadow and fired a bullet through the hyena's brain.

Still the foul-smelling animal would not die, but it was no longer a danger to any living thing. It lay on the ground twitching its life away and Adam returned to his blanket, pausing to calm the horse on the way.

He slept no more that night. Instead he spent the remaining hours of darkness sitting hunched with his back against a rock, rifle in hand, his blanket thrown about his shoulders.

At first light Adam saddled up and rode south. Behind him the first vulture dropped from the sky. Soon the scavengers of the veld would complete their grisly task, leaving nothing behind to show the hyena had ever existed.

That night Adam stayed in a small *kraal* on the extreme edge of the Matabele sphere of influence. The *kraal* headman offered him food because such hospitality was traditional to the tribe, but the manner of the Matabele men was surly to the point of open hostility.

At first Adam thought their manner was due to news of the Boer war, but then the headman mentioned that Adam was the first white man they had seen since he and his people had broken away from the main tribe after the death of Lobengula. When Adam mentioned that his father and Lobengula had been friends, and that as a child he had walked and talked with Lobengula, he found he had the immediate attention of every man in the headman's group. Most still wore the out-dated 'warrior ring' in their short, curly hair, signifying that they had proved their manhood in one of Lobengula's fighting regiments.

Adam was questioned closely about the identity of his father. Then, suddenly, the mood of the Matabele tribesmen underwent a dramatic change. Daniel Retallick had been known to many of them. Indeed, his friendship had been highly valued by the headman himself. Suddenly, from being an unwanted visitor, Adam found himself being fêted as an honoured guest. One of the headman's cattle was slaughtered for meat, huge containers of native beer were dug out from their hiding place within the headman's stockade, and soon Adam was surrounded by young Matabele youths and girls impressed by his command of their language and eager for his reminiscences of the last Matabele king.

During the course of the evening Adam learned that the village headman was in fact one of King Lobengula's sons-in-law. The reason for his self imposed exile to this remote part of the country was because he had played a prominent role in a battle in which all the men of Major Allen Wilson's patrol were defeated and killed in the uprising of 1893. The incident was one that many Rhodesians would dearly have liked to avenge.

The time spent at the Matabele *kraal* dispelled all the fears and uncertainties Adam had experienced the previous night. When he rode away the next morning he sat tall in his saddle, as a man should. He rode away without a backward glance, even though he knew that among those watching him go was the young Matabele girl who had shared his blanket. She had risen before dawn to light a cooking-fire and provide him with a meal that would sustain him on that day's journey. There had been other Matabele girls in Adam's young life. They meant nothing to him. He had not even asked this one her name.

Adam hoped to cross the Limpopo river to the Transvaal that evening, but he discovered that the border was being patrolled by Rhodesian volunteers, supported by troopers of the British South Africa Company police. Only his natural caution prevented him from riding straight into a camp occupied by these border guards. A slight breeze from the camp brought him the whiff of wood-smoke in time and he was able to back away without being seen.

Leaving his horse a mile back, Adam climbed a nearby rocky *kopje*. From here he could see the wide, muddy river. The churned up banks on either side indicated the crossing-place used by Africans and Europeans over the years. Adam was also able to pin-point the camps of the men guarding the river border and gain some knowledge of their patrolling routine.

He quickly learned that guarding the border was a fairly relaxed duty for the men involved. The Boers were not expected to attack here, certainly not in any strength. The result was that the men on border duty were not as alert as they might have been. Crossing the river to the Transvaal should not prove too difficult, but it would need to wait until early morning. The light was already fading and Adam would not risk crossing during darkness. Fed by the rain-swollen streams and rivers of the western highveld, the Limpopo was higher than Adam would have liked. There was also the danger posed by crocodiles. He could see many of these dangerous creatures lying on the mud banks of the great brown river.

It rained a little during the night. Adam had a cold and comfortless camp and he saddled his horse ready to move off as soon as there was enough light behind the grey clouds to guide him on his way.

Adam believed that even if sentries were set on the crossing overnight they would not be at their most alert after such a wet and miserable night.

He was right. The crossing he had chosen was reached without incident and Adam rode his horse straight into the water. It was shallower than he had expected. Although the horse was soon wading chest deep, the water never rose any higher.

When Adam was almost midway across the half-mile wide crossing-place he saw a huge crocodile ease its bulk from a mud bank and slide gently into the water. As it disappeared beneath the surface, Adam urged his horse on, desperately hoping the crocodile would drift away down-river with the languid current. His hopes were dashed almost immediately. Rising to the surface of the water, the ugly reptile sped towards horse and rider.

Adam had his rifle cleared in an instant, all caution thrown to the wind. With the crocodile no more than ten feet away, he hastily aimed between the two protruding eyes and sent a bullet crashing through the bony skull.

The creature did not die quietly. Expelling breath in a prolonged moan, its death throes churned the water to a bloody foam.

Terrified by the gyrations of the crocodile, Adam's horse plunged into deeper water, but Adam managed to guide it back to the crossing almost immediately and urged it on. As he did so, he heard the crack of a rifle-shot from the Rhodesian side of the river. He did not turn around, but concentrated his efforts on the horse, goading it forward.

Adam expected to feel the impact of a Rhodesian bullet at any moment, but the horse was in shallower water now and gained the bank in a series of great bounds that splashed water up about horse and rider, making them a more difficult target. Then the horse was on land, slipping and sliding as it surmounted the high river bank.

When the horse was on level ground, with hard turf beneath its hooves, Adam kicked back with his heels and let out a loud yell of elation. He had made it! He was on Boer soil.

Seconds later, Adam galloped headlong into a party of horsemen, and thirty Mauser rifles were being aimed at him.

'Stop! I'm on your side!' Adam shouted the words in Afrikaans, the language of the Boers, alarmed that he might have escaped the guns of the Rhodesians only to be shot down by the men he had come to join.

Most of the Boers lowered their guns. A few did not.

'What's going on? What is all the shooting about?'

'It's Rhodesian border guards. They were shooting at me. I would have got across without being seen if it hadn't been for a damned crocodile.'

One of the bearded men looked at Adam from beneath bushy black eyebrows. 'What's so important about you, boy? Why should they be so anxious to kill you – and where do you think you're going in such a hurry?' The man's accent was the heavy, almost unintelligible Afrikaans of the *takhaaren*.

'They were shooting because I was crossing the river. I'm on my way to join a commando.'

'You, join a commando . . .?' One of the Boers, a coarse-faced bearded man, kneed his small wiry pony forward until he was looking into Adam's face. 'You haven't started to grow hair on your cheeks yet, boy.'

'He's not one of us, that's certain. He could be a spy. We ought to shoot him.'

The alarming suggestion came from a *takhaar* who could not have been more than a year or two older than Adam, and whose 'beard' was a fringe of down about his face.

'Shot? With skin like this?' The coarse-faced Boer leaned across and pinched Adam's cheek between finger and thumb.

Adam caught the smell of stale brandy on the man's breath. I think it's *vrou* dressed up as a man. I say we keep her and find out.'

The *takhaar* reached across again and, suddenly angry, Adam struck out at him. Caught off balance the man fell from the saddle, frightening his pony.

The animal reared and backed away. Unfortunately for the *takhaar*, he had caught one foot in a stirrup as he fell and he was dragged through a small, immature thorn bush. The Boer's cries of pain and rage only frightened the animal more and it plunged and reared in a bid to rid itself of the unseated rider.

None of the *takhaaren* went to the aid of their unfortunate companion. Instead, they hooted with laughter and their shouts caused the horse to gallop away with the angry man.

Eventually the Boer managed to free his boot. Catching his pony, he belaboured the animal about the head with his fist before swinging back into the saddle. Then he returned his attention to the cause of his discomfiture and Adam saw murder in the *takhaar*'s eyes.

'I'm going to kill you . . .'

One of the men of the Boer commando rode his horse between Adam and the angry *takhaar*.

'That's enough, Arni. You asked for what you got. The boy's proved he's old enough to join a commando. Willie Joubert wasn't as old when he was wounded at Ladysmith last month, and he's one of the Commandant General's own family. Come, leave the boy alone. We'll need every man and boy we can get when the British land more troops. If he can use a gun as well as he uses his fists it doesn't matter whether he's sixteen years old, or sixty.'

For a moment it looked as though the dangerous 'Arni' might disregard the advice given to him by the other man. Then he jerked on his reins so hard that his pony gave a snort of pain, and the angry *takhaar* horseman rode back to his grinning companions.

'What's your name, boy?' The man who had intervened on Adam's behalf appeared to be the leader of the commando.

'Adam. Adam Retallick.'

The Boer commander frowned. 'That's an English name. Why should you want to fight for us?'

'I'm not English. I was born in Matabeleland. I'm here because I think you're right and the British are wrong.'

There were murmurs of approval from the Boers and the commandant nodded. 'Men have killed each other for less reason. I am Louis du Plessis. This is my commando. Do you want to join us . . . or do you have a particular commando in mind?'

'I'm heading south to join up with General De la Rey.'

'Koos De la Rey? You know him?'

'I met him some weeks ago, when I and my brother were at Mafeking.' Adam deemed it wiser not to disclose any more details of their meeting.

'You'll need a fast horse to find Koos – you ask the British. He'll be knocking hell out of 'em one minute but by the time they start shooting back he's fifty miles away.' The colourful information was volunteered by another member of the *takhaaren* commando .

'I'm heading for a farm at Lichtenburg, near Koos De la Rey's home. The Viljoen family live there. They'll know where I can find him.'

CHAPTER TWELVE

Adam Retallick was dusty and travel-weary when he rode up to the Viljoen farmhouse ten days after crossing the Limpopo river. The house was deserted except for an aged woman who came to the door leaning heavily on an elaborately carved stick.

'The Viljoens, you say?' The woman spoke in a high, cracked voice in answer to his question. 'Which of the Viljoens would you be seeking? If it's my son Cornelius, or young Lucas, you're out of luck. They're both away fighting in the war – though why they should be away when there's so much work to be done about the farm, I don't know. It doesn't need *both* of them to beat the British.'

'I rather hoped I'd find Johanna here . . .'

'Johanna? You've come calling on Johanna? Who are you? I've never seen you about here before. Why aren't you off fighting, like the others? Calling on our Johanna, indeed – without permission from her father, I don't doubt! I don't know what you young people are coming to. No respect for the old ways. Get off with you, and don't let me see you here again or I'll turn the dogs loose on you, just as I would on a no-good kaffir.'

'But where is Johanna . . . and her mother?'

'Over at the De la Rey farm, comforting poor Nonnie on the loss of her son. He was a good boy, that Adaan. Now there was a young man who would have asked permission before he came calling . . .'

With this final observation the old lady slammed the door shut and Adam heard her stomping away into the house.

Adam was sitting in the shade on the wide wooden *stoep* when Sophia and Johanna Viljoen arrived home in a light wagon pulled by a single mule. Adam had been waiting for five hours and he was feeling both tired and hungry. Although he would never have admitted it, not even to himself, the thought of Johanna's delighted reaction when he told her he had ridden from Insimo to join a Boer commando and fight for her people had played no little part in his decision to leave home. Hardly a day had gone by since their first meeting when he had not thought of her.

He took off his hat and stood on the wide verandah, momentarily tongue-tied and awkward as the light wagon came to a halt in front of the house.

Mother and daughter did not immediately step down. From their expressions it was evident that they had not recognised him. Then Adam realised he was standing in the deep shadow of the *stoep* and he stepped forward into the sunlight.

'Adam!' Johanna's reaction was more in keeping with the dream Adam had been cherishing. 'What are you doing here? Is Nat with you?'

The mention of his elder brother temporarily soured the moment for Adam. He was not yet ready to think of all he had left behind.

'I've come to join Koos De la Rey's commando. Nat is still at Insimo.'

'You've come to join a commando? Why? This isn't your war. *Your* home isn't threatened. *Your* friends aren't being killed. Why should you want to fight . . . either *for* or *against* us? All this fighting and killing is . . . *sickening*. If everybody who had no business in South Africa packed up and left there would *be* no war. We could all go on happily, just as we were before Adaan and Pieter and all the others were killed . . .'

Suddenly Johanna's face crumpled. Pushing past Adam she ran into the house, the door banging shut behind her.

An African servant had run from the rear of the house. He held the mule's bridle as Sophia Viljoen handed him the reins and stepped heavily on to the *stoep*.

'You mustn't take too much notice of Johanna right now. We've just returned from the memorial service for young Adaan De la Rey, killed on the Modder river. He and Johanna

92

were great friends. I had hoped . . . Agh! This accursed war has destroyed so many dreams, and broken the hearts of so many mothers. Adaan has been buried at Jacobsdal. So far from his home and his poor mother . . .'

Sophia Viljoen was close to tears. Wiping her eyes with a fierce movement of her hand, she said, 'These are unhappy times . . . But life must go on. Come inside, young man. If you're going to war you'll need fattening up. It doesn't look as though you've met up with a good meal for weeks. Come, boy. What did you say your name is . . .?'.

Supper at the Viljoens' was a strangely unreal affair for Adam. After thanks had been given to God for His bounty, and prayers offered up for absent members of the family, they sat down to a meal as filling as Sophia Viljoen had promised. During the meal Johanna said hardly a word, and she ate only a fraction more than she talked. By way of contrast, Granny Viljoen talked through the whole meal, occasionally glowering at Adam and muttering about young men who came calling on girls without first obtaining parental permission or observing the accepted formalities of courtship.

Undeterred by either garrulous mother-in-law or silent daughter, Sophia Viljoen questioned Adam closely about his family background, learning of the farm at Insimo and his reasons for leaving home to come and fight for the Boer cause.

When the meal was over and the women began clearing the kitchen table, Sophia Viljoen reminded Johanna that she had to check that the fowls were locked away for the night, and the horses and cattle safely penned in.

'When the menfolk are home it isn't necessary,' confided the Boer woman to Adam. 'The kaffirs do everything required of them. But now . . .' She shrugged her shoulders in a gesture of helplessness. 'No one knows when the men will be back and the kaffirs get lazy with no one around to boss them up. This war . . .! But you'll see enough of it yourself before long. Go out and help Johanna. If you find anything not done *you* can shout at the kaffirs for me. They take more notice of a man than of a woman.'

Adam hurried after Johanna and found her gathering up the chickens, a task that should have been done by the African farm-hands. Seeking out the man responsible, Adam gave him a tongue-lashing in a mixture of Matabele and Afrikaans. The farm-hand may not have understood all that was being shouted at him, but he did not doubt its meaning.

'Thank you, Adam.' Johanna spoke almost grudgingly. 'It *does* need a man about the place. We had a hired hand, Jacob, until a few weeks ago. He was a bit simple, but could handle things about the farm. Now he's gone off to war too. How long will *you* be staying with us?'

'Only until I learn the whereabouts of General De la Rey. I hope I'm not too late. I met a *takhaaren* commando when I was on my way here. They reckon the British will be asking terms for a ceasefire before Christmas.'

'Since when have the *takhaaren* known what is going on in the world? They're used to fighting kaffirs armed only with spears. The British have guns – *and* more men than we can imagine. We're winning now, but we're losing too many men. We can't afford such a loss. I . . . I'm worried for my pa, and Lucas.'

Unexpectedly, Johanna turned and took both of Adam's hands in hers. 'Don't get involved in this war, Adam. Go home. Go back to where you belong. This isn't your fight.'

Thrilled by the fact that Johanna was holding his hands, Adam said boastfully, 'I've come here to fight with Koos De la Rey – and your father. I'll go back when we've won.'

Much to Adam's disappointment, Johanna set his hands free. 'You make it sound, oh . . . so *easy*! I only wish it were, then Pa and Lucas would be home again soon. Have you discussed this with Nat?'

The old jealousy Adam had always felt for his older brother flared up again. 'No, why should I? He wouldn't understand. All he thinks about is Insimo. To listen to him talk you'd think the land there was sacred . . .'

'Adam! That's the way every burgher in Transvaal and the Orange Free State thinks about *his* land. That's what this war is all about!'

'I want to fight the British. They came and took over Matabeleland and stirred up the Matabele. If they hadn't, my pa would be alive today. It sickens me to see Nat running errands for British soldiers, as though we were all the greatest of friends. I'd rather *fight* them.'

Johanna turned away from him and looked over the rolling countryside to where the sun was sliding beneath the horizon, spilling a crimson stain across the darkening sky.

'Look across there, isn't that beautiful? How many people do you think there are in Mafeking looking at the same sunset and wondering if they'll be alive to see another one? Sometimes you can hear our big guns firing into the town. The other night I went to bed early – about this time of day – and I could hear the bombardment going on for an hour. I wondered how many girls like me were lying in bed praying a shell wouldn't land on *their* house. I got out of bed, went down on my knees and prayed for them all.'

'I don't think there *is* another girl like you, Johanna. Not in Mafeking, nor anywhere else.'

Johanna looked at Adam sharply, believing he was ridiculing her. She saw he was serious.

Uncharacteristically nervous, Adam looked to the ground at his feet as he spoke. 'When I arrived your *ouma* thought I'd come calling on you. She was angry because I hadn't asked your pa's permission.'

'She gets some peculiar ideas in her head. It's because she's getting old, I suppose.'

'It's not *really* so peculiar . . .' Adam wanted to take this opportunity to speak his mind, but the words tumbled over each other. 'I . . . What would *you* have said . . . if I *had* come calling on you?'

'I'd have told you not to be so silly. You're too young to be thinking of such things, Adam – and I'm too young to take any man seriously.'

'Your *ouma* was married when she was your age. She said so at the supper table tonight.'

'Things have changed a lot since she was young,' retorted Johanna, 'and it's a good thing too. Her father was one of the early *takhaaren* – a *really* wild Boar. The Zoutpansberg was no place for a young girl in those days – or for any woman. When *ouma* was twelve years old her mother died. A week later her father sold her off as wife to a *voortrekker* who was heading south after losing all his family up in the tsetse country. He was four times her age, but before he died he'd given *ouma* four children. Not one of them lived longer than a

95

month. When she married my grandpa she'd been widowed two years, had lost four children – and she was still only twenty! Since then she's lost my grandpa and two more sons fighting Zulus. When I'm her age I want to be able to look back on better times than she's known. I'll marry when I've learned a bit about life. Not before.'

Listening to Johanna's tirade, Adam grew more and more dejected. His misery showed and Johanna said softly, 'I hope all this talk of joining the Boer army isn't just meant to impress me, Adam Retallick?'

'Of course not,' said Adam indignantly. It was only a half-lie. 'I came here because I believe in what your people are fighting for.'

'That's all right then. I wouldn't want to think of you risking your life because of some foolish notion you might have in your head about me. You won't have met many girls at Insimo . . .'

'I've met *lots* of girls,' lied Adam. 'There are plenty of them in Fort Victoria – and Bulawayo too. They come to Insimo sometimes.'

A girl *had* come to Insimo, six months before. A German archaeologist had brought his family to Insimo and left them there while he scoured the surrounding country for traces of an ancient civilisation. During the archaeologist's absence Adam had seduced his grossly overweight seventeen-year-old daughter and come close to being shot by the irate father when he suspected the truth.

But in spite of his bravado, Adam *had* been disheartened by Johanna's words. She was not his *sole* reason for wanting to join a Boer commando, but she had been an important factor in his decision. On the long journey from Insimo he had often tried to imagine Johanna's reaction when he told her he had come to join the Boer army and fight for her people.

Reality had come as a disappointment, and he had never imagined that disillusionment would be as bitter as this. He tried hard to recover something from the ashes of his dream.

'Will you let me come and visit you sometimes, when the commando returns here?'

'*Visit?*' You'll *stay* here. Where else would you go?' Johanna knew she had hurt Adam's feelings. She did not wish to make it worse. Besides, she *was* fond of him, and he *had* ridden five hundred miles to go to war because of her. She could not fail to be impressed by Adam's devotion to a girl he hardly knew.

Warming to him suddenly, Johanna took Adam's hand and said, 'You'll always be welcome here while you're fighting in our cause, Adam. Afterwards too. Now we'd better return to the house before *ouma* comes looking for you wielding a *sjambok.*'

CHAPTER THIRTEEN

The Insimo valley was raided by a Boer commando at dawn, thirty-six hours after Nat's return from guiding Thomasina to Fort Victoria. It was the same thirty-strong *takhaaren* commando encountered by Adam when he crossed the Limpopo river on his way south.

The commando had crossed the river in the opposite direction during darkness, avoiding the Rhodesian border patrols with as much ease as had Adam. They kept clear of settlements until they were well inside Matabeleland and then began attacking stores and isolated farms in a frighteningly swift series of raids. So quickly did they move that news of their presence in the country had not reached Insimo when they struck.

Nat came awake suddenly, brought out of a deep sleep by an unfamiliar sound. It took a matter of only seconds to shake off sleep and realise he was hearing the screams of his Matabele farm workers and their families. There was another sound too. The crackle of flames consuming dry thatch and timber.

Thinking a fire had broken out in the Matabele compound, Nat dressed hurriedly and rushed through to the kitchen. He had almost reached the back door when he heard his mother calling from her bedroom, demanding to know what was happening.

Nat stepped back to the main part of the house to call out a reply – and the few paces saved his life. He had hardly left the kitchen when the back door was splintered by a fusillade of shots from outside. Then Nat heard glass shattering in the shuttered windows and the fall of plaster, torn from inside walls by rifle bullets.

Nat threw open the door to his mother's room and saw her standing beside the bed.

'Get down on the floor. Ma. Quick!'

Elvira Retallick didn't move, not understanding. Nat sprang across the room and dragged her to the floor as glass and bullets exploded into the room through the shuttered window. Pointing beneath the stout brass bed, Nat ordered his mother to remain there until he returned for her. His rifle was in his own room loaded ready for just such an emergency and Nat reached it on his hands and knees.

He had the gun and a belt of ammunition when he heard the sound of something heavy battering at the back door. He returned to the kitchen just as the door flew open and a bearded Boer fell through the door.

The Boer spotted Nat before he fell to the floor, but his mouth had hardly opened to shout a warning when Nat's bullet pierced his brain. A second Boer was close behind and Nat's second bullet was close enough to tear tiny, dart-like splinters from the door frame and scatter them in the intruder's face.

The Boer dropped out of sight and then two hands reached through the doorway in an attempt to grab the fallen man's ankles and pull him outside. Nat fired again and the Boer retreated, nursing a shattered wrist.

Suddenly a stick wrapped in dried grass and burning furiously arched through the open doorway. It landed on a dry rush mat and seconds later it seemed as though the whole kitchen was ablaze.

Another volley of bullets sprayed the kitchen through the doorway and the windows, forcing Nat to crouch close to the floor. When he rose to his feet a flurry of wind cleared the smoke from the doorway and Nat saw the body of the Boer raider had gone.

From somewhere outside Nat heard the boom of a large-bore hunting rifle. It was followed by shots from smaller calibre guns. It sounded as though Jaconus Van Eyck had been woken by the battle and come from his cabin to take a hand.

There was a sound behind Nat and he swung around to see

Ben standing in the doorway behind him, looking in horror at the conflagration.

'It's a Boer raid,' snapped Nat tersely. 'Ma's beneath the bed in her room. Get her in here and tackle this blaze. I'm going outside.'

Fighting his way through smoke and flames to the door, Nat paused to wipe his streaming eyes before plunging outside.

He went through the door hunched as low as he could make himself, but caution was no longer necessary. The only Boer close to the house was the man Nat had shot through the head. He was quite dead and a crowd of Matabele workers were gathering about the body, expressing vengeful satisfaction.

The other members of the commando, many of whom had never left their saddles, were galloping away southwards along the valley. One of them was turned towards the house and sighting along a gun barrel, but his shot smacked harmlessly against the wall of the house. Nat took aim more carefully and fired a return shot. He had the satisfaction of seeing his target sag in the saddle, but the Boer raider kept his seat and was soon out of range.

As Nat organised the Matabele workers into fire-fighters, Jaconus Van Eyck came limping to the house, a heavy elephant gun in his hands.

'Are you all right?' Nat asked anxiously, believing the old hunter must have been wounded.

Jaconus Van Eyck grimaced. 'I twisted my ankle when I jumped out of bed. But the house . . .! Is your mother all right?'

'Yes, but we'll need to come to grips with the fire quickly. You organise the boys out here. I'm going back inside . . .'

It was two hours before the fire was finally extinguished. The kitchen had been gutted and much of the roof destroyed. Looking at the damage, Elvira Retallick fought back her tears as she said, 'The house was built for me by your father. All the hard work he put into it. All gone . . .'

Nat put an arm about his mother and did his best to comfort her. 'It might have been far worse, Ma. None of us is hurt. That's all that would have mattered to Pa. He'd have shrugged this off and repaired the damage. We'll do the same.'

'Why did they do this to Insimo, Nat? Why should Boers ride all this way just to attack us?'

'I don't know . . .' The words Sophia Viljoen had spoken to him in the Boer camp at Mafeking suddenly returned to Nat with ominous clarity. '*You're part of southern Africa . . . You won't be allowed to stay out of this war . . .*' He had taken little notice of her then. Now, with Adam gone to war and Insimo attacked by a Boer commando, it seemed she was right.

The cost of the Boer commando's surprise raid was high. Apart from the damage to the house, half the huts in the workers' compound had been burned. They had also killed three Matabele herdsmen, run off all the horses they could find, and set fire to a number of outhouses.

Nat was forced to change his mind now about Insimo's involvement in the war between Great Britain and the Boer republics. While the Boer was being buried in an unmarked grave on the hillside, away from the house, Nat took a decision he had hoped would never be necessary. Sending some of the Matabele herdsmen to round up horses grazing farther along the valley, he went to his smoke-blackened room and began packing saddle-bags.

His mother came into the room as he worked and the fear on her face when she realised what he was doing would have deterred a less determined man.

'Nat . . . You are going away?'

Reaching down a spare ammunition belt from the wall, Nat said, 'I'm taking some of the Matabele with me to track down the Boer commando. I must try to prevent this from happening to anyone else. When I'm through I'll send the boys back. Then I'll go and find Adam. When he learns what's happened here he might see sense and come home.'

'You can't go to Transvaal! Jaconus told me what was said when you were released before. If you return you'll be shot.'

'That was just talk, Ma. From a man trying to impress others with his importance. While I'm away Jaconus and Ben can start work repairing the house. I'll send one of the Matabele to Fort Victoria and have new windows made up and brought here. Ben can keep the farm running while I'm away. He knows as much about the business as I do . . .'

Elvira Retallick fell upon her son and hugged him. With tears running down her face, she cried, 'Where is all this madness going to end, Nat? It has taken me all this time to recover from the loss of your father and Wyatt . . . and now *this* happens. You and Adam leaving Insimo. The house set on fire by raiders. What is happening to us . . .?'

'Try not to worry too much, Ma. When Adam and I are back everything will be as it was before.'

Elvira Retallick released her son. Standing back from him she shook her head sorrowfully. 'No, Nat. *Nothing* will ever be quite the same again. But you must do what needs to be done. I will try to understand. I *do* understand. But you are my son. My *oldest* son. I will miss you. God go with you.'

Nat set off with ten mounted Matabele from his compound. Most had seen their houses burned by the Boer commando and they were bent on revenge. All had once been warriors in Lobengula's army and had fought white men before, but now they were armed with modern breech-loading rifles.

The trail was already five hours old, but to the Matabele it was as though the Boer commando had sign-posted their movements. So clear was it that Nat thought the Boers might have deliberately set a clear trail in order to lie in wait for any pursuers. However, as the day progressed and more than one excellent ambush spot was passed, Nat realised the commando leader did not expect pursuit. He had taken more than sixty of Insimo's best horses and doubtless thought there were no more.

The Boer commando travelled fast, pursuing a curving course to the south-east that would take them within ten miles of Fort Victoria. It appeared the Boers might have completed their deep foray into Rhodesia and were now heading for one of the most desolate areas of the Zoutpansberg, where the borders of Rhodesia, Mozambique and Transvaal met. It was wild, empty country. A sanctuary for renegades from all three countries. Only men who lived outside the law – and the *takhaaren* – were familiar with such a land, as untamed as the *takhaaren* themselves.

Writing a hasty note to Captain Carey Hamilton, Nat gave him news of the attack upon Insimo, together with details of the commando and the direction the Boers were taking. Delivery of the note was entrusted to one of the Matabele warriors, who was told to ride to Fort Victoria as fast as he could go.

Nat followed the trail of the commando until darkness overtook him. He was convinced that he and the Matabele were closing on the Boers, who were pushing a horse herd before them.

They were now in an area of high, boulder-strewn *kopjes*, dotted haphazardly across the veld. Convinced that he might have caught up with the Boers given another couple of hours of light, Nat sent one of the Matabele men on foot to the top of the nearest *kopje*, with instructions to look for the tell-tale light of a cooking-fire. Boer commandos usually carried a good supply of *biltong*, the spiced, dried meat of the *voortrekker*, but the commando must have been away from home for a long time. It had probably run out of *biltong* and the Boers would need to cook.

The Matabele warrior was away for a long time but he returned with exciting news. He had seen no fire – the Boers were too cautious to give away their camp in such a manner – but he *had* smelled smoke.

After a few minutes of quiet argument, the Matabele warriors agreed on the direction of the wind, and the most likely location of the commando's camp.

Two of the warriors slipped away into the darkness, leaving the remainder to await their return. Against such men as the *takhaaren* it was not wise to take chances.

The two Matabele scouts did not hurry their task and it was two hours before they returned and reported to Nat. The Boers' camp was no more than five hundred yards away, in a small, steep-sided valley, blocked halfway along its length by a rock-slide. With the camp guarding the only entrance, the Boers had been able to turn the horse herd loose in the valley without posting a guard upon them.

The Matabele scouts confirmed that there were twenty-eight men about the camp-fire. The odds were three to one in favour of the Boers – and they were probably the best shots to be found anywhere in the world. But Nat knew that if he placed his men in carefully concealed positions on the low hills about the valley it would level out the odds. The Matabele warriors had been taught to shoot by Jaconus Van Eyck, by Adam, and by himself. They were capable marksmen, although no match for the Boers. However, the commando would be fighting from the worst possible position, over-looked from the heights all about them, unable to adopt their favourite tactic of hitting hard, then riding away before an enemy was able to gather his wits.

There was little sleep for the Matabele this night. Once Nat was satisfied they knew what was expected of them, he moved them quietly and carefully into position and settled down to wait.

The Boers came close to spoiling Nat's plans. They were led by Henrik Meyer, a wily old *takhaar* who had fought against hostile natives for twenty-nine of the last thirty years. For the other year he had fought the British during the first Boer war, nineteen years before. Henrik Meyer knew that the most vulnerable time for any fighting unit was dawn. This was especially true for a commando operating many miles inside enemy territory.

Commandant Meyer roused his commando half an hour *before* dawn and the Boers made ready for departure in practised silence. By the time men and horses were vague shapes moving about in the grey pre-dawn, the commando was mounted and ready to move off – or to fight.

There was no breakfast. Those who still had *biltong* in their saddle-bags would chew or cut off plugs of hard, sun-cured meat as they rode along. Those who had none would go hungry.

Henrik Meyer also sent out scouts to climb the rocky *kopjes* on either side of the valley. He wanted to be certain the way was clear before his men resumed their homeward ride. It was one of these Boer scouts who stumbled across a Matabele guard dozing over his rifle behind one of the balancing rock formations. The Boer wasted no time seeking an explanation from the armed tribesman. He put a bullet in him at point-blank range before scrambling back down the steep hillside.

The shot killed the Insimo Matabele warrior and warned Henrik Meyer and his commando. It also proved fatal for the scout.

A single shot was the pre-arranged signal for Nat's men to open fire on the commando, and the startled Matabele war-riors began firing on the shadowy, indistinct figures below them in the valley. The Boer scout, moving faster, was easier to see than his companions and at least half the Matabele rifles were turned on him. He fell the last twenty yards to the valley floor and lay on the ground, an indistinct, dark form.

Somewhere in the still-dark valley Nat heard the drumming of hooves. The Boers were determined to take the horses stolen from Insimo with them. Nat was equally determined they would not.

Leaping from his rock cover he shouted at his men, 'Keep firing at the commando. Make them shoot back at you. The noise will turn the horses. I want those horses turned.'

The Matabele warriors answered his call readily, but by leaving his own cover to call the order, Nat had exposed himself to the view of the Boers.

With terrified horses milling about him, Henrik Meyer raised his rifle and took careful aim at the indistinct figure on the slopes above him. As he squeezed the trigger of the government-issued Mauser, a horse was felled by a Matabele bullet and fell against the Boer commandant's mount.

The sudden movement saved Nat's life. Henrik Meyer was a crack shot, even in such light as this, and the bullet would have pierced Nat's heart. As it was, he felt a blow in his side, just above his leather belt. It was powerful enough to spin him around and dump him to the ground, but it was not especially painful.

When Nat picked himself up his side felt numb, as though he were bruised. He thought the blow must have come from a thrown boulder. Then he put his hand to the spot and felt blood oozing between his fingers. With a feeling of increasing incredulity he realised he had been shot!

The Boer commando could not make a stand against riflemen hidden in the rocks above them, and to attempt to climb the steep valley sides would be suicidal. Henrik Meyer shouted his orders and the *takhaaren* commando moved out of the valley. It was not a rout, nor even a flight. It was an orderly retreat. Three of their men had been killed and they were left where they lay. Others had been wounded, some badly, but not one wounded man was left behind. Those too badly hurt to ride by themselves shared another's horse.

A number of horses had also been killed, but the Boers were not short of mounts. They had saddled some of Nat's horses in the darkness, leading their own horses as remounts, it being their intention to drive the remainder. As Nat had hoped, the shooting had driven many of the unsaddled horses back along the valley, but the commando still had mounts to spare.

The Matabele warriors fired at the commando until the hoofbeats faded into the distance of the morning, and not until Nat began the descent to the valley did the wound in his side begin to give him any pain.

He was losing a great deal of blood and needed to be helped the last few yards to the valley floor. Once there he sat breathing heavily, his back against a crumbling ant-hill, and gave instructions for the Matabele to bury the dead Boers and round up the frightened horses.

As his order was being carried out, Nat realised that the dead Boers were being stripped of their clothing and belongings by the Matabele burial party, but by now it did not matter. Nothing seemed to matter any more. His head swimming, Nat leaned back against the ant-hill, fighting hard for every laboured breath.

One of the Insimo warriors had been watching Nat anxiously. When he began to slide sideways the warrior was there to catch him. The same man now began to snap out his own orders. The burial party hurriedly completed its task while another two men trotted away to fetch the party's horses, hidden outside the valley.

It was mid-morning when Captain Carey Hamilton and a combined force of hussars and Rhodesian volunteers met up with the Matabele warriors riding towards Fort Victoria, one of them holding Nat in front of him on his horse.

Four of the Rhodesian volunteers took Nat from his men and returned to Fort Victoria while the angry Matabele led the mounted force on the trail of the commando.

CHAPTER FOURTEEN

Nat remained in a semi-conscious state for three days. For the first two the doctor at Fort Victoria was pessimistic about his chances of recovery.

For Nat this was a strange and unreal time. When his senses swam close to consciousness he was confused by strange surroundings and strange faces. Yet always there was one face that had become so much a part of his foolish fantasies in recent days that he *knew* he was suffering hallucinations. He even believed he felt Thomasina's touch during bad moments when pain alone bridged the gap between reality and the twilight world where Nat's mind lurked.

Then, late in the evening of the third day after his fight with the *takhaaren* commando, mind and reality came together. Nat opened his eyes to see Thomasina Vincent gazing down at him.

'Well! Doctor Dymond said you would regain consciousness today. I was beginning to doubt him.'

Nat tried to smile at her, but he was only partly successful. 'It seems Doctor Dymond can work miracles.' His mouth was parched, talking an effort. 'How did he manage to bring you to me?'

'He didn't. You were brought to Fort Victoria. This is Carey's house.' Thomasina saw his tongue exploring dry lips and filled a glass from a water jug. 'Here, drink this.'

Nat tried to reach up to take the glass from her, but his arm felt ridiculously heavy. It only just cleared the bedsheet before dropping back helplessly.

'I . . . I can't.'

Thomasina showed immediate concern. 'Of course you can't. I'm sorry. You have lost so much blood you will be as weak as a new-born kitten for a day or two. You are very lucky to be alive. Here, let me help you to sit up.'

Leaning over Nat, she put an arm about him and heaved him awkwardly to a sitting position. Nat tried to help her but he ended up leaning back against the pillow, gasping for breath, feeling totally exhausted.

When he saw Thomasina's anxiety he managed a weak smile. 'It must have been a very large Boer bullet to let out so much blood.'

'I don't doubt it.' Thomasina was holding the water to his lips, when her face suddenly screwed up. 'God! You don't know how close you came to being killed. Doctor Dymond said the bullet needed to be no more than an inch higher or to the side, and you would have been dead long before you reached Fort Victoria. What on earth were you doing taking on a Boer commando with only a handful of natives to help you? You must be quite mad.'

'They attacked Insimo. Burned the house and compound, killed some of my men and ran off the horses.'

'Oh! I didn't know this when I sent off to tell your family you are here. Were any of them hurt?'

Nat shook his head weakly. 'We were lucky. Others might not have seen. The Boers had to be chased back across the border.'

'It was still foolish. But all this talking will tire you. I'll lay you down to sleep for a while.'

As Thomasina slid him down in the bed her face was very close to his. For a moment their eyes met and he knew she too was remembering the moment they had both promised to forget.

'I'll leave you now . . .'

'No!' Somehow he summoned the strength to take her hand as she tucked the sheet about him. 'Don't go . . . Stay a while longer.'

For a moment she hesitated. Then, giving his hand a gentle squeeze, she said, 'All right. I'll read to you – but I want no foolishness.'

Thomasina began to read to him from a book of poems by

Yeats. Two pages later he was asleep but Thomasina waited a few minutes longer before releasing her hand from his.

Nat slept until the following morning. When he awoke this time sunlight was streaming through the window and his mother, Ben and Jaconus Van Eyck were seated patiently at his bedside.

As Nat struggled in a vain attempt to sit up, Elvira Retallick reached out a hand to stop him.

'You stay where you are, my son. That young lady has been telling me how close to death you've been. I don't want you undoing all her good work now.' Leaning across the bed she kissed him. Behind her his young brother Ben had a relieved grin on his face.

'That young lady is Thomasina Vincent, wife of Colonel Vincent, soon to be the commanding officer here. She's the one I brought from Umtali.'

'So? When your father met me I was Elvira Costa Farrao, daughter of the Captain General of the North-West District of Mozambique and Commandant of Sena. Title and rank mean little to a young man and a young woman when they are thrown together. Once we were married your father would never have allowed *me* to travel halfway across the country in the company of an impressionable young man.'

'I'm sorry you don't like her, Ma. I was hoping we might invite her to Insimo . . . When the house is repaired.'

'I do not say I don't *like* the girl. I was merely expressing my thoughts, as a mother should. Thomasina Vincent has worked harder than anyone to save your life. For this she will always have a place in my prayers. She can visit Insimo whenever she wishes. As for the house . . . It already has a new roof and I am going out to buy new things for my kitchen today. You will also be pleased to know the Matabele returned with the horses before we left. But *you* need fattening up, my son. There is no more flesh on you than on a maggot. It's as well I came. This Thomasina may be a very good nurse, but I doubt if she's familiar with a cooking pot. I'll go and see what I can find.'

When their mother had gone from the room, Ben spread his arms wide and with an apologetic grin said, 'Sorry, Nat, but you know Ma. Anyway, cooking for you will be good for her.

She's been worried sick about you all the way from Insimo.'

'How *are* things at Insimo? Who's looking after the place while you're all here?'

'Don't worry none about Insimo,' Jaconus Van Eyck replied. 'We've left Victoria in charge. The boys fear her more than they fear any of us — and Ben's told her exactly what needs doing. As for the house . . . it wasn't as bad as it looked. It will stink of smoke for months, but with a coat of whitewash and new windows it will be better than new.'

Nat was relieved to know there was nothing he needed to worry about at Insimo. 'Help me sit up, Ben. Has there been any word of Adam?'

'No.' Ben helped Nat to a sitting position. 'The pair of you will turn Ma grey. I swear that if she didn't have *one* steady son in the family she'd go out of her mind. But I'd go out and get a wound myself if I could be sure of getting a nurse like yours . . .'

Nat said nothing. He did not feel inclined to joke about Thomasina.

Nat returned to Insimo after hardly more than a week at Fort Victoria. He rode in a light, leather-sprung wagon that had been made by the town's first carriage maker. Unable to sell his vehicles because of the absence of a reasonable road, the man had run up many debts before fleeing the country on a stolen horse, leaving all his unsold stock behind him.

Elvira Retallick travelled in the wagon with Nat. So too did Thomasina Vincent. Nat's mother had issued a surprise invitation the previous evening, when Nat was seated outside enjoying the breeze for the first time since his arrival.

Looking back on the moment, Nat thought it had sounded more in the nature of an order. Carey Hamilton had just returned after fruitlessly tracking Henrik Meyer and his commando all the way to the Transvaal border. All they had found along the way were two graves adorned with wooden crosses. The Boers had no gentle-touched woman to tend *their* wounded. For them it had been a one hundred and fifty mile flight through hostile country, spending twelve hours a day in the saddle. Those who survived would boast of the exploit for the rest of their lives. Those who did not would be quickly forgotten by their fellow *takhaaren*. Their world was for survivors.

After hearing Captain Hamilton's story, Elvira Retallick had turned to Thomasina and said, 'Nat tells me you would like to see Insimo. This is as good an opportunity as you're ever likely to have. We'll be leaving soon after dawn. You can help me take care of Nat on the journey. Once there you'll have Jaconus to show you around – he's the finest hunter in Matabeleland.'

What Elvira was really saying was that Nat would be convalescing, and too weak for he and Thomasina to go off on long rides together. Nat knew this, so too did Thomasina. But she expressed her delight and promptly accepted the invitation.

The journey was made in a single day and despite the comparatively soft springing Nat was in a great deal of pain by the time they reached the remote farmhouse and were met by Victoria.

Victoria looked curiously at Thomasina as she was handed down from the wagon by Jaconus Van Eyck. Few women visitors came to Insimo – and there had never been one quite like this. Victoria viewed the newcomer from head to toe, taking-in the smart hat with its brim turned up at one side, the expensively tailored riding dress, and the specially made boots of soft leather. When she returned her gaze to Thomasina's face, Victoria saw that the object of her scrutiny was inspecting *her* in an equally interested manner.

Victoria took an immediate and totally unreasonable dislike to the other woman. Victoria had an instinctive nose for trouble – and she smelled it on this attractive and elegant young woman whose life was everything that Victoria's had never been.

Unaware of Victoria's thoughts, a tired Nat was left to make the introductions.

'Victoria, I'd like you to meet Thomasina Vincent, my nurse. Thomasina – this is Victoria, the Retallick family's oldest friend.'

The two women nodded coolly at each other and Victoria said, 'Now I can understand why you've been in no hurry to return to your duties in the valley.'

'You echo my husband's sentiments, Miss . . . Victoria. He swears that if sick soldiers were nursed by sergeant majors instead of women, the time they spend in hospital would be reduced by three-quarters.'

'Your husband must be quite exceptional to *want* to keep his men out of hospital, Mrs Vincent. Reports reaching us here suggest that British officers in South Africa are feeding their men on a diet of Boer bullets.'

Turning to Nat, Victoria explained, 'A police patrol came through here looking for that Boer commando. The trail was five days old by the time they got here, but they *did* have news of the war. It seems British casualties are being counted in thousands. The police captain said their officers form their soldiers into long lines and throw them at the guns of the Boers. He called it sheer bloody murder.'

Tight-lipped, Thomasina said, 'Our soldiers are the bravest in the world. If they are suffering heavy casualties it must mean they are carrying the fight to their enemies.'

'If they are to survive this war they'll need to learn the Boer way of fighting and let their *bullets* carry the fight to the enemy.'

Before Thomasina could reply again, Elvira Retallick came from the house and hugged Victoria. The first one off the wagon, she had immediately hurried inside to check what had been done. Her delight was evident.

'Victoria, you have performed a miracle. It's so bright and clean. No one would ever know there had been a fire.'

Victoria smiled. 'All the thanks are due to the Matabele. Every one of them in the valley must have been here painting, thatching and cleaning up. The windows were all fitted on the day they arrived from Fort Victoria. You've even got some new furniture. It's a present from the Administrator, in Bulawayo. He had the furniture put on a train to the railhead, then brought by wagon the remainder of the way.'

'Do you think someone might help the master of this wonderful house down, so he can see the transformation for himself . . .?' Nat was on his feet in the wagon. One hand clutching his wounded side, he was bent over like an old man. The jolting ride had caused his barely healed wound to stiffen painfully.

Jaconus Van Eyck and Ben lifted Nat between them to the ground and helped him inside the house.

Everything was as Elvira had described. Restored to its former glory, Insimo once more fulfilled the Matabele description of 'The Great House in the Valley'.

CHAPTER FIFTEEN

Nat made steady progress to recovery and within a week of his return he was taking Thomasina on short rides to show her the valley's features. The waterfall where Nat's father had first camped, the gold-mine, and the small, fenced-off plot of land where Daniel Retallick was buried with Wyatt, his eldest son.

There were other wooden crosses in the burial ground, and standing before them with Nat, Thomasina learned much of the history of Insimo and those who had lived there.

Thomasina would think of Insimo often during the days ahead, and always her thoughts would come back to this quiet spot. She would remember Nat's voice filled with emotion as he told her of the grief and sacrifice that had helped make Insimo home for the Retallicks and their friends.

During their rides Thomasina grew to appreciate Nat's love for the beautiful valley. She and Nat never went riding unless they were accompanied by Ben, or Jaconus Van Eyck, and although Nat would have preferred to have Thomasina to himself, theirs was an easy, uncomplicated relationship.

'Almost as though they are brother and sister,' Elvira remarked to Victoria as the two women stood together at the kitchen window one morning, watching Nat and Thomasina riding away from the house ahead of Jaconus Van Eyck and Ben. They were on their way to search for a number of cattle, believed to have strayed from the north end of the valley to the hills beyond.

Victoria snorted derisively. 'If you believe *that* you'll believe anything. Nat is infatuated with the girl – and she loves the attention he gives her, for all that she's got a husband somewhere else.'

'She nursed him when he was so ill, that's all. It brings people closer. Had I thought it more than that I would never have invited her to Insimo.'

'The lack of an invitation wouldn't have stopped that one, not once she'd taken it into her mind to come to Insimo. She is used to having her own way – in everything.'

'Wilful she may be,' agreed Elvira. 'But she comes from a good family and is married to a senior British army officer. What would a woman like that want with Nat?'

Victoria's reply was a snort that would have shamed a warthog. 'Have you looked at your son lately? He's a handsome, virile young man. Everything her husband isn't, likely as not. That's enough in itself for any lonely and bored young woman. If she were shrewd enough to be looking to the future she need look no farther than the two hundred square miles of Insimo – not to mention a gold-mine as rich as any in Matabeleland.'

Elvira did not want to believe the words of the long-standing family friend, even though too much of what she said rang true.

'Rhodesia isn't a country to suit Thomasina Vincent. She's used to society life, and having folk look up to her. She'd find none of that here.'

But Victoria had an answer for this too. 'Rhodesia's a young country, but it won't be very long before it's too big to be run by a company. When that day comes they'll be looking for men to share in the government. Men like Nat, with a large stake here. With an ambitious young woman urging him on he could one day govern this land. I fancy such a prospect might appeal to your Thomasina more than being the wife of a soldier – whatever his rank.'

Nat was certainly infatuated with Insimo's guest, but he would not have agreed with Victoria's assessment of Thomasina's aims. No matter how hard he tried, it proved impossible to get her alone. When Nat complained quietly that Thomasina seemed scared of him, she gently reminded him of the promise he had made. Pulling her horse to a halt, she called to Jaconus Van Eyck, and when he caught up with them she asked him the prospects for hunting in the hills to which they were riding.

'Depends what you're hoping for. There are plenty of buck. I've seen eland, and there's no shortage of lion.' Jaconus Van Eyck glanced from beneath shaggy, greying eyebrows to where Nat waited for Ben to catch up with him. As the two brothers rode on together, he added, 'If it's anything else you're after, I don't think I can help.' Jaconus Van Eyck's words were so pointed that Thomasina's head came up and she adopted what Nat would have called her 'colonel's lady' attitude.

'I'm hoping to have an enjoyable day's *shooting*. I'll be happy with an eland – and delighted with a lion.'

Nat looked back again and Jaconus Van Eyck saw Thomasina's expression soften. Pulling a soft leopardskin pouch from his pocket, the old Boer hunter began packing tobacco into a short-stemmed pipe. 'That young man is very fond of you. Too fond for his own good.'

Her head came around angrily, but when Jaconus Van Eyck met her gaze, the anger evaporated as suddenly as it had appeared.

'I'm fond of him too. Far too fond to allow him to delude himself about our relationship. I don't doubt it's to this you're alluding? I am not a cheat, Jaconus. I won't cheat on my husband. Neither will I cheat Nat.'

Puffing noisily on his pipe, Jaconus Van Eyck waved away a cloud of blue smoke. 'I've never doubted it for a minute. I only hope it's as clear to Nat.'

Thomasina Vincent shot an eland within an hour of leaving the Insimo valley behind. It was a shot made from a distance of five hundred yards and the bullet went straight through the heart of the great half-ton antelope, killing it instantly.

Before leaving the valley, they had called in at the Matabele compound and had almost a hundred of the Matabele employees with them to help in the cattle round-up. The tribesmen stood around the eland, loud in their praise of the woman who had made a kill at such a range.

Leaving two of the Matabele to skin the animal, the remainder went on to scour the hills for cattle. It was a highly successful round-up, more than four hundred Insimo cattle being collected. The bleached bones of many more provided a grim reminder of the penalty paid by the cattle who had wandered away from the protection of the Insimo valley.

It was a happy party which returned to the house at Insimo that evening, with the hide and the long, spiral horns of the eland as proof of Thomasina's marksmanship.

They were still half a mile away from the house when Nat noticed a number of unfamiliar horses turned out in the paddock adjoining the house.

Pointing them out to Thomasina, he said, 'Unless I'm mistaken those are cavalry horses. Most likely it's your brother. He's chosen a good day to come visiting. I doubt if he'll ever see a finer pair of eland horns than these. Who's going to be the first to tell him . . .?'

The race to the house was won by Ben, riding a spirited little Botswana pony, but Thomasina beat him to the doorway.

Nat, Ben and Thomasina entered the house in a happy, noisy group, with Jaconus Van Eyck bringing up the rear more sedately. Laughing and jostling each other they crowded into the living room – and the hilarity died away instantly. Carey Hamilton was there. So too were a number of other officers. One, a rather portly, balding and heavily-moustached officer with pale, almost colourless eyebrows and wearing the insignia of a full colonel, stepped forward and stretched out his hands towards Thomasina.

'Thomasina! I thought I would give you a surprise.' Stepping forward, he caught her in a stiff embrace and kissed her cheek. 'My dear, you're positively radiant. This colonial life appears to suit you.'

Not tall enough to look over his wife's head, Colonel Digby Vincent peered around her shoulder at Nat. He was older than Nat had imagined. Much older. Probably more than twice Thomasina's age. The revelation shocked Nat and he felt a totally unreasonable anger at this man who had the *right* to hug Thomasina.

'Digby! You should have let me know you were coming. I would have returned to Fort Victoria and not made you ride all this way to find me.'

'My dear Thomasina, I would ride half-way around the world to be with you, as well you know' – while he spoke, Colonel Digby Vincent was looking at Nat, and he added, 'I believe you've been doing a fine job of nursing this young man back to health. Unless I'm mistaken, the army will have cause to be grateful to you before very long.'

Thomasina did not understand the implication of her husband's words, but she hastened to introduce her husband to Nat.

Colonel Digby Vincent shook hands warmly with Nat. With no apparent guile, he said, 'I'm delighted to meet you, young man. I would like to thank you for escorting my wife to Fort Victoria, and for ensuring that her visit to your country is a memorable one. I've also been looking forward to congratulating you in person for your exploits against the Boers. The story of your return visit to Mafeking raised our spirits at a time when everything else seemed to be going wrong. Carey tells me that since then you've sent a Boer commando scurrying back to the Transvaal to lick its wounds. Well done, young man. Well done indeed.'

Thomasina slipped her arm through her husband's. 'Nat has also found me the largest eland in the whole of Africa. I have the hide and horns as a trophy. Come outside and see for yourself, Digby. It really was a *magnificent* animal.'

Smiling indulgently, Colonel Vincent murmured apologetically to the others and allowed himself to be led outside. When he had gone, Carey Hamilton commented wryly that if the Boers had a dozen women like Thomasina to marry off to senior British officers, they would have little need of an army.

During the ensuing laughter, Nat slipped out of the house through the kitchen door as a Matabele servant brought drinks to the room. Victoria saw him leave and her heart went out to him for what she knew he was suffering inside. At the same time she breathed a prayer of relief for Colonel Digby Vincent's timely arrival. Had Thomasina been allowed to spend another week or two in Nat's company, Victoria was convinced she would have broken Nat's heart.

Nat did not return to the house until darkness had fallen. The serving of the evening meal was delayed to await his arrival.

Victoria and Elvira had kept the drinks flowing and in the convivial atmosphere Nat's explanation about needing to pen the recovered cattle was accepted without comment.

Over the meal table Colonel Vincent revealed that his visit to Insimo had not been made with the sole intention of effecting a reunion with his young wife.

When the talk turned to the progress of the war with South Africa, Colonel Vincent said, 'The British people are shocked by the setbacks our army is suffering at the hands of untrained Boers – and there are no two ways about it, they have been severe defeats. However, the British government has finally woken up to the situation and General Sir Redvers Buller has arrived in the Cape to take charge of operations. There are forty thousand men on the high seas from Britain. Thousands more have already arrived from India. Troops are being sent from every country in the British Empire. We now have enough men to begin fighting a *real* war. In a month or two we will have enough soldiers to crush the Boers once and for all.'

Beaming at those about the table, Colonel Vincent's good humour faltered when he saw the expression on Elvira Retallick's face.

'Excuse me ... The kitchen ...' Elvira Retallick left the table in such haste that her chair would have fallen from the floor had not one of the young officers caught it. A moment later Victoria stood up and hurried after her friend.

Bemused, Colonel Digby Vincent asked Nat, 'I'm sorry, have I said something wrong?'

'My young brother ran off to join a Boer commando a few weeks ago. We haven't heard from him since he left.'

'Oh dear! Your mother must find my visit most distressing.'

Addressing Thomasina, the Colonel said, 'My dear, will you see if you can be of assistance to Mrs Retallick? Please offer my sincerest apologies for speaking as I did.'

When Thomasina had followed the other women to the kitchen, Colonel Vincent returned his attention to Nat. 'It must be in the interest of *everyone* to have this war brought to a rapid conclusion. Do you agree?'

'I certainly wouldn't argue.'

'Good! Then I am hopeful that you will give very careful consideration to the request I am about to make. I have been ordered to take a force into Transvaal. I would like you to act as a guide and scout for me.'

Nat took a deep breath before replying, 'This isn't my war,

Colonel. I have a farm to run . . .'

From the corner of his eye Nat saw the flare of a match as Jaconus Van Eyck lit up his pipe and looked thoughtfully down at the flame.

'Your brother is fighting in the war – and I regret to say he has chosen the wrong side. The Boers cannot possibly win. His best chance of survival lies in being found quickly and brought back to Rhodesia. I doubt whether anyone but you can do this.'

There was some truth in what Colonel Vincent was saying. Nat had given the problem of bringing Adam back to Insimo a great deal of thought. He had wondered about going to Transvaal, finding Koos De la Rey and asking him to order Adam home.

The idea had many flaws. First, Nat would have to make his way through the Transvaal, convincing every commando he met that he was not a spy. Then he had to find Adam. If, as Nat suspected, Adam was with Koos De la Rey's hard-hitting commando, he could be anywhere between the Cape Colony and the Rhodesian border – almost two thousand miles of country. It was an impossible task. Even if Nat *did* find De la Rey, he would still need to persuade the dedicated Boer commander to release Adam.

Nat knew his best chance would probably lie in accompanying British troops. A British force would draw Boers to them and there could be Boer prisoners, some of whom might have news of Adam. It was a remote chance, but the only practical one he had. On the other hand he would be leading a British force to fight against Boers. Possibly against Adam himself.

As though reading Nat's mind, the British colonel said earnestly, 'We are taking the war to the Boers in Transvaal, whether or not you accompany us. I believe that by bringing this war to a rapid close we will save many thousands of lives on both sides, and so prevent lasting bitterness between our two countries.'

Nat was still undecided, and Colonel Digby Vincent added quietly, 'There is one more consideration. Another Boer commando from Northern Transvaal has crossed the Limpopo river. It is attacking settlers on our side of the border at this very moment. Your family has experience of what this means.

You were strong enough to run them off. Many others are not. I want to take my full regiment to the border area and give them battle experience by driving this commando back across the Limpopo. Then I will follow them into Transvaal and eliminate their base – if they have one. In any case, I will ensure that they never raid into Rhodesia again in any force. But we need you. Will you come with me as my scout . . . please?'

For the first time, Nat was aware that the women had re-entered the room. They had been listening to Colonel Digby Vincent and now they awaited Nat's reply. Nat tried to will his mother's eyes to meet his. He wanted to know her thoughts.

She would not look at him. Only Thomasina met his gaze with a bold, challenging look.

Nat knew what he had to do. Perhaps he always had. Sophia Viljoen had been right. There was no way he could stand back and watch other men fight a war around him.

'All right. I'll come with you.'

CHAPTER SIXTEEN

Adam remained at the Viljoen farm for only three days before being taken to Mafeking with three other young men of his own age from the Lichtenburg area. In charge of the small party was Theunis Erasmus, an old man who held a corporalship in the Lichtenburg commando. Almost seventy years of age, Theunis Erasmus had been wounded in the neck by an English lance in one of the very first skirmishes of the war. Sent back to his home to recuperate by General De la Rey, the ageing Boer now felt sufficiently well to return to the fray.

One of the other new recruits whispered to Adam that Theunis Erasmus was a widower with eleven daughters and no sons. Ten of the girls were married and some had brought their families to see Theunis while he was recuperating, each hoping to be the one to whom he would leave the farm when he died. The informant said the old man was returning to the war because he found more peace on the battlefield than at home.

Whatever his reason for going to war, there was no doubting Theunis Erasmus's devotion to his general. As they rode to join the men investing Mafeking, he regaled his young charges with stories of Koos De la Rey's personal bravery and inspired generalship.

As the small party approached the beleaguered town Adam could see the empty railway line stretching away to the north. He could not help remembering the last time he was here. The thought that Insimo was only a few hours' ride from the end of the line gave him an uncomfortable feeling.

Adam had not been looking forward to a reunion with

Field-Cornet Ignatius Lemmer, in view of the circumstances of their last meeting. But Lemmer was not there, and neither was the Lichtenburg commando. They had been sent south to join a major Boer army headed by Boer General 'Piet' Cronje. The Boer intention was to oppose British General Lord Methuen, who was advancing northwards along the line of rail towards Kimberley, another of the towns invested by the Boers.

Lord Methuen's khaki-clad army of some fifteen thousand men was known to contain many of Great Britain's finest regiments. Half were Scots. The Black Watch, Seaforth Highlanders and Gordon Highlanders. There were Guards too – Scots, Coldstream and Grenadiers, together with representatives of many other British infantry regiments, as well as the 9th Lancers, and batteries of the Royal Field Artillery.

Pessimists in the Boer ranks were convinced that such an army was unstoppable – but no one dared to air such an opinion in the presence of Koos De la Rey. He was determined to stop Methuen – and he wanted the men of his home commando to share in the victory. Adam and the others were ordered south to join him.

Adam rode from Mafeking with a number of other reinforcements. He went with mixed feelings. Excited at the prospect of his first battle, he was apprehensive too. He could not confide his hopes and fears to his companions. With the possible exception of the other youngsters from Lichtenburg, the Boers seemed distrustful of him. Adam was not one of them. He was not even a 'burgher' – a citizen of one of the two South African republics. The men with whom he rode considered the war to be a tragic but necessary thing that interfered with their lives. That anyone should actually *choose* to fight was beyond their comprehension.

Only the young men of the Boer reinforcement kept up a steady chatter as they rode along. Koos De la Rey had already succeeded in slowing Methuen's advance force. With so many Boer reinforcements on the way they would surely turn Methuen and his army about.

The older burghers were less certain. Boer forces headed by Piet Cronje, General De la Rey's senior, had already inflicted heavy casualties on the British, killing or wounding close to fifteen hundred of their men. Yet, constantly reinforced by the troops who were arriving daily at Cape Town, the British army still edged forward.

The older burghers pointed out gloomily that even with God on their side the Boers too were suffering casualties. Hadn't Koos De la Rey lost his own son? The British were as numerous as flies on a day-old carcass. They could afford to lose hundreds of men – thousands, even. Not so the Boers. As likely as not, a dead burgher would be a farmer – and to many families the loss of their man meant the loss of the farm.

The reinforcements from Mafeking reached the siege lines about Kimberley in the early morning of 10th December, 1899, having covered the two hundred miles from Mafeking in three and a half days. They were immediately ordered to Magersfontein Farm, fourteen miles to the south of the besieged town. Here Cronje and De la Rey were making another stand against General Methuen.

An attack by the British force on the Boer positions was thought to be imminent. British artillery had been pounding out a warning for most of the afternoon, the sound heard by all those in and about Kimberley.

As the reinforcements neared Magersfontein the sound of the bombardment grew terrifyingly loud and the tongues of even the most enthusiastic of the young men fell silent.

Looking in their direction, Theunis Erasmus grinned his understanding. 'Agh! You won't want to let the *khakis*' shelling bother you. It's hitting no one. They are shelling the place where *they* would make a stand, on the *ridge* of the *kopjes*. But we're not there. Old Koos has had trenches dug at the *foot* of the *kopjes*, so we can pick off the *khakis* long before they get to us. It works every time. The *khakis* are so busy looking up they never see us. Not only that, they go into battle packed so close together that not one of our bullets is ever wasted. If it misses one man it's bound to hit another. It beats firing from a hilltop where a bullet just buries itself in the ground if it misses its target. I tell you boys, if you're in Koos De la Rey's army all you need to do is shoot. All your thinking is done for you.'

His words failed to reassure anyone, and the weather did little to restore their failing spirits. It had been raining since they first arrived in the vicinity of Kimberley. As the horses of the sodden riders plodded through the mud the men thought longingly of the comparatively cosy positions they had left behind at Mafeking.

Adam and the other reinforcements stopped and made an uncomfortable camp when they were still a mile short of the line of shell-battered hills. Breaking open some of the stores brought with them from Kimberley, they picked at a cold and tasteless meal.

When darkness fell they were taken forward to join the Boer forces manning the trenches at the base of the far side of the hills. They could not see the men about them, but whispered questions and answers marked their progress. After stumbling through the darkness for more than a mile, they reached their allotted place in the long line of trenches that curved along the base of the Magersfontein hills.

The trenches were carefully prepared. Deep and narrow, there was barely room for one man to squeeze past another. They were also cunningly sited. Although darkness prevented a full appreciation of De la Rey's military genius, it was apparent that the trenches had been dug to give maximum concealment from the enemy, while allowing the occupants a wide field of vision. Also, by virtue of their depth and narrowness, nothing short of a direct hit from an artillery shell would dislodge the men in occupation.

Many other men from Lichtenburg were here, and in the darkness men crawled from other trenches to hear news of home and receive verbal reassurance that the loved ones left behind were keeping well.

Adam had brought messages for Johanna's father and Lucas, her brother. After a whispered explanation of his presence he passed on the love and good wishes of their family, with a reminder that they were remembered in the family's prayers.

If the Viljoens failed to understand Adam's reasons for involving himself in their war, they refrained from comment. Both father and son had fought in two battles against Lord Methuen and his army. They knew the odds against them. Every additional rifle was important to the Boer army.

Adam also carried a message for Jacob Eloff, the Viljoens' hired hand.

A simple young man of about twenty years of age, Jacob had appeared at the Viljoen farm almost ten years before. Dressed in rags, the young boy told an incredible story. His parents had farmed in a remote area of North Transvaal until his mother's death while Jacob was still small. The tragedy prompted Jacob's father to turn to religion for consolation. Deserting the farm, he had set off to take religion to the natives of the lands bordering the blistering Kalahari desert.

For years father and son led a nomadic existence, travelling from *kraal* to *kraal*, trusting to the generosity of the tribesmen for food. One day, when Jacob was eight years old, they were mid-way between two villages when Jacob's father complained of feeling unwell. Sitting down on the ground, he died.

Jacob had wandered alone for days until, starving and near-demented, he was found by a family of Bushman hunters. They cared for Jacob, teaching him to hunt and track game. He remained with them for two years. Then the rains failed and the animals upon which the nomadic tribes lived either moved many miles away, or died. The Bushman family faced the same prospect. One day they took the simple-minded white boy many miles away, to the top of a hill. They would go no closer. Regarded as 'vermin' by these outlying farmers, a Bushman was shot on sight. The gentle little men from the desert knew they were doomed, but there was no need for Jacob to share their fate. Telling him it was time he returned to his own people, they turned their backs on him and walked back to the parched desert lands of the Kalahari.

The farmstead belonged to Cornelius Viljoen, and here Jacob Eloff found a home. Never quite one of the family, he was happy to sleep in the barn and tend to the domestic animals. The proudest moment of Jacob's life came when Cornelius Viljoen presented him with a piglet to do with as he wished.

It was the first actual possession Jacob Eloff had ever owned. If ever he went missing from about the house, the family knew Jacob would be found at the sty, just looking at his piglet. The animal quickly grew to be a prime, healthy sow, but when the family suggested she should be killed and the meat sold, the simple-minded young man threatened to run away, taking the sow with him.

The Viljoen family resigned itself to having Jacob's sow around the farm until it died of old age. However, Jacob *did* agree that the sow should be mated – and the message for him was that the sow had produced a litter of seventeen healthy piglets.

'Seventeen!' Jacob Eloff whispered the number, then repeated it in awesome disbelief. 'Seventeen?'

'That's right – and not a runt among them.'

'Is she all right? The sow, is she well?'

'As lively as a *klipspringer*,' Adam assured him. 'Giving birth came as natural to her as feeding.'

'You've seen her yourself?' Jacob Eloff asked excitedly.

'Shh! There might be a *khaki* patrol out there.' The hissed warning came from farther along the trench.

Crouching down beneath the rim of the trench, Jacob repeated, 'You've seen Victoria . . . and the piglets?'

'I've seen her – and picked up every one of her piglets.' Adam was glad his simple companion could not see the smile on his face. 'But why "Victoria"?'

'Lucas called her that.' There was resentment in Jacob Eloff's voice. 'He says she looks like the Queen of England. But we're fighting the English, aren't we?'

There was stifled laughter from others in the narrow trench, and Adam realised with some embarrassment that his conversation with Jacob Eloff was being followed with great amusement by the burghers around him.

'That's right, Jacob, we're fighting the English – and they might be creeping up on us at this very moment. Keep your voice down and your wits about you.' The not unkindly warning came from Theunis Erasmus. The ageing Lichtenburg farmer had been put in charge of this section of the line.

For the remainder of the night hours Jacob Eloff hugged thoughts of 'Victoria' to himself. On the few occasions when he spoke, it was to ask Adam a question in a low whisper. The questions were all about his pig and many went unanswered as Adam dozed intermittently, crouching in the wet and uncomfortable trench as he awaited his first taste of battle.

Jacob Eloff's resentful declaration that Victoria was Queen of England fell short of the whole truth. Queen Victoria was also monarch of Scotland — and it was Scots soldiers who formed up to launch an attack on the Boer lines, believed by Lord Methuen to be on the peak of the hills in the rear of the unseen narrow trenches.

The Highland Brigade was roused from a fitful sleep soon after midnight. As they prepared for battle the kilted Scotsmen grumbled about the rain, the darkness, and the N.C.O.s and officers who moved among them giving orders and urging greater haste.

Rifles and ammunition were checked as in the confusion of the darkness the officers tried to gather their own men. Colour sergeants shouted for their regiments to muster on them and, gradually, order was brought to the midnight chaos.

The Scots soldiers were formed in a tight rectangle, four thousand men packed forty abreast. The 2nd battalion of the Black Watch was first, followed by the 2nd Seaforth Highlanders, the 1st Argyll and Sutherland Highlanders, and finally the 1st Highland Light Infantry. Each regiment was separated from the one ahead by its own officers and senior N.C.O.s. To ensure the men maintained close formation, officers holding long ropes marched at each end of the human columns. Leading the whole brigade was Major-General 'Andy' Wauchope. One of the richest men in Scotland, the commanding officer was adored by his men.

Advancing with the Scotsmen, but to their right and slightly to their rear, was the Guards Brigade.

As the tight formation began to move forward in the darkness, a thunderstorm broke over their heads, lightning playing over the *kopjes* towards which they were being led. The deluge would continue until daybreak, but that was still a long way off and for more than three hours, in fearful conditions, the Scotsmen stumbled towards their destination.

Dawn comes early in Africa. By four o'clock it was possible to see the dark outlines of the *kopjes* against their backcloth of dark, grey sky as the rain ceased.

At the head of the close-packed soldiers, Major-General Wauchope questioned his guide about their position. The guide replied that they had gone slightly off course in the darkness, but suggested it would make little difference to the final assault. He also thought it time the Brigade assumed open formation, in order to present a less compact target to the enemy.

The Scots major-general agreed, but the soldiers had just encountered a dense thicket. Wauchope wanted his mean clear of this before they deployed to commence their attack.

With the thicket behind them and close formation resumed to his satisfaction, Major-General Wauchope gave the order to deploy. It was the last command many of his men would ever hear. Even as they moved to obey it was too late. Suddenly the fading darkness erupted in a holocaust of bullets.

To the accompaniment of the screams of the wounded and dying men, order and counter-order were shouted. The men were to fix bayonets and charge . . . They were to retire . . . Return the fire . . . Get up . . . Lie down.

At first it was impossible to obey this last order, so thickly packed were the ranks of the Highland Brigade. But some men managed. In fact, during those first chaotic minutes, separate groups of Highlanders obeyed every single conflicting order that could be heard above the din of death and battle. Soldiers lay down, or charged the Boer trenches. They fired on an unseen enemy, or cursed him and ran. They screamed in agony, or sat in shocked disbelief, watching blood gushing from a mortal wound.

Here, in the half-light of a South African dawn, thousands of miles from their cool highland hills, many brave men died. Among them was Major-General Andrew Wauchope, the pride of Scotland.

CHAPTER SEVENTEEN

Adam was thoroughly miserable and dejected by the time dawn began to lighten the heavy grey clouds over Magersfontein. He was wet, hungry and tired, sleep having proved to be nigh impossible. The rain had turned the bottom of the trench into a quagmire, with a depth of up to six inches of muddy water in places. This was not how he had imagined war would be. He had not even sighted a single English soldier yet.

The thought had scarcely passed through his mind when Jacob Eloff suddenly raised his head and whispered, 'What was that? I heard a noise . . .'

'It's probably Victoria, bringing her piglets to show you . . .'

The mumbled reply provoked subdued and tired laughter in the trench.

'Shut up!' Adam's order was urgent enough to stop the laughter instantly. 'I heard something too . . .' Standing up he suddenly exclaimed, 'My God!'

The last words escaped from him in an explosion of surprise that brought every man in the trench to his feet in instant wakefulness.

Theunis Erasmus was one of the last to struggle stiffly to his feet. A veteran of the first war against the British, standing or squatting in a wet trench was not for him. He had been seated upon an up-ended ammunition box, his feet resting on another. Looking out across the veld he saw the tightly-packed mass of Andy Wauchope's Highland Brigade just as the first ranks began to extend in open formation. His mouth dropped open . . . then clamped tight shut.

Lifting his rifle over the edge of the trench, he pulled back the bolt and rammed a cartridge home.

'What are we going to do, Theunis?' The anxious question came from Jacob Eloff.

'Do? We're going to kill them *khakis* before they get here and kill us. All of you . . . Get to shooting!'

Setting an example, Theunis Erasmus squinted along the barrel of his government-issue Mauser rifle and fired into the close-packed ranks of the Scots soldiers. Adam and the others of De la Rey's commando followed suit.

Alerted to the sudden danger, the whole of the Boer lines opened fire, each man sending bullet after bullet ploughing into the milling Scots soldiers, increasing the initial confusion. Some of the soldiers detached themselves from the mass of men and ran forward, firing at an unseen enemy as they came. Few reached the Boer lines. Many of the soldiers, confused by conflicting orders and faced with such a murderous barrage of bullets, broke and fled back the way they had come. The remainder dropped to the ground and returned the fire, frustrated by not being able to see the men at whom they were shooting.

Adam emptied his magazine into the anonymous mass of soldiers, his emotions a tangled mixture of excitement and fear. He was pushing another ammunition clip into the magazine of his rifle when he heard a sound from Jacob Eloff that was half-cry, half-gasp. Thinking the simple young farmhand had been hit by a British bullet, Adam looked up quickly.

Standing looking down into the trench was a kilted soldier. He was trying to fire his rifle, but it had jammed. Adam rammed the last bullet home and brought his weapon up just as the Scots soldier lost patience with his rifle and lunged downwards with his bayonet at the fear-frozen Jacob Eloff.

Adam fired at the same time as a dozen other Boers, and the Scots soldier fell forward into the trench, his body riddled by bullets. He fell upon the slightly built Jacob Eloff, carrying him to the bottom of the trench with him.

But Adam had no time to observe the whole of the incident. The courageous Scots soldier had not been alone. Four more of the kilted soldiers appeared on the rim of the trench and fired down at the men below them.

It was a valiant but futile charge by a handful of Seaforth Highlanders and they all died for their bravery, Adam killing one and contributing a bullet to the death of another.

Meanwhile Jacob Eloff lay moaning in the mud at the bottom of the trench, pinned to the ground by the body of the Scots soldier. Roughly, Adam pulled the body from the young hired hand. In the dim light he saw Jacob Eloff's face covered in blood.

'Jacob! Where are you hit, man? Where's the pain?'

Instead of answering, Jacob began shaking violently. Taking the young Boer orphan by the shoulders, Adam dragged him to a part of the trench where a rocky outcrop protruded above the level of the bottom of the trench. It was reasonably dry here. Adam laid Jacob down and began wiping his face with a handkerchief.

As he worked, Adam became increasingly puzzled. He had wiped almost all the blood away now, but had not found a wound. There was a sound from farther along the trench and Adam looked up to see some of the Lichtenburg men heave the body of the dead Scots soldier over the parapet of the trench — and realisation of the truth dawned. The blood on Jacob Eloff's face came from the Scotsman.

All gentleness forgotten, Adam lifted Jacob Eloff's head clear of the ground and shook him violently.

Moments later, Jacob Eloff was fighting to free himself from Adam's grip. Adam stopped shaking the other man only when he saw tears coursing down Jacob Eloff's cheeks. Then a shout went up, 'They're attacking again . . .'

Leaving Jacob Eloff where he lay, Adam snatched up his rifle and peered over the edge of the trench. The Scotsmen were not attacking, but were running forward to help one of their wounded officers. His knee shattered by a Mauser bullet, he had been trying to crawl to the shelter of a small cluster of rocks when his men had seen him. A number of soldiers led by a sergeant went to his aid. With bullets flying all around them they tried to reach him as he clawed his way along the ground. Two minutes after the vain rescue attempt began, every one of the would-be rescuers had been downed, most of them mortally wounded—yet still the wounded officer continued his slow and painful progress.

All along the long line of trenches the combatants faced each other, but for a moment there was a lull in the battle as it seemed that both Boers and Scotsmen were willing the wounded Scots officer to claw his way to safety. Even Jacob Eloff had risen to his feet and was soundlessly mouthing words of encouragement.

The wounded officer had almost reached the safety of a lone boulder when quite suddenly and unexpectedly Adam's rifle kicked in his hands, the report startling the soldiers of both sides. The head of the wounded Scots officer jerked back momentarily, then fell forward, his face sinking in the soft mud of the battlefield. The fingers that had been clawing at the earth in his painful progress now relaxed in the idleness of death.

A sound, as though of a great sigh, rose from both armies before the battle resumed with increasing fury as the British artillery brought their guns to bear on the Boer positions.

Ducking down below the parapet of the trench, Adam came face to face with Jacob Eloff. He crouched in the mud at the bottom of the trench, quivering with fear.

'Why did you do that, Adam? Why, man?' Jacob Eloff got the question out between chattering teeth.

'Why did I do what?' Adam growled, although he knew very well to what Jacob was referring.

'Why did you shoot him? Another few seconds and he'd have been safe. Out of the battle for good.'

Adam rammed a clip of bullets home and gave a tight-lipped reply. 'He was a *khaki*. An officer. He'd have killed me or you, given the chance.'

Grabbing Jacob's rifle which someone had propped against the side of the trench, Adam thrust it in Jacob Eloff's hands. 'Here, starting shooting. If the *khakis* get close enough they'll kill *you*, that's for sure. If you want to live you'll need to learn to kill them first.'

Jacob Eloff took the rifle from Adam as though fearful of what might happen to him if he refused. Pushing it over the edge of the trench he pulled the trigger again and again, not caring where the bullets were going.

Adam shook his head in disbelief at the simple farm boy's fear. It was a feeling he could not understand. He was gaining a fierce exhilaration from killing. Shooting the soldier who had toppled into the trench had been one of the most satisfying moments of his life. Killing the wounded Scots officer had been another. For the moment before pulling the trigger he had been a god, deciding whether the officer should live or die. Adam had chosen to kill him. Had he known that the vast majority of his comrades-in-arms deplored his action it would not have concerned him unduly. Adam *knew* he had been right. The officer was an enemy. He needed to be killed.

During a brief lull in the shelling a shout went up farther along the line that the British had over-run a section of the trenches and men of the Highland Brigade were fighting their way up the slopes of the Magersfontein.

The cry caused a ripple of fear to run through the long line of Boers. A large enough British force established on the crest of Magersfontein would dominate the trenches and reverse the course of the battle.

As it happened the rumour was an exaggeration of the truth. About a hundred Scots soldiers led by an enterprising young lieutenant had found an inexplicable gap in the Boer line of defenders. Perhaps General Cronje had intended putting a commando here, but had sent them on other duties. More likely, the men holding this section had become discouraged by the bad weather during the night and gone home. The free-thinking burghers never felt under any obligation to remain in a given spot if conditions were not to their liking, whatever the occasion. Such determined and unpredictable individuality was the bane of every Boer commander's life.

Whatever the reason, the Scots soldiers had breached the Boer lines and more were heading for the gap. As field-cornets and corporals shouted orders, a few men climbed out of each Boer trench. Bent low to escape British bullets, they doubled across the ground in order to plug the gap in their defences.

For many of the Scots troops, pinned down in open country in front of the trenches, it was their first glimpse of the enemy and in their frustration and anger they threw caution to the wind and fired at the running burghers. The British artillery too was brought to bear with impressive accuracy on the running men.

The flurry of British activity brought a quick response from the entrenched Boers and a furious action was fought, with casualties heavy on both sides. In the midst of this fierce exchange a messenger delivered a verbal message to old Theunis Erasmus. Looking along the line of men in his section of trench, the aged Lichtenburg corporal beckoned for three men to follow him. One of them was Adam.

The four men made their way from the trenches towards the line of *kopjes*, seeking every scrap of cover they could find against the bullets of the pinned-down Scots soldiers and the sharp-eyed British artillerymen. Around them groups of men from other trenches were heading in the same direction as themselves.

'Where are we going?' Adam asked the question as he and Theunis Erasmus rested for a few moments among broken rocks, after sprinting across a patch of open ground.

'General Cronje and his staff are holding off the *khakis* who broke through our lines. He's asked for help.'

'Then what are we waiting here for?' Eagerly, Adam set off, leaving Corporal Erasmus and another older man to come on more slowly.

At first, Adam followed other burghers, not knowing where he was supposed to be going, but it was not long before he heard gunfire coming from a slope close to the Magersfontein crest and he headed in this direction with a few of the others.

Closer to the crest he came upon a squat, full-bearded Boer crouched behind a rock and peering along the barrel of a Mauser rifle. Other burghers were in position about him, but there were only six or seven in all. The amount of gunfire coming from a short distance away, and the number of bullets ricocheting angrily off the rocks, suggested that the burghers were engaging a much larger British force.

Darting to the side of the thick-set burgher, Adam said breathlessly, 'Don't worry, help is on the way.'

Without waiting for a reply, Adam thrust the barrel of his rifle around the side of the rock and fired off two quick shots at a number of Scots soldiers who were moving towards him. The nearest of the soldiers dropped to the ground, attracting yet more fire from the Boers hidden among the boulders.

'I'm not in the least bit worried, young man. Who are you? Where are you from?' The burgher asked the questions without turning around, his gaze firmly fixed in the direction of the Scots infiltrators.

'Adam Retallick from Matabeleland. I'm with the Lichtenburg commando.'

The Scots soldiers tried another rush but many more Boer reinforcements had reached the scene now and a devastating volley downed most of the kilted men.

Theunis Erasmus crawled to the shelter of the rock and spoke to the heavily-built burgher. 'You all right, General?'

As Adam stared open-mouthed, the burgher snapped off a quick shot at an incautious Scot and levered another cartridge into the breech of his gun before nodding in affirmation.

'Of course. I've got a young *uitlander* here to protect me.' General Piet Cronje, commander-in-chief of the Boer forces, inclined his head in Adam's direction. 'Does he belong to your commando?'

Theunis Erasmus glanced briefly in Adam's direction. 'That's right, General. He enjoys killing *khakis*.'

General Cronje's glittering black eyes dwelled on Adam a moment. 'I sometimes wish I enjoyed it more. Take charge here, Theunis. I'm going to find out what's happening elsewhere.'

Gunfire was brisk on the hillside now, but enough Boers had reached the scene to confidently contain the Scotsmen as Cronje and his staff made their way from the scene of the hillside battle.

The Scots soldiers fought bravely, but their position was hopeless. When the young Scots lieutenant eventually ordered his men to lay down their arms, only a third of his original force remained.

Elsewhere the battle went on all day. In the early afternoon a commando from Ficksburg began to move in on the flank of the attacking force. Lieutenant-Colonel Hughes-Hallett of the Seaforth Highlanders was the only Scots commander still alive. Although wounded, he called on two of his companies to retire from their forward positions and meet the Boer advance. Many other Scots soldiers, seeing the Seaforths pulling back, thought a retreat had been ordered and began to withdraw from their positions. The entrenched Boers poured a murderous fire into the retreating Scots and in a short time the retreat had become a rout.

Once out of rifle range the Scots officers tried to rally their men. No sooner had they begun to re-form than the Boer artillery opened up with great accuracy, scattering the battle-weary Scots soldiers once more.

On the battlefield many men still lay in the open, justifiably afraid of leaving their positions. The victorious burghers were firing at anything that moved on the blood-stained veld.

The Scotsmen lay on the open veld while the blazing sun shone down on them, drying the mud on their clothes and blistering the tender skin exposed between tartan-topped gaiters and plaid kilt. All the while, displaying incredible courage, British medical orderlies crawled about the battle-fields, doing what little was possible to ease the lot of the wounded men.

When night fell, those men who were capable of walking rose painfully to their feet and stumbled back to the British lines. In the light of the camp-fires their dull eyes shuttered an experience that would bring them awake bathed in the perspiration of fear long after Magersfontein had been left behind.

Adam and the burghers of the Boer army spent another uncomfortable night in their trenches. Their water was exhausted and no arrangements had been made to bring up more. Some men merely complained, others left their positions and silently made their way to the rear of the Magersfontein heights. Here they located their horses, saddled up and turned their faces towards home.

But most of the burghers remained crouched in the narrow, damp confines of their trenches. It was a disturbed night. On more than one occasion the whole of the Boer lines was brought to its feet by a sudden sound. The groan of a wounded man, or a pitiful plea for water. Each sound began a chain-reaction as men started to their feet, convinced a British attack was under way.

Dawn came as a relief for the burghers. Their field-cornets and corporals brought them to readiness, peering into the waning gloom towards the scene of the previous day's slaughter.

It soon became apparent that only the wounded and dead remained. Thinking the battle for Magersfontein was at an end, many of the burghers wanted to quit their trenches and move among the prone Scotsmen. A few were eager for loot, or a British rifle to take home as a souvenir. Many more were aware of the plight of the Scots wounded. Some of them had lain unattended for twenty-four hours. The burghers wanted to give whatever aid a Christian could give to his fellow men.

All were held back by the Boer officers. Such caution was well-founded. An hour after dawn the British mounted a new attack. Under cover of artillery fire, Lord Methuen moved up his Guards brigade. The Grenadiers, Coldstreams and Scots – the latter eager to avenge the bitter defeat suffered by their countrymen.

The attack was not pressed home. The Guardsmen, cream of Great Britain's army, were halted when they came close enough to exchange rifle shots with their sharp-shooting adversaries. Gradually the sheer futility of the exchange became apparent to both sides and the firing petered out and died away.

Suddenly, as though the whole thing had been prearranged, medical orderlies moved on to the battlefield, British and Boer together.

No armistice had been agreed, and when the first khaki-clad figures with their stretchers moved forward from the British lines, Adam's finger curled about the trigger of his rifle and he took aim. Before he could fire, a large, rough-skinned hand closed about the sights of the Mauser. It was Theunis Erasmus.

'There's been enough killing. These are white men, not kaffirs. Let them tend their wounded and bury their dead.'

There was no shortage of work for the stretcher bearers and burial details. The British had suffered close on a thousand casualties – more than a third of them men of the Black Watch, the regiment which had spearheaded the first disastrous attack.

Ambulancemen and burial parties toiled under a hot African sun until well into the afternoon. Then, their grim work completed, they retired from the battlefield. So too did the whole of Lord Methuen's army.

As the Boer artillerymen fired their guns, more in the nature of a celebration than with the intent of killing their fellow men, Lord Methuen's badly-mauled army retreated. The Guards Brigade formed the rearguard, marching with a parade-ground precision that smacked of ill-deserved contempt for the marksmanship of the Boer gunners.

The victorious Boers allowed the Guards regiments this show of salvaged self-respect. It was all they had. The British army was in full retreat, defeated by an untrained, unpaid and undisciplined force of men who came to war dressed in their everyday working clothes.

As each burgher gravely shook hands with his neighbour in the Boer trenches, he tried hard to contain the pride that welled up inside him. Pride was sinful, and the victors of Magersfontein were God-fearing men. Their victory belonged to the Lord – helped by some inspired planning on the part of General Koos De la Rey.

CHAPTER EIGHTEEN

After the defeat of Lord Methuen's army, the Lichtenburg commando went south with General De la Rey. Cornelius Viljoen did not go with them. He and a few others in the commando had contracted enteric fever as a result of drinking the heavily contaminated water of the Modder river. They returned to their farms about Lichtenburg to recuperate, and showed no eagerness to return to the battlefields of the Orange Free State.

One man who would never again return to Lichtenburg was Field-Cornet Ignatius Lemmer. He had been with the burghers who went to the aid of General Cronje on the Magersfontein. He was killed there – shot in the back. No one saw him die and most of his men assumed he had injudiciously shown his back to the *khakis*. Others, remembering how Lemmer would have dealt with the Retallicks at Mafeking, looked thoughtfully in Adam's direction, but they kept their own counsel.

Koos De la Rey's style of fighting appealed to Adam and the younger men of the commando. Ranging over wide areas of the veld, the Transvaal commander rode fast and hard, hitting the British when and where an attack was least expected. During the first week of February, 1900, De la Rey's commando extended their activities to the British Cape Colony, south of the Orange River. Here they attacked British supply columns, tore up railway tracks, and took a number of prisoners. Only a few days later, but many miles away, he surprised and overwhelmed a whole British garrison, capturing much needed stores and ammunition.

Field Marshal Lord Roberts, V.C., was now the Commander-in-Chief of the British forces in South Africa, and he had as his Chief of Staff Major General Lord Kitchener of Khartoum. Both officers had made their way across Africa in great secrecy to join Lord Methuen on the Modder river. They now amassed thirty thousand British troops in the area and with this force they launched a surprise attack on General Cronje. The siege of Kimberley crumbled away and Roberts and his great army quickly pinned Cronje and five thousand burghers into an untenable position on the Modder river, close to Paardeberg.

Ten days later came news that rocked the men of Koos De la Rey's commando. After enduring a devastating artillery bombardment, General Cronje and his men had surrendered. Nothing now stood between Lord Roberts and Bloemfontein, the capital of the Orange Free State.

To the commandos fighting in the wide open spaces of the veld it seemed unbelievable that Cronje should allow himself to be backed into a trap from which he and his men had no escape, but this was exactly what he had done. The truth was that as a result of his earlier resounding victory over Lord Methuen, and an overlong sojourn at Magersfontein, Cronje and his burghers had almost forgotten they were still involved in a bitter war.

The families of many of General Cronje's burghers had joined them with their wagons. Cronje's own wife and other family members were there too. Other burghers, solicitous of the welfare of their horses, had sent them home, away from the heavily overgrazed veld around Magersfontein.

So it was that many of the men with Cronje were unable to break out because they had no mounts. Others would not go and leave their wives and children behind.

For nine days General Cronje, his army and the women and children suffered a fearful bombardment in their *laager* on the banks of the Modder river. Fifty pieces of British artillery pounded away at them for every hour of the day. Wagons were reduced to shattered, smouldering heaps of ash. Oxen and horses were killed in hundreds, their carcasses either left to rot where they lay, or thrown into the sluggish Modder river where the current was not strong enough to carry them away. The stench was indescribable. It sickened the besieging army and seeped into the farthermost corners of the tunnels dug into the river banks. Here the Boer women and children spent both their waking and sleeping hours.

Such conditions could not be endured for ever. On 27th February, 1900, the tenth day of the siege, white flags fluttered from poles above the Boer *laager*. The defenders of Paardeberg could take no more.

The commanders of the two opposing forces met in the British headquarters camp, and the dapper little British field marshal extended his hand to the squat, heavily-built Boer commander who was dressed in a tattered green coat, frieze trousers and heavily scuffed boots.

'I am glad to see you. You have made a gallant defence, sir.'

The sixty-four year old Boer general sunk his hands deeper in his coat pockets, glowered at his sixty-seven year old conqueror and said nothing. Behind him, under the watchful eye of a battalion of the Buffs, four thousand burghers shuffled from their stinking *laager* and stacked their arms. All around them ragged and dirty women and children wept openly to see their menfolk humbled.

'Damn this country!' Adam grumbled to Lucas Viljoen. Rubbing rain from his eyes with the heel of his hand he slouched lower over his horse's neck, the better to protect his face from the driving rain.

'Agh! This is a *good* year. Sometimes you can't see ten feet ahead of you for dust in this part of the country. I've seen grown men on their knees crying as they prayed for rain.' The reply came from Theunis Erasmus, riding close on Adam's other side.

Boers from all the battlefields of South Africa were gathering ten miles east of Paardeberg to make a stand against the British advance upon Bloemfontein, capital of the Orange Free State. Adam and Lucas were members of a small commando, only a hundred strong, sent out under Theunis Erasmus's command to scout the movements of the British army. So far the commando had not found the British. For the past twenty-four hours their battles had been only against the atrocious weather.

'You people talk as though God listens to every word you say. Why shouldn't He treat you as He does the rest of us and turn a deaf ear on you once in a while?'

'Don't make jokes about such things.' Theunis Erasmus glared at Adam from beneath the sodden rim of his slouch hat. 'God is the only true friend we Boers have. He hears us because we live according to *His* rules – and we need Him now as we've never needed Him before.'

'I reckon General Cronje must have broken the rules then,' retorted Adam. 'God didn't hear *him* at Paardeberg.'

'That's right . . . Piet Cronje *did* break the rules and anger the Lord.'

A horseman who had been riding close behind the others drove his horse forward between them. It was Predikant Paul Maritz, a minister of the Dutch Reformed Church, from Pretoria. A small, wiry man, he had a fiery temperament that many men found difficult to equate with his calling. He was one of a small group of men who had broken out of General Cronje's *laager* shortly before his surrender.

Bringing his horse alongside Adam, he said, 'Piet Cronje had forgotten that we are all equal in the sight of God and our fellow burghers. There are few luxuries that come the way of the men in our army. Those that did always went to Cronje and the men he gathered about him. These same men always managed to remain well fed when others were going hungry. *Oom* Niklaas had a vision about his downfall, but General Cronje was too stubborn to listen to him.'

Adam felt a flicker of interest. *Oom* Niklaas was Nicolaas Van Rensburg, the mystic whose visions were treated with great respect by Koos De la Rey. He had foreseen the British advance on Bloemfontein many weeks before, but no one had wanted to believe him then.

'Where is *Oom* Niklaas now?'

Predikant Maritz shook his head. 'No one knows. We broke out of Cronje's *laager* together, but then he went off somewhere on his own. *Oom* Niklaas says the Devil likes the company of men, so he goes off on his own every so often, to escape from him.'

Adam squinted through the rain to see if Predikant Maritz was being facetious, but the preacher was a humourless man and was perfectly serious.

Adam had seen Nicolaas Van Rensburg once. A small, almost frail man, *Oom* Niklaas had been riding with General De la Rey.

'Does *Oom* Niklaas see us winning this war soon?' Theunis Erasmus asked the question hopefully. He was seventy years old now, and of late he had begun to feel and look very tired.

'*Oom* Niklaas's visions of the progress of the war are shared only with Koos De la Rey – and *he's* still carrying the fight to the British. Have faith, Theunis. The Lord is surely on our side.'

'I'm not short on faith, Predikant. It's *time* that's running out for me. I've had a long life and I'll not complain when the Lord calls me to Him, but I'd rather not make my way to heaven spitted on some *khaki*'s bayonet.'

'That's not very likely, Theunis. You've been weathered by so many seasons your hide's tougher than that of some old rhino.' The cheeky retort came from Lucas Viljoen.

Theunis Erasmus spat expertly past the pipe clenched in his teeth. 'Time was when no young man would dare talk to his elders that way. Like I said, the sooner this war's over the better it will be for everyone.'

Lucas Viljoen and Adam grinned at each other. Theunis Erasmus was always complaining that he despaired of the younger generation ever becoming good burghers. For all that, he had proved himself a sound leader. The men of his commando, young and old, were proud of *Oom* Theunis. They boasted that the old veteran could out-ride and out-think any other commando leader, many of whom were no more than a third his age.

However, this was not to be one of the ageing commando leader's good days.

Towards late afternoon the rain which had hung like a thick blanket over the veld suddenly lifted. To their astonishment the men of the commando discovered they were not alone.

Heading towards them, not a thousand yards away, was a very large British scouting party of mounted infantry. Behind the scouts was what appeared to be the whole of the British army! They were making camp and the tents and picket lines extended for as far as the eye could see!

For a long, incredulous moment the opposing forces stared at one another in disbelief. Then, as though an order had been given, the men of the Boer commando wheeled their horses and fled, pursuing the rain across the veld.

The British scouting party gave chase immediately, but their mounts were no match for the wiry, veld-bred ponies of the Boers. The horses used by the British army had been hurriedly purchased from all over the world, rushed to Africa and put to work before they had the opportunity to acclimatise to the new country, or even recover from the long sea voyage.

The British scouts gave up the chase when the Boer commando began drawing away from them. But if the horses of the British soldiers could not match those of the Boers, there was little discrepancy in the velocity of their respective bullets.

As the Boers increased the distance between the two groups of horsemen, the British hauled their horses to a halt and some of them leaped to the ground to fire at the departing enemy.

It was almost maximum range for the ·303 Lee-Enfield rifles, but at least one of their bullets reached its target, severing the ham-string in a rear leg of Theunis Erasmus's pony. The animal went down in an awkward fall with the commando leader still in the saddle.

Adam glimpsed the fall from the corner of his eye and looked back in time to see horse and rider skid to a halt in an ungainly heap, the horse with all four legs in the air. By the time Adam brought his own mount to a halt, Theunis Erasmus's horse was trying unsuccessfully to regain its feet while Theunis Erasmus lay unmoving on the ground.

As Adam leaped down beside the Lichtenburg corporal, Theunis Erasmus stirred and groaned with sudden pain.

Putting an arm beneath him, Adam hauled the old commando leader to his feet, ignoring his cry of pain.

'My leg, man! My leg . . . It's broken.'

For the first time since the fall Adam looked back towards the British scouting party. Most sat their blown horses, watching his rescue attempt, but others were cantering towards him.

Supporting the crippled commando leader, Adam reached his own horse.

'Get up . . . quick!'

'I can't.'

'*Get up!*'

Somehow Adam lifted Theunis Erasmus to the saddle. Taking his rifle from its holster he kneeled beside the horse and took careful aim, firing at the nearest of the British soldiers, now no more than three hundred yards away.

The soldier slumped over the neck of his horse and Adam took aim and fired again. This time he brought a horse to the ground, its rider tumbling over the animal's dipping head.

The remaining riders reined in and went to the aid of their wounded and injured companions. Adam fired again, downing a second horse before returning his attention to Theunis Erasmus.

The commando leader was sagging in the saddle and Adam mounted up behind him. With his arms about Theunis Erasmus he put the horse to a canter, gritting his teeth against the injured man's groans. Others of the commando had turned their horses now and their long-range shots succeeded in keeping the pursuers at bay.

The commando rode into the hills, pursuing a tortuous route towards the place where the Boer army was camped. But darkness was almost upon them and after riding for no more than an hour they set up an uncomfortable camp in a shallow, wind-swept valley. They were afraid a fire might give away their position to a prowling enemy, but nevertheless a low fire was lit in order that Predikant Maritz might examine Theunis Erasmus's injuries.

The commando corporal's leg was broken, as he himself knew, but he also complained of severe pain in his stomach and chest and it was this that caused the Dutch Reformed Church minister most concern.

'He should see a doctor. I think he has broken some of his ribs, but I'm not skilled in such matters.'

'Can he hold on until morning?' queried Adam. 'There will be no moon until after midnight. We can't travel before then.'

From the ground Theunis Erasmus gasped, 'Never mind about *me* . . . Get word to Koos. Tell him about the *khakis*.'

The burghers looked at each other uneasily. Koos De la Rey was at the small village of Poplar Grove, many miles away. There was no telling how many British scouting parties were camped along the way.

'I'll go,' said Adam. '*And* I'll find a doctor too. I'll bring him back tomorrow morning. We haven't come all this way together to lose Theunis now.'

'Good boy. But you take care, you hear?' The old man reached up and gravely shook hands with his rescuer.

When Adam had ridden off into the night, Theunis Erasmus called Predikant Maritz to him. Breathing noisily, the injured commando leader said, 'I'm going to die, Predikant. You know it, and so do I.'

'We all have to die some day, Theunis. *When* is for the good Lord to decide . . .'

Theunis Erasmus waved the preacher to silence impatiently. 'Don't play word games with me, Paul Maritz. I've played too many of them with dying men in the past. I'm dying, I tell you.'

Predikant Maritz shook his head. 'I'm a simple preacher, Theunis, not a seer or a medical man. You're hurt, yes, I can set your leg, but I can't right the pains in your chest, and I don't know how bad it is.'

'It doesn't matter . . . I want you to write a will for me . . .'

'We'll think about that tomorrow, after you've seen a doctor.'

'Tonight . . . *Now!* I want to leave everything I have . . . My possessions . . . The farm . . . *everything*, to that young boy who went back for me today. To Adam Retallick.'

'Are you sure you know what you're saying, Theunis? What about your daughters?'

'They've all got husbands, except Esme. Most of them are good for nothing. They never let a day pass without squabbling with someone. They sent their mother to an early grave and would have done the same to me if I hadn't been away so much. No matter how I tried to divide the farm, it would be wrong. If I left it to Esme they'd find some way of robbing her. The farm is for that boy, Predikant. Tell him to provide for Esme, that's all I ask of him. Have you got that?'

'If it's what you wish, Theunis. I'll put it all down in writing just as soon as I've set this leg for you. Now, I'm going to need two strong men to help me . . .'

CHAPTER NINETEEN

Adam and the doctor met up with the commando again in the early morning, four hours out from Poplar Grove. Excitedly, Adam spoke to Lucas Viljoen and Jacob Eloff. 'I've seen President Kruger! Stood as close to him as I am to you. He wanted to make a speech but General de Wet made him go back to somewhere safer . . .'

As he was talking, Adam's eyes were searching the ranks of the commando. Suddenly the excitement left him and he looked accusingly at Lucas. 'Where's Theunis? I've brought a doctor . . .'

Adam's question was answered by Predikant Maritz. 'Theunis died during the night, Adam. He was hurt far more seriously than any of us realised. We buried him in the hills.'

For a moment Adam's face showed his feelings, then he scowled. 'Damn! He was a good corporal. We needed him.'

Taking a folded piece of paper from a pocket, Predikant Maritz held it out to Adam. 'Before he died he asked me to write a will and witness his signature. He's left his farm and everything he owns to you.'

Adam took the piece of paper and read, his expression one of bewilderment. 'Why to me . . .'

'You went back for him when his horse was shot. Theunis admired a brave man.'

'I can't accept *this*. He has family . . . daughters.'

'Theunis meant for you to have his farm, Adam. His daughters are all married, except for one. It's in the will that he trusts you to make provision for her. I think he gave you the farm to give you something to fight for and to keep you in the

148

country. He said Transvaal needs young men like you.'

Adam made no reply, but his mind was ranging ahead. *Far* ahead. Now he owned a farm not too far from the Viljoen family. *His* farm. He had something to offer Johanna ... He became aware that the Predikant was still talking to him.

'Where is General De la Rey? Is he going to make a stand at Poplar Grove?'

'Yes, but not at the place where I found him. Anyway, General de Wet's in charge and I doubt whether he'll be able to hold the burghers together long enough for a battle. When I told them about the *khakis*' cavalry it put the fear of God into most of his men ...' Adam saw Predikant Maritz frown at the mild blasphemy. 'I think General Cronje's defeat has knocked the fight out of the whole Boer army. Unless someone can stop them they'll run right through Bloemfontein and out the other side.'

'What will *we* do?'

The burgher who asked the question did not think it incongruous for a mature man to ask the question of a boy of sixteen. Adam had fought in battle with the commando and proved himself more of a man than most.

Adam shrugged off his thoughts of Theunis Erasmus. 'We follow after the others. When they decide to make a stand, we'll stand with them. We can't do it alone. Come on, we'd better move or we'll never catch up with Koos and de Wet.'

The Boer general upon whose shoulders rested the near-impossible task of preventing the British from taking Bloemfontein was General Christiaan de Wet. A farmer, and the father of sixteen children, de Wet had joined the Heilbron commando with three of his sons on the outbreak of war. His rise through the Boer ranks had been spectacular, to say the least. Now, after less than six months of war, he was Commander-in-Chief of the forces of the Orange Free State.

Deceptively mild-mannered, de Wet was a determined yet practical man. The surrender of General Cronje with more than four thousand burghers had temporarily unnerved the Boer army. He would need to delay a battle with the British for another day. For the moment it was enough to withdraw his troops to safety before the advance of the British army.

Adam and the burghers of his commando formed part of de Wet's rearguard. While the vulnerable Boer army streamed eastwards in disarray, the rearguard launched an attack on the British cavalry. The cavalry were slow to retaliate, believing the commando must have the might of the Boer army behind them. By the time they learned differently the Boer rearguard was gone, their mission completed. The Boer army was well on its way to Bloemfontein, leaving the British cavalry to curse the jaded horses that made pursuit impossible.

The immediate problem for General de Wet was to persuade his fleeing army to halt and make a stand. It was not to prove easy, especially after Oom Paul Kruger, President of Transvaal, and a man of legendary stature among the burghers, tried – and failed – to halt their flight.

Heading back towards the capital of the Orange Free State, Oom Paul became alarmed at the increasing numbers of armed burghers overtaking his light Cape cart. Ordering his escort to halt, the seventy-five year old Head of State climbed down and appealed to the fleeing horsemen to stop and make a stand to save the capital of his fellow president. Shamefaced, the demoralised burghers averted their gaze from the old man in the long black coat who leaned on his stick and appealed to their patriotism.

Furious at their refusal to obey him, the Transvaal president called on his police to open fire on the 'cowards' who refused to stand and fight for their country. The Pretoria police wisely kept their guns slung over their shoulders. President Kruger could only fume at his impotence as the Boer army continued its flight.

Not until a few Transvaal men came upon the scene did the president begin to gather a small force about him. Then an unexpected new arrival changed the situation in an instant. General Koos De la Rey came from the direction of Bloemfontein, accompanied by a police commando. He was soon joined by Adam and the men from Lichtenburg, and suddenly new hope replaced despair. Gathering about General De la Rey, the burghers pledged to do battle with the advancing British army.

The Boers knew they were heavily outnumbered. At the final count they numbered about fifteen hundred. Opposing them were more than ten thousand British troops determined to break through to Bloemfontein. But if the thought of the odds bothered them, not one of the burghers with Koos De la Rey allowed it to show as they prepared their positions on a ridge overlooking Abraham's *kraal*, on the Bloemfontein road.

The British were in no hurry. Each new day brought them fresh reinforcements and supplies. Their advance was agonisingly slow. For three days Koos De la Rey's small force waited for the enemy. On the 10th of March they arrived – in their thousands. The tense burghers gasped in alarm as file upon file of mounted men came into view. Among them were many lancers, and the sight of the red and white pennons fluttering at the end of their ancient cavalry weapons struck a chill into Boer hearts.

A battery of Boer artillery was supporting the men on the ridge, and they too saw the mounted men. Their shelling was both prompt and accurate. The shells scattered the cavalrymen and they retreated to re-group well out of artillery range.

The Boer artillery kept the British troops at bay until early in the afternoon, when infantry was moved up to make an assault on the *kopje* where Koos De la Rey's men were preparing to resist the British advance.

By the end of the afternoon Adam and his commando had fought off two determined assaults on their position. Then, with almost half their men wounded, they began to fall back. The British artillery was in action now and as afternoon became evening the ridge of the *kopje* became untenable, filled with exploding shells, smoke, the crackle of rifle fire, and the screams of wounded men. Suddenly, from out of the swirling smoke, came a line of bayonet-wielding khaki-clad soldiers. Scrambling over the ridge they fell upon the Lichtenburg commando.

Adam had not experienced a full British bayonet charge before – and he hoped he would never have to face another.

In front of him a group of six soldiers appeared, all seemingly determined to spit him on a bayonet. He shot the first two, someone beside him killed a third, but still the three survivors came on. One lunged forward and Adam heard a gasp of pain from Lucas Viljoen. Adam promptly shot the man who had bayoneted his friend. As another *khaki* lunged forward Adam pulled the trigger of his rifle again – and nothing happened. The rifle was empty! Before the British soldier could lunge again, Adam had reversed the Mauser rifle and slammed the brass-bound stock into the face of the *khaki*.

Even so, the remaining soldier would have spitted Adam had not two shots from behind downed him. Turning, Adam saw Koos De la Rey standing behind him, a rifle in his hand.

'Well done, young man – but now it's time to go. Take him with you . . .' Koos De la Rey pointed to Lucas, then, peering closer, asked, 'Isn't it Cornelius Viljoen's son?'

On one knee beside Johanna's brother, Adam nodded. Lucas Viljoen had been bayoneted in the chest. The blood trickling from a corner of his mouth was an indication of the seriousness of the wound.

'You . . . Help him.'

General De la Rey snapped the order at Jacob Eloff who had spent the last few minutes cowering behind a boulder. The simple-minded young farm-hand was no soldier and the sound of the first shell exploding on the ridge had reduced him to a trembling heap.

As Jacob Eloff scurried to obey De la Rey's order, the general said to Adam, 'Get him off the *kopje* and to the hospital at Bloemfontein – but don't remain there too long. We have no hope of holding the town against the British . . .' For a moment the weariness of the Boer general showed – but only for a moment.

'When he's seen a doctor, send him home. Better still, go with him.'

'But the war . . .'

'The war is over here, young man . . . But it's only just beginning in Transvaal. There will be fighting enough for you there. Go now.'

As Adam turned to help Lucas Viljoen to his feet, Koos De la Rey added, 'Tell Cornelius I am sorry his son has been hurt. There are times when I wish I were a burgher and not a general. Tell Cornelius that . . . He'll understand.'

There was a sudden increase in the sound a little farther along the ridge. Many shots and screams, and finally a man pleading with God to allow him to die quickly. Adam hoped God understood Afrikaans. He was beginning to doubt it.

As the light faded, the *kopje* took on an air of unreality. Lucas Viljoen was in great pain as Jacob Eloff and Adam helped him down the slope. Uncertain of their direction, they hoped they were heading away from the British army.

Adam and his party were not the only men lost on the slopes above Abraham's *kraal* as darkness began to cast its pall over the scene of battle. A shell suddenly burst against a rock, sending small, sharp-edged stone splinters in a wide circle and making Adam's ears hurt.

As the smoke cleared, a khaki-clad figure stumbled through the gunpowder smoke.

Adam released Lucas Viljoen and cocked his rifle, the sound lost in the explosion of yet another shell. The British soldier stopped as he saw Adam and his companions. He was a boy of no more than fourteen. He held out his hands and it could be seen that he carried no weapon, only a brightly polished but battered bugle.

Suddenly the bugler attempted a smile. It was the smile of a young, scared boy, not that of a soldier. Jacob Eloff answered the smile – and at that moment Adam fired. The bullet opened a red chasm between the bugler's eyebrows and, as a muscular twitch wiped the smile from his face, he dropped dead to the ground.

'You had no need to kill him . . .' Jacob Eloff's anguished cry was directed at Adam. Even Lucas Viljoen gave Adam a brief, pain-filled look of accusation.

'Had he sounded that bugle we'd have had half of Roberts's army here. Anyway . . . he was a *khaki*.'

Adam defended his action with sufficient vehemence to silence the simple-minded farm-boy and his pain-racked companion. 'He was a *khaki*, that's reason enough,' he repeated – but somehow the words did not wipe out the memory of the young, freckled face, split in a smile.

Of a sudden, Jacob Eloff ran back to the body of the bugle boy and began stripping off his khaki tunic.

'Jacob! What are you doing?'

Looking back over his shoulder as he fumbled with the buttons at the dead bugler's throat, Jacob called, 'I need a coat. Look . . .'

Holding up his arm he showed Adam his sleeve, ripped from

wrist to elbow and almost severed from the remainder of the coat. The clothes of many men in the Lichtenburg commando were in a similar state. They had been campaigning for many months far from home, in appalling weather and rugged country. General De la Rey's force had become an army of ragged vagrants.

Jacob Eloff returned, pulling on the khaki tunic. Brushing it with his hand, he said apologetically, 'There's not much blood on it. In a few days you won't even notice.'

Just before they reached the foot of the hill they saw some British soldiers, but they were some distance away and in the poor light the soldiers saw Jacob's newly-acquired tunic and waved cheerfully, believing him to be a British soldier helping a wounded companion off the hill.

When they reached the place where the horses had been held, they found all but two of the mounts had been taken. Cursing their companions, Adam and Jacob lifted the now semi-conscious Lucas Viljoen to the saddle of a horse. Adam climbed up behind him, and with Jacob Eloff following on behind they set off to ride the few miles to Bloemfontein.

CHAPTER TWENTY

Before reaching the Orange Free State capital, Adam, Jacob Eloff and Lucas Viljoen caught up with Predikant Maritz. He too had left the ridge with a wounded burgher. Unfortunately, the condition of his companion had worsened along the way, forcing him to stop at the side of the Bloemfontein road. Within minutes of their meeting, the burgher died.

When Adam suggested the Predikant ride on with them, he declined. Recovering his coat from the dead man, he said, 'I'll stay and bury him. You take his horse. He wouldn't have begrudged it. He was a good man.'

In the faint moonlight Adam thought he could see tears glistening on the Predikant's cheeks. The preacher's next words confirmed the suspicion. 'It's been a bad night for our people, Adam. More than three hundred dead and many more wounded. It's a tragic loss . . . Tragic. One the country can ill afford.'

'But it's delayed the British and given our army time to strengthen the defences at Bloemfontein . . .'

'Defences? There *are* no defences. Once an army starts running there's no stopping it. They certainly won't be hanging around building defences.'

Adam did not believe the Predikant's words until he reached Bloemfontein, the next morning. There were no fortifications – and very few burghers. It seemed that the whole Boer army, together with many of the residents of the Orange Free State capital, were trekking northwards. They followed the panoply of government which had already been moved to the town of Kroonstad, a hundred miles to the north-east – and no more than a day's ride from the Transvaal border.

Adam soon found the Bloemfontein hospital, but the medical staff were surprisingly reluctant to help Lucas. One of the orderlies told Adam it was because so many wounded burghers had reached the town that they had overwhelmed the hospital's limited facilities.

However, when Adam insisted that Lucas Viljoen be treated, a doctor was found to examine him. Exposing the wound, the doctor pursed his lips and looked from one to another of the young men. Jacob Eloff was the oldest and he was no more than twenty.

'Was it a bayonet caused this wound?'

Adam nodded, and to his surprise the doctor's manner underwent a change. 'Well, at least you've been *close* to the enemy. Most of your friends seeking treatment have been wounded by shrapnel, wounds they received while running away.'

'Is Lucas going to be all right?'

The doctor shrugged. 'I can only treat what I see – and I can't see into the future. It depends on a great many things. Whether the British soldier kept his bayonet clean – and how much damage it's done to your friend's lung.'

'How long before you know?'

'I'm a doctor, young man, not a fortune-teller. What's your hurry?'

'I want to take Lucas home to the Transvaal before I join up with Koos De la Rey again.'

'So you're General De la Rey's men? I should have known . . .' As he spoke the doctor applied a dressing to Lucas Viljoen's wound and bound a bandage tightly about his chest. 'All the same, you've probably fought your last battle. We have no army left . . . certainly not in the Orange Free State. Presidents Kruger and Steyn have asked the British for peace, but Lord Roberts refuses to parley – and why shouldn't he? He's winning!'

On the bed Lucas tried to sit up. The movement caused him to grunt in pain. Lying back, he gasped, 'We can't give up now. We can still beat them . . .'

The doctor placed a large hand firmly on Lucas Viljoen's wounded chest and held him down. 'Your fighting days are over for a while, young man. You need rest and some fattening up. I'm keeping you in hospital for at least a week.'

Adam was dismayed. 'The British will be in Bloemfontein within a week. We'll all be taken prisoner.'

'I'm not keeping *you* here,' retorted the doctor. 'You can go whenever you wish. At least you'll have the satisfaction of knowing your friend is a *live* prisoner.'

Adam and Jacob Eloff managed to find a room in a Bloemfontein hotel. Neither man had money, so Adam sold the horse that had been the property of the dead burgher.

They returned to the hospital that evening to visit Lucas – and met President Steyn and some of his grave-faced advisers leaving. The president had been visiting a dying, past member of the Orange Free State government.

As they stood respectfully to one side, President Steyn stopped before them and frowned. 'What are two strong young men doing skulking around here? Why aren't you out fighting the British, eh?'

'We've done as much fighting as any Free State burgher,' declared Adam, stung by the president's question. 'We saw precious few of your men yesterday at Abraham's *kraal*, and they were long gone when we brought a wounded Lichtenburg man here this morning.'

'You're De la Rey's men?'

Bursting with pride at talking to the Orange Free State president, Jacob Eloff blurted out, 'I got this jacket from a *khaki*. Adam shot him. It fits me good.'

Resting a hand on Adam's shoulder, President Steyn saw how young he was – and how tired and strained he looked. 'I'm sorry. You and your comrades did well. With twice your number ...?' He shrugged. 'Who knows, we might have turned the British back from Bloemfontein. As it is, there's no one left here to fight. Bloemfontein is theirs ...' Overcome by sorrow, President Steyn began to walk away. He had taken no more than a dozen paces when he stopped and looked back.

'What will you two boys do now?'

'Take Lucas Viljoen home to Lichtenburg when he's a bit better. Then rejoin General De la Rey.'

'You'll need to leave Bloemfontein quickly if you want to

fight again. The British will be here in another twenty-four hours — thirty-six at the most. I'm taking a train for Kroonstad in the morning. Be at the station and I'll find a place for both of you.'

'We can't leave without Lucas.'

President Steyn nodded. 'If your friend is fit enough to travel we'll take him too.'

The doctor was adamant that his patient was *not* fit enough to travel, but Adam pre-empted all argument by arriving at the hospital at dawn and removing Lucas Viljoen.

Later that morning, after Lucas had coughed up blood, Adam was questioning his own wisdom in taking Johanna's brother from the care and attention he had been receiving at the hospital. They were travelling in a closed wagon, towards the rear of the Orange Free State president's train, sharing the space with a mound of hastily loaded government papers and documents. Their two remaining horses were accommodated in the next wagon.

When Adam voiced his misgivings, Lucas Viljoen reached up and gripped his arm tightly. 'I'm glad you brought me with you, Adam. I'd rather die a free man than live as a prisoner of the British.'

Another trickle of blood escaped from Lucas's mouth as he spoke. Wiping it away, Adam said, 'That's enough talk of dying. You're going to live. You've *got* to live. I promised Johanna I'd bring you home safely. She'll never forgive me if I don't.'

'You're fond of Johanna, aren't you?'

'We'll be married one day . . . and I have my own farm to take her to.'

'I knew soon after you and your brother were captured near Mafeking that she'd fallen for one of you *uitlanders*. At the time I wasn't sure whether it was you or your brother.'

It had been a long time since Adam had thought of Nat. But listening to Lucas, all the old jealousies and rivalries flooded back with renewed strength.

At Kroonstad, President Steyn stepped down from the train and was immediately surrounded by members of his government's administration. They bombarded him with questions . . . His signature was required on a dozen documents, each of the utmost importance. There were decisions to be made . . . orders to be given. The army . . . Housing for his staff. President Kruger had requested an urgent meeting . . .

With questions and pleas coming at him from all sides, the president of the war-torn republic still found time to look in on the three young men in the covered wagon at the rear of the train. He informed them that the train was going on to the Transvaal capital of Pretoria to load guns and ammunition for the Boer army. Once the papers had been removed from their wagon the wounded Lucas Viljoen and his two companions could continue their journey with the train.

It was a great stroke of luck, and this luck held good. Adam left the wagon at Johannesburg to water their horses and learned that another train, standing alongside, was heading along the West Transvaal branch line within the hour. Its route would take it to within fifty miles of Lichtenburg – and no more than forty from the Viljoen farm.

Adam had intended that Lucas should rest for a few days at Pretoria, for by now he was a very sick young man, but such an opportunity was too good to be missed. If their luck held Lucas could be home in three days.

An hour later they were rattling around in an open truck, heading west. All thoughts of dying behind him now, Lucas was dreaming of home. Meanwhile Adam was thinking of the reception Johanna would give him, and Jacob Eloff was doing his best to hide his excitement at the thought of seeing Victoria, his pig, and her offspring.

CHAPTER TWENTY-ONE

When the three companions left the train to begin their overland journey, they were faced with a sudden deterioration in Lucas's condition. He had been bleeding for some days and now he developed a fever.

There was a solitary farmhouse nearby and Adam went for help, only to be greeted by a tall, gaunt Afrikaner woman armed with a large-bore elephant gun. She demanded to know who he was, whence he had come, and what he was doing at her farm. The woman wielded the gun as though it had a bayonet attached, prodding him to emphasise her words. Her finger was curled about the trigger and Adam was more scared than at any time during his battles with the *khakis*. Had the large-bore gun gone off – accidentally or otherwise – it would have made a hole through him large enough to take a man's fist.

Not until Adam mentioned the name of Theunis Erasmus was the big gun lowered, and the stern-looking woman looked suddenly vulnerable.

'Theunis is dead, you say?'

'I dragged him clear of a fallen horse myself.'

'He was a good man. A really good man.'

'You knew him well?' Adam was reluctant to drop the subject of the late corporal for fear she might raise the gun and point it in his direction once more.

'I nursed his wife when she lay dying. He and my husband fought together in the first war against the British.'

'Is your husband here now?'

'He was killed on the first day's fighting in this war . . . at

Mafeking. But you're not here to chat about my family. Where is this friend of yours?'

'By the railway line. We've just got off a train.'

'Is he hurt bad?'

'He was bayoneted through to the lung. All the travelling we've done has made him bleed and brought on a fever.'

The woman grimaced. 'It doesn't sound good, but bring him in, he'll be well nursed here.' Raising her voice, she called, 'Margret. Gezima. Come.'

Two young girls appeared at the doorway. One was aged about eighteen, the other probably three years younger. Both were very pretty.

Adam returned his gaze to their mother and saw she had been watching for his reaction. 'Now you know why strangers to the Coetzee house are greeted with a gun. Go and fetch your friend.'

When Adam and Jacob Eloff returned to the house carrying Lucas Viljoen between them, the two girls hovered around him expressing concern at his pale face and the blood that still leaked from the corner of his mouth. Lucas was taken to a bedroom, and when Mrs Coetzee had ushered her daughters from the room, Adam and Jacob Eloff undressed their wounded companion and put him in the bed. Then the two Coetzee girls returned to the room with their mother and it was the turn of Adam and Jacob Eloff to leave.

The two young men sat aimlessly on the *stoep* for a long time before Margret, the older of the Coetzee girls, came out and said she would cook a meal for them.

It was the first proper meal Adam had enjoyed for many days and he and Jacob Eloff did it full justice, praising the skill of the cook. When Mrs Coetzee came to the kitchen she looked suspiciously from Margret's flushed face to Adam.

'I was telling Margret it was the best meal I've had since I left home, months ago. It was almost worth the waiting.'

Mrs Coetzee snorted, still not convinced. 'As long as that's *all* you were telling her. You behave yourself while you're under my roof, young man. If you don't, you and your friends will be out, wounded man or no. Margret, go out and shut up the stock. It will be dark soon.'

'I'll do it.' Adam rose from his chair. 'It's the least I can do.'

'I'll come too,' said Jacob Eloff, rising clumsily to his feet. 'I'm good with animals. That's my job on the Viljoen farm, when I'm not fighting. I've got my own pig. Her name's Victoria. She's got seventeen piglets. *Seventeen!* I haven't seen them yet, but I will soon.'

Marie Coetzee's expression softened as she listened to the simple young man. 'Whoever sent you off to war ought to be ashamed of themselves, Jacob. Never mind, you'll soon be back home with your pig. Margret, show these two young men what to do – but don't be too long about it, or I'll be out looking for you.'

Outside the house, Adam spoke quietly to the girl. 'I don't think your mother trusts you, Margret. I wonder why?'

'I'm sure I don't know what you're talking about,' said Margret, indignantly. But Adam was left with the impression that she was not offended by his question.

'I suppose it gets lonely living so far away from other folks?'

'Then you suppose wrong. Since the war began we see lots of people here. The Johannesburg commando always stops by on its way to Mafeking.'

'I doubt if you get to speak to any of them. Not with your ma being so strict about such things.'

'Wrong again. I get to speak to lots of them. Why, there's at least two of the Johannesburg boys want to marry me. They've told me so.'

'Do you have any pigs? I like pigs.'

For a moment, Margret looked startled at Jacob Eloff's unexpected question. Then she giggled. 'Yes, we have four sows and a young boar. They're penned on the low ground down by the river. You can go and lock them in for the night if you want.'

Watching Jacob Eloff going off happily on his voluntary task, Margret said, 'He's a bit simple, isn't he?'

'He has the mind of a child. Your ma is right. Jacob should never have been sent off to war. The noise of battle terrifies him.'

'Have you been in many battles? My pa was only in the one and he was killed by a British shell.'

Adam's expression tightened and for a moment he looked much older than his years. 'It seems to have been one battle after another since I came south. The last one was the worst, the one where Lucas was wounded. Too many of our men were killed that day.'

'Did you kill any British soldiers?' Margret asked the question eagerly.

'A few . . . including the *khaki* who bayoneted Lucas.'

There was a strange look on Margret's face as she said, 'Most of the men of the commandos who come through here have never been in a proper battle . . . they're just boys, really. I'm *glad* you've killed Britishers.'

'How glad?'

Margret Coetzee gave a quick glance over her shoulder to check if they could still be seen from the house. Then she took his hand and led him inside a windowless, mud-walled barn that smelled of straw and grain. Closing the door behind her, she turned towards him in the darkness. '*Very* glad, Adam Retallick. Very glad indeed . . .'

The three young men remained at the Coetzee farm for a week. Then, one evening when Adam, Margret and Jacob Eloff left the house to shut away the domestic animals, Marie Coetzee gave them a few minutes and followed after. She saw Jacob Eloff making his way happily towards the river bank to shut away the pigs and she made for the feed-barn. In her hands she carried the large-bore elephant gun.

Fortunately for Adam he had spent many nights on sentry duty, his ears tuned to the slightest sound. When Marie Coetzee pushed open the barn door he was kneeling in the straw, cutting open a grain sack. Margret was beside him, hidden from her mother's view as she hurriedly adjusted her clothing.

Looking up in feigned surprise, Adam said, 'I'm just opening a grain sack for the chickens, ready for the morning . . .'

'You won't have to concern yourself about feeding chickens in the morning. You'll be on your way.'

'No, Ma! Don't send him away. Please don't do this to me again . . .'

'Shut up, girl. Get outside. You hear me? Get out! I've something to say to this young man.'

Crying in vain frustration, Margret was bundled outside.

When her mother returned her attention to Adam, he asked, 'What about Lucas?'

'He's well enough to travel. You can borrow the light wagon. It's behind the house. Send it back with one of the Johannesburg commandos – or any other way you like, but I don't want to see *you* in my house again.'

When Adam began to protest his innocence, suggesting she had gained a wrong impression, Marie Coetzee cut him short.

'I've gained no "wrong impressions", as you put it – only right ones. Think yourself lucky I'm packing you off and not making you stay and marry her, as her father would if he were alive. You're not the first, and try as I will I doubt if you'll be the last. Get out now, before I change my mind.'

In truth, the order to leave the Coetzee farm came as a relief to Adam. The excitement of the hurried meeting of hot bodies in daily ritual inside the feed-barn had already begun to pall. Adam had accepted Margret's 'gratitude' to a man who was avenging her father's death, but he realised she wanted more than a few moments of stolen passion. Apart from her lack of morals – most unusual in a girl brought up in the strict religion of the Dutch Reformed Church – Margret was no different from any other farm girl. Constantly under pressure from her mother's scrutiny and supervision, she wanted to break free in the only way open to a girl in that time and place. She wanted marriage.

But if the sudden departure suited Adam, it did not please Lucas Viljoen. He had enjoyed the attentive nursing of Gezima, Margret's fifteen year old sister. Marie Coetzee had no qualms about leaving her younger daughter and the wounded patient alone, and the two were together for hours at a time. Gezima sometimes read to him. At other times they would talk, about themselves, their families, and their dreams for the future.

Lucas Viljoen's sudden departure brought an abrupt end to their shared confidences, and there were tears on Gezima's cheeks as she stood in the doorway, waving to the departing trio.

In the back of the wagon, propped up by Jacob Eloff, Lucas waved until the farmhouse was lost to view behind a small, tree-covered *kopje*.

Sinking back on his uncomfortable blanket bed, Lucas Viljoen said fiercely, 'I'll be back here for Gezima, one day.'

'Have you told her?'

'No, but she knows.'

The heavy old wagon creaked up to the door of the Viljoen farmhouse soon after midday, four days after leaving the Coetzee farm. It had been a long, slow ride. The wagon had not been used for so long that parts of its woodwork had begun to rot away. One of the wheels had twice collapsed.

It had also been a painful ride for Lucas. The bleeding from his lung had not resumed, but he was having difficulty with his breathing.

Cornelius Viljoen, looking fit and well, had been the first to see the wagon approaching, and he had called out the remainder of the family. But it was not until it drew close that he recognised Adam and Jacob – and he became alarmed because he could not see Lucas.

When the wagon came to a halt the family crowded around and saw Lucas lying inside. He was pale and thin, his face registering the pain he had known, but there was nothing wrong with his smile.

Adam and Jacob Eloff, helped by Cornelius, lifted Lucas down, and as he grasped his mother's hand she began to cry.

'My boy . . . Oh, my poor boy.'

'Poor boy nothing, Ma. I'm alive – thanks to Adam. Now I'm home again I'll get well quickly, you'll see.'

Once inside the house Lucas refused to go to bed. Instead he lay on a hard settle and joined in the babble of conversation that erupted. Exchanging news of the war for details of life on the farm, and hearing the names of the men from the area who had been confirmed as casualties of the war.

The figure was high. Tragically high. There was not a household within fifty miles of Lichtenburg which did not have a casualty among its family members.

'. . . And for what?' asked Sophia Viljoen bitterly. 'Are we winning this war? While our men are dying the British are quietly bringing in more troops. One of our commandants who was here last week said there are now two hundred thousand *khakis* in South Africa – with fifty thousand of them in Bloemfontein. *Fifty thousand!* That's more fighting men than the Transvaal and the Orange Free State can muster between them right now . . . and those we *have* got won't stand and fight. It's stupidity to continue this war, I tell you.'

'We've won some great battles, Mrs Viljoen.'

'But we're not winning the *war*, don't you see? If we carry on the way we are there won't be enough young men left to put our country back together again. It will be taken over by *uitlanders*. Is *this* what we're fighting for?'

Aware that he too was an *uitlander*, Adam did not reply, and Sophia Viljoen's expression softened. 'But why am I arguing with *you*? You've brought our Lucas home. This is your home too, Adam. Everything we have is yours.'

Lucas had been unaware of the drama behind their sudden departure from the Coetzee farm. Wan from the excitement of being home, he managed a smile. 'Go careful with your generosity, Ma. You might find you're giving our Johanna away.'

Cornelius Viljoen looked from Adam to his daughter, who was scowling furiously at her grinning brother.

'Adam and Johanna . . .? Well . . . She could do worse. They could *both* do worse.'

'Pa!'

'Eh? What's this about Johanna and the young man? I knew it. I knew he'd come calling the first time I set eyes on him. You didn't believe me then. Perhaps you'll listen to me in future . . .'

The laughter that greeted *Ouma* Viljoen's outburst cleared the embarrassment that had followed on Lucas's disclosure, and Johanna asked, 'Where's Jacob? He should be here with us.'

Adam said, 'I can hazard a guess. He'll be with his precious Victoria and her seventeen offspring. He's talked of little else since we began the journey home.'

Cornelius and Sophia Viljoen exchanged glances, and Cornelius said, 'So help me, I'd forgotten about Jacob and that precious pig of his.'

'Has something happened to her?' Adam knew that if some calamity had befallen 'Victoria' the simple young farm-hand would be heartbroken.

'The pig's all right, but her litter is long gone. It was more than four months ago Victoria had them. Pa couldn't have

166

eighteen pigs around the place as well as our own. We kept one young sow for him and sold fourteen for Jacob at a fair price. The other two are hanging up in the smoking-shed. Jacob will see them on his breakfast plate on Sunday.' Johanna made the explanation.

'I'd better go and explain things to him,' said Adam. 'He's going to be very upset at not seeing his precious Victoria surrounded by seventeen little piglets. It hasn't occurred to him they'll have grown.'

'I'll come with you,' said Johanna, unexpectedly. When her newly returned brother raised his eyebrows, she added, 'The pig pen has been shifted. I'll need to show Adam where it is now.'

'Of course,' grinned Lucas. 'What other reason could you have?'

Johanna pulled a face at Lucas before leading Adam from the room.

On the way to the pig pen, she suddenly asked, 'Was it a hard-fought battle . . .? The one where Lucas was wounded?'

'The hardest we've ever fought. We were lucky to escape with our lives. Many didn't.'

'From what Lucas has said it wasn't luck but *you* who saved his life.'

'We might all have been dead had it not been for Koos De la Rey. He was everywhere at once.'

'Adam . . . I *am* grateful to you for saving Lucas's life, and for bringing him home. I want you to know this.'

'Are you, Johanna?' Looking at her, Adam remembered Margret Coetzee's 'gratitude' and his pulse began racing. He dismissed the thought immediately. Johanna was the girl he would one day marry. 'Does this mean there can be an . . . an "understanding" between us?'

Her answer was a long time coming. 'If it's what you want.'

'It's what I've wanted since I first saw you.'

'All right.'

Adam was elated. This was the reason he had left Insimo to come to South Africa. The moment he had dreamed of on cold, wet nights, crouched in muddy trenches, when love and happiness seemed very far away. Johanna had agreed she would be his wife one day . . . and her father had already given his tacit agreement, back in the house.

'Johanna . . .' Adam took her uncertainly by the shoulders. 'I . . . I love you.'

'Do you?' He felt her trembling in his grip. Pulling her clumsily towards him, he kissed her full on the mouth.

Johanna had never kissed anyone in this way before but she responded instinctively and Adam's restraint snapped. His kiss became demanding as his hands moved over her body. Suddenly Johanna squirmed in his arms and she pushed him from her with a surprising strength.

'Don't you *dare* do that! Don't you *ever* dare . . .' She was angry. More angry than Adam had ever seen any girl.

'I'm sorry . . . I thought you were expecting me to.' Adam spoke stiffly. He was unused to offering apologies. It came hard.

'You thought . . .?' The remainder of the sentence was never uttered. A distraught Jacob Eloff came running around the corner of a nearby barn, almost bowling them over. Breathlessly, he gasped, 'It's Victoria . . . *She's* there . . . but there are no piglets.'

Johanna looked from Adam to Jacob Eloff and back again. Suddenly all the anger drained from her and she collapsed against the side of the barn and began laughing.

Both young men looked at her in consternation. Seeing their expressions, Johanna laughed all the more.

Finally she stood away from the wall and wiped the tears of mirth from her cheeks. 'Jacob, you're priceless. You really are. I get a proposal of marriage; a protestation of love; my first kiss – and have a quarrel with the man who wants to marry me, all in the space of a few minutes. Then you come along and everything must take second place to that wretched pig of yours . . .'

Still giggling uncontrollably, Johanna explained. 'Of course there are no piglets. They were born months ago and they grew into pigs. That's one of them in the pen with Victoria. The others are . . . are sold. Pa's kept the money for you. They fetched a good price. Victoria has earned you some money, Jacob – and now you have *two* sows to have piglets. If things go on like this you'll have the largest pig-farm in Transvaal by the time this war is over.'

She linked an arm through Jacob's, then held out her other hand to Adam. 'Come on, let's go back to the house and Pa can tell you everything that's been happening while you were away.'

CHAPTER TWENTY-TWO

After he had been back from the war for a week, Adam decided it was time to claim the farm that had been willed to him by Theunis Erasmus. It was only about thirty miles from the Viljoen farm, in the hilly country to the north.

There were few settlers here, the early trekkers preferring the richer soil to be found in the flatter land. However, Cornelius Viljoen assured Adam there *was* good land in the hills, and he drew Adam a map, showing him how to reach the farm. Cornelius also said he had heard that the remaining Erasmus daughter was now married. Adam should have the farm to himself.

It was an easy ride to the farm. Setting off in the early morning, Adam came within sight of it by mid-afternoon. The farmhouse was larger than Adam had thought it would be. Large and dilapidated. It was also occupied.

Adam smelled wood-smoke from a long way down the valley, and as he drew closer he could see smoke trickling from the stone-built chimney at one end of the farmhouse.

Adam was puzzled, and he took no chances. There was a small clump of thin trees not far from the farmhouse and he tied his horse there before advancing cautiously towards the house, rifle in hand. He kept the ramshackle farm buildings between himself and the windows of the house, hoping he had not been seen riding along the valley.

He slipped quietly between two outhouses, one with a collapsed mud wall, the other with a threadbare thatched roof. He could see the house from here. A short dash across a patch of sunlit yard would bring him to the back door . . .

'Drop your gun and raise your hands above your head.' The soft-voiced order, given in Afrikaans, came from the shadows of one of the derelict outhouses.

Adam hesitated, weighing up his chances of diving clear of whoever was there.

'Do as I say – *now*, if you understand me. If you don't it means you must be English, in which case I'll shoot you anyway.'

Adam dropped his rifle to the ground and raised his hands high in the air. Turning to the ruined outhouse, he said, 'We're on the same side, unless I'm mistaken . . .'

'I'm on *my* side. Keep your hands up where I can see them.'

Dressed in ragged fustian trousers and faded shirt, a slight, barefooted figure stepped from the shadows holding an ancient percussion rifle that was pointing at Adam.

Adam thought at first it was a young boy, but then, as the armed stranger moved closer, he realised it was a girl of about his own age.

He began to lower his hands and the girl stopped, the rifle once more coming up to the aim. Adam raised his hands again quickly.

'Who are you? What are you doing here?' Adam queried as the girl edged towards the Mauser rifle lying on the ground. She never took her eyes from him and at no time moved close enough for him to attempt to snatch the gun from her.

'*I'll* ask the questions.' Reaching Adam's gun, the girl pushed it backwards with her foot until it was well clear before picking it up. Checking the magazine, she rested her own ancient gun against a pile of crumbling wooden logs.

'That's better. Now I have five chances instead of only one. I'll ask you the same question you put to me. Who are you, and what are you doing sneaking around here?'

'My name is Adam Retallick – and I'm not sneaking around anywhere. I came to have a look at my farm.'

'*Your* farm? It belongs to my pa, Theunis Erasmus – and no one's going to steal it from him. Not while I'm here.'

Adam began to breathe more easily. 'Then you must be Esme. Cornelius Viljoen told me you were married.'

'It doesn't do to believe all you're told – and I don't know any Cornelius Viljoen.'

Adam took a chance and lowered his hands. The barrel of the Mauser came up threateningly, but Esme Erasmus said nothing.

'Look . . . can we go inside the house? We need to talk about one or two things. First of all I think you should see this . . .'

Reaching slowly and carefully inside the breast pocket of his jacket, Adam held out the piece of paper on which was written Theunis Erasmus's will.

Ignoring the piece of paper, Esme said, 'I can't read. Tell me what it says.'

'It's your pa's will. He left the farm to me.'

The gun came up again. 'Try again. Pa couldn't write nothing but his name.'

'A Predikant from Pretoria wrote it for him. He was with your pa when he died.'

Esme Erasmus studied Adam's face for some moments. Then she said, 'So Pa *is* dead.' Theunis Erasmus's daughter was unnaturally composed. 'Someone told me so a few days ago. I didn't believe them, even though Pa's never stayed away this long before. How did he die?'

'His horse was shot and fell on him. I got him free but he didn't last the night. I'm sorry. In the will he asked me to make provision for you . . .'

'Pa said that . . .?' Esme blinked rapidly, then responded angrily. 'How did he think you'd make provision for *me*? You're hardly more than a boy. Besides, this is *my* home. I was born here.'

'It can remain your home . . . at least, for a while. I'm not thinking of marrying and coming up here until the war ends. You might be married yourself by then . . .'

Esme Erasmus gave Adam a look that silenced him immediately. 'My sisters found *one* man for me. I'll not be taking another. But you'd better come into the house and tell me more of how you came by that piece of paper from Pa . . .'

Much to Adam's relief the girl lowered the Mauser and handed it back to him. Picking up her ancient percussion rifle she preceded him into the house.

The inside of the Erasmus farmhouse was as untidy and neglected as the exterior had promised. But there was a fire in the kitchen and a smell of coffee came from a pot on the fire's edge.

'Take some.' Esme nodded in the direction of the coffee and slid a tin mug along the table in his direction.

The mug was reasonably clean and Adam filled it from the pot.

'Tell me about my pa, and where you first met him.'

Adam told Esme of his arrival from Matabeleland and of joining the Lichtenburg commando under her father's corporalship, and of the skirmishes and battles they had fought against the British. Finally he told her of the unlucky incident which had resulted in the death of Theunis Erasmus.

As he spoke, Esme came very close to tears. But none came and when he told of going back for Theunis and pulling him from beneath the horse, Esme asked, 'Why? Why did you do that? Why did you go back for him?'

'I liked him. He was a fine fighter and a good leader. I don't doubt he'd have done the same thing for me.'

Esme nodded. 'Show me Pa's will again.'

Adam took the paper from his pocket and handed it to her. 'I thought you couldn't read?'

'I can't. Does this mention me by name?'

'Yes.'

'Where? Show me my name . . . and tell me what Pa said about me.'

Adam leaned over the slightly-built girl and pointed out her name on the paper. Then he read, 'If my daughter Esme is still unmarried it is my wish that Adam makes all reasonable provision for her.'

With her finger Esme traced two words in the will. 'Is this the bit that says, "my daughter"?'

'That's right, "my daughter, Esme".'

She handed the paper back, then abruptly turned away and walked to the window. Looking out at the broken-down farm buildings around the yard, she said, 'It's not much of a farm. Everything's run down. There's no livestock. Not even a chicken.'

'It will need some work done around the place,' Adam agreed.

'Not much of a place for a wife, even when it's done up. There are no neighbours. There *were* two other farms, but the womenfolk went to Mafeking with their men when the war began. They didn't come back.'

'They're probably still there. The siege is still going on.'

'All right, the farm is yours.' Esme relinquished her claim to the farm with no more emotion than she had shown when offering Adam a cup of coffee. 'I might come around occasionally, but I've been spending much of my time in the hills anyway. I only come down here when I feel like having a roof over my head . . . and to tend Ma's grave. None of the others ever comes back to do it.'

She looked at Adam sharply. 'Was Pa given a proper burial?'

Adam nodded. 'The Predikant dug the grave himself.'

'Pa would have liked that. He was strong for marriages and Christian burials. That's why it would have upset him to know what happened to me . . . He wasn't so strong on family, though. Not after Ma died. Still, he was a Christian, all the same.'

It seemed that now she had begun to talk, Esme did not want to stop. 'He always hoped I'd be a boy. Told me so, often. Said he thought that after ten daughters the Lord might have seen fit to have given him a son. It seems the Lord thought different. I was born the eleventh daughter. Mind, I can shoot and ride just as well as any son might have done. Pa said so himself . . . But I don't think it was enough. I expect that's why he went away so much, us all being girls. I wish he'd have taken me with him sometimes, though, I'd have gone to war with him. I could fight and kill the British as well as any man. But I'm not a son. I'm a daughter. "My daughter Esme", isn't that what he wrote?'

Once again Adam felt she was very close to tears.

'That's right, Esme. That's exactly what he wrote . . . But tell me how you've been living up here – and what happened to your husband?'

Esme's expression hardened. 'He wasn't really my husband, although my sister swore he would be, as soon as a preacher could be found. It was all Zipporah's idea. She's the next-but-one-youngest to me. She and that husband of hers came and took me back to their place. There was a man there. He was hairy, and ugly . . . and nigh as old as Pa. He came from the Zoutpansberg – a *takhaar*. I don't suppose he was any worse than most of the men from there, but he stank. He smelled worse than any old hyena . . . But he's dead now and they say you shouldn't talk ill of the dead, don't they?'

'So I've heard said.'

'What do you plan to do now? Will you stay on for a while?'

'I want to have a look around and maybe fix up a few things that need mending.'

'You won't mind if I stay too? I'll sleep in my old room and try not to cause you any trouble.'

'It's your home too, Esme. You stay for as long or as short a time as you like.'

'I'll get us some food. I *can* cook, and I've got a young buck hanging out back. I shot it farther along the valley this morning.' Suddenly Esme seemed to have warmed to Adam. She even smiled in his direction. 'There's a half-barrel of Cape brandy out back too. Pa traded for it when he went to Johannesburg years ago. I know where it's hidden.'

'Esme, I think I'm going to enjoy having you around.' As he spoke, Adam put a hand on the girl's shoulder. She stiffened immediately, the smile leaving her face, and Adam removed his hand quickly.

Theunis Erasmus's daughter fulfilled her promise as a cook, although it took much longer than Adam expected. The Cape brandy was also all it should have been, and Adam swore it had improved with age. He was not used to strong drink and by the time Esme put food on the table before him the room was beginning to swim.

Esme saw his glazed expression and took the brandy glass in exchange for his plate. 'You've had enough to drink. You're looking just the way Pa did when he'd been drinking too much. Get some food down you and you'll feel better.'

The meal was eaten in comparative silence as the shadows lengthened outside and dusk successfully disguised the shabbiness of the farmhouse kitchen. Across the table Esme leaned over her plate, streamers of long hair escaping from the leather thong tying it at the back of her neck. She had undone the top two buttons of her shirt while cooking at the hot fire, leaving no possible doubt that she was a young woman and not a boy.

Esme was an attractive young girl in an unsophisticated way and Adam felt a familiar stirring of his body.

'What are the sleeping arrangements for tonight?'

'You can have Pa's room — but you'll need a blanket. Have you got one?'

He nodded, his mouth too full of meat to reply.

'Good. One of my sisters must have taken all the bedding on a visit to the house.' Esme smiled suddenly as a memory returned to her. 'Pa used to tell us girls off for talking at table. He'd say mouths were for talking *or* eating, and not for doing both at the same time. Meal times were for *eating*, he'd say. Mind you, I suppose eleven girls all talking at the same time would have been a bit much!'

'Your pa was something special for you, wasn't he?'

The stiffness returned to her again. 'Not particularly. He was just a man, that's all. No better nor no worse than any other man.'

Pushing her plate away from her, Esme stood up. 'You'd best get your blanket before it gets too dark. There are no candles in the house, and no lamps. There used to be, but I expect my sisters took them too.'

Downing his meal quickly, Adam went out to the stable to where he had brought his horse. His saddlebag was there, together with a roll containing two blankets. It was early winter and nights were cold in these hills.

Slinging the tight roll over his shoulder, Adam went back inside the house. In the kitchen he removed his boots before walking along the passageway. When he reached the door where he knew Esme was sleeping he saw the door was badly warped and did not close properly. Pushing it open a few inches, he called softly, 'Esme?'

'What do you want?'

There was no fear in her voice, but neither was there any particular friendliness.

'I've got two blankets here. I wondered whether you wanted one of them. It's a chilly night.'

'I'm all right.'

He pushed the door open wider. He could just make out her outline now. There was no bed, only a heap of dried grasses – and there was no blanket covering her.

'Here, I don't need two.' He crossed the room, unrolling the blankets, and draped one over her. As he leaned down to straighten it, he said softly, 'Good night, Esme.'

When she made no reply he leaned lower and kissed her. He was unsteady with drink and the kiss only brushed the corner of her mouth, but when she made no move to repulse him the blood began pumping faster through his veins.

Dropping awkwardly to his knees he kissed her again, harder this time. Still she made no move, either to escape or to push him away. Encouraged, he slid beneath the blanket and ran his hand over her body. She was fully clothed, but it would not take him long to do something about that . . . First he unfastened his own trousers, slipping the buckle of his heavy leather belt and undoing his buttons. Suddenly he froze, as something cold and very sharp cut through the delicate skin covering a very tender part of his body.

'That's as far as you go with me, Adam Retallick. Try anything more and it's as far as you'll ever go with any girl. This is a skinning-knife and it was sharpened only today.'

'Don't do anything foolish. I'm sorry . . .'

'Pick up your blankets and stand up – slowly! This knife is liable to slip at the slightest sudden movement. Keep going – and stay out of my room. I've had enough of drunken men treating me as though I were some kaffir girl. You understand me?'

She accompanied the question with a jab of the knife, and he was quite certain she drew blood.

'I hear!'

'Good.'

They were at the doorway now and Adam backed into the narrow passageway outside. Much to his relief, Esme and the skinning-knife remained in the bedroom.

'I'm sorry, Esme. I thought you . . .'

'I know exactly what you thought – and you thought wrong. Go to your room and stay there. The only company I'll have in bed tonight will be my gun, and I warn you, I'm a very light sleeper.'

When Adam awoke in the morning Esme had gone. She was nowhere in the house and a search of the outbuildings and repeated shouting of her name brought no results.

He did not know whether to be pleased or sorry. His head throbbed from the amount of brandy he had consumed the night before and her absence saved him the embarrassment of making an abject apology. Yet he felt somehow . . . cheated.

Esme Erasmus was a remarkable girl. Not in the same way as Johanna, of course. Nobody could ever be *her* equal, but Esme was certainly unlike any other girl he had ever known.

Adam remained at the house for over a week and frequently caught himself looking out over the surrounding hills, hoping in vain to catch a glimpse of Esme.

On his return journey to the Viljoens, Adam met a burgher with his family. They were heading for a farm about seven miles away. They were some of the absent neighbours Esme had mentioned, returning from the siege of Mafeking. He told Adam that relief was imminent for the residents of Mafeking. Field Marshal Roberts had three columns heading northwards, one of them following the railway through Bechuanaland. Meanwhile, other columns had moved south from Rhodesia.

The Boer farmer had another item of news that startled Adam far more than the progress of the war. When he heard Adam had been willed the farm that had belonged to Theunis Erasmus, and had just spent a week there, the bearded farmer said jocularly, 'I hope you didn't see anything of Theunis's youngest while you were there?'

'Esme? Why?'

Nudging the large woman who sat on the high wagon seat beside him, the burgher grinned slyly. 'You hear that, Christiana? He hasn't heard about Esme Erasmus. He wouldn't be sitting that horse so comfortably if he had now, would he?'

Beneath her bonnet the large woman's face reddened. 'Hush, Arne. Think of the children in the back of the wagon.'

'What haven't I heard about her?' Adam asked impatiently.

'Folks are saying she was married and widowed within the space of only twelve hours,' said the burgher dramatically. 'Twelve hours!'

'I blame her sisters,' said the woman. 'All they were interested in was palming her off on the first man who came along, so they could shed all responsibility for her. That sort of thing might have been all right fifty years ago. You can't do it today.'

The burgher snorted. 'So? It wasn't her sisters who cut him up on his wedding night.'

'Esme killed him?'

'As good as.' The burgher was finding Adam's curiosity highly satisfying.

'He was no good,' declared the burgher's wife. 'A *takhaar*. A wild one. He could give her nothing . . .'

Her husband interrupted her with a hoot of raucous laughter. Slapping his thigh with a rough hand, he exclaimed, 'You've said it, Christiana. He had *nothing* to give her after she'd finished with him. Nothing to give *anyone*. Cut it right off, she did. Right off. He ran out of the house and stuck a gun barrel in his mouth. Blew half his head away . . . Hey! What's the matter with you? You feeling all right, man . . .?'

CHAPTER TWENTY-THREE

Adam said nothing about Esme on his return to the Viljoen farm. He spoke only of the ruinous state of his inheritance and of the isolation of the property. He hastened to add, for Johanna's ears, that the farm had tremendous potential. He thought it needed only a resident farmer – complete with wife, of course.

Adam also began to tell the Viljoens what he had heard of the movements of the British army, but over the heads of the remainder of his family Cornelius Viljoen signalled him to silence, then led the conversation in another direction.

Later, when they were alone, Cornelius Viljoen said he had a proposition to put to Adam and asked him to ride out with him to inspect some cattle he had grazing on the farthermost section of the farm.

When they were well clear of the house, Cornelius Viljoen explained his reason for wanting Adam to keep silent. Koos De la Rey was back in the area, rounding up members of his commando, and recruiting new men. Organised Boer resistance had finally collapsed in the Orange Free State and De la Rey wanted men to help in the defence of Pretoria, an aim that already seemed doomed to failure. Roberts and the British army had taken Bloemfontein and were now half-way to Pretoria, the capital of Transvaal. Many British troops were already in the Transvaal Republic, having crossed the Vaal river in strength.

As if this news was not bad enough, the Rhodesian Field Force, numbering some six thousand men, was massing to the north. Meanwhile in the east General Redvers Buller and his ponderous army of almost fifty thousand men was lumbering towards the Transvaal. To the west, where the forces of the Transvaal had expected to notch up a much needed victory, the small town of Mafeking still held out against them.

'If Koos or his recruiters come here Lucas will want to go and fight again – and he's not yet fit. That *khaki* bayonet has left him with a serious weakness. The slightest exertion brings on a coughing fit and he's in pain for hours. Going to war again just now would kill him.'

'I'll say nothing to make him think he should be fighting again,' agreed Adam. '. . . But you said you have a proposition for me.'

'Yes. This farm of yours . . . Will it support my cattle?'

Puzzled by the question, Adam nodded. 'Easily. But what's this to do with keeping Lucas out of the war?'

'I'll tell you. If . . . No, *when* the British relieve Mafeking, their troops will advance into Transvaal for a link-up with Field Marshal Roberts. It's the only logical thing for them to do. When this happens they're bound to come this way, because Koos's home is here. They will want to make his family and friends suffer on his behalf. When they do come I don't doubt they'll take all our cattle to feed their army – but they won't go up into the hills looking for them. I'd like to send the cattle up to your place with Lucas and a couple of kaffirs to guard them. They can graze the cattle in the hills about the farm and do a bit of work about the house. I'll give you half of all the calves born there. That should give you a useful start towards stocking up.'

It was a generous as well as a sensible offer. Adam agreed immediately, but added, 'I want Jacob to go up there with Lucas too.'

'Jacob? But why? He's able-bodied. He can fight.'

Adam shook his head. 'Jacob is too gentle and simple to make a fighter. The noise of battle terrifies him. Sending Jacob to war is like giving a gun to a seven year old and expecting him to be a warrior. But he's a sound worker. He'll do more good up at the farm fixing things and keeping an eye on Lucas.'

'All right, but we'll need to send them off quickly. Another couple of days and it might well prove too late.'

* * *

Lucas Viljoen and Jacob Eloff left for Adam's hill farm the next day. They travelled in a wagon, driving the Viljoen herd of about a hundred and sixty cattle ahead of them. Two horses were tied behind the wagon, and two kaffirs ran on the flanks of the herd to keep them bunched.

As it happened, an emissary from Koos De la Rey did not reach the Viljoen farm for another ten days, but when he arrived his news was grim.

Field Marshal Roberts and the main British column were advancing steadily along the central railway line through Transvaal, towards Johannesburg and Pretoria. They were now only forty miles from the capital. The siege of Mafeking would continue for the time being, but relief was only a matter of time and the Boer troops investing the town were urgently needed elsewhere. Transvaal was coming increasingly under British domination, columns of British troops criss-crossing the Republic almost at will and, in most cases, unopposed. Koos De la Rey wanted all the commandos which could be mustered to assemble on the Klip river, south of Johannesburg. Here, on the *kopjes* overlooking the river, he intended taking on the British army.

But the news carried by Koos De la Rey's messenger was already out of date. In spite of the last-minute arrival of the Boer general on the scene, Mafeking had been relieved. After a fierce fight only eight miles from the beleaguered town, the Boer line collapsed. At 7 p.m. on the 16th May, 1900, Major Kerri Davis and ten troopers of the Imperial Light Horse rode into Mafeking. The seven-month siege was over and the British army of the west began spilling over the border into the Transvaal homeland — with tragic consequences.

It was one of Johanna's chores to secure the fowls and the farm animals each evening, and Adam had taken to helping her. It was the only opportunity he had of talking to her without others being around to hear.

The evening after the visit from De la Rey's emissary, the two were in the stables, rubbing down the horse on which Cornelius Viljoen had just returned late, after visiting a neighbour.

'When are you and Pa setting off to join up with the commando?'

'Just as soon as your pa can persuade some of the others to come with us. That's where he's been today. I expect we'll be off in the next day or two. Why, are you going to miss me?'

Johanna shrugged off-handedly. 'I got along well enough before you came. I'll do the same when you've gone.'

It was meant as a joke, but when Johanna looked up she saw the hurt on Adam's face and laid a hand on his arm. 'I'm sorry, Adam. Of course I shall miss you. You're a great help around the farm and . . . I enjoy talking to you.'

'Is that all?'

'Why, what else do you want me to say?'

Adam shrugged, still unhappy. 'You know how I feel about you. I've told you often enough.'

'I know you have. You've spoken enough about such things for both of us. I've told you I'll marry you – and I'll keep my word. There's time enough to think of other things when we're wed.'

'When will that be?'

'Not until things are more settled and this war is over.'

Suddenly she stopped talking. 'Listen! What's that?'

'It's a horse . . . and it's coming fast.'

They ran outside just as Lucas galloped into the farm yard, scattering long-striding, complaining chickens in every direction.

Lucas was crouched over the neck of the horse, swaying in the saddle, and there was blood on the front of his shirt. Adam thought at first he had been shot, but then realised it was blood coughed up from Lucas's barely healed lung. It had occurred before when Lucas over-exerted himself.

Cornelius Viljoen came running from the house, followed by Sophia Viljoen and Lucas's grandmother.

As the two men lifted Lucas from the horse he tried to speak, but for some minutes no sound came.

'Don't try to talk. We'll get you into the house.'

As they helped him to the door, Lucas's voice returned. 'It's Jacob . . .' he gasped. 'He's been shot . . . By the *khakis*. He's dead.'

Startled, Cornelius Viljoen exclaimed, 'The British are near here?'

'No . . . in the hills.'

The two men helping him into the house looked at each other in sudden understanding. It was hardly surprising that Lucas had been reeling in the saddle. The unwell young man had just galloped thirty miles to bring them news of Jacob Eloff's death.

Lucas Viljoen and Jacob Eloff were repairing the farm buildings when a small troop of British mounted infantry took them by surprise. They were questioned by the young lieutenant in charge of the soldiers, but it soon became clear that the two young men could tell him nothing of importance. He would have left them and ridden away had not the remainder of the British army column, more than three hundred strong, arrived. The commanding officer was Major Frederick Wills, a fusilier officer.

Taking one look at the khaki tunic worn by Jacob Eloff, the major angrily demanded to know how it came to be in his possession.

While the simple-minded Jacob Eloff floundered for a reply, Lucas interceded, explaining that the jacket had been given to Jacob by a friend.

Glaring at Lucas, the major snapped, 'I was talking to him, not to you. Let him speak for himself.'

'He's a bit slow in thinking,' explained Lucas as patiently as he could. 'If you shout at him you'll only confuse him.'

'He's intelligent enough to realise he shouldn't be wearing a British army tunic,' retorted the major. Brusquely he ordered Lucas to be taken some distance away, adding that they might then obtain some sense from his 'uncommunicative friend'.

Protesting vainly, Lucas was led some distance away and the major returned his attention to the bewildered Jacob Eloff.

'Now, where did you get this tunic?'

Following the lead given to him by Lucas, Jacob Eloff said, 'It was given to me.'

'Don't lie. You shot a British soldier for it, isn't that so?'

'No! Adam shot him. I only took the tunic. He was dead and didn't need it. There wasn't much of my own coat left . . .'

'Ah!' The British officer was triumphant. 'Now we're approaching the truth. So you took the tunic in *battle*? Which

183

battle would this be, eh? Come on, man. Which battle?'

Jacob Eloff shook his head. He could not have told the British major the names of any of the battles in which he had cowered in the bottom of a trench – even had the major's bullying not confused him.

'You realise of course it's a very serious offence to wear a tunic and impersonate a British soldier? It's a *capital* offence. You can be shot for it.'

Jacob Eloff was Afrikaans-speaking and he did not understand English too well, but he caught the gist of the English major's words and looked at him in wide-eyed fear. Even some of the British soldiers listening to the exchange began to look uneasy.

'I just needed a coat, that's all.'

'Which regiment does the tunic come from? You there, trooper. Take off the tunic and check for a name and regiment.'

One of the British soldiers peeled off the khaki tunic and found a faded name penned inside the collar.

'Can't find no regiment, sir. Just a name. "J. Brimble Bugler".'

Major Wills went puce and he scowled furiously at Jacob Eloff. 'You killed an unarmed bugler in order to steal his tunic?'

'I didn't kill no one. I didn't.'

The major looked disdainfully at the frightened hired hand. 'You're not even man enough to own up to what you've done. Very well . . .'

Turning to the young lieutenant, he said stiffly, 'Take this man away – and shoot him.'

The lieutenant looked at the major in disbelief. 'We can't do that, sir. He's not even under arms . . . If he were he'd be a prisoner-of-war.'

'A Boer wearing a murdered British soldier's tunic can claim no right to the niceties of war. You have my orders, Lieutenant Ashby. See they are carried out. *Immediately*, if you please.'

The young lieutenant had gone as far as he dared in Jacob Eloff's defence. Junior officers did not argue with their superiors in the British army. Turning to the troopers, he barked, 'You heard what the major said. Sergeant! Fall in a firing-squad.'

The sergeant had been in the army too long even to think about an order given to him by an officer. Orders were given to be obeyed.

Lucas Viljoen saw the arrangements being made for the execution and he tried to break way from the men who guarded him. 'They can't do this to Jacob. He's been our hired hand since he was a boy. He's never killed anyone. Never.'

One of the mounted infantry, a long-serving soldier, held Lucas back. 'Get a grip on yourself, lad. You'll do him no good. Yourself neither. Once Major high-and-mighty Wills has made up his mind he listens to no one. Turn away, son. Don't watch.'

Lucas *did* watch. He saw Jacob Eloff, hands tied behind his back, and blindfolded, supported between two men against the mud wall of the stable.

The soldiers of the firing-squad raised their rifles and took aim as the young lieutenant raised his arm. He nodded to the men supporting Jacob Eloff and they quickly moved away from the condemned young man.

Still protesting his innocence, Jacob Eloff took a pace forward and began to turn. At that moment the lieutenant's arm dropped and fingers were squeezed on a dozen triggers.

Only two bullets hit Jacob Eloff, the others being deliberately aimed to one side of him. But two bullets were enough. Both pierced Jacob Eloff's heart and he slumped to the ground.

In the hush that followed there was another shot. The flat crack of an older weapon echoed around the valley and the lieutenant who had signalled the execution clutched his chest and looked in disbelief at the blood that seeped through his fingers. Then he too pitched forward to the ground.

Lucas had seen the faint puff of black powder smoke from high on the hillside above the farmhouse. One of the soldiers had seen it too and he pointed upwards, shouting to his companions. Running to his horse, the major called on his men to follow him up the hill.

At the height of the confusion the soldier holding Lucas Viljoen whispered in his ear, 'Get the 'ell out of 'ere, young 'un. If you've got a horse jump on it and ride – no matter where. Just get away from 'ere. Go on now.'

Lucas Viljoen needed no second bidding. Trying not to look

at the blindfolded body lying on the ground, he ran to the stable, thankful that his horse was already saddled. He had expected to ride out and look at the cattle again before bedtime.

As he galloped away from the farm he hoped whoever had fired the shot would escape from the British soldiers.

Adam was in no doubt about the identity of the unseen sniper. As he rode into the valley and neared the farmhouse he too hoped the soldiers' search for Esme Erasmus had proved fruitless.

He approached the farm cautiously, fearing the British might have left some of their men behind. But the place was empty. After searching the house and outbuilding, Adam stopped by a long, low mound of earth on the hillside. Someone had made a crude cross of the two tree branches. At least the British had given the simple farmhand the decency of a burial before they went away. Adam wondered about the lieutenant. He must have only been wounded and carried away.

Adam had ridden through the night to reach the valley as early as possible. His was a mission of vengeance. He had liked Jacob Eloff, in spite of the simple young man's aversion to war. He had not nursed Jacob Eloff through so many battles to have him murdered by a British officer.

The trail left by the mounted British soldiers was broad and clear, leading away from the hills. After a couple of miles it swung south-east, heading across the veld in the general direction of Mafeking. Adam soon became aware of something else. Another horseman – or horsewoman – was following the British soldiers. It was a light pony with distinctive tracks and at times it took short cuts, without its rider losing touch with the British soldiers.

Adam rode hard and by the time the sun was nearing the horizon he spotted the lone rider a couple of miles ahead. Having followed the British soldiers for so long Adam was confident he knew the direction in which they were heading. Taking advantage of a rise in the ground he took a short cut that would take him ahead of the lone rider.

His initiative almost proved his undoing. He had covered

some four miles when he emerged from thick scrub and broken rock to discover he was no more than five hundred yards from the camp made by the soldiers he was following.

Hurriedly backing his horse into the scrub again, Adam wondered where Esme Erasmus had gone – and by now he was convinced it *was* Esme. The chances were that she too would come upon the camp unexpectedly – and she might not be as fortunate as he had been. When he thought himself well clear of the British he put his horse to the slope and rode over the low ridge.

He almost rode headlong into Esme. She was also heading for the ridge from the other side and she drew her rifle from its saddle holster with a speed that alarmed Adam.

'Esme . . . Don't shoot! It's me. Adam.'

For a moment he thought she would shoot anyway and his stomach muscles contracted in anticipation of the bullet. Then she up-ended the percussion rifle and thrust it back in its holster.

'You'll get yourself shot one day, coming up on folk like that.'

'And so will you. The British have made camp just off the end of this ridge. You'd have been seen by them had you carried on.'

'You came to warn me? How did you know I was here?'

'I've been following you from the farm. Your tracks were as clear as those of the *khakis*. What do you think you're doing?'

'I saw them murder a young burgher at the farm. Was he a friend of yours?'

When Adam nodded, Esme continued, 'It made me think of Pa, and of all the others who have died fighting the *khakis*. I was mad and I wanted to fight too. I shot one of them, but I didn't kill him. I'm following them now in the hope that I might get a shot at the one in charge. The one who ordered the shooting of your friend.'

'That's why I'm here. I suggest you leave it to me now.'

'Suggest away – but don't expect me to do as *you* say.'

Adam shrugged. 'Please yourself, but if we don't work together then one of us is likely to land the other in trouble.'

'True. Do you have anything planned?'

'Perhaps. How well do you know this part of the veld?'

'Well enough. It depends what you have in mind.'

'I plan simply to shoot the officer who ordered Jacob's killing and then make my escape. But we've both got tired horses. We'll need to lose anyone who's chasing us pretty quickly.'

'Our horses are in better shape than those of the *khakis*. I'll lose them.'

'Then what are we waiting for?'

It was not difficult to gain a good vantage point overlooking the British camp. The mounted infantry had set sentries, but only around the perimeter of their camp. There was no one posted on either of the two *kopjes* that dominated the camp.

To Adam's surprise the commanding officer of the mounted infantry had a tent pitched for himself. He must have been inside, because he was nowhere to be seen. Adam and Esme settled down to wait, hoping the officer would emerge before it became too dark for accurate shooting.

They had been waiting for half an hour and Adam was beginning to doubt whether they would achieve their objective, when another group of horsemen cantered up to the camp. It was evident they were British soldiers too, but they were a different breed to the mounted infantry.

The newcomers did not have their horses cluttered with all the paraphernalia that made British cavalrymen audible to sharp ears for more than a mile away. All except one of the newcomers wore khaki uniform, but it was of a tough, durable material, and they wore crossed ammunition belts, in the fashion favoured by the burghers of the Boer commandos. The man not wearing uniform was apparently a scout. He wore civilian clothes, although he also favoured the wide-brimmed felt hat, turned up at one side, worn by the remainder of his party.

Esme looked enquiringly at Adam.

'It makes no difference and it should bring the officer out. When I shoot him, you get the scout who's just arrived. He's probably the only one down there capable of tracking us . . .'

Even as Adam spoke the British army major ducked out from beneath the flap of his tent and the officer in charge of the new arrivals dismounted and shook hands.

Adam had just taken aim at the major when he saw the scout remove his hat and run a sleeve across hs forehead. There was something familiar about the gesture and suddenly Adam grabbed the barrel of Esme's gun, forcing it downwards.

'*Don't shoot!*'

He had spoken loudly – too loudly. The sharp-eared scout was looking up to where the two would-be snipers lay, and now Adam knew without doubt.

Esme was looking to him for an explanation and Adam said, 'The scout . . . It's my brother, Nat.'

CHAPTER TWENTY-FOUR

When Nat left Insimo with Colonel Digby Vincent he had only a vague notion of how long he would be away from home. The most optimistic estimate of the duration of the war was three months. A more 'realistic' opinion suggested it might continue for some six to nine months.

Nat hoped to find Adam before the war's end and bring him back to Insimo. Hopefully, Adam would have had his fill of adventure by then. In the meantime young Ben was quite capable of running the farm, assisted by Jaconus Van Eyck.

Carey Hamilton rode with his brother-in-law and Nat. He was coming along to familiarise himself with the country along Rhodesia's border with Transvaal, leaving behind some of his troopers to escort Thomasina from Insimo to Fort Victoria.

Nat guided the soldiers down from the heights of Insimo to the lowveld, following the course of the Lundi river. They were now in the lowveld and the temperature rose by almost thirty degrees Fahrenheit. Here they began searching for the marauding Boer commando. It was not known where it was operating, or even if it was still in the country. Nat thought his best plan was to take the soldiers straight to the Limpopo, find the men who were guarding the border, and ask them.

However, they were still a day's ride from the river when Nat called the column to a halt before they reached a small stream.

'What is it?' Colonel Digby Vincent walked his horse to where Nat had dismounted and was examining the ground closely.

'A large party of mounted men crossed here, probably some time yesterday evening. They were heading westwards.'

'How many were there?'

Nat shook his head. 'Could be as many as sixty. Might be as few as forty.'

Colonel Vincent frowned. 'If it's forty it might be a police patrol. I'd say sixty would be too many. What's your own opinion?'

'I don't know . . . but I've got a gut-feeling that this is a small commando.'

The middle-aged colonel sighed and ran a damp and grubby handkerchief over his shining face. With his pale colouring, Digby Vincent suffered in the heat and sunshine.

'We'll follow it up, if you like, but I don't want to dash off on a damned wild goose chase in this heat.'

Nat looked to where the five wagons accompanying the column were being manhandled down a slope towards the water's edge. With these to hold them back the column would not be making a 'dash' anywhere.

'Stay here and have your men cook a meal. I'll follow the tracks for a couple more hours. If I can find where they spent the night it might tell me something. Post sentries while I'm gone. If the tracks *were* made by Boers they might come back this way – and there are enough of them to take you on and give you a mauling, at least.'

'Thank you for the warning, but I'm not out here to stay clear of Boers. I'll carry the battle to *them*, whether there are forty or four hundred.'

There were two troops of cavalry with Colonel Vincent, less those troopers who had been left behind with Thomasina. In all, it meant a little over two hundred soldiers, all relatively inexperienced. For Digby Vincent's sake, Nat hoped that when they had their first brush with a Boer commando it might number forty, and not four hundred.

Nat followed the trail with some difficulty, and the farther he rode the more convinced he became that this *was* a Boer raiding party – most probably they were *takhaaren*. The men rode an instinctive and unerring path, picking terrain that would make tracking difficult. These were men who had fought tribesmen from the time they could first hold a gun.

Covering their tracks came as naturally to them as breathing.

Confirmation of Nat's theory came after two hours of riding. The tracks led to a mine, tucked away in a hidden valley. Here, outside an earth-walled hut, lay three bodies, surrounded by the ejected cartridge cases of Mauser rifles.

Looking down at the bodies of the three men, Nat felt very, very angry. This was not war, it was murder. The three miners had been living lonely, secretive lives, far from any form of civilisation. They had probably never known that a state of war existed between Great Britain and the Boer republics. Even had they known it would have made little difference to their way of life. Their battle was with the earth, reluctant to give up its treasure to man.

Leaving the bodies where they lay, Nat turned his horse and rode back to the bank of the stream where he had left Colonel Vincent and his soldiers.

They camped that night at the mine and the grim-faced cavalrymen buried the three miners within yards of the tunnel they had dug into the hillside. They erected three crude crosses to mark their graves, but the crosses were unlettered. There was nothing at all among the scant possessions of the miners to show who they had been. The secrets of the miners were buried with them.

The next morning Nat set off with Colonel Vincent and half his force in a fast pursuit of the *takhaaren* commando. The remainder of his force would follow with the wagons as fast as they were able.

The pursuing force had travelled for no more than a mile before Nat called a halt.

'Colonel, if you're serious about catching this commando then you've got to get rid of all the useless bits and pieces your men are carrying. Those tin cans clanging together can be heard three miles away in this type of country.'

'Those "tin cans" are army issue mess tins and water bottles,' replied the colonel stiffly. 'They are regulation issue for cavalrymen.'

'I'm sure they're fine when you're fighting an enemy carrying the same gear and who wait for you to line up against them in battle – but you're not fighting that kind of war now. You're up against Boers. Men who fight to *win*. If you're serious about wanting to beat them you'll need to learn to think and behave the way they do. Outsmart them. You'll never do it if you give them three miles' warning that you're on the way.'

'I thought when we came here we'd be fighting white men. The Boers are trickier than Indians.'

'The Boers are fighting for their land and their homes, Colonel. They don't care *how* they fight. For them nothing counts but winning.'

'One could almost believe you are sympathetic to the Boer cause, Nat. After what you discovered at the mine yesterday I must confess I'm surprised.'

'No ordinary Boers did that, Colonel. That was done by the *takhaaren*. They don't behave like human beings, even in their own country. As for sympathising with the Boers . . . I can sympathise with any man who's fighting to keep a way of life that he and his family have made for themselves – no matter whether he's a Boer, or a Matabele. Besides, who knows, we "Rhodesians" may find ourselves in the same situation one day.'

General Digby Vincent looked at Nat thoughtfully for a few seconds, then he snapped an order to Carey Hamilton. 'Tell the men they are to discard everything that's likely to make a noise when they're riding. Detail two or three troopers to return the discarded items to the wagons.'

There was some grumbling from the men, but they were quickly silenced by the officers and N.C.O.s who were relieved to have someone with them who knew something of the enemy.

The soldiers made good time that day, and evening saw them on the banks of the Limpopo river. It seemed that after killing the miners the *takhaaren* commando had gone straight back to Transvaal, travelling fast.

When the troopers reached the river crossing, Colonel Digby Vincent called his officers together to tell them what he intended doing.

While the officers talked, Nat sat his horse, quietly gazing across the wide river from beneath the brim of his felt hat, and the troopers watered themselves and their horses from a stream which flowed into the Limpopo just below the crossing place.

When Digby Vincent finished talking to the officers, he called to Nat and told him, 'I intend crossing the border and pursuing this party of Boers until we find them. Will you guide us into Transvaal?'

'I will, Colonel, but you won't need to travel far to find the Boers we've been following. When all your men are strung out across the river they'll *show* you where they are.'

'You think they are over there waiting for us?'

'I *know* they are. I wondered why they came straight back to the river leaving such a clear trail. They *want* us to go across after them.'

'Then, dammit, I'll be pleased to accommodate them . . .'

'Do it their way and *you'll* never reach the far bank alive.'

Digby Vincent was inclined to be impetuous, but he was not a fool. He knew Nat was right. If the Boers were waiting across the river, he and his fellow officers would be their first targets.

'Do you have a better idea?'

'Yes. Beat them at their own game. Make them come to us.'

'How?'

'Let them believe we don't know they're waiting for us. Choose a camp – choose it well, and close to a *kopje*. Send out hunting parties and let the Boers see our men settling down for the night. When the fires burn low begin moving your men off, leaving their bedding behind – and make sure there's a strong guard on the horses. Send the remainder of the men to the *kopje*. If the Boers run true to form they'll come across the river during the night and attack at first light – and their first target will be the horses. They need to replace all those they've lost in the lowveld – and without horses they know you're at their mercy.'

'I don't like this kind of warfare. I prefer to meet my enemy face to face – and in daylight.'

'The Boers don't give a damn what you "prefer", Colonel. A burgher doesn't go into battle seeking glory. He fights to win. Whether he does, or whether he doesn't, the chances are that afterwards he'll climb on his horse and go back to his farm. You won't find him doing anything that's likely to interfere with that – not if he can help it.'

Colonel Digby Vincent gave Nat another of his strange, searching glances. Then he smiled. 'You make the Boer sound an eminently sensible fellow. It's certainly an important thing to remember when trying to anticipate Boer strategy. I'm grateful to you. Very well, we'll do as you say. I suggest we camp on that open piece of ground along the river bank. Then we can picket the horses with the river behind them, giving us less area to guard. During the night most of the men can go back to that hill – *kopje*, I believe you call it – about a half-mile away. If the Boers take advantage of any cover it will probably be that broken area of ground. Command of the *kopje* should mean we'll be able to flush them out quickly.'

'I'll leave those details to you, Colonel. While you work it out and fix up a camp I'll go hunting.'

Nat took some troopers with him to help carry back their evening meal. They were gone for little more than an hour, returning with enough fresh meat to ensure the camp would have the air of celebration Nat intended.

Nat's plan was well executed. As the fires burned low the cavalrymen were roused from their blankets and each man made his way quietly and secretly to a pre-arranged rendezvous.

The last change of sentries was made about an hour before dawn, but the incoming watch did not remain at their posts for long. Carefully making up rolls of blankets topped with hats to give a fair imitation of sleepy sentries sitting hunched inside blankets against the chill of early dawn, they slipped away to reinforce the men guarding the horses.

Nat had hidden himself close to the river crossing earlier in the night and he had a long wait. It was not until there was the faintest hint of dawn above the eastern hills that he heard a faint, incautious splash of water, as though an animal had slipped on a pebble in mid-stream. It might have been any one of the wild animals in the habit of using the crossing, but Nat had a feeling this was no wild animal. Easing himself carefully from his cramped position, he moved quietly away.

A few minutes later the shadowy figure of a man leading a horse loomed out of the darkness. He was followed by many others, but Nat did not stay to count their numbers. Already he was working his way back to the *kopje*, pausing along the way to warn the men guarding the horses.

Colonel Digby Vincent and his men were fully awake and

alert and Nat's information sent a ripple of excitement along their waiting lines. For most this would be their first action, and their anticipation was accompanied by a mixture of emotions.

The *takhaaren* commando wasted little time before going into action. When the whole force had forded the Limpopo river they split into two forces without a word being spoken. Then, as though the whole operation had been well rehearsed, the first half of the commando set off to secure the horses of the cavalrymen they believed to be blissfully unaware of their presence.

The commando, originally almost sixty strong, had been joined by another twenty men for this attack. By the time the first half reached the horses in the grey morning light and fired what was intended to be a demoralising volley, the remainder of the commando hit the camp.

The morning light was by now just sufficient for the *takhaaren* to be visible in shadowy outline to the men on the *kopje*, and the commando was ripped apart by the volley which met them as they charged into the deserted camp. Many men were knocked out of their saddles and others wounded. As their horses trampled the empty blankets the *takhaaren* realised they had run headlong into a trap, and many sought shelter from the bullets among the broken rocks and began to return the fire of their unseen ambushers.

Others fled for the river crossing, only to find their escape blocked by a detachment of British troopers led by Captain Carey Hamilton. More Boer saddles were emptied until, realising they were hopelessly outnumbered, many of the Boers raised their arms, surrendering to the British soldiers they had expected to take by surprise.

The Boers who had taken refuge among the rocks held out only until full daylight arrived. Then, surrounded by Colonel Vincent's men and fired upon if they so much as moved an uncomfortable, cramped limb, they too gave up the fight.

It had been a disastrous raid for the Boer commando. Of the eighty *takhaaren*, thirty-six had been killed and twenty-two wounded. The remainder now stood in a numbed, disarmed group, having thrown themselves upon the mercy of the men they had hoped to slaughter in their sleep.

* * *

The cavalrymen had lost only two men killed and another seven wounded, but among the latter was Colonel Digby Vincent, a Boer bullet lodged in the flesh of his left arm. In spite of this, Colonel Vincent was in a cheerful mood. He had defeated a commando of the dreaded *takhaaren* in his very first engagement on African soil.

The report of his victory would bring great joy to the War Office in London, and receive maximum publicity in the British newspapers, starved of good news from South Africa for so long. The British colonel was generous in his praise of Nat for helping to turn the tables on the commando. Captain Carey Hamilton also came in for mention for his quick thinking in cutting off the Boers' escape route and so bringing about their surrender.

As the unwounded Boers squatted in a disconsolate circle guarded by victorious cavalrymen, Nat assisted the British army medical orderlies who were treating their wounded. Hardly any of the *takhaaren* spoke English and they sat in stoic silence as their wounds were dressed, only occasionally grunting a guarded reply to Nat's questions.

'You'll get no information from these men,' Nat told Colonel Digby Vincent, while the cavalry commander was having his wound bound. 'They say little enough to each other. They'll tell us nothing.'

'It doesn't matter.' The Colonel pulled his tunic gingerly over the wounded arm. 'We'll send a couple of Boers home to pass word of what's happened here today. Perhaps they'll think twice before raiding in Rhodesia again.'

'What of the rest of them?' Nat nodded to where the Boers of the *takhaaren* commando were sipping coffee given to them by their captors. 'What will you do with them?'

'They are prisoners-of-war. They will be interned until the end of the war. I understand the British government is setting up prison camps on the island of St Helena. No doubt they will go there.'

Nat wondered how many of the *takhaaren* commando would survive internment. They were used to a life that was as free and untrammelled as that of the Bushmen of the Kalahari. Internment would cause them particular hardship. Then he remembered their raid on Insimo and shrugged off such uncomfortable thoughts.

That night three of the *takhaaren* escaped. Colonel Digby Vincent was philosophisical about the incident, commenting wryly that it saved him from having to make a decision about which of the prisoners to release. It was also a lesson to the inexeperienced cavalrymen of the resourcefulness of their Boer adversaries.

The British soldiers were to gain more experience of their enemies during ensuing weeks as they hunted down more Boer commandos in the border areas. For the most part these were smaller than the *takhaaren* commando had been, but they were nevertheless effective. One such small commando ambushed the cavalry column and inflicted a number of casualties before escaping in the direction of the richly wooded hills of the nearby neutral territory of Mozambique.

With Colonel Digby Vincent and his cavalry, Nat fought the Boer commandos along a two-hundred-mile front, ranging from the hills of Mozambique to Bechuanaland and the hot sands of the Kalahari desert.

During these weeks Nat grew to like and respect Thomasina's balding husband. Cool in the heat of battle and personally brave, Digby Vincent always listened courteously to any advice Nat had to offer. If he felt the advice was sound, Colonel Vincent was quick to act upon it and give credit where it was due. He was also a very good tactician and well liked by the officers and men under his command.

Because of his regard for the cavalry commander, Nat was particularly concerned about the wound Digby Vincent had received at the riverside battle. It was still troubling him long after it should have healed. The bullet had been dug out of his arm, but on many occasions as they rode along Nat would see the Colonel nursing his arm, as though it pained him. Once when he entered the Colonel's tent without warning he saw the officer examining an ugly swelling beneath the armpit of the wounded arm.

When Nat expressed his concern, Digby Vincent assured him it was no more than a trifling infection, aggravated by the heat of the lowveld, and he made Nat promise not to tell Carey Hamilton or the other officers.

Nat agreed, but only after the Colonel promised he would

see a doctor as soon as they reached a place where one was available.

'That time isn't far off,' Nat said grimly. 'We're losing too many horses. The lowveld is notoriously bad for horses in certain years. I'm afraid this is one of them.'

'Can we keep them going for a few more days? With any luck we'll be up with the next Boer commando by then.'

Nat shrugged. 'They're the army's horses, Colonel, not mine. If you're lucky you might get three more days from them – just so long as we don't need to chase anyone.'

They came upon a Boer commando on the second day in the foothills of the highveld, mid-way between Bulawayo and the Bechuanaland border. The Boer horses were in a worse state than those of the British column, making flight impossible for the raiders. The Boers put up a desperate fight, but the outcome was never in doubt. After three hours of furious fighting almost half the Boers were casualties. With no hope of winning and all chance of escape cut off, the remainder surrendered.

These men were not *takhaaren* and many could speak English. Within minutes of the battle's end Boers and cavalrymen were kneeling side by side to tend the wounded. Water bottles were passed from mouth to mouth, irrespective of nationality. A Boer thirst was every bit as demanding as that of a British soldier. Watching them, Nat felt a great sadness that such men should be enemies.

Something of his thinking must have showed in his face, because Digby Vincent came to stand beside him and said, 'The battle is over. *Nos amis, les ennemis.*'

Nat looked blank and the cavalry colonel translated. 'It means, "Our friends, the enemy". The words of a Napoleonic poet and humanitarian. It sums up the essence of war against a civilised foe.'

'If you're both so civilised, why fight at all? Couldn't the leaders of both countries have talked until they arrived at a "civilised" solution to each other's problems?'

'We've been talking to the Boer leaders for years, Nat. Unfortunately, all too often talk merely begets more talk among politicians. There comes a time when they need to call in their armies to settle matters for them.'

Nat shook his head sadly. 'I'm glad you can make sense of it, Colonel. I'm damned if I can.'

Reaching up to his shoulder, Digby Vincent kneaded it with the heel of his hand and made no reply.

'It's high time you had something done about that wound.'

'You're right, of course. We'll soon be back at Bulawayo. I'll see a doctor there.'

Twenty-four hours later Colonel Digby Vincent collapsed with a high fever while the column was on the move. He would have fallen from his horse had not Captain Carey Hamilton been by his side to catch him.

As the column came to an abrupt halt. Nat helped the alarmed officer to lay the cavalry commander on the ground. As Carey Hamilton called for brandy and water to be brought, Nat undid Colonel Vincent's tunic and eased the shirt down over his shoulder and upper arm. It was not easy. The arm was swollen to twice its normal size. It was also badly discoloured, the hue of the taut skin about the grubby bandage having the appearance of tarnished copper.

While they were examining the unconscious commanding officer, a young Boer prisoner talked his way through the soldiers about him. Kneeling at Digby Vincent's side he began to unwind the stained bandage.

'Are you a doctor?' Carey Hamilton eyed the bearded Boer sceptically.

'No, but I had completed a year's medical training in Holland when the war began. Do you have anyone here with higher qualifications?'

The last few turns of the bandage were removed with great difficulty and the young Boer wrinkled his nose in disgust as he looked at the ugly, puffy skin around the wound. 'This is not good. Not good at all. The wound is seriously infected, possibly gangrenous. Unless something is done, here and now, your colonel will certainly lose his arm. Probably his life too.'

'What can you do?'

'I can cut the wound open and let out some of the poison, but it needs more than that. What medical supplies are you carrying with you?'

Carey Hamilton called on one of his sergeants to provide an answer.

'A few field-dressings, that's all, sir. The rest are in the wagons the colonel left behind.'

The burgher attending Colonel Vincent looked to Nat. 'The Zulus make use of a special plant to draw out poison. Is there a kaffir *kraal* near here?'

'There's a small Matabele village about three miles away.'

'Can you take me there? They'll have what we need. Sure to.'

Nat looked at Carey Hamilton and the captain nodded.

The village headman was surly and unhelpful until Nat mentioned the name of his father. Then, as had occurred on so many other occasions, the Matabele headman's attitude underwent an incredible change. For a man whose father had been one of Lobengula's true friends nothing was too much trouble. The headman's wives were sent to gather herbs while Nat and his Boer companion were informed that everything the village possessed was at their disposal.

Explaining that they were in a great hurry to return to a very sick companion, Nat promised to sample the headman's hospitality at a later date.

The herbs were procured and prepared by the Matabele women, and the entire population of the village turned out to see Nat and the Boer medical student leave.

As they rode to where they left Colonel Digby Vincent, the Boer asked, 'Is Retallick a common name in Rhodesia?'

Nat shook his head. 'The only Retallicks are from Insimo. My home.'

'Then the Adam Retallick who fights with the Lichtenburg commando must be related to you?'

'My younger brother. You've met him? Where is he now? I was hoping he might have had enough of fighting with the Boers and be ready to return home, where he belongs.'

The Boer looked at Nat curiously. 'You might as well try to stop a *meerkat* from hunting. Your brother is a natural fighter. I would go as far as to say he *enjoys* killing.'

'That doesn't sound like Adam,' said Nat, defensively. 'He enjoys *hunting*, he always has. But killing men . . .? I can't believe that of Adam. Why, he's not seventeen yet!'

The Boer shrugged. 'Then we must each be talking of a different sixteen year old Adam Retallick.'

Suddenly, Nat realised he did not really know Adam at all.

For the past few years he had been too busy with the affairs of Insimo really to observe what manner of man his brother had become.

'No, there can only be one Adam Retallick,' he conceded. 'What do you know of him?'

The Boer medical student had been with another commando at Magersfontein. He had witnessed the killing of the wounded Scots officer and the name of his slayer had been passed from trench to trench along the Boer line. He had also heard of Adam's bravery in rescuing old Theunis Erasmus near Poplar Grove and the tenacity he and his companions had displayed in the bloody battle of Dreifontein had become a legend.

'Where is he now?' Nat asked the question, still incredulous at the picture that had been drawn of his younger brother.

The Boer shook his head. 'He probably went with the Lichtenburg commando when Bloemfontein fell. I believe most of them went home.'

Home! Mention of the word conjured up a picture of Insimo. Home for the Retallicks – *all* the Retallicks. It seemed a lifetime since Nat had left the green and peaceful valley. He wondered how long it would be before the family would gather there again. Whether they would *ever* be there together. Somehow it did not seem possible that anything could ever be the same after this war.

Colonel Digby Vincent completed the journey to Bulawayo strapped in a hastily constructed travois. Pulped into a poultice, the herbs had been applied to the ugly wound on his arm. Although they did not bring about a miraculous cure, the wound was certainly no worse by the time Bulawayo was reached.

Digby Vincent was hurried into the tiny field hospital established in the town that had once been King Lobengula's capital. The partly trained Boer doctor, his purpose served, was bundled inside a prisoner-of-war camp with his fellow-countrymen. While Captain Carey Hamilton went to the army headquarters to make his report and send a telegraph message to Thomasina, telling her of Digby's condition, Nat made for the town's largest hotel and booked a room. Here he had a bath and then went to bed.

Nat was deadly tired as a result of weeks and months spent acting as a guide to Colonel Digby Vincent. He was tired too of always having so many men about him. But most of all he was weary of watching men kill and maim each other with such an incomprehensible lack of malice. But his last waking thoughts were of none of these things. They were of Thomasina Vincent, who would soon be arriving in Bulawayo to nurse her wounded husband back to health.

CHAPTER TWENTY-FIVE

Thomasina Vincent never came to Bulawayo. The doctor who examined her husband in the field hospital was of the opinion that the arm required amputation, and he had neither the experience nor the facilities for such an operation. Colonel Vincent needed to go to Salisbury and, if necessary, on to Beira to be taken on board one of the fully equipped hospital ships currently cruising off the East African coast.

Digby was to be taken by train to the head of the railway line that was being gradually extended towards Salisbury from Bulawayo. Thomasina would ride the hundred miles from Fort Victoria to meet him there spending a night at Insimo along the way.

The thought of Thomasina at Insimo was all the added incentive Nat needed to return home. That night, when Carey Hamilton came to the hotel room to see him, Nat told him he intended leaving in the morning.

To Nat's surprise, the captain pleaded with him to change his mind and remain with the cavalry. Carey Hamilton had been given temporary command of the two cavalry troops, with orders to check and report on the railway line through Bechuanaland as far south as Mafeking. He would be scouting in advance of a much larger force which had orders to secure the early relief of Mafeking.

'I've been made an acting-major, Nat. If this mission goes well I'll be confirmed in the rank. It's all-important to my future career.'

Nat was rolling up a soft leather jacket prior to stuffing it inside his already bulging saddlebag. Now he threw the jacket to the floor in disgust. 'That's taking unfair advantage of our friendship, Carey. My place is at Insimo. That's where *I* want to be.'

'Insimo is in good hands. You've said so yourself many times. The best thing anyone can do right now is help bring this war to an end as soon as possible.'

'I wish I was convinced you mean what you say, Carey. But the longer the war lasts the better are your promotion chances. You're a professional soldier. War is your business.'

'No, Nat.' Carey Hamilton spoke quietly and with total conviction. 'Soldiering *is* my business, but as a professional soldier I have a duty to my men. The sooner we bring this war to a close the more of my men will be alive to celebrate – myself included. Remember, I don't *send* my men into battle. I *lead* them.'

The saddlebags joined Nat's coat on the floor. 'Damn you, Carey! Why are you so uncomfortably logical? All I want from life is to be allowed to live in peace at Insimo and forget this war.'

'You might as well be an ostrich sticking its head in the earth in the middle of a veld fire, pretending it's not happening around you. This war has already touched you and your family. There's no going back until it's over.'

'The last person to say the same thing to me was the wife of a Transvaal Boer. All right, how long before we set off?'

'Good man! I knew you wouldn't let me down. We set off tomorrow. Mafeking has been under siege for more than four months and the British government is becoming uneasy despite Colonel Baden-Powell's light-hearted messages of reassurance.'

'Tomorrow? I thought I might at least have got in a quick visit home.'

'It shouldn't be too long before you're back there again. By the way, Digby would like to see you before he leaves. I think he's due to be put on the train any time now.'

Colonel Digby Vincent had already been placed on board the train. Another ten minutes and Nat would have been too late. Colonel Vincent's fever had broken, but he looked a very sick man and older than his fifty-two years. Clasping Nat's hand in a tight grip the wounded soldier first thanked him for his work as his scout, then suggested that Nat would soon be returning to Insimo.

'That's what I thought too, Colonel, but it seems Carey still has need of me.'

Digby Vincent nodded. 'I don't doubt it – but you'll be returning to Insimo soon. It's a wonderful place. Thomasina fell desperately in love with it, you know?'

Nathan found it uncomfortable listening to Digby Vincent talking about his wife, but he replied, 'Thomasina will meet you at the railhead. No doubt she'll stop at Insimo before she gets there.'

'Good! Good! I hope she'll become a regular visitor . . .' Still holding Nat's hand, Digby Vincent said, 'Thomasina is very fond of you too, Nat. She sees you as a quite exceptional young man – and so do I. Should anything happen to me I would wish her to turn to you for help and comfort. She has Carey, of course, but his first duty is to his regiment. You and Insimo could do far more to help her forget her sorrow . . .'

'Thomasina will feel no sorrow, because nothing is going to happen to you.' Nat spoke more harshly than he had intended in an effort to hide the embarrassment he felt. 'When you're better you will *both* be welcome visitors to Insimo.'

'Of course.' Digby Vincent's hand dropped back to the wooden-sided bunk and he closed his eyes. 'Goodbye, Nat. Good luck . . .'

Nat watched the train until it disappeared from view. He had been disturbed by Digby Vincent's words. They might have been spoken by a father giving away his daughter and not by a husband who was concerned for the future well-being of his wife.

Carey Hamilton had grossly over-simplified the task allotted to his two-hundred-strong column. It was not merely to survey the line, but also to clear the Boers from its length and secure all bridges and cuttings. It was a near-impossible task. Some of the bridges had been destroyed by Boer commandos in the early days of the war and never repaired. Nevertheless the small column did manage to prevent more damage being caused while the engineers of the main force repaired the existing damage.

Occasionally Acting-Major Hamilton's column came under attack from Boer commandos. More than once they fought brief but ferocious battles, but most of the time Nat was ranging far ahead of the column, seeking out any Boer encampments likely to pose a threat to Carey Hamilton's two troops of cavalry.

The distance between Bulawayo and Mafeking was five hundred miles and it took Carey Hamilton's column two months to complete the journey. For the last weeks they formed part of a much larger force which had been sent from Rhodesia. Together they fought their way to within six miles of Mafeking before the Boers mustered in strength and pushed them back again, keeping them fifteen miles from their destination.

By now Bloemfontein, capital of the Orange Free State, had fallen and Field Marshal Roberts had divided his forces into a number of strong columns intent on taking Pretoria and relieving Mafeking. It was widely believed by the British government that when Pretoria fell into British hands all Boer resistance would come to an end.

Nat did not share this view, but he kept such thoughts to himself. In the euphoria following their recent victories no one in the British army wanted to listen to the cold voice of reasoned dissent.

When it was apparent that the British had mustered sufficient troops to relieve the town, the Boer troops surrounding Mafeking saddled their horses and rode away. It was not Boer policy to fight unnecessary battles. They could not hope to defeat the army advancing upon them and it was foolhardy to throw away the lives of burghers when the end was never in doubt. Besides, Mafeking was in neither of the South African republics. Pretoria was.

With Mafeking relieved, a number of cavalry columns were sent into the Transvaal to test Boer strength in the area between Mafeking and Pretoria. Carey Hamilton's two troops of cavalry formed one of these columns, and Nat went with them.

While the Boers gathered their forces about Pretoria and the neighbouring gold-mining town of Johannesburg, ready to take on Field Marshal Roberts and the British army, those troops who had relieved Mafeking roamed the Transvaal countryside virtually unchallenged.

Carey Hamilton's column neared the Lichtenburg region and, knowing there was a possibility of Adam being at the Viljoen's farm, Nat was anxious to pay them a visit. However, he was reluctant to lead British troops through the Boer farmlands.

Carefully skirting the farms in the Lichtenburg area, Nat took Carey Hamilton and his troopers through the rugged hill country to the north. In answer to the acting-major's query about the reason for pursuing such a tortuous course, Nat replied that if Johannesburg and Pretoria fell to Field Marshal Roberts the Boer army would probably fall back to these hills. It would be as well to have at least *some* knowledge of the country.

Carey Hamilton had faith in Nat and said no more. As it happened, Nat was not alone in his thinking. In the hills they met with a column of mounted infantry making a similar sortie. Detached from Field Marshal Roberts's army, the mounted infantry were commanded by Major Frederick Wills.

When Nat led Carey Hamilton into the camp set up by the mounted infantry he was impressed by the smartness of the sentries on duty at the edge of the camp and posted outside the tent of Major Wills. He was less enthusiastic when he learned no sentries had been posted on the nearby *kopjes*, one of which overlooked the camp.

When the introductions were made Wills was quick to seize upon the fact that he was a *substantive* major, while Carey Hamilton was merely acting in this rank.

'I'm glad you've found us, Hamilton. Your men can link up with mine and we'll put on a good show for the Boers in the farming areas. It might make them think twice about leaving home to fight before Lord Roberts reaches Pretoria.'

'Thank you for your offer, Major Wills.' Carey Hamilton was polite but firm. 'Unfortunately I am on a mission for Colonel Mahon. My orders are to report back to him.'

'I see . . .' Major Wills was disappointed. With Carey Hamilton's men added to his own he would have commanded the best part of a full regiment. This would have been sufficient strength to track down and defeat the troublesome commandos of General De la Rey, who had been operating in the area. Such a feat would speed up his promotion chances. After taking more than twenty years to reach his present rank, Major Wills felt his career needed a little help – especially when there were youngsters like Carey Hamilton, men with only a quarter of his service, enjoying a similar rank, albeit it in an *acting* capacity.

'Well, I'll borrow your scout for a while instead. I intend scouring these hills for Boers. I caught one impersonating a British soldier yesterday. I executed him, of course.'

'*Impersonating a British soldier?* What was he doing?'

Major Wills's expression made it clear that Nat had not been included in the conversation.

'He was wearing a British army tunic. Taken from a bugler he'd killed – *murdered* would be a more accurate word, I've no doubt.'

'If every Boer who wore British army clothing was executed you'd need to kill half your prisoners. They *need* the clothing. They've got no stores, as you have. For them the British army is a fair source of supply.'

Some of Major Wills's officers exchanged glances. They had said the very same thing among themselves. But the mounted infantry officer was unperturbed. 'There are rules that must be obeyed in war. They apply to Boers as well as to us. However, I don't expect you to understand such matters. All I ask is that you prove an efficient scout and maintain the standards I set for every man under my command.'

Nat shook his head. 'Sorry, Major. I'm not scouting for you. I came down from Matabeleland at Major *Hamilton's* request. I'll stay with him.'

Major Wills bristled with anger and opened his mouth to speak. The words never came. A bullet struck him in the right temple and he fell dead at the feet of Carey Hamilton.

Nat spun round in time to see two figures scrambling over the top of the *kopje* where a sentry should have been posted.

Soldiers were snatching up their rifles and firing haphazardly towards the top of the hill, while others ran for their horses, convinced the shot heralded an attack.

'There are only two Boers. Keep everyone down here while I

find out which way they've gone.'

Running to his horse, Nat set off to ride around the *kopje*. The two Boers would have kept their horses nearby and it would not be necessary to climb the steep slope. Besides, it was the end of the day. His horse was tired.

He rounded the *kopje* just in time to see the two Boer horsemen disappearing into a wide valley that was cluttered with stunted trees and great piles of balancing rocks, some towering more than a hundred feet from the valley floor.

Nat headed for the valley, but once there he advanced using the utmost caution. It might easily be a trap, awaiting the arrival of the British troops. The valley was ideally suited for such an ambush. A hundred men skilfully positioned among the stacks of great boulders could hold off an entire army.

But there were no hundred men posted here, and after passing a dozen places where an ambush might have been laid Nat began to relax a little and concentrate on the job in hand. The tracks left by the two Boer horsemen were not easy to follow, especially on the rocky ground. But Nat had learned his skills from the Matabele. Each crushed blade of grass or displaced stone passed on a message to him.

After Nat had tracked almost two miles along the slowly widening valley he looked up at the sky anxiously. It would not be long before the sun dropped down over the low hills to the west, leaving the valley in shadow. There was no chance of catching up with the Boer marksmen now, even had his horse not been so tired. It was time to turn back.

No sooner had the thought crossed his mind than a voice from above and behind him called softly, 'That's far enough, brother – and please don't reach for your rifle.'

'*Adam!*' Nat's gasp was half-shock, half-delight. Turning, he saw his brother standing in the space between two rocks high on a pile of boulders, a rifle cradled in his arms and a shadowy figure standing behind him.

'I'm coming down, but don't move until I reach you. Esme has no family ties with us and she's still sulking because I stopped her from shooting you back at the *khaki* camp.'

Startled, Nat stared at the blonde, sun-tanned girl who stepped forward as Adam scrambled down the rocks. She returned his stare with an animosity that sent shivers down his spine at the thought of her looking at him over the sights of a rifle.

'Was it you who shot the major?' For some inexplicable reason Nat had to ask the girl the question, but it was Adam who answered.

Stopping ten feet from the ground, he said, 'Murderers don't get *shot*. The major would have told you that. They get *executed* – as he executed Jacob Eloff, a poor, half-witted orphan who had never harmed anyone in his brief, unhappy life.'

'Major Wills said he shot a Boer for wearing the tunic of a bugle boy he'd killed.'

'Jacob didn't kill anyone – and I should know. I stood beside him many times during a battle while he cowered at the bottom of a trench.'

Dropping lightly to the ground, Adam wiped his hands on his trousers. When he looked at Nat again his expression carried a challenge. '*I* shot that bugle boy. Jacob merely took the tunic because his own coat was in tatters. Which of us do *you* think should have been executed?'

This was a new Adam. Harder. He was no longer the boy Nat had left behind at Insimo.

'I told Major Wills I thought what he did was wrong. But that doesn't excuse what you did. That was murder.'

'No, Nat. What *I* did was *war*. In war you kill the enemy and he tries to kill you. The bugler was an enemy too.'

Adam was standing by Nat's horse now. Looking up he asked, 'How's Ma . . .?'

Suddenly they were brothers once more. Nat swung down from his horse and they embraced.

'Ma misses you, Adam . . .' Holding his brother at arm's length, Nat felt the hard shoulder muscles beneath his hands. 'But she misses a young boy who ran away. You're a man now.'

Adam successfully hid the pleasure Nat's words gave him. 'I was a man before I left. You just didn't notice, that's all.'

'Come back to Insimo, Adam. Let's *both* go back. It's Ma's birthday next month. We'll give her a day to remember.'

Adam's expression showed his conflicting emotions, but he shook his head. 'My future's here now, Nat. I've even got a farm of my own, left to me by a burgher who died down near Poplar Grove, in the Orange Free State. He was Esme's father. When I've got it together I'll be married and then we'll move in.'

Nat looked to where Esme stood high above them, staring out along the valley. 'You're too young to think of marrying . . . and she's no older.'

Following his brother's glance, Adam grinned, 'Tell that to the last man she killed . . . But Esme's not the girl I'm marrying. I'll be wed to Johanna Viljoen. You remember her?'

For a moment more Nat looked up to where Esme stood silhouetted against the darkening sky. She did not seem *capable* of killing a man. Then he remembered her eyes when she had looked down at him. He returned his attention to Adam, and frowned. He had thought of Johanna Viljoen frequently lately, probably because the Viljoen farm was near. She was a fine girl, yet the news that she was to marry his brother failed to please him.

'You're still far too young to think of marriage.'

'*You* told me many times I was old enough to take responsibility for running Insimo while you were away. The Boers — and the British — know I'm old enough to fight a war and kill men. I'll marry Johanna *and* provide for her when this war's over. Tell Ma I'm sorry if she's upset about my leaving, but I'll be back to see her one day — bringing Johanna with me.'

'Adam! There are horsemen coming.'

The warning came from Esme, and she began scrambling to the ground.

Adam looked accusingly at his brother and Nat shook his head. 'I told them to stay where they were. They are probably worried about me. I'll go and tell them I lost you.'

Adam smiled. 'I doubt if they'll believe you, big brother. You're too good a scout. No one knows the earth and its ways better than a Matabele.' Adam spoke the last sentence in Ndebele, the language of the Matabele tribesmen from whom they had both learned their tracking skills. 'Good luck — go home to Insimo *now*. If you stay here until this war's over you'll likely forget what the place looks like.'

Before Nat could reply Adam had run to the deep shadows behind the tall pile of balancing rocks. A few moments later

Adam and Esme emerged on their horses. Pausing a moment to wave, Adam dug his heels into his horse and galloped away. The girl looked at Nat for a moment. Then she too turned her horse and rode off into the gathering dusk.

CHAPTER TWENTY-SIX

The armies of Field Marshal Lord Roberts were on the move everywhere. The commander-in-chief himself led two great columns upon Johannesburg and Pretoria. Other columns swung eastwards from Mafeking to link up with the British commander. Even the ponderous, overburdened army of General Sir Redvers Buller which had taken so long to relieve Ladysmith was pursuing its hesitant course through the coastal province of Natal, heading vaguely in the direction of Pretoria.

Meanwhile smaller columns of British cavalry and mounted infantry were operating with official sanction in many parts of the Transvaal. Nat and Acting-Major Hamilton remained in the hill country to the north and east of Lichtenburg, occasionally flushing out small bands of armed burghers.

Then word reached them that Pretoria had fallen without a fight. The young lieutenant who brought the news jubilantly declared that Lord Roberts had set up his headquarters in the Transvaal capital and was confidently predicting that the Boers were ready to surrender. The war was almost over.

The lieutenant had been sent out to find Carey Hamilton and the other mounted units to issue them with new orders. They were to tour the countryside offering a full amnesty to those burghers who handed in their rifles and signed a pledge not to resume hostilities.

Nat did not share Lord Roberts's view that the Boers were ready to lay down their arms. However, the new orders from the British commander-in-chief provided him with a reason for visiting the Viljoen farm.

Acting-Major Hamilton halted his two troops of cavalry a half-mile short of the Viljoen farm, leaving Nat to go on alone to speak to the family who had shown him kindness when he was captured outside Mafeking.

The British army officer was not entirely certain he knew Nat's true reason for wanting personally to inform the Viljoen family of the truce offered by Lord Roberts, but he was aware it was important to his friend from Insimo.

Carey Hamilton thought he understood a little more when he saw a young, slim girl leave the low, single-storey farmhouse to await Nat's arrival.

Nat had not seen Johanna's expression of pleasure when she recognised the rider approaching the house, and it had disappeared by the time he reined in before her.

The whole Viljoen family had seen the approach of the British soldiers and Johanna's first words referred to their presence.

'Have you brought the British army with you to burn *our* farm, Nat Retallick?'

'The British army doesn't wage war on civilians.'

Nat knew he should have expected to hear hostility in her voice. After all, he was a scout for the *British* army. All the same, it stung him.

'Tell that to Nonnie De la Rey,' Johanna retorted. 'British soldiers set fire to Koos's farm and turned her out on the veld with six of their children. Tell *her* the British don't take out their spite on women and children.'

Nat did not doubt Johanna's words, but he was equally certain the action had not been taken by regular troops.

'It must have been one of the irregular units. There are a few of them around . . .'

Johanna's derisive snort broke in on his words. 'Is your General Lord Methuen an "irregular"? He was the one who ordered the soldiers to burn the farm.'

'Such things happen in war, Johanna. My own farm at Insimo was attacked and burned by a *takhaaren* commando.'

Now it was Johanna's turn to show dismay. 'I'm sorry. I didn't know. Adam didn't say anything about it after you'd spoken to him. Was anyone hurt?'

'None of the family – and there wasn't time to tell Adam

very much news when we met . . .' He was reminded that she was to marry his younger brother. 'But the war is almost over now, Johanna. It's time to stop fighting and learn to get along with each other again. Lord Roberts is offering an amnesty to all burghers who hand in their guns. They'll be allowed to return to their farms. I'd like you to tell Adam, and your pa and brother.'

'It's a pity I'm not able to tell Jacob Eloff too,' said Joanna bitterly. 'He'd stopped fighting – Adam says he never really started. Yet your *khakis* stood him up and shot him. This war isn't over yet – not by a *long* way. We're going to fight it *our* way. Three days ago our burghers cut the railway line south of Johannesburg. They took nearly a thousand *khakis* prisoner and captured enough stores and ammunition to keep our whole army going for a year. Does *that* sound as though we're beaten?'

'Johannesburg is a hundred and twenty miles away. How have you learned of the raid so quickly?'

Johanna's dismayed expression gave Nat his answer. 'It must have been Adam. Is he here now?'

Johanna's glance moved to where Carey Hamilton's cavalrymen were watering their horses at a small stream within rifle range of the farm. She said nothing.

'Tell Adam what I've said, Johanna. Persuade him to hand in his gun, then ask him to take you to Insimo. It will be the proudest moment of Ma's life when one of her sons brings home a wife.'

Nat saw a movement in a window of the house behind Johanna and the afternoon sun glinted on something metallic. He did not doubt it was a gun barrel, and he knew he made a tempting target. One of the Boer leaders had suggested that if his men wiped out the men who scouted for the British army and spared the British generals, a Boer victory would be assured. Nat did not fear a shot from his brother – but there could be other Boers inside the farmhouse.

'Why don't *you* go home to Insimo, Nat? This isn't your war. You told me so once – and I admired you for it.'

'A lot has happened since then. I still don't believe there should have been a war, and the longer it goes on the worse it will be – for everyone. It's time to end it now. I'll stay to see it through . . . *then* I'll go home. I'd like to see you and Adam there. Goodbye, Johanna.'

'Nat!' She called after him as he turned his horse. '. . . You'll be welcome to call on your way home. When you don't have the *khakis* with you.'

Nat shook his head. 'This war has brought too much bitterness with it, Johanna. No one who fought with the British will be welcome in Transvaal for many years to come. Take care of Adam . . .'

Leaving Johanna standing in front of the Viljoen farmhouse, Nat rode back to Carey Hamilton and the cavalrymen. The British army officer could see the meeting had not been a happy one for Nat, but said nothing to him. Calling on his men to mount their horses he set off with Nat at his side.

As they rode together Nat gave Carey Hamilton news of the attack on the railway line, south of Johannesburg. As a result of this information, the acting-major decided to head for Johannesburg to learn for himself what was happening there. They had been patrolling the veld for many months now. It was time his men had a rest.

Unfortunately for the saddle-weary cavalrymen, Carey Hamilton was not sufficiently senior to take such a decision on behalf of his men. When they reached Johannesburg they were ordered to Pretoria. Here they enjoyed no more than twenty-four hours of the Transvaal capital's limited delights before receiving new orders.

Confirmed in the rank of major, Carey Hamilton was given two troops of mounted infantry to supplement his hussars and sent eastwards to reinforce Field Marshal Lord Roberts.

The hopes of the British commander-in-chief had not yet been realised. The capitals of both Boer republics were now in his hands and many burghers had handed in their rifles and returned to farms and homesteads. Yet still the war dragged on. In the Orange Free State, dramatically annexed to the British Crown by Lord Roberts on Queen Victoria's official birthday, President Steyn still headed a Boer government, the seat of which was wherever he chose to rein in his horse.

Meanwhile, in the Transvaal, *Oom* Paul Kruger was still the president of his invalid republic. Lampooned by the cartoonists in the British press, Kruger represented the archetypal burgher to his enemies. Yet this huge, ugly, uncouth and bigoted man possessed an awesome, rough-hewn grandeur that dominated all who knew him. In common with his fellow Boer president, *Oom* Paul ruled his country from a constantly changing 'capital'. In his case it was a railway car retreating along the line that led from Pretoria to Portuguese Africa, the coast . . . and inevitable exile. At seventy-five years of age and suffering from diseased eyes, President Kruger was no longer able to withstand the rigours of campaigning on the open veld.

Field Marshal Lord Roberts was aware of this and he was determined to push Kruger all the way to the borders of Portuguese territory. By so doing he would also seal off the sole outside source from which the Boer republics were able to receive aid. This, surely, must force the Boers to their knees and so bring the fruitless and increasingly costly war to an end.

But the British commander-in-chief's advance had ground to an unexpected halt. The Boers were in a strong defensive position along a line of hills straddling the railway line no more than ten miles outside Pretoria. Lord Roberts decided on an immediate attack.

Carey Hamilton and his four troops of horsemen followed the wide trail left by Roberts's fourteen-thousand-strong fighting force until they reached the scene of the battle, guided for the last few miles by the sound of fierce gunfire.

The newly promoted major hardly had time to give his name and the details of his command to one of the commander-in-chief's staff officers before the dapper little field marshal waved him into battle in support of the hard-pressed cavalry brigade. Nat turned his horse to go with Carey Hamilton, but once again the energetic British commander intervened personally.

Calling Nat to him and eyeing his civilian dress suspiciously, he snapped, 'Who are you?'

'Nat Retallick. Scout for Major Hamilton.'

'Retallick? You're English?'

'No, I was born in Matabeleland.'

'Ah! One of *Rhodes's* men. Major Hamilton has no need of a scout in this battle. You can remain with me and carry out messenger duties.'

Nat restrained the urge to correct the commander-in-chief.

He was neither Rhodes's man, nor anyone else's, but Field Marshal Lord Roberts was fighting a grim battle. A moment later an urgent request was received from the battlefield and the little field marshal was issuing new orders.

For a couple of hectic hours Nat watched in increasing fascination as the British commander-in-chief controlled the battle, directing attack and counter-attack. Listening to the calm and decisive sixty-seven year old field marshal it would have been easy to believe the war was all part of some elaborate game being played out on the South African veld. Only the constant noise of gunfire and the growing stream of wounded men being helped to the rear of the British lines provided a grim reminder of reality. This was a desperate battle in which men were being maimed and shot to death.

Late in the afternoon, when the battle showed no sign of slackening, Lord Roberts turned to Nat. 'Nothing has been heard of the cavalry since Major Hamilton went up to reinforce them. Do you think you can locate them and ask General French to send me a detailed report of his situation as soon as possible?'

Nat nodded, trying to appear as calm as the field marshal. Inside he was a strange confusion of emotions. Working with Carey Hamilton he had been engaged in several skirmishes with Boer commandos, but he had never taken part in a battle of such magnitude as this.

Nat was shown a map by one of Lord Roberts's staff officers, giving the position where he might expect to find General French and the British cavalry.

As he neared the spot Nat realised the map bore little resemblance to the actual terrain. However, he was soon attracted to a fierce action raging independently of the main battle and, topping a low ridge, he came upon the horses of Carey Hamilton's command. The sergeant in charge of the soldiers guarding them told him what had happened.

Carey Hamilton had gone to the aid of General French's cavalry brigade, only to find them dismounted and surrounded by Boers who had led them into a trap. In order to dislodge the Boers from their positions, Hamilton's troopers had also been forced to dismount and fight as infantrymen.

Leaving his horse with the others, Nat made his way to

where the hussars and mounted infantrymen were fighting their way up the side of a rocky *kopje*. Dodging from boulder to boulder he eventually found Carey Hamilton.

When Nat explained his mission, the major cursed. 'Damn! I sent a messenger an hour ago. He must have been taken or killed by the Boers. If I write another will you take it back?'

Nat nodded, keeping his head down. The last couple of hundred yards to the position held by Carey Hamilton and his men had been traught with danger. Boer marksmen on the ridge commanded most of the slope. However, Nat preferred to take his chance and return, rather than remain here with the dismounted cavalrymen. The Boers were on the ridge in force. Dislodging them would not be easy.

Beyond the *kopje* a valley opened out to a width of perhaps two miles, and it was here that the whole of General French's cavalry had been encircled by a strong Boer force. Caught in a vicious fire from all sides when strung out along the valley floor, they had dismounted and found whatever cover was available. Sent by Lord Roberts to roll back the Boer flank, they had walked into a well-set trap.

'This looks like Koos De la Rey's work,' said Nat as Carey Hamilton scribbled his note and bullets winged off the rocks above them. 'I can't think of any other Boer general with the nerve to set a trap for the *whole* British cavalry.'

'Tell that to Lord Roberts when you give him this.' Carey Hamilton handed Nat the folded message. '. . . Good luck. I don't need to tell you how important it is that we get some help from the infantry. If the Boers move up artillery they will annihilate our cavalry.'

By the time Nat reached the spot where he had left his horse he was more convinced than ever that Koos De la Rey was leading the Boers who dominated the surrounding hills. The marksmen who had fired at him on his way up the slopes of the *kopje* had been reinforced, and the intensity of their fire left him in no doubt that they had been awaiting his return. He covered the final few hundred yards on his stomach, wishing the grass were long enough to hide his progress.

When he recovered his horse Nat did not ride directly back to the British headquarters. Instead he led the horse on a roundabout route that took him through thick scrub at the foot of the hill. His caution was justified. A light breeze carried the aroma of tobacco smoke to him when he was a quarter of a mile from the *kopje*. There was a Boer ambush on the route he might have been expected to take. Increasing his caution, Nat walked his horse for another quarter-of-a-mile before mounting and riding hard to find Lord Roberts.

The British commander-in-chief read the note before brusquely questioning Nat about what he had seen. When Nat repeated his belief that Koos De la Rey was in charge of the Boers who had General French trapped, Lord Roberts nodded. 'I don't doubt it. I don't doubt it at all. The man's a brilliant general. I wish I had him in my army. However, he's the enemy, so I had better do something about getting him out of our way.'

Half an hour later Nat was guiding two regiments of infantry to the spot where the British cavalry was pinned down. Ahead of them a mounted artillery battery had already reached the scene. By the time the infantry arrived the British gunners were laying down an impressive barrage along the long ridge.

Yet again the Boer commander had anticipated such a move, and his own artillery bombarded the British infantry before they could reach the beleaguered cavalry.

On this occasion, however, the Boer general was unsuccessful. The infantrymen were veterans of a dozen battles and led by experienced officers. Deployed along the slopes of the hills held by the Boers they worked their way methodically towards the ridge under cover of their own artillery fire. Meanwhile, Carey Hamilton had seen what was happening and was able to give some covering fire from his own position.

One of the British regiments was composed of Highland Scots. For the first time in his life Nat heard the skirl of bagpipes as the barrage ceased and the Scots soldiers fixed bayonets and prepared to charge the last few yards to the ridge. It was a sound that sent cold shivers up his spine. He wondered what effect it was having upon the Boers.

Leading his horse, Nat was following in the wake of the infantry when the pipe music suddenly ceased in a discordant wail and the piper fell to the ground, his bagpipes falling from his grasp, not thirty yards away.

Nat reached the spot as the Scotsman stirred and tried to rise. A bullet had shattered his knee and there was no way he could stand unaided. Dropping down beside him, Nat urged the piper to stay still, promising to send a medical orderly to him as soon as he could find one.

'Damn the medics!' The Scotsman took a tight grip on Nat's arm. 'Help me sit up . . . over there, against that rock . . . and pass me my pipes.'

Nat opened his mouth to reason with the piper. Then he saw the expression on the man's face. Reaching down he began to drag the Scots soldier towards the rock. It was not easy. The Scot was a big man and in considerable pain.

When Nat released his grip the Scotsman pulled himself to a sitting position, then held out his hands for the bagpipes. Moments later an unmusical wail rose above the gunfire on the *kopje*. Then the wail became a tune. The sound brought a great cheer from the advancing Highlanders and suddenly they were running for the ridge, all caution thrown off.

It was an attack that would have broken the nerve of the strongest men. When the Highlanders reached the ridge the Boer defenders were in full flight. But many of the burghers found their escape cut off by Carey Hamilton's men, who swarmed along the broken ridge at right angles to the Highlanders. Moments later the attack became a series of disconcerted and desperate small battles.

Carey Hamilton had led his men in person in support of the infantry and now he sent off an orderly to tell General French of his success. By clearing this ridge the infantry had opened a gap through which the cavalry brigade could fall back and reform, in order to play a more positive part in the battle.

Cutting across the hillside to where Carey Hamilton stood, Nat heard a noise from behind a pile of rocks. It sounded as though someone had tried unsuccessfully to stifle a groan of pain.

Dropping the reins of his horse and holding his rifle in readiness, Nat went in search of the source of the sound. Walking with a soft tread he rounded the rocks and almost fell over two Boers. One was lying on the ground, and it was he who was groaning. One leg of his trousers had been ripped open to expose a bloody kneecap, shattered by a jagged piece of shrapnel. There was blood on the man's shirt too. The second man was kneeling on the ground, trying to pour water into the wounded man's mouth.

Not until the water bottle was removed did Nat see the Boer's face clearly. He gasped in surprise. It was Cornelius Viljoen! At the faint sound the other man turned towards Nat and he saw it was Lucas, Johanna's brother.

At that moment one of the British mounted infantrymen came upon the scene. He had seen Nat's horse standing beside the rocks and decided to investigate. He saw Lucas Viljoen standing facing Nat and his rifle came up. As his finger tightened on the trigger Nat knocked the gun down and the bullet burrowed into the ground at his feet.

Still holding the rifle barrel towards the ground, Nat said, 'These men are prisoners – and they're both hurt.' He had seen the blood staining the shirtsleeve of Lucas Viljoen.

The British soldier was a young recruit, straight from England. This was his first battle and when he looked at Nat there was fear in his eyes.

More gently, Nat said, 'Find a doctor and bring him here. Quickly now.'

The soldier had seen Nat riding and talking with the major. He did not doubt his authority to issue orders and went off to do as he had been told.

'Is he badly hurt?'

Nat put the question to Lucas Viljoen as he crouched down beside the Lichtenburg boy. When he did not receive an immediate reply, Nat looked up sharply. He doubted if Lucas Viljoen had heard him. The young Boer's face wore the dazed expression of a man who had been subjected to an intensive artillery bombardment. Nat had seen similar cases before. He would get no sense from Lucas Viljoen for a while.

Ripping Cornelius Viljoen's shirt apart to check on the source of the blood, Nat saw a gaping wound parting the muscles of the burgher's stomach. He was only semi-conscious and Nat could do no more than attempt to make him comfortable before turning to Lucas Viljoen.

Johanna's brother's wound was worse than a first glance had indicated. There was a deep, jagged gash below the elbow and, from the way Lucas was holding the arm, Nat suspected it was broken.

His diagnosis was confirmed by the doctor of the Army Medical Corps who arrived some minutes later, but the doctor was far more concerned with the condition of Cornelius Viljoen.

'He needs urgent hospital attention,' he declared. 'Have him taken to the railway line. A special train will be coming to collect casualties before evening. It will take them to Pretoria.'

'Can they both go together? They're father and son.'

The medical officer nodded. 'Yes. No doubt the boy will want to be with his father when he dies – that's if *he* has recovered some of his wits by then.'

Nat winced at the mention of Cornelius Viljoen's probable death and the army doctor asked, 'Do you know the family?'

'Yes. I visited their farm only a few weeks ago.'

Stuffing instruments inside a surgical bag, the doctor stood up. 'They should have stayed on their farm instead of leaving it to fight a damned silly war that they can't possibly win. That *nobody* will win. They are killing and maiming us, we're killing and maiming them – and this God-forsaken country is killing more than either side.'

'I doubt if the Boers would agree about their country being "God-forsaken". They are convinced this is God's own country and they are His chosen people.'

'Then they'd better pray that this personal God of theirs can bring about a peace pretty damned quickly. If He doesn't they'll be left with a land that the Devil would scorn. At a recent staff meeting it was suggested the farms and crops of fighting Boers should be burned – "for strategic reasons". *Strategic reasons!* We pride ourselves on being the product of thousands of years of civilisation, yet we can still find a sound reason for setting fire to a man's home and his stock. God! I should have been a veterinary surgeon. Animal behaviour at least is comprehensible.'

Nat helped two Indian medical orderlies to take Cornelius Viljoen and his son to the railway line. When he left them Lucas was showing signs of regaining his senses. There were many other wounded Boers here, and Nat asked a slightly wounded Boer corporal to do his best to ensure father and son remained together.

The battle raged until dusk. The threat to the cavalry had been removed, but it would be a long time before the British army realised just how lucky they had been. It was indeed Koos De la Rey who had trapped the cavalrymen and he had called on the supreme Boer commander to send him a few more men, in order that he might deliver the *coup de grâce*, and thus eliminate the whole of Lord Roberts' cavalry.

Failing to grasp the importance of such a masterstroke, the Boer commander-in-chief let the opportunity pass and the British cavalry survived to fight again.

Despite such a reprieve, Lord Roberts was pessimistic about the prospect of dislodging the Boers from their defensive positions, even though his own troops outnumbered them by more than three to one. This was the kind of warfare in which the Boers excelled, and they were fighting on a battlefield of their choosing.

The diminutive English field marshal called on all available reinforcements and spent much of that night planning his strategy for the next day.

As morning came, the army of Field Marshal Lord Roberts moved forward cautiously to join battle with the enemy once more. Up the slopes of the waiting hills the British infantry advanced with bayonets fixed, apprehensive for the first shot that would herald the slaughter of another day of battle.

The shot never came. As the first brave men scrambled to the summits of the hills they looked about them in disbelief. There was not a Boer to be seen. The battle was over. The hills were theirs. The way to the coast was open.

CHAPTER TWENTY-SEVEN

Nat had been scouting for Carey Hamilton for nine months. Now, heartily sick of the war, he wanted to return to the peace of Insimo. But first he had to speak to Johanna Viljoen.

Since the arrival of the British army in Transvaal the countryside had been criss-crossed by the wires of a military telegraph system. With the express permission of Lord Roberts, Nat had telegraphed a message to the Viljoen family, informing them that Cornelius and Lucas were wounded and in hospital in Pretoria. Nat's hope was that Adam had returned to the Viljoen farm from the hills and would accompany the womenfolk to the capital. He had been relieved to learn that Adam had not been with the Lichtenburg commando during their recent battle, having not returned from his farm when they set off for Pretoria. Nat still entertained the hope that if he spoke to his brother again he might persuade Adam to return home with him, if only for a visit.

In spite of the army doctor's gloomy prognosis, Cornelius Viljoen was not only still alive, but was improving. He would be permanently lame in the wounded leg, but his stomach wound had not affected any vital organs and he was as cheerful as any wounded prisoner-of-war might expect to be. Lucas too was much better. It was at first thought he would have to lose his wounded arm, one of the bones being sheared through. However, skilful surgery had saved it, although it would never be as strong as his other arm.

Nat estimated it would take Johanna and her family a week from receipt of the telegraphed message to reach Pretoria — longer if *Ouma* Viljoen insisted upon travelling with them.

They would probably make the journey by ox-wagon, and oxen were renowned for patience, not for speed.

On the fourth day after the battle, orders came for the prisoners-of-war to be sent by rail to the Cape Colony. Once there, they would be shipped to a new camp being built for Boer prisoners-of-war in the hills of Ceylon, five thousand miles from the homeland for which they had been fighting.

Nat protested first to the medical officer, then to the officer in command of the prisoners-of-war, that Cornelius, in particular, was unfit to travel. The medical officer shrugged his shoulders. Cornelius Viljoen was just another wounded prisoner. There was no shortage of them. A doctor would be travelling on the train with the prisoners. No doubt he would do his best . . .

The officer responsible for the Boer prisoners was no more helpful. His orders were to send *all* prisoners-of-war to the Cape Colony and close down the Pretoria camp. When this was done the officer could return to his own regiment. He would do nothing that might interfere with these orders.

In desperation Nat went direct to Lord Roberts. The British field marshal listened courteously to Nat's plea that the Viljoen father and son be allowed to remain at Pretoria, if only on medical grounds.

Lord Roberts pushed a bulky sheaf of papers across the desk towards Nat. 'This is a report about the deficiencies in my army's medical services. It's being quoted in British newspapers, and in the House of Commons. On my way to Pretoria I've lost a quarter of my army through disease alone. British wounded are lying on the floors of hospitals without pillows or blankets – it says so right here. There are few nurses . . . doctors are worth their weight in gold, and the Boers are constantly cutting the railway lines and preventing medical stores from reaching me. I can't justify keeping a medical officer in Pretoria solely for Boer prisoners-of-war when there are better facilities in the Cape Colony.'

'I'm willing to arrange civilian medical attention for the Viljoens while they are in Pretoria, and you have my word that they won't attempt an escape. Their family is on its way here and will remain with them until both Cornelius and Lucas are well. After that I'm sure they'll be content to be treated as any other prisoners-of-war.'

Lord Roberts looked at Nat curiously. 'What's your particular interest in these two prisoners?'

Nat told the British commander-in-chief of his journey from Matabeleland to Mafeking during the first days of the siege; of his capture, and of Cornelius Viljoen's intervention when Nat and his companions were threatened with death. Finally he mentioned Koos De la Rey's part in allowing him to return home.

Lord Roberts was fascinated by Nat's story. He was also puzzled. 'You have a great deal of sympathy for the Boers, Retallick – and understandably so. I have always admired De la Rey as an adversary, and the Viljoens would also seem to be fine people. Why are you fighting against them when you might have stayed out of this conflict with a clear conscience?'

Nat told the field marshal of the *takhaaren* attack on Insimo, of his own wound, and how his scouting career had begun as a bid to drive the *takhaaren* commando from Rhodesia.

The British commander-in-chief relaxed visibly. To his orderly mind a man needed a good reason to go to war. Whether it was for his country, his home, or his family. An Englishman's duty in this war was clear. His duty lay with Queen and country. Nat's reason for fighting had always been less clear to him.

In the reports reaching the commander-in-chief from Carey Hamilton's column, Nat's skill as a scout had been commended to him with such frequency that Field Marshal Roberts had caused inquiries to be made about the scout from Matabeleland. He had learned that Nat's father had been living in the country now called 'Rhodesia' long before Cecil Rhodes had first set foot in Africa and had quarrelled with Rhodes over 'the empire-builder's' attitude towards the Matabele king. Despite his immense power and influence, Rhodes had not been able to take one acre of land from the Retallick family. They still lived in the valley given to them by the last Matabele king and were the largest land-owners in the immense kingdom ruled over by Cecil Rhodes and his British South Africa Company. Furthermore, Nat's father had been killed many years before during a war believed by many men to have been deliberately engineered for the furtherance of Rhodes's aims.

Field Marshal Lord Roberts would have expected the sympathies of a man with such a background to lie with the Boers, even if his vast land-holding demanded that he remain neutral, at least. Now he understood why Nat had entered the war on the side of Great Britain. Until the war against the Boers was won his huge farm would never be free from the danger of attack. Indeed, it was a prime target for any Boer commando operating north of the Limpopo river.

'Your concern for the Viljoens is commendable, Retallick. However, they saved your life, so you could hardly do less. How many of the family are on the way from their home to see these two men?'

'Three, most probably. Cornelius Viljoen's wife, his mother and daughter.'

There was speculation in Lord Roberts's eyes once more. 'How old is his daughter?'

'Old enough to be marrying my brother before very long.'

'I see.'

Lord Roberts stood up and walked to a map on the wall. It was a large map of southern Africa and included Rhodesia.

'Where is this farm of yours?'

Towering over the diminutive field marshal, Nat placed a finger on an unmarked section of the map.

'It's here. Twenty miles long and ten across.'

'Hmm! Very impressive. You intend to return there soon?'

'As soon as I've settled the problem of the Viljoen family.'

The British field marshal traced a line down the southern part of Rhodesia and through the Transvaal to the Orange Free State. His finger stopped at the edge of Basutoland. Looking up at Nat, he asked, 'I don't suppose you've ever been here?'

Nat shook his head. 'My father travelled in that area. I never have.'

'Do you have any knowledge of the native language spoken there?'

'I could get by.'

Lord Roberts walked away from the map, nodding his head vigorously. 'That's what I thought.'

He sat down at his desk again and waved Nat to a chair on the other side. 'There's a situation building up on the Basutoland border that might bring the end of this war closer if only I can take advantage of it. President Steyn of the Orange Free State, General de Wet, and almost ten thousand Boer fighting men are camped there, among the mountains. I believe it possible to bottle them up and force their surrender – probably without a shot being fired, and so saving thousands of lives. I am sending all my available troops to the area. Major Hamilton will be among the first. His mounted men will form a reconnaissance column, finding the passes through the mountains in order that other troops might seal them. I was hoping you would accompany him as his scout.'

'There are other scouts. Probably some who know the area.'

'No doubt. But you are known to Major Hamilton. He trusts your judgment. Full confidence in his scouts is most important for a reconnaissance commander.'

'I'm sorry, I'm going home to Insimo.'

'Very well.' The field marshal stood up and extended a hand. 'Thank you for your services in the past, Retallick. I am sorry I am unable to do anything for your friends.'

Something in the commander-in-chief's voice made Nat pause before taking the proffered hand.

'Would you help the Viljoens if I agreed to go with Carey Hamilton as his scout?'

Field Marshal Lord Roberts shook his head. 'The rules regarding prisoners-of-war are dictated by international agreements. I cannot interfere with them.'

'Then there is nothing more to be said. Goodbye, sir.'

'Wait! Are you intimating that if I do something for these Boer friends of yours you *will* act as a scout for Major Hamilton?'

Nat paused and drew a deep breath before replying. He desperately wanted to return to Insimo.

'Yes.'

'I see.' Lord Roberts smiled. 'How badly wounded are they?'

'Very badly. Cornelius will never be able to walk properly again. Lucas, who can be no more than fifteen or sixteen, has almost lost the use of one arm.'

'Ah! Then I might be able to intercede on *humanitarian* grounds. I will have a medical officer look at both men. If he supports the view that they are no longer able to fight I will authorise their release. Will this meet your demands?'

Nat nodded, at the same time hoping the doctor would not examine Lucas too closely. If he did he would discover the scar left by a British bayonet only months before. Nat consoled himself with the knowledge that a British doctor would not expect a man to recover from such a wound and return to fight again so quickly. But the Boers had always known that the exceptional climate of their country helped even the most serious wound to heal remarkably quickly if there were no complications. Burghers were often able to return to the saddle only weeks after receiving wounds that would have made an invalid of a soldier serving in another land.

If all went well, Nat knew he had gained more than he had expected for the Viljoens — but he had also committed himself to a far longer absence from Insimo than he had anticipated.

Johanna, accompanied by her mother and grandmother and a Bantu servant, reached Pretoria exactly a week after Nat's message was received. Greatly relieved to discovered that Cornelius was no longer in danger, the family were delighted that the two men were to be allowed to return home with them. The head of the Viljoen family would always have a stiff leg to remind him of the part he had played in the war against the British, but Sophia Viljoen felt it was a small price to pay to have her husband and son home and alive. The Lichtenburg commando was always in the forefront of every battle in which it took part, due to its close association with General De la Rey. Because of this there were few farms in the area where a member of the family was not mourned.

Nat was not at the hospital when the family arrived. He would be leaving Pretoria with Carey Hamilton the next morning and there was much to be done before then. Not least of his chores was to write a long letter to his mother, explaining the reasons for his long absence from Insimo.

When Nat learned that Johanna was in Pretoria he went to the hospital to see her, but his reception by the female members of the Viljoen family was decidedly cool. In view of his own sacrifice on their behalf, Nat was both surprised and hurt. Finally, after bidding them an unusually formal goodbye, he left the members of the Viljoen family to enjoy their reunion.

He had reached the corridor outside the room where the Lichtenburg men were housed before Johanna came hurrying after him, ignoring the call from her grandmother to return to the room.

'Nat . . . I'm sorry. We should all be grateful . . . I know we owe you so much. It's just . . . Oh, it doesn't matter. Pa told me how you had him and Lucas brought to safety after they'd been wounded. He says it's only through your efforts that they're being allowed to come home with us instead of going off to a prisoner-of-war camp. We *are* grateful.'

Nat nodded acknowledgement of her thanks. He had not told the Viljoen men of the bargain he had struck with Field Marshal Lord Roberts in order to secure their release. They believed they were being allowed to go home because they were too disabled ever to ride with a Boer commando again.

'Pa says you'll be returning to Insimo soon.'

'That *was* the idea. Now I've agreed to act as a scout for one more campaign.'

'Do you enjoy fighting Boers *so* much?'

'I don't enjoy fighting at all. I *do* believe what Lord Roberts says. The sooner this war is over the better it will be for everyone.'

'Your brother wouldn't agree with you. He would rather fight than do anything else . . . Well, *almost* anything else.' She spoke with an inexplicable bitterness.

'Adam didn't come with you? Is he still up in the hills, on his farm? The farm that's going to be home for both of you?'

Johanna's head came up suddenly. 'You don't know? No, how could you? No wonder you don't understand why the Retallicks aren't popular with my family . . . I won't be seeing Adam again. If he comes to the farm *Ouma* Viljoen has threatened to take a *sjambok* to him.'

'But . . . I thought you were to be married?'

'That was *before* . . . Oh, it doesn't matter any more. He's married to someone else. The Predikant and some burghers left behind by the commando made him marry the girl.'

'Made him marry *which* girl?' Nat was dumbfounded. 'Not the girl who was with him in the hills?'

Now it was Johanna's turn to look puzzled. 'In the hills . . .? I don't know. I can't even remember her name!'

At that moment there was an angry call from the doorway of the room they had just left. *Ouma* Viljoen was standing in the doorway, hands on hips, the face looking out from beneath the stiffly starched Cape bonnet red and angry.

'Come in here this minute, girl. What are you thinking of, standing out here in the dark passageway with a young man — a *Retallick* at that. Haven't we had problems enough with that family? Come in here this minute, I say.'

'Yes, *Ouma*.' Johanna's reply was all that might have been expected from a dutiful grand-daughter, but as Johanna turned to go, she said, 'Will you come to see us again, Nat? When this war is over? When you come to visit Adam, perhaps?'

'Yes . . . But first I need to find out what's happening to Adam . . .'

'Things might be different when the war is over. Perhaps I might even be able to forgive you for fighting on the side of the *khakis*. I'll try.'

Then Johanna was gone and the door of the room in which the Viljoen family were gathered was very firmly closed.

CHAPTER TWENTY-EIGHT

After their encounter with Nat, Adam and Esme rode through the hills in the wake of the soldiers who had shot Jacob Eloff to death. They hoped to catch some of them straying from the main body of men, but the British cavalrymen had learned their lesson. They sent out scouts in strength and their camps were well guarded. Eventually, Adam and the Boer girl tired of their fruitless mission and turned their horses towards Adam's farm.

Adam expected Esme to remain with him at the farm for a while, but when they were no more than a half-day's ride away they camped for the night, and in the morning Esme had gone. Adam followed her trail as far as an area where the hills seemed to be carved from solid rock, but here he lost the trail, as Esme must have known he would.

Adam turned back towards the farm filled with a grudging admiration for the strange, independent girl. She could track and shoot as well as any man. Had she been a son, old Theunis Erasmus would have had just cause to be proud of his offspring.

Once back at his farm Adam worked hard for ten days. By the seventh day he was heartily sick of his own company, but he still believed Esme might return. When it became increasingly apparent that she was not coming back Adam packed his saddlebags and rode on to the Viljoen farm.

Much to his chagrin he learned that General De la Rey had been to the Lichtenburg area in Adam's absence, gathering members of his commando. Cornelius and Lucas had ridden off with him to Pretoria, ignoring Sophia Viljoen's protest that her son was still not fully fit. Adam also learned of Nat's visit to the Viljoen farm. He told Johanna of his own meeting with his brother in the hills, taking care to make no mention of Esme Erasmus. He was relieved to learn that Nat had not spoken of her either. It made embarrassing explanations unnecessary.

Adam decided he would leave for Pretoria in the morning, to catch up with the remainder of the commando . . . but fate had other plans.

Adam was sitting down to a lamp-lit supper with the Viljoen family later that evening when they heard the sound of horsemen and the creaking of a light wagon outside in the darkness.

'Are you expecting callers?' Adam asked the question of the women.

Sophia Viljoen shook her head. 'We don't welcome visitors at this time of night.'

Adam was on his feet and halfway to the corner where he had placed his rifle when there came a heavy knocking at the door. Without waiting for a reply the late caller opened the door and came inside.

'Predikant Maritz! I thought you'd be with General De la Rey . . . Did you know he'd been here? He's on his way to take back Pretoria. We can travel together in the morning . . .'

Adam was walking towards the Dutch Reformed Church preacher as he spoke, and then he became aware there were others with him.

Predikant Maritz did not reciprocate Adam's pleasure at their meeting, and as he advanced farther into the room a number of burghers crowded into the house behind him. Adam recognised a few of them as having served in the Lichtenburg commando.

Then three women filed in through the door and Adam's mouth dropped open in utter dismay. It was Mrs Coetzee and her daughters, Margret and Gezima.

Seeing Adam, Gezima gave him a nervous half-smile. Her sister kept her glance fixed firmly upon the floor at her feet. Margret's face was streaked with dust from the trail and her eyes were puffy, as though she had recently spent a great deal of time crying.

But Adam barely had time to register such details before Mrs Coetzee pushed her way across the now-crowded room towards him, the force of her anger driving him backwards before her.

'That's him! That's the filthy little animal who took advantage of my hospitality.'

Addressing herself to Sophia Viljoen, Mrs Coetzee said, 'While I was fighting to save the life of your son this one was out in the hay barn with my Margret, seducing her with talk of how he'd avenged her poor father's death by killing *khakis*. The poor girl never stood a chance against such talk. He made her feel she *owed* herself to him, he did. And her an innocent, God-fearing girl who thought every man was as honourable as her poor, dead father. Now look at her. A disgraced girl – and with his *baster* in her belly. My God! I'll kill him, so help me, I will . . .'

'Now, now. Let me handle this.' Predikant Maritz stepped in front of the menacingly advancing woman as one of the other men took hold of her arm.

With the immediate threat temporarily in check, Predikant Maritz turned his attention to Adam, and there was no trace of their former friendship in his expression. 'You've heard what Margret's mother has said. Do *you* have anything to say about the matter?'

Adam could see Johanna standing on the far side of the room, her face unnaturally pale, her expression one of acute distress.

'I reckon Mrs Coetzee has said it all.'

'You're not denying you're the father of the child Margret is carrying?'

Adam remembered Mrs Coetzee's own words when she had surprised Adam and Margret in the feed barn. '. . . *You're not the first . . . I doubt if you'll be the last . . .*' He opened his mouth to repeat what she had said. Then, looking at the disapproving expressions on the faces of the men crowding behind the Predikant, he changed his mind. No one would believe him and he had no doubt that Mrs Coetzee would deny ever making such a statement to him. Her daughter was expecting a child. Mrs Coetzee was determined it should have a father.

'I'm not denying I *could* be the father . . .'

The tension in the room suddenly lessened. Adam had not denied paternity. It made what was to follow much easier.

Margret Coetzee's glance was raised momentarily from the floor to Adam. He thought he detected triumph in her eyes.

'If you want me to support the child I'll not quibble about the amount . . .'

'Support? There's only one way to support a child in the Transvaal Republic. By marrying its mother!' As one of the men behind the preacher spoke, the tension returned and one or two of the men fingered their guns angrily.

'But I can't. I'm marrying Johanna . . .'

Adam realised the futility of his outburst, even as it was being made. Margret Coetzee and her mother had come after him with marriage firmly in mind, and the men in the room were all relatives of the pregnant girl, determined to see justice done. Even in the improbable event that he could evade his responsibilities there would be no marriage with Johanna now – as Sophia Viljoen was quick to confirm.

'You'll never be welcome in this house again, Adam Retallick – no matter what happens here tonight. You've abused our trust . . .' Sophia Viljoen choked on her words, temporarily overcome by emotion.

Ouma Viljoen suffered from no such problem. 'I told you! I said the boy was no good when I first set eyes on him. Coming here calling on our Johanna without so much as a by-your-leave. Good riddance to him, I say . . . and I pity the girl who's getting him – though I doubt she's any better, by the sound of things.'

Having expressed her opinion, *Ouma* Viljoen glared around the room as though challenging anyone to argue with her. No one did. Instead, one of the men cleared his throat noisily and said, 'We've come here to see our Margret decently married. Let's get on with it.'

Adam's acquiescence was neither sought nor deemed necessary. Within ten minutes of Sophia Viljoen bundling Johanna from the room, Predikant Maritz had joined Adam Retallick and Margret Coetzee in matrimony, according to the laws of the Dutch Reformed Church.

When the brief ceremony came to an end, everyone seemed

at a loss about what was to be done next. It was left to *Ouma* Viljoen to make the decision for them.

'You can all clear out of the house now and let decent folk go to bed and sleep. If you've no place to go you can sleep in the barn. There's plenty of room since my son went off with all the horses. You'll find all the water you need in the *spruit*, but be off this farm first thing in the morning. There's work to be done, and breakfast is only for those who belong here.'

Adam and his unexpected bride spent their wedding night apart. It was cramped in the barn, even with the horses gone, and Adam and the Boer men crouched uncomfortably at one end of the building while the women laid down at the other. At first light Adam caught his horse and packed his saddlebags with the few possessions that had been dumped by someone – probably *Ouma* Viljoen – on the covered *stoep* that extended the length of the house.

'Where you taking our Margret?' The question was put to Adam by a short, squat, rifle-carrying Boer with a bushy black beard that reached halfway down his chest.

'To my farm, up in the hills.'

The heavily bearded Boer was joined by two other men and one of these spoke now. 'We'll be around to see you're treating her right. We look after our own.'

'Visitors won't be welcome on my farm. That means members of the Coetzee family in particular.'

'A man's entitled to do what he wants on his own land,' agreed the heavily bearded Boer. 'But we'll call just the same.'

'And don't think to get out of your responsibilities by going off to war. The Lichtenburg commando got on well enough before you came here. We'll manage without you again.'

Adam said nothing, curbing the anger he felt. If he started anything here and now Margret's kin would delight in joining together to give him a beating. There would be other occasions.

'Since you're so keen Margret shouldn't be left behind, perhaps you'll tell her to move herself and get out here.' Adam addressed his words to the man who had first spoken.

'I'm here, Adam.' Margret stood in the doorway of the barn, a large, heavy-looking bundle clutched in her arms.

Without another word, Adam jerked his horse's head around and rode off. After a moment's hesitation his bride of only a few hours clutched the bundle to her and laboriously set off after him. There were no farewells, and no one waved her goodbye. Only Gezima stood in the doorway and watched her sister set off to begin married life. Behind her in the barn their mother still slept.

Not until they reached a stream, about five miles from the Viljoen farm, did Adam look back. Margret and her large bundle were about half a mile behind. Slipping to the ground, Adam led his horse to the stream to drink, quenching his own thirst up-stream of the animal.

When Margret caught up with him he was chewing on a thick strip of *biltong*. She dropped her bundle to the ground with great relief. The muscles of her arms ached and her legs were already tired. She looked at Adam, but he was gazing out across the veld in front of them. Dropping to her knees at the side of the fast-moving stream she put her face down to the water and sucked noisily. Then, her thirst quenched, she sat back on her haunches.

Adam was already mounting his horse and he moved off without a glance at Margret. For a moment her lower lip trembled and it seemed she might break down and cry. Instead, she sat down and took off the high, buttoned boots she had worn especially to impress Adam. She rubbed her feet gingerly, feeling the blisters. The high leather boots were too small and had hurt her feet, but the pain would have been worthwhile had Adam only noticed.

Heaving a great sigh, Margret stuffed the boots inside the bundle containing her other possessions and picked it up, heaving it awkwardly to her shoulder. Then, barefoot, she set off after Adam.

The young bride staggered in through the doorway of her new home an hour before dark, more dead than alive. Her feet were bloody and torn and every muscle in her body cried out for rest.

A mile from the farm, Adam had ridden off and left her. There was no fear of Margret becoming lost now. The faint track led only to the farm. Adam entered the house as Margret supported herself against the rough-hewn table and he threw a small, freshly killed *klipspringer* to the packed earth floor.

'Here. Cook it.'

They were the first words he had spoken to her since repeating the words dictated by the Predikant, the previous evening.

By a supreme effort Margret pushed herself upright from the table. In a voice that she thought as shaky as her legs, she said, 'You get a fire going and I'll cook a meal.'

Adam glared at her for a few moments. Then he uttered an ambiguous grunt and stalked from the room. A few moments later she heard him chopping kindling wood.

It was dark by the time a meal was ready, but Margret had brought candles with her and she lit two of them for the table. There was mealie-meal in the bundle and from this she made a good, belly-filling paste which tasted delicious with *klipspringer* gravy.

The meal was good, and in any other circumstance Adam would have told her so, but he was still filled with a bitter resentment that would not allow him to say anything that might possibly give her pleasure.

Not at all sure of their sleeping arrangements, Margret had gathered coarse, dry grass from outside. While the meal was cooking she had made up two beds on which she laid their blankets.

Before the meal Adam had brought in the Cape brandy. He set some on the table and drank without offering any to Margret.

When the meal was over he continued drinking while she cleared away the dishes. She was so tired she could hardly keep her eyes open, but she made him a coffee and set it on the table. Then, hesitantly, she said, 'I'm very tired, Adam. I'd like to go to bed now.'

When he made no reply Margret left the room and made her way to the room where she had made up the beds. Undressing in the darkness she slid between two soft Basuto blankets. Suddenly the heartbreak of her present circumstances overcame her and she began to cry.

Ever since she was a young girl Margret had dreamed of

marriage and all it entailed. Never had she imagined the dream would in reality prove to be a nightmare. She did not blame Adam. He had been forced into the marriage — but so had she. If he only gave her a chance she would be a good wife to him. They could both salvage something from the situation and have a reasonably good life together.

Despite her weariness she was still awake when Adam came into the room. She could not see him but she knew by the way he kept bumping into things that he had drunk far more than was good for him. Then she heard him drop on his bed, his breathing deep and uneven.

She waited for the sound to become steady, a sign that he was asleep. Suddenly, he said, 'Come here.'

When she did not reply immediately, he repeated, 'I said, come here. I know you can hear me.'

Pushing back the blanket that covered her, she put her feet to the ground and winced. Her feet and legs were very painful.

Going to Adam's bed she lay down beside him, not sure what to expect.

'Adam . . . I'm sorry things have happened this way. But I'll make you a good wife. Things will turn out all right for us. I know they will . . .'

She waited for him to say something. To kiss her as he used to in the barn at her home. But still Adam said nothing. Then, rolling on to Margret, he took her without a word. As Adam used her with all the resentment and frustration that was in him she cried for the second and last time in her married life. When it was done he lay still, her body pinned beneath him, his head lying beside hers and his drunken snores in her ear.

It was July 14th, 1900 — Adam Retallick's seventeenth birthday.

Adam was sitting down to breakfast in the kitchen when Esme arrived. His head felt as though it was packed with boulders, and the sour taste of stale brandy tainted his food. The brandy had dulled his senses too; he had not heard Esme ride up to the farmhouse.

She walked into the kitchen in her usual, free-limbed way, but stopped short when she saw Margret. For some moments the two girls stared at each other. Margret was older by at least three years, but she lacked the arrogant self-assurance of the younger girl.

'Who's this?' Esme put the question to Adam.

'*I* should be asking that question. I'm his wife.'

Esme looked at Adam incredulously. 'A wife . . .? You've gone and got yourself married?' Esme's reaction might have been amusing in other circumstances.

'I didn't get *myself* married. I was standing at the wrong end of half-a-dozen guns at the time, all held by her uncles and cousins.'

'You were *made* to get married — you mean you've fallen for that "I've-got-your-baby-in-my-belly" trick?' Suddenly Esme's astonishment changed to mirth. 'Yes, you would. Your brains stay on the floor with your trousers when you go to bed.'

'I didn't trick Adam into doing anything. I don't want a baby any more than he does. But he *is* my husband now. We'll make a go of things.'

Ignoring the outburst, Esme said to Adam, 'I want to talk to you.'

Pushing his plate from him, Adam stood up. 'We'll go outside. I could do with some air.'

'Adam . . .'

Whatever Margret intended saying was lost as Adam rounded on her. For a moment she thought he would strike her and she shrank back from the sheer hatred she saw in his eyes. Margret had hoped Adam's rough usage of her during the night might have purged some of the resentment he felt against her. In spite of such a disastrous start she still hoped they could make something of their marriage. It *would* have been possible, she was sure . . . but that was before the arrival of this self-possessed young girl.

Outside the house Esme looked at Adam more closely. 'You look *awful.*' For a moment her grin returned as she added, 'I should have used my knife when you tried it on me. It would have saved you a whole lot of trouble.'

'I'm in no mood for jokes. You said you wanted to speak to me.'

Esme became serious immediately. 'I've been visiting one of my sisters. Her husband was with her. He said Christiaan de

Wet is putting together a great army to fight the *khakis* in the Orange Free State. He has almost ten thousand men gathered in the Brandwater basin, close to the Basutoland border.'

Christiaan de Wet was commander-in-chief of the Orange Free State army.

'My brother-in-law says if the Transvaal burghers rally to him as well, the *khakis* can still be beaten. De Wet needs every man he can get. *I'm* going. I had thought you might want to go too.'

'*You're* going?' Adam squinted at Esme. He wished his head did not ache so much. 'But you're a woman.'

'So? I can shoot, ride and fight as well as any man, can't I?'

Adam nodded. Esme had all the qualities needed for the Boer army. But she *was* a woman, and women did not take up arms.

When he put this to her, Esme said, '*You* know I'm not a man, but if you cut my hair and I dressed in men's clothes would anyone else know? There are thousands of unshaven young boys in our army. I could pass as one easily – even more easily if you were with me. You could say I was your younger brother. No one would think of doubting you.'

Adam was forced to concede that she was right. Esme had a slim, under-developed figure and a deeply tanned face.

'Why do you want to join the Boer army? You could stay here out of trouble and see the war out.'

'So could you, especially now, but you won't – and I've far more reason to want to kill *khakis*. Will you help me? Cut my hair and loan me some of your clothes? They'll fit well enough. If you're not coming you can give me a letter of introduction instead. You've fought with the Boer army, you must know some of the Orange Free State men.'

Adam had met enough Orange Free State fighting men to do as Esme asked, but his thoughts were speeding along different lines.

'The Brandwater basin is almost three hundred miles away. To get there you'll need spare horses – and a better gun than that old muzzle-loader you're carrying.'

'There's a horse herd in the hills, and half are already saddle-broken, I can catch what I need. I don't know about the gun though . . .'

'It won't be too difficult. We can take what we want from the British along the way.'

'You're coming? What about *her* . . .? Your wife?'

'She'll have as much say in my leaving as I had in marrying her. The baby will have a name when it comes and that's the main thing as far as her family is concerned. If she doesn't like it here on her own she can go back to them. There seem to be enough of them about Lichtenburg.'

'When do we leave?'

'Right now.'

Adam cut Esme's hair with his hunting-knife and grimaced at the result. It was the manner of haircutting practised by the *takhaaren*. However, when Esme dressed in a shirt and trousers belonging to Adam and an ancient hide jacket left in the house by Theunis Erasmus, Adam admitted Esme would pass for a fifteen year old boy with no difficulty.

The main problem was finding a pair of stout boots to fit her. Esme was used to going barefoot. Eventually she agreed to wear a pair of her father's boots. They were a couple of sizes too large, but smaller than those offered to her by Adam.

Her outfit completed, Esme went to her horse and was seen by Margret from the kitchen. Margret immediately went in search of Adam and found him in the bedroom.

'Who's that outside? Where's the girl . . .?' Then she realised that Adam was stuffing clothes into saddlebags and her puzzlement became alarm.

'Adam! What are you doing? You're not leaving me here alone?'

'We're at war, remember? You ought to. It was your "gratitude" to a fighting man that got you into trouble.'

'But . . . the war's almost over. Everyone says so. Please, Adam. You can't leave me here alone.'

'Women are being left alone all over South Africa. You'll find plenty of cattle higher up the valley – milking cows among them. Cut out one or two and bring them back here. There's a flintlock musket that belonged to Theunis hidden on a beam just inside the stable door, and powder and shot buried in a barrel beside the kitchen fireplace. You've even got a vegetable plot that's run wild at the back of the house. You'll find seed enough to raise a crop by the year's end. If you don't like it up here by yourself you can go and stay with some of your folk, nearer your own home.'

'But what about the baby? It *is* yours, Adam. Truly it is.'

'Tell it that its pa has gone off to war.'

CHAPTER TWENTY-NINE

The mountainous area about the northern border of Basutoland was some of the most breathtakingly beautiful country Nat Retallick had ever seen. The Drakensberg range of mountains reached more than eleven thousand feet into the African sky. Strewn in profusion about them were lesser mountains, cliffs, ravines, and an occasional lush, wide river valley.

In the midst of this grandeur was the Brandwater basin. Here General de Wet had mustered nine thousand Boer fighting men, the bulk of the Orange Free State army, together with many burghers from Transvaal. Securely surrounded by mountains, with only four passes to guard, General de Wet thought his army would be safe from attack while he laid plans for the liberation of the two Boer republics. Only after Field Marshal Lord Roberts had despatched sixteen thousand British troops to the area did General de Wet realise that his mountain 'refuge' might prove to be the graveyard of the Orange Free State's hopes.

Fortunately for Christiaan de Wet, Lord Roberts did not think this particular campaign required his personal attention. The Orange Free State was already conquered. The field marshal was intent on pushing *Oom* Paul and the Transvaal army all the way to the sea. *This*, he believed, was the way to bring the war to a close. He was convinced the Orange Free State army had retreated to the mountains on the Basutoland border in order to lick its wounds. If the British soldiers he was sending to the area could bottle them up they would eventually surrender without a fight — and casualty figures weighed heavily upon the thinking of the little field marshal.

However, the general sent to the area by Roberts was displaying little sense of urgency about his assignment. He made his headquarters in a village some fifteen miles from the nearest pass, and here he settled down to await supplies and more accurate maps.

Nat was sent into the mountains to map out the areas around the passes. While here it occurred to him that if de Wet became aware of the British intentions he could march his men out of the mountains, leaving the British army sitting in the middle of a beautiful but strategically useless wasteland.

When he put this view to the general's officers he was politely but firmly told by a British staff officer that he was not qualified to make such an assessment.

This opinion was shared by the British staff general himself. However, when Carey Hamilton and a few of his fellow-officers expressed their misgivings, the general airily agreed to send a column to blockade the passes as he had been instructed. Carey Hamilton and Nat were sent with the column, but Major Hamilton was not in command. This was given to Lieutenant-Colonel Merriweather Fordyce, an unimaginative infantry officer, newly arrived from England.

In common with many other officers who had not done battle with the Boers, Lieutenant-Colonel Fordyce was contemptuous of the ill-disciplined burghers. He was convinced that the reverses suffered by the British army in the past had been due to bad British generalship and had nothing to do with the fighting abilities of the raggle-taggle Boer army.

When the column came within sight of the Slabbert's Nek pass and Lieutenant-Colonel Fordyce saw the weather closing in around the mountains, he turned his column about and made camp on lower ground.

When Nat suggested he should check on the pass first, Fordyce dismissed such a reconnaissance as a waste of time.

'Look at the weather up there. Nothing will be moving in this. Leave it until tomorrow morning.'

'If it's all the same to you, Colonel, I'll go and have a look anyway. I'd like to know whether there's been any movement through the pass.'

Lieutenant-Colonel Merriweather Fordyce shrugged his shoulders indifferently. 'Please yourself, Retallick. It's your own time you're wasting, not the army's.'

The British army officer's scorn for civilian scouts almost equalled that he had for the Boers. Armies should line up and face each other on a field of battle. Infantry facing infantry, resplendent in colourful uniforms, with cavalry in support. This was the way his father had fought in the Crimean War, and his grandfather at Waterloo. Face to face with one's enemy was a *man's* way of fighting. None of this hide-and-seek, ambushes, and civilian scouts who could walk away from a battle and go home if they didn't feel like fighting.

Nat set off in a steady drizzle to gain the heights above the pass and see whether there was any Boer movement in the area. He had not gone far when he saw a small Boer scouting party keeping observation on Lieutenant-Colonel Fordyce's column. They did not see Nat and he kept well clear of them, but he soon discovered there were other Boer scouting parties in the vicinity, ranging over a large area. One such party sighted him and he was forced to turn back. Riding for his life he was pursued all the way by Boer bullets.

The sentries posted about the British camp exchanged a few long-distance shots with the Boers before the horsemen pulled their mounts in and rode away towards the snow-mantled higher slopes of the mountains.

Nat told Lieutenant-Colonel Fordyce what he had seen, adding, 'The Boers are up to something. Their scouts are not merely checking on *our* progress. They're checking out the whole countryside. In my opinion they intend either mounting an attack, or breaking out of the mountains.'

'Indeed? Would you also hold an opinion on how best to thwart either contingency?'

'Yes – shift our camp up to the pass. Drive off their look-outs, replace them with your own, and send off a message to the general requesting that he send troops to do the same with the other passes.'

'Ah! So you offer advice to generals, as well as to field officers? You are extremely presumptuous for such a young man, Retallick.'

'No, Colonel, I offer advice based on what I see, and on my knowledge of the Boers. You're up against General Christiaan de Wet here. He and Koos De la Rey are two of the cleverest generals in any army, anywhere. I doubt if he'll allow you to bottle him up inside these mountains.'

'You are not here to give advice, or offer opinions, Retallick. You are a scout, and while you are under my command you'll report to me only what you *see*. No more, and no less, you understand? It might interest you to know I *have* taken the trouble to study the backgrounds of all the Boer generals I am likely to meet on the battlefield. De Wet is a farmer and has been one for most of his life. He began this war serving in the ranks of a commando and in less than five months rose to command the army of the Orange Free State. From farmer to commander-in-chief in twenty weeks! Good God, man, it takes longer than that to teach a soldier ceremonial drill! I've spent twenty *years* learning my business, and no twenty-week general is going to out-think, out-fight, or out-run me. Look at the weather up there. De Wet is not going to move his men anywhere for a very long time. He'll sit tight and while his men are up there shivering we'll be in a snug camp, putting hot food in our bellies. When the weather lifts we'll move into the passes. Fresh, well-fed soldiers eager for a fight against tired and dispirited men who must be aware that they have already lost this war. Dammit, Retallick, if this weather persists for much longer I'll be accepting surrender terms from de Wet, not an invitation to do battle.'

'If you really believe that, Colonel, then all your studying has been wasted. "Surrender" is a word no one dares to mention when either de Wet or De la Rey is around.'

During that night, General Christiaan de Wet and two thousand six hundred men broke out of the mountain stronghold through the pass known as 'Slabbert's Nek', taking with them four hundred wagons and five field guns. The three-mile long Boer column moved with a disciplined silence that would have confounded Lieutenant-Colonel Merriweather Fordyce. Passing only a mile from the sleeping British camp, they were not heard by a single sentry.

Nat found the Boers' trail about two hours after daybreak. Although they were able to travel with an uncanny silence, the army of Christiaan de Wet could not hide the wide path of churned-up mud it made across the water-logged veld.

Nat saw the trail from a half-mile away and at first he thought the whole Boer army must have escaped from the Brandwater basin. As he drew closer he saw that, although they had cut a wide swathe across the veld, there had probably been less than three thousand men. Even so, it was a considerable triumph for the Boers who had been waiting in the pass for nightfall. The unexpected arrival of Lieutenant-Colonel Fordyce's column must have come as a nasty shock to them.

When Nat informed Lieutenant-Colonel Fordyce of the Boers' escape the infantry officer seemed incapable of taking the unpalatable news. Then he demanded that Nat take him to see the tracks for himself.

Viewing the muddy tracks that extended north-west from the pass for as far as the eye could see, Fordyce asked, 'How many men do you estimate to have been in the Boer party?'

Nat shrugged. 'It's difficult to say. More than a thousand, certainly. Probably closer to three thousand, together with wagons numbered in their hundreds. I found the tracks of at least one field gun too – a certain sign that the Boers are in strength.'

Lieutenant-Colonel Fordyce looked back to the wide and muddy trail and shook his head in disbelief. 'I can't believe such a large party of men could pass so close to our camp without *someone* hearing them. It must have been a much smaller party. A hundred . . . two hundred perhaps.'

'No, Colonel, there were more than two hundred.'

'Very well . . . *three* hundred. I'll send a message to General Hunter that some three hundred Boers are believed to have broken out of the Brandwater basin.'

'There are *three thousand* Boers out there, Colonel – and God knows how many more have escaped through the other passes. For all we know the whole Boer army might be out on the loose.'

'It's possible . . . but I doubt it very much. I'll take my infantry and chase these Boers. Major Hamilton can divide his men and seal off the remaining passes. You go with them and check for any Boer movement. Keep General Hunter informed of your findings, if you please.'

In a hard day's riding Nat ascertained that no Boers had left the Brandwater basin through the other passes. He also learned that the passes were well guarded by the Boers, indicating that at least a part of the Boer army remained in the mountains.

It was four days before Carey Hamilton's hussars and mounted infantry were reinforced by the army of General Hunter. Another three days passed before their combined forces advanced on the passes under cover of heavy artillery fire.

If Lieutenant-Colonel Fordyce's theory had been correct, the Boers should have been too weary to put up a fight. The weather in the mountains had been atrocious for days. Gale-force winds had brought both rain and snow sweeping through the mountains, transforming the ground into a slippery morass of mud. But in spite of bad weather and a heavy artillery bombardment the Boers in the passes beat off the British attacks.

Had it not been for the arrival of Lord Lovat's Scouts, resourceful Highland Ghillies, recruited in their native Scotland for their tracking skills, the passes would have remained in Boer hands. All that day, with Nat, they climbed the dominating heights above Slabbert's Nek, and that night they guided troops to the places they had marked out. When morning broke, the Boers found their positions rendered untenable by British marksmen manning the heights above them. Abandoning their suddenly exposed defences, they retreated into the heart of the Brandwater basin.

Suddenly the whole character of the war in the Orange Free State had undergone a change. While General de Wet and his two thousand six hundred men successfully eluded Lieutenant-Colonel Fordyce and the other pursuers, those he had left behind fought a battle for survival among the hills and valleys of the Brandwater basin.

Finally, sick of war and unable to agree among themselves, the beleaguered Boers sued for peace. Once more Nat's services were in demand, this time as a messenger and negotiator between Boers and British.

The Boers wanted time to discuss all the implications of surrender among themselves. They requested a cease-fire in order to reach agreement on the terms they would seek.

The request was telegraphed to Lord Roberts, and his reply was swift. There was to be *no* temporary ceasefire and he would accept no conditions from the Boers trapped in the mountains. For them it was to be unconditional surrender and subsequent internment. Either they agreed immediately or the war would be carried to them.

They chose surrender.

More than four thousand men handed over their weapons, horses, oxen and wagons. As they did so many of them wept bitter tears of despair and frustration. For them it was the end of a long and desperate road.

Not *all* the Boers surrendered. During the night preceding the surrender, one and a half thousand of them set off along narrow paths to achieve the impossible. Their intention was to scale the mountains and escape from the Brandwater basin along routes no man had taken before. By morning they had succeeded. Even though forced to discard most of their equipment and stores along the way, they were free to fight on.

Behind them, inside the Brandwater basin, the scale of the British victory was sufficient cause for celebration in the camps of the 'khakis'. Fires burned brightly and soldiers were generous in their praise of the resourceful enemy.

Nat was camped with Carey Hamilton and his hussars in a small valley that night, sheltered from the chill wind by a series of small hills. The rain clouds had long since rolled away and the night was crisp and cold, with a strong hint of frost in the air.

A number of civilian scouts were attached to the regiments camped about the hussars and during the course of the evening many of them strolled across to chat with Nat. Because of this he was not surprised when he saw a rifle-carrying civilian picking his way through the camp-fires towards him. The man's coat collar was turned up about his ears, protecting them from the cold, and he had his hat pulled low over his features, yet there was something familiar about the figure, even in the uncertain light of the camp-fires.

The visitor halted some distance from the camp-fire. Thinking the man had not seen him, Nat rose and walked forward to meet him.

'Hello, I'm Nat Retallick. Are you looking for me?'

'That's right, brother, and I'm in need of your help — urgently!'

It was Adam.

CHAPTER THIRTY

None of the Boers in the Brandwater basin questioned the right of 'Arne Retallick' to be with them. 'He' could shoot and ride as well as any burgher. Arne's voice was thin, but no thinner than the voices of the many thirteen and fourteen year olds who fought alongside brothers, fathers and grandfathers.

'Arne Retallick' was the name adopted by Esme, and she had time on the three hundred mile ride through Transvaal and across the Orange Free State to get used to it. Esme's ancient rifle was exchanged for a brand-new British issue Lee-Enfield ·303 when they crossed the railway line, south of Johannesburg. They had no need to shoot the sentry to whom the rifle had been issued. They surprised him bathing in the *spruit* that ran beneath a small bridge he was supposed to be guarding. For good measure they took his uniform too, leaving the naked soldier to walk back to his unit and report on his lapse of duty.

Esme and Adam fell in with a number of armed Boers when they were still seventy miles short of their destination. On their way to reinforce commandos in the Brandwater basin, they had a number of young boys with them and Esme no longer felt conspicuous. Just before they passed into the mountains around the basin the party acquitted themselves so well that when they reached the army of Christiaan de Wet they were able to take their pick of the commandos. They chose to join the local men, Adam believing their knowledge of the territory would provide a guarantee of success in future actions.

They were disappointed. General de Wet moved out of the Brandwater basin with Marthinus Steyn, President of the

Orange Free State, leaving behind him instructions for the remainder of the Orange Free State army. They were to follow him out the next day and link up with fresh commandos coming in from the east.

Unfortunately for the Boer cause, no sooner had de Wet gone than a leadership dispute broke out behind him. While the British soldiers seized the passes and their patrols began probing the Boer defences, the bitterest battle was that for leadership of the encircled Boers. Eventually the leadership issue assumed such grotesque proportions that the Boers asked the British general for an armistice in order that the matter might be settled without any outside distractions.

By way of reply the British general called upon the Boers to surrender, with or without a leader. His demand was echoed by many of the quarrelling burghers.

'What's happened to the army that was meant to sweep the British out of the country?'

Adam put the bitter question to Esme when he returned from look-out duty on the hilltop behind the camp shared by four of the commandos. Helping himself to a mug of coffee from the pot hanging over the fire, he squatted on the ground beside her. It was dusk and the Boers did not bother to maintain look-outs after dark.

'Things are worse than you know. There's been a meeting this evening. They are going to surrender. All that remains to be done is to work out the final terms.'

'Surrender? I came here to fight.' Adam was appalled by the news. 'There are six thousand burghers here, with all the food and ammunition they could possibly want. It . . . it's *unthinkable*. Surely some of them will fight?'

'No one's prepared to make a stand here – but the Rouxville commando is going to try to break out of the basin tonight.'

'How? The *khakis* have the passes sealed so tight I doubt if a mouse could squeeze through.'

'They're not going to use the passes. One of the Brandwater men is going to try to take them over the mountains.'

'Then I'm going with them. Are you coming?'

Esme grinned. 'I've already packed our saddlebags, and our horses are picketed with those of the Rouxville commando.

We leave as soon as it's too dark for the *khakis* to see what we're up to.'

The escaping Boer commandos moved fast and quietly towards the high mountains over which lay freedom from captivity. It was a frosty night, but the moon was not yet up. A number of smaller scouting parties moved ahead of the main body, in case there was an ambush waiting for them. Bringing up the rear were more burghers, detailed to hold back possible pursuers.

Adam and Esme were in one of these latter groups and theirs was destined to be the only one to see action this night.

Riding well to the rear, on the right of the main Boer column, they were following the slope of a hill when suddenly a party of riders loomed out of the darkness. A challenge from the newcomers identified them immediately as British soldiers and there was a quick, confused outbreak of gunfire before the engagement was abruptly broken off and each party cantered off in the direction in which it had originally been travelling.

Adam was fairly certain he had shot at least one British soldier from his saddle, but when he turned to tell Esme, he could just make out her outline doubled over the neck of her horse.

Riding alongside her he called, 'Are you all right?'

'No . . .' The pain in her voice alarmed him. '. . . I've been shot.'

'Where?' Reaching out quickly he was in time to prevent her from falling from her horse.

'In . . . my chest. It hurts, Adam. I feel as though I'm on fire.'

'Can you ride on . . .? Get over the mountains?'

He sensed she was shaking her head, but it was too dark to see.

'I don't think I can ride very much farther. Don't let me fall. Adam . . .'

'Oh God . . .!'

'Is something wrong?' The question came from the corporal in charge of the small party.

'My brother's been shot.'

The corporal swore in the darkness. 'How bad is he hurt?'

'Too bad to ride. I'll need to take him on my horse.'

'No. You know the orders.'

Adam knew only too well. The escape across the mountains would be both hazardous and taxing. It had been ordered that if anyone were to be injured, or wounded, he must be left behind.

'Can he ride back? If he surrenders with the others the *khaki* doctors will take care of him.'

'I'm not handing him over to the *khakis*,' Adam declared defiantly. 'Besides, I doubt if he'd make it.'

'Then you'll need to go with him. I'm sorry, but there's too much at stake for the rest of us.'

Adam nodded acceptance of the situation. The order had been necessary. A wounded man – or girl – might cry out in pain on a difficult mountain pass and put the whole escape in jeopardy. But he knew the situation would have been easier to accept had anyone else but Esme been wounded.

'There's a farmhouse less than a mile back. Take him there. They might look after him for you. We've got to go on now. Good luck.' With this, the rider was gone.

'Leave me, Adam. Leave me and ride off with the others. I'll make it to the farm.'

'Of course you will . . . and I'll be with you.' Adam felt Esme sway and he swung her from her horse to his own, surprised by the lack of weight in her body.

The move hurt, but Esme stifled her cry before it escaped.

Soon Adam could make out the faintly lit farmhouse and he headed his horse in that direction. His arm was about Esme and he could feel her warm blood on his hand.

By the time they reached the farmhouse Esme was fast sinking into unconsciousness. After knocking twice at the door, Adam opened it and carried the wounded girl inside.

There were three occupants inside the house. Two women who looked as though they might be mother and daughter, and an old man.

'I've someone here who needs help . . .' No sooner had Adam begun his explanation than the older woman interrupted him.

'We want no trouble here . . . from anyone. You go out and fight your war elsewhere.'

'Ma! It's only a boy and he's hurt bad.' The younger woman

looked anxiously from Esme's blood-soaked shirt-front to her mother.

'It's nothing to do with us. We've lived at peace here with everyone – including the Basuto – for thirty-five years. In a few days' time the Orange Free State army will be gone ... surrendered. The British will remain. We'll need their goodwill if we're to run our farm as we always have. Taking care of a wounded burgher is not the way to get it.'

'My son wouldn't have agreed with you.' The old man spoke for the first time in a thin, tired voice.

'Your son was killed fighting the British fourteen years ago – and what did that achieve? He left me with a daughter to raise and a half-won farm to run. I succeeded with both. I'll not throw everything away now for a stranger.'

While Adam's attention had been on the old man, the younger woman had unbuttoned Esme's shirt and now she gasped in surprise. 'Ma! It's not a boy ... it's a *girl*!'

'A girl! Are you sure?'

The old man started forward, but the older woman planted herself firmly in his way. 'You keep your eyes where they belong, *Oupa*. You'll be meeting the Good Lord before very long. You don't want to add lustful thoughts to all your other sins, not at your age.'

Turning to Adam she asked, 'Did you know?'

Adam nodded. 'She wanted to pay back the British for killing her father.'

The woman snorted. 'Her pa would feel she'd paid them back if he could see her lying at death's door, I'm sure.'

'She's not going to die.' Adam spoke vehemently.

'Oh?' The Boer woman eyed Adam, from his scuffed and broken boots to the crossed ammunition belts with half the pouches empty. 'Suddenly you're a brilliant surgeon and *not* one of Christiaan de Wet's defeated burghers, running from the British?'

'The *khakis* have done their share of running – but I didn't bring Esme here to discuss the war. She needs a doctor. Where can I find one?'

The Boer woman had torn Esme's shirt open and peeled back the wide strip of cloth Esme had bound tight about her breasts to conceal them. The woman frowned. 'The nearest

Afrikaner doctor is at Fouresberg. She'll be dead long before you reach there.'

'There must be someone else. There *has* to be.' Adam could see the blue-tinged bullet wound, oozing blood. He had seen many men die from such a wound, but it distressed him to think of Esme ending her life in this manner.

'There *is* another doctor. A *British* doctor. He's in the camp not a mile away. Take her there and see if he can do something.'

'A *khaki* doctor? And have us both spend the rest of the war in a prison camp?'

'She'll be longer in a grave than you'll be in a prison camp.' The Boer woman's face was expressionless as she looked at Adam.

'There *is* another way. Instead of taking her there, I'll bring the doctor *here*.'

'What . . . and bring us trouble? Oh no you won't!'

'There's a cave half-way up the *kopje*. I'll show you where it is. You can take here there.' The old man started to his feet eagerly.

But the older of the two Boer women was looking down at Esme, and suddenly her face softened. 'You'll do nothing of the sort. All right, young man. Go and fetch your doctor . . . but think of a good story along the way. All I'll admit to is taking her in when you knocked at my door. Is that clear?'

'Yes.' For a few moments Adam looked like any other vulnerable seventeen year old, but he recovered quickly. 'I'll think about that later. The *khakis* will look after her, I don't doubt that . . . but they'll not make a prisoner out of me.'

The British had a field hospital set up in their camp and Adam had no difficulty in finding his way there. Indeed, he was never challenged. However, there was no doctor in the camp, only medical orderlies busily tending their patients, almost all of whom were suffering not from bullet wounds but from illness.

Adam became impatient. Esme lay clinging desperately to life. She needed a doctor's attention – and needed him urgently. He saw the officers' tents and knew the doctor must be here somewhere. Nevertheless, finding him would not be easy.

It was at this moment that he saw Nat.

Surgeon Captain Richard Crawford, attached to Carey Hamilton's hussars, was the same army doctor who had spoken bitterly to Nat of the follies of war when he was treating Cornelius and Lucas Viljoen, after the battle that followed the fall of Pretoria. Captain Crawford treated wounded British and Boer fighting men alike and never tired of telling ayone with time to listen of the futility of such battles. Nat liked the army surgeon and the two men had become good friends during the current campaign.

It was to Captain Crawford that Nat took Adam's request that he treat the wounded Esme.

In his tent the army surgeon frowned. 'Let me hear this again. A girl was out at night and was caught up in a battle between a British patrol and some prowling Boers . . . When and where did this happen?'

'What does all this matter?' asked Adam angrily. 'She needs your help – and she needs it *now*. Are you coming?'

'Will you call another doctor if I say no? Yes, I'll come . . .' The doctor looked at Adam suspiciously. 'All the same, I don't think I am being told all I should know about this young Amazon who goes riding in the dead of night and ends up in the middle of a battle.'

There was nothing Amazonian about Esme Erasmus. The British army surgeon pulled back the blanket and signalled for Nat to bring the candle-lit lamp closer. When the light shone on the slim, still figure, Captain Crawford drew in his breath sharply. 'Why, she's no more than a child! She shouldn't have been out after dark.'

'There was no one to stop her,' said Adam. 'Her mother died when she was a baby and her father was killed when a British soldier shot his horse from under him.'

'It would appear that getting in the way of bullets runs in the family,' said the doctor sarcastically. 'No doubt this one is British too.'

Removing the blood-soaked cloth placed on the wound by the Boer woman, he took the lamp from Adam's hands. 'I'm going to need help, but not from you. Send in the women.'

The elder of the two Boer women entered the room carrying

the contents of her own medicine chest, and Nat suspected that the British army doctor was about to witness something of *voortrekker* medicine.

Not wishing to talk in front of the old man, Nat and Adam went outside and stood in the cold of the clear, starlit night.

'What is the girl to you, Adam?'

Adam shrugged. 'I feel responsible for her, I suppose. When her father willed me his farm he asked me to look after her.'

'Dressing her in a man's clothes and taking her off to war is a strange way of accepting your responsibility.'

'It wasn't my idea. If I hadn't brought her she'd have come anyway. This way I was able to look after her for part of the time, at least.'

'What does your wife think about it?'

Adam's head jerked up in surprise.

'The Viljoens told me. They were in Pretoria. Cornelius and Lucas were both wounded and in hospital.'

'Then you'll know *why* I was married. She trapped me.'

'But it is *your* child she's carrying?'

'So she tells me.' Adam was silent for a few moments before adding grudgingly, 'Yes, it's mine. Margret is many things, but she's not a liar.'

'Where is she now?'

'At my farm, up in the hills.'

'Alone? What if the baby comes early? She's miles from anywhere in those hills.'

'There are hundreds of women in a similar situation ... thousands. She can go back to her family if she doesn't like being alone.' Adam displayed the defiance of a young man who knew he had done something wrong.

'Ma would want her first grandchild to be brought up at Insimo.'

There was another long silence before Adam replied. 'I can't think of Margret's baby as being one of the family. A Retallick. Had I married Johanna it would have been different.'

'Would it have stopped you coming here with Esme?'

'Johanna realises we're fighting a war.'

'It's not the war I'm talking about, Adam. Where does Esme fit into your life?'

'She doesn't. Esme Erasmus goes her own way – and she will

kill any man who thinks otherwise, believe me.'

Nat wondered how it was Adam could speak with such certainty, but he did not pursue the subject. 'What are you going to do when this war ends?'

'I'll think about that when it happens. There is going to be a lot more fighting before then. Fifteen hundred men went out over the mountains tonight. Added to the two thousand six hundred who went with Christiaan de Wet, it makes a good fighting force. Almost the same number are giving up their guns here in the basin, but most of these were ready to stop fighting anyway. How about you? Are you going to carry on scouting for the *khakis*?'

'No, I've had enough of this war. Besides, I don't agree with you. I think the fighting *is* pretty well over now. I began scouting because a *takhaaren* commando raided Insimo. I stayed on in the hope of finding you and persuading you to return to Insimo with me. I'd still like you to come back, Adam. I don't have to tell you how happy it would make Ma.'

'I'm sorry, Nat . . . I really am. But my future is in Transvaal now, whatever happens . . .' Suddenly, Adam said, 'Take Margret back to Insimo with you. Let Ma have her grandchild and bring him up to be a true Retallick. When the war is over I'll decide what to do about Margret . . . and everything.'

The door of the house creaked open and the Boer woman was silhouetted in the dim light of the lantern in the room behind her.

'The girl is conscious. the doctor says you can see her . . . *Doctor*, I say!' She made a disapproving sound with her tongue against the roof of her mouth. 'How he can call himself a "doctor" when he knows nothing of herbs, I don't know. It's no wonder so many British soldiers die here.'

Adam slipped past the woman while she was still talking. By the time Nat reached the place where Esme lay Adam was already assuring her that all was going to be well.

'How is she?' Nat put the question to Surgeon Captain Crawford.

The army doctor shook his head and Adam said, 'You can speak quite freely. Esme doesn't understand English.'

'That explains why I've had no cooperation from her . . .' Looking across the room at Esme who lay still, weak and pale, the doctor continued. 'There's a bullet lodged somewhere inside her that must come out. Until it does her life is very much at risk. Thanks largely to the Boer woman the bleeding has stopped – externally, at least. I dread to think what might be going on inside her.'

Adam rose to his feet and spoke to the army doctor. 'What will happen to her? Is she going to recover?'

'Not without surgery to remove the bullet – and anything else it might have carried inside her. I would expect her to develop a high fever some time in the next twenty-four hours. I'd like her to be in my hospital when this happens. If I can contain the fever I will send her by rail to Durban where there's a hospital ship which carries all the facilities of the most up-to-date city hospital.'

'What will happen to her if she *doesn't* go to your hospital ship? If she stays here with the old lady and her daughter to take care of her?'

'Unless the bullet is found and removed, I believe she will die. I *might* be wrong. I have been before and no doctor is infallible. But I've had an awful lot of experience of bullet wounds since this war began.'

'I believe you.' Adam spoke gruffly. 'Have you told her?'

'I haven't been able to tell her anything. As you just said, she doesn't understand English and I don't speak Afrikaans.'

'I'll tell her, if you like.'

'By all means. I've done all I can here. I'll go back to the camp and arrange to have her taken there. Oh, and if anyone should ask, tell them she was an innocent bystander caught in crossfire between Boers and British soldiers . . . That is true, is it not?'

'Yes . . . and thank you.'

When Adam told Esme what had been decided he expected her to argue against being placed in the care of the British. To demand that Adam arrange something else. But Esme Erasmus was far too weary to fight any more battles. Besides, the opium-based potion given to her by the army doctor was having its effect.

'Will your brother be with me?'

'For a while, I expect, although he's talking of going home to Insimo.'

'What will you do?'

'I'll go over the mountains and join up with the others.'

'When I'm well enough I'll come and find you.'

'No. Go back to the farm. I'll see you there when I return.'

'What of your wife . . . and the baby?'

'Nat is going to take Margret to Insimo. You'll be there on your own, just like before.'

Esme closed her eyes and Adam thought she had gone to sleep, but just as he was about to leave her side, she opened her eyes again.

'Nothing can *ever* be "just as it was before", Adam. Far too much has happened . . .'

Twenty minutes later Adam was riding away, following the path taken by the escaping Boers. Nat had made another attempt to persuade Adam to return to Insimo with him, but Adam remained firm. His future lay with the Boers. Yet now, riding away in the darkness, he felt more alone than he ever had before. Empty. Seeing Nat again had brought back memories of all he had put behind him. His mother; Ben; Insimo . . . Johanna – and tonight it was Johanna he was wanting most of all.

CHAPTER THIRTY-ONE

Orders were received for the wounded and sick soldiers from the Brandwater basin to move off only two days after Esme was wounded. With a great many misgivings, Surgeon Captain Crawford took Esme with them and Nat went along too.

Carey Hamilton travelled with them for part of the way. He had received another promotion, this time to lieutenant-colonel. He was to command a new regiment of mounted infantry, currently at Harrismith, where the hospital train was waiting.

It would be a sad parting in many ways for Nat and Carey Hamilton. They had become good friends during the months they had spent together. Nat admired Carey Hamilton because he was an excellent officer in an army where few rose above mediocrity. Carey Hamilton, in his turn, knew he was losing probably the best scout working for the British army.

The forty-odd mile journey to the rail-head at Harrismith would take the convoy four days, and it would be an uncomfortable journey for Esme and the wounded British soldiers. Mercifully, when they set off Esme had lapsed into a feverish coma, but her condition caused grave concern to Surgeon Captain Crawford.

After the convoy's first halt, the army doctor spoke pessimistically to Nat. 'I will be very surprised if she survives to board the train. With a wound of this type the chances of survival for a strong, fit young man is no more than fifty-fifty. For a young slip of a girl who has obviously been pushing herself far too hard, the odds are far less favourable.'

'Then we'll both need to give her all the help we can,' said

Nat, determinedly. He spoke with more confidence than he felt. He too had seen many die from gunshot wounds and Esme appeared far too fragile to survive such an experience, with the bullet still lodged somewhere inside her body.

Nat felt both a sense of helplessness and an absurd responsibility for this young Afrikaner girl. He felt he would be failing both her *and* Adam if he were to allow her life to ebb away. Yet he had known Esme only briefly, and Adam already had a wife – who was expecting his child in the hills beyond Lichtenburg.

Nat decided he would not contemplate the complications of Adam's life. Instead, he resolved to direct all his efforts towards Esme's eventual recovery.

Tying his horse behind the slow-moving hospital wagon, Nat climbed inside the canvas cover. There was water here and, soaking a towel, Nat laid it across Esme's forehead.

The army wagons had been built to withstand the rigours of a campaign, with no thought of passenger comfort in mind. At the next stop Nat had some of the medical orderlies gather all the dried grass they could find. It would provide a mattress to cushion Esme from the worst jolts, but it was a small comfort and Nat winced on Esme's behalf each time the cumbersome vehicle jolted over another rocky obstacle.

On the third day the convoy crossed a gully where torrential rain had washed out a two-foot deep channel across its path. Most of the drivers managed to slide their wagons gently to the bottom of the channel and call on their soldier-escort to help pull them free.

For some reason this method of crossing did not appeal to the driver of the wagon in which Nat was travelling with Esme. Suddenly whipping up his startled mules, the driver managed to coax them to a trot. His intention seemed to be to use the mule's momentum to pull the wagon up the far side of the gully, unaided by the perspiring, hard-swearing soldiers. He succeeded in his aim, but his choice of a crossing place was unfortunate. The spot he chose had a sheer drop to the bottom of the gully. As the wagon hit the unseen, boulder-strewn ground in the gully bottom, Nat was sent sprawling and Esme was thrown from her improvised bed and landed on top of him.

Shouting furiously at the driver, Nat held the wounded Afrikaner girl while the wagon bounced across the river-bed and up the steep slope on the far side.

When the wagon finally lurched to a halt, the wagon driver turned a white and frightened face towards Nat. 'I'm sorry . . . I wasn't thinking. I'm a transport driver . . . I forgot I was driving an ambulance and not a supply wagon.'

'Shut up and fetch the doctor . . . Quickly, man!'

As the frightened soldier scrambled down from his seat and ran to find Captain Crawford, Nat began unfastening the bandage bound around Esme's body. The jolting, coupled with her fall, had caused the wound to begin bleeding again.

Surgeon Captain Crawford cursed the driver of the wagon soundly as he worked to staunch the blood, but at the same time he expressed satisfaction with the state of the wound.

'There's no obvious sign of infection,' he said as he re-bound the wound. 'But it's what's going on inside that troubles me. If only we could find that damned bullet and remove it.'

When Esme was bandaged once more the wagons resumed their journey and Nat continued his anxious ministrations.

It must have been two hours after the crossing of the gully when Nat first noticed that Esme appeared to be less feverish than before. It was another hour before he was quite certain, and then he called excitedly for Surgeon Captain Crawford.

The army doctor was guarded in his reaction to the unexpected change in Esme's condition.

'Her temperature has certainly gone down,' he agreed, after examining her. 'But it's far too early to assess its significance.'

'You said if her temperature came down she would improve. Well . . . it *is* down.'

'She's lost a lot of blood since I made that statement,' said Captain Crawford. 'It might be that her body no longer has the strength to support a fever.' Seeing Nat's concern, he smiled. 'On the other hand it's also possible that all the jolting she's received has caused the bullet to move slightly, perhaps easing the pressure on some vital organ. It will still have to come out, of course, but she'll be more comfortable in the meantime.'

'How will we know which it is?' Nat was thoroughly confused.

'You'll know. Either she'll regain consciousness and complain of feeling hungry . . . Or she'll die.'

Leaving the stark prognosis hanging in the air behind him, Surgeon Captain Crawford climbed down from the wagon and plodded away to his next problem. The army doctor had left the Brandwater basin with eighty-seven wounded and seriously sick men. Seven had already died along the trail and he was working day and night to save many more.

At the next stop Nat took a bucket to a cold spring that tumbled down from the mountains and replaced the tepid water with which he had been bathing Esme's forehead. Returning to the wagon he climbed inside and placed the bucket on the floor. Not until then did he look up, and he was startled to see Esme watching him.

Her glance shifted to the canvas cover of the wagon above her and, as her eyes widened, Nat explained, 'You're in a hospital wagon, on your way to Harrismith. From there you'll be put on a train and taken to a British hospital ship in Durban.'

Esme's eyes dulled. 'I'm a prisoner. Tell me, was Adam taken too?'

'You're not a prisoner, and neither is Adam.' Nat told Esme all that had happened since the night she was shot.

'Will I be allowed to go free when I'm better?'

'Yes . . . if you don't start boasting of how many *khakis* you've killed.'

Esme lay staring up at the roof of the wagon for a few minutes. Then she said suddenly, 'I'm hungry.'

Nat grinned with relief. If Surgeon Captain Crawford could be believed, Esme was on the mend. He went off to beg some soup from the army cooks, and word that Esme had regained consciousness was quickly passed along the line of stationary wagons. Suddenly it seemed there was a grin on every British face and Nat realised for the first time how much interest there was in the progress of the young, wounded Boer girl.

Feeding Esme was not easy. When Nat tried to lift her to a sitting position she cried out in pain. Surgeon Captain Crawford came to Nat's aid, but there was no way Esme could sit up without suffering excruciating pain. Eventually the two men succeeded in laying Esme back with the upper part of her body raised slightly. In this position she was able to take the soup very slowly.

Afterwards an exhausted Esme went to sleep, and in answer to Nat's question the army doctor explained, 'The bullet must have shifted close to a nerve. It means that every movement is going to prove painful for her and makes the removal of the bullet even more urgent, before it does some permanent damage.'

When the convoy reached Harrismith they found the hospital train waiting in the station. Half the train consisted of open carriages. Into these went the walking wounded, to face an uncomfortable two-day journey to the Indian Ocean port of Durban. Esme was given an officer's compartment to herself in which to travel. Nat was allowed to go with her, but only after considerable argument – and not until it was discovered that no one else on the train spoke Afrikaans.

It was a slow journey to Durban, the two hundred tortuous miles taking twice as long as anticipated, mainly because the train did not travel at night. The scattered Boer forces were re-grouping in small commandos, attacking railroads almost at will. No train anywhere in southern Africa was entirely safe, and in the darkness the large red crosses painted on the hospital train could not be seen.

At every stop medical orderlies came into the carriage to attend to Esme's needs, and each night the army surgeon changed her dressing and checked on her condition.

During the long journey Nat became very fond of the young Afrikaner girl, and she came to rely heavily upon him.

On the last night the train was shunted into a siding at Pietermaritzburg, the capital of Natal. Here the sick and wounded soldiers enjoyed fresh fruit and vegetables, and home-made cakes, sent to them by the ladies of the town. As the cooking-fires burned beside the railway track, those wounded who were able to walk sat around the fires, more contented than they had been for very many months, in spite of their wounds and sickness.

The soldiers expressed their contentment in traditional soldier fashion, by singing. The sound took Nat back to another night, on the Rhodesian veld, when he had shared a fire with Thomasina Vincent. It was the first time he had thought of her for many weeks.

'What are they singing about?' In the carriage lit only by a low-burning oil lamp, Nat had thought Esme asleep.

Nat listened for a while before replying. 'They are Irish soldiers singing about their land, their homes, and the wives and sweethearts they've left behind.'

'Irish? But I thought they were fighting *against* the English and trying to free their own land.'

'Some of them are, I believe.' Nat had only a sketchy knowledge of the affairs of the British Isles. 'Perhaps they just enjoy fighting.'

'You mean like Adam?'

'I think Adam just got tired of farming at Insimo,' said Nat, defensively. 'The war has given him an opportunity to see something of the world outside Matabeleland.'

'*You* don't enjoy fighting?'

Nat shook his head. 'No.' The soldiers were singing one of the songs he remembered from the night at the hot springs now.

'Tell me about Insimo. Adam would never say very much about it to me.'

The Irish soldiers began another song, one that Nat had not heard before, and he asked, 'What is there between you and Adam?'

'Nothing. Certainly not in the way you mean. One day I returned home and found the farm didn't belong to me any more. Pa had given it to Adam. I didn't mind *too* much. I hadn't been spending much time there – and Adam had tried to save Pa's life. For doing that *I'd* have given it to him. Adam and I get along together because we both want to fight *khakis*, that's all.'

'You'd better watch that tongue of yours, young lady. You're in Natal now. Many folk here can understand Afrikaans. If it's learned you were fighting with a commando you'll spend the rest of this war in a prison camp, taking orders from those "*khakis*" you hate so much.'

Esme tried to ease herself into a more comfortable position on her uncomfortable bunk and her body suddenly contorted in pain. Nat quickly put an arm about her and took some of the strain from the tortured muscles.

'*Oh Jesus!*' Some of the pain escaped in Esme's cry. She looked into Nat's face and for a few moments he saw the fear in her eyes. 'What's wrong with me, Nat? Why does it hurt so much.'

'Captain Crawford says the bullet must be touching a nerve somewhere in your body. This is why you're being taken to a hospital ship. They've got some wonderful surgeons on board. They'll be able to put you right.'

'I hope so . . . God! I hope so.'

Gradually the pain-induced tension in Esme's body seeped away and the tortured look left her face. 'Are you going to be in Durban for long, Nat?'

'I'll stay long enough to see you on the mend. Then I'll go back to Insimo.'

'You really love that place, don't you? Adam once said you think more of Insimo than you do of your family.'

The bald statement stung Nat. It stung because he realised it came close to the truth. He had idolised the father who had carved Insimo from virgin land to make it one of the largest and finest farms in southern Africa. When his father and elder brother were stabbed to death by the *assegais* of the Matabele impi, Nat had transferred his love to Insimo, determined to run it as his father might have done. He had succeeded, but it seemed there was a price to be paid.

'I've done my best to run Insimo *for* the family. Just as Pa would have wished.'

Even in the dim light of the carriage Esme could see how much her words had hurt Nat. More gently, she asked, 'Is there anyone waiting for you back at this farm of yours?'

'There's my ma . . . and another brother, Ben.'

'No wife . . . or a girl? Perhaps there isn't room for both Insimo *and* a girl in your life?'

The question came out even though Esme knew it was rubbing salt in the wound she had made by repeating Adam's words. But she wanted to know the answer.

Esme was asking questions about things that were none of her damn business, but Nat controlled the urge to tell her so. 'Insimo's in the middle of nowhere, and not all women want to spend their lives galloping around the veld on a horse, waving a gun . . .'

Nat's outburst tailed away as he remembered how much Thomasina had enjoyed hunting. But Thomasina was in the past. He would probably never see her again.

CHAPTER THIRTY-TWO

Exactly twenty hours later the hospital train steamed slowly into Durban, the steam whistle on the locomotive giving hoarse notification of its arrival. As the train ground to a screeching halt at the siding where the casualties were to be off-loaded, Nat swung the carriage door open – and the first person he saw was Thomasina Vincent.

She appeared to be in charge of a large party of nurses and nursing auxiliaries, directing them to various sections of the train. She was stooping to listen to the query of one of the nursing auxiliaries when she saw Nat standing in the doorway of the carriage.

Thomasina straightened up, all interest in the nursing auxiliary's query forgotten. She stared in disbelief for some seconds. Then, as Nat began to descend the iron steps of the compartment he had shared with Esme, she ran forward to greet him.

'Nat! What a *wonderful* surprise! My dear, what *are* you doing *here*?' Then she was hugging him, her delight at seeing him so unexpectedly causing many raised eyebrows among the interested nursing staff.

Suddenly Thomasina released him and stood back, fear replacing delight. 'Why are *you* on this train? Are you with Carey? Has he been wounded?'

'Carey's fine – and fairly racing up the promotion ladder. He'll be a general by the time the war is over. But how is Digby? Is his arm better . . .?'

The sudden expression of grief that crossed Thomasina's face cut Nat's question short, giving him the tragic answer even before she spoke.

'Digby lost his arm. Then . . . when he was still weak, he caught a fever. He died a week after we reached Durban.'

'I'm sorry, Thomasina. I really am. Digby was a good man . . . a fine officer.'

'Thank you, Nat.' Aware for the first time of the curious stares of the British nursing staff, Thomasina regained control of herself quickly. 'But why *are* you here? You've not been sick?'

'I've come from the Brandwater basin with a young Afrikaner girl who speaks no English. She has a bullet somewhere inside her that needs to be removed as soon as possible.'

'You've travelled all the way from the Brandwater basin with her?'

'Someone had to.'

'I see.' Thomasina was once more the efficient organiser. Calling to an army medical orderly corporal, she snapped, 'There's a girl in here who needs to be taken on board.' Beckoning to a nurse, she said, 'Miss Drake. There's a girl in this compartment. Stay with her and tend to her needs until she's safely on board. Oh . . . and she doesn't speak any English. The Indian orderlies speak Afrikaans. Be sure one of them is among her stretcher bearers.'

Thomasina turned back to Nat. 'Now, let's have a look at this Afrikaner girl of yours.'

With Nat's help Thomasina entered the railway carriage compartment. Nat followed her, noticing for the first time how untidy it was after the long journey from Harrismith.

Looking down at Esme, Thomasina commented, 'Why, she's rather a pretty little thing – but she could do with some fattening-up. What's her name?'

'Esme. Esme Erasmus. She's from the Lichtenburg area, but was shot while she was with friends in the Brandwater basin.'

'I see.' Thomasina realised that Nat was not telling her everything, but she gave a mental shrug. There was no reason why he should.

Nat knew this unexpected reunion with Thomasina was going wrong, and he desperately wanted things to be right between them. He wondered whether he should tell her the truth about Esme – but he immediately dismissed the thought.

Thomasina would feel obliged to tell the army authorities. He could not do that to Esme.

Tucking the blanket tidily about Esme, Thomasina said, 'You're in safe hands now. Once we have you on board the surgeons will find that bullet and have you well in no time, you'll see.' Thomasina had said similar words of comfort to hundreds of wounded men during the past few weeks.

Nat translated Thomasina's words, and as Esme studied the older woman's face, he added, 'Thomasina will take good care of you, Esme. She'll see you have the best possible care.'

'You know her?' Esme's eyes widened as she gazed up at Nat. Looking at Thomasina again, she said, 'She's beautiful, Nat. *Really* beautiful. But I can't imagine her settling down to life on a remote farm. Not even one as wonderful as Insimo.'

'What is the girl saying?'

'Esme thanks you for your words of comfort. She also thinks you're beautiful . . .' Nat hesitated. 'So do I, Thomasina.'

Thomasina looked at him sharply and Nat thought he had gone too far. At that moment a party of stretcher bearers arrived at the compartment door with the nurse detailed by Thomasina to take care of Esme.

As the men crowded into the cramped compartment, Nat said, 'Be very careful how you lift her. The bullet's lying on a nerve. It causes her great pain.'

'Don't you worry, sir. I've lifted hundreds of wounded men. *Thousands*. This young 'un will be no problem. Why, she can't weigh no more than a rasher of bacon . . .'

Before Nat realised his intentions, the orderly put his arms beneath Esme and lifted her from the hard train bunk.

Esme's scream of pain would have unnerved a more sensitive man, but the stretcher bearer was used to the screams of wounded men. As Esme writhed in agony in his arms, he lifted her from the carriage and laid her on a stretcher.

His clumsy task completed, the orderly looked up at Nat. 'It isn't as bad as it seems, sir . . . and it's better to have it all done with at once, if you understand . . .'

But Nat was kneeling beside Esme. She was fighting for breath as her body contorted with pain. The stir caused by Esme's screaming brought Surgeon Captain Crawford running to the scene.

'What the devil's going on here?' He made no apology for his language to Thomasina, pushing her to one side in his haste to reach Esme.

'One of the orderlies lifted her bodily from the carriage . . .'

'Lifted? It sounds as though he threw her out.'

'I did my best, sir . . .'

'Your best, man? Get out of my sight. Go and offload ammunition . . . or stores – anything! But don't you *dare* to touch another of my patients.'

As the still-apologising medical orderly backed away, Surgeon Crawford took a hypodermic syringe from his bag, checked the contents, then injected the needle into Esme's arm.

Gradually the injection took effect, and as Esme's writhing subsided, the army doctor stood up, saying, 'Too many incidents like this and the shock will kill her. We'll need to find that bullet quickly, but I fear it won't be easy.'

'Perhaps easier than you think,' declared Thomasina. Having witnessed Esme's very real pain she had lost her faint air of indifference and had held the Afrikaner girl's hand very tightly while the morphine injection was being administered, at the same time murmuring sympathetic, albeit unintelligible words to the young, wounded girl. 'We have some marvellous machines on board the hospital ship. They can actually look inside the body and show where a bullet is lying.'

'X-ray machines? I can hardly believe it! Up at the front we're desperately short of everything – sometimes no drugs of any kind – yet here you are with *X-ray machines*! I've said it before, this is a crazy war! Will you see the girl is taken on board as quickly as possible? She's having a hard time.'

As Surgeon Captain Crawford walked away shaking his head, Esme called to Nat.

Thomasina stood away as the Afrikaner girl reached up and clutched Nat's arm. 'What's happening? What are they going to do with me?'

Nat told Esme about the hospital ship and did his best to explain the X-ray machine – something about which he had no knowledge at all.

'Will you stay with me . . . please?'

It was the first time he had seen beneath the veneer of total indifference she showed to all that went on about her.

'Don't worry, Thomasina or a nurse will never be far away.'

'I don't want them. I want *you*.' Esme's grip on his arm tightened. 'Please, Nat ... You promised Adam you would take care of me ...'

'All right. I'll stay around for as long as they'll let me. Just you hurry up and get well, that's all.'

Esme released her hold on his arm and her eyes closed. After a few minutes she opened them again and focused on him with some difficulty as the morphine took its course. 'It's hard to think of you and Adam as brothers.' She was drowsily enigmatic. 'You are different ... Very different.' Closing her eyes, Esme slipped away into sleep, her breathing coming deeply and easily.

'That was a touching little scene.' Thomasina was unusually tight-voiced as she waved up some Indian stretcher bearers. 'You need not worry, your young friend will receive excellent care on board the *Maine*. It has more facilities than any shore hospital in Africa.'

'Good, she's been in a lot of pain. But Esme's not *my* friend. My brother asked me to take care of her ... But this is neither the time nor the place to talk about it.'

'I'm sorry, Nat. I had no right to make any comment. No right at all.'

One of the stretcher bearers put a question to Thomasina and she said, 'She's to go to a private ward. The one nearest the Sister's quarters ...'

Before Thomasina could return her attention to Nat another orderly came to her with a list of names in his hand.

As Esme was carried away, Nat began to follow. But Thomasina broke off her conversation with the orderly and came after him, 'She'll be all right, Nat – I promise you. Besides, the morphine will put her out for a long time and I will ensure you are called the moment you are needed. Where will you be staying while you are in Durban?'

'I don't know. I haven't had time to think about it yet.'

'Find your way to the house of Madame Claris. She takes the occasional paying guest and you'll find it far more comfortable than any hotel. You had better tell her I sent you or she might think you belong to some Boer raiding-party.'

Catching his reflection in the carriage window, Nat knew Thomasina was right. Just before the train had pulled in to

Durban Nat had donned his crossed bandoliers and he was carrying a Mauser rifle, of the type used by the Boers.

Giving Nat one of her most dazzling smiles, Thomasina said, 'We'll have dinner together tonight and you can tell me what you and Carey have been up to.'

The house occupied by Madame Claris was a two-storey wooden structure set among low trees, beyond which could be glimpsed the blue sea, fringed by sun-bleached sand.

A coloured girl opened the door to Nat, but she would not allow him to cross the threshold. Nervously eyeing the way he was dressed, she ordered him to wait while she fetched her mistress.

A few minutes later Nat heard voices raised in rapid French drawing nearer along an unseen corridor. Then the largest woman Nat had ever seen filled the doorway in front of him. Nat was six feet tall, but the woman looked down at him. Her girth more than matched her height and Nat estimated she weighed more than three hundred pounds.

Contrasting strangely with her vast bulk, her voice was unusually soft. 'I am Madame Claris. You wish to see me?'

'Yes. I understand you take paying guests. I am in Durban for a while . . .'

'I am so sorry. *Every* room is taken. Even if my poor, dear husband were to return to me tonight I would have to send him away.'

'Can you suggest anywhere else I could try?'

The huge woman spread her hands wide. 'Closer to the docks, perhaps? There are many hotels there. You will find something to suit your pocket, I do not doubt.'

Nat lifted his saddlebags from the ground. They were heavy because he had stowed his ammunition belts inside one of them. As he slung the bags over his shoulder he suddenly remembered Thomasina's last words to him.

'Can you give Thomasina Vincent a message for me?'

'*You* know Thomasina?'

Eyeing Nat from head to toe, Madame Claris expressed her disbelief.

'She recommended that I try to get a room here. We were hoping to have dinner together tonight. I've just arrived from the Brandwater basin on the hospital train.'

'You have come from the war? But you are not in uniform.'

'I'm a scout. I've been working with Thomasina's brother.'

'A scout! But of course. Come in, do not stand out here. Henrietta . . . tell Thadeus to take the gentleman's bags upstairs. To the *best* room. The one with a bath.'

As Nat wondered what was going on, Madame Claris reached out a great hand and literally dragged him inside the house, at the same time relieving him, with unbelievable ease, of his heavy saddlebags.

'But . . . you said you were full.'

'That is before I know you are a friend of Thomasina. You have known each other long?' The Frenchwoman asked the question as she steered Nat firmly towards a flight of wide stairs that spilled into an impressive, high-ceilinged hall.

'We met when I guided her from Umtali to Fort Victoria – in Rhodesia. Later she stayed at our farm . . .'

'Of course, I should have guessed before. You are Nat Retallick.'

Madame Claris stopped on the stairs and, cupping Nat's face in her hands as though he were a young child, kissed him enthusiastically on both cheeks. 'Thomasina has spoken of you very often. So many times I have wished you would come to Durban. She is so unhappy. The death of her husband, you understand? Now you are here. This will be your room. You like it?'

Madame Claris held open a door and Nat entered. It was a large room, somewhat feminine in décor, with much chequered gingham in evidence and two large french windows opening to a wide balcony from which there were magnificent views of the sandy coastline.

'It's a beautiful room . . .' Remembering her words of only a few minutes before, Nat grinned. 'But I don't want to deprive your husband of a bed, Madame Claris.'

The large Frenchwoman snorted. 'My husband ran off ten years ago, with a Zulu girl young enough to be his daughter. No doubt they suited each other well. Zulu women are used to working hard while a good-for-nothing husband lounges around waiting to be fed. Simon is now probably squatting around some smoky fire surrounded by half-caste brats, waiting for his woman to return from the fields and brush the flies from him. I am well rid of him. If ever he has the courage to return to me I will break him into tiny pieces and feed him to the dogs.'

The tirade over, Madame Claris shrugged apologetically. 'Yet I still miss him! I am a stupid woman, no?'

Suddenly she smiled. 'But today is not for the reminiscences of an old woman. *You* have arrived in Durban. Perhaps tonight I will hear Thomasina laugh again.'

An hour later Nat lay back in a deep slipper-bath, filled for him by a grumbling Zulu garden-boy. The house servant had been sent off to the Indian shops to buy new clothes, taking Nat's threadbare shirt and trousers as a size guide. After almost a year spent scouting on the veld Nat was in desperate need of new clothes – and a bath. Nat carried no money with him, but he did have letters of credit from the British South Africa Company's bank. He would have no difficulty in obtaining all he needed whilst in Durban.

The grumbling garden-boy was mollified when he discovered Nat spoke Ndebele, the language of the Matabele and a dialect of the Zulu language. Through him Nat learned much about Madame Claris and her household. As Nat had already suspected, inside her large, man-size body there was the heart of a kind and generous woman. It came as no surprise to learn that he was the only guest in the house. A room was kept for Thomasina, but it seemed she spent most nights on board the hospital ship. It appeared that Madame Claris was very selective about her guests. Those she took were usually non-paying friends.

Thomasina was late arriving for dinner and Nat spent a long time talking to Madame Claris. She asked a great many questions, ostensibly about the progress of the war, but by the time Thomasina's carriage drew up at the door of the house the Frenchwoman knew a great deal about her latest guest.

Thomasina looked very tired. Helping the occupants of the train to settle in on board the hospital ship had kept her very busy.

Nat's first question was about Esme – and Thomasina's reply took him by surprise. 'The operation to remove the bullet has been performed – and it was entirely successful. The X-ray machine located the bullet lodged against her right shoulder-blade. It clipped the bone and the surgeon who carried out the operation believes it was this that caused her so much pain.'

'They operated so soon? But she wanted me to be with her. I must go . . .'

'It would be a waste of time, Nat. They operated before the morphine had time to wear off properly. Esme would not have known whether or not you were there. She was sleeping soundly when I left the hospital and the surgeon assures me she will not wake until some time tomorrow morning. You can see Esme then. In the meantime I suggest you relax and enjoy Madame Claris's cooking. I can assure you it is the finest in Durban.'

'Esme? Who is this Esme?'

Madame Claris looked from Thomasina to Nat. She had made 'plans' for the couple who shared her table. Those plans did not include an 'Esme'.

'You'll need to ask Nat that question,' replied Thomasina. 'All I know is that she is an Afrikaner he brought from the Brandwater basin with a serious bullet wound. He claims she is a friend of his brother, but I sense some mystery.'

'This "Esme" . . . how old is she?'

Nat shrugged. 'Fifteen . . . sixteen perhaps. No more.'

'Why, she is no more than a child!' Relief cleared the furrows from Madame Claris's brow. 'But you say she was shot? Who would shoot a child . . . and what is this mystery?'

Nat had decided to keep the secret of Esme's involvement in the war to himself. It would not be fair to share it with these two women.

'My brother is fighting with the Boer forces. He risked his life to come and find me and ensure that Esme received medical attention. She has no parents. Her mother died when Esme was young and her father has been killed in the war. He left his farm to my brother because he risked his life to save him on the battlefield.'

'This girl and your brother . . . They are in love? They will marry one day?'

'No, my brother is already married.' Nat saw Thomasina's surprise and realised he would have to give an explanation. 'It seems the marriage was forced upon him by the other girl's relatives. She is expecting his child.'

This time it was the turn of Madame Claris to raise her eyebrows. 'How old is your brother?'

'Seventeen.'

Madame Claris's eyes opened wide in disbelief; then she laughed. 'So young! Yet he fights the British, risks his life for a young girl . . . and still finds time to father a child by someone else. Such a young man I dreamed of finding when I was a girl. Instead I found Simon Claris. No matter. This Esme . . . What will become of her when she leaves the hospital ship?'

'I hope to be able to send her back to the Lichtenburg area. Perhaps I'll take her there myself, on my way to Insimo.'

'You are returning to Insimo?' The question came from Thomasina.

'As soon as I can . . . Come with me. Ma would enjoy having you there, I know.'

'Excuse me . . .' Madame Claris levered herself from her chair. 'I think I am needed in the kitchen.'

As the Frenchwoman retreated from the room, Thomasina smiled. 'Madame Claris is a romantic, Nat. She sees you as a knight in gleaming armour, riding in to rescue me from the tower I have built around myself since poor Digby died.'

'The colonel was a good man. He wouldn't have wanted you to mourn him for ever.'

'No.'

Nat waited for Thomasina to say more, but as the silence grew with time, he urged, 'I issued an invitation to you.'

'I know . . . Thank you, but I'll need to think about it.'

'I'm happy to wait for an answer . . . as long as it's "Yes".'

'We shall see.' Thomasina looked across the table, and when she smiled he could see the tiredness in her eyes. 'It *is* good to see you again, Nat. Truly it is.'

'I'll take encouragement from that and just sit here and look at you. It's better than sitting around a camp-fire thinking about you.'

Changing the subject quickly, Thomasina said, 'Tell me about that brother of mine . . . and all the things you have done together since you rode away from Insimo.'

While Nat was speaking Madame Claris returned to the room and listened to his story of the battles being waged in Transvaal and the Orange Free State. Later, when Thomasina announced she was going to bed, Madame Claris kept Nat talking for many minutes, asking questions about Pretoria, where she had lived for two years with Simon, her errant husband.

When Nat finally escaped to his room he found the oil-lamp burning low and smoking, the servant-girl having forgotten to fill it. Cupping his hands over the glass, Nat blew out the low and ragged flame. There was a smell of paraffin fumes in the room and Nat went to the window to draw the curtains and open one of the french windows. As he was about to turn back into the room he saw a movement on the balcony.

During the months he had spent on the veld Nat's life had often depended upon a quick reaction, and he instinctively dropped to a crouch.

'Who's there?' His hoarse question silenced a noisy cricket which was serenading the world from the bougainvillaea entwined about the balcony.

A soft voice replied. 'I'm glad you asked first, Nat. After some of the experiences you've been through you couldn't be blamed for shooting instead of questioning.'

It was Thomasina.

Embarrassed, Nat said, 'I'm sorry, I didn't expect anyone to be out here. My lamp has been smoking and I opened the window to let the smell out.'

'Ugh! I hate the smell of paraffin smoke. Your room will be uninhabitable for a while. Sit here and talk to me.'

As he stepped on to the balcony Nat saw another door next to his own and the faint glow of a lamp beyond the heavy curtains. He had not realised Thomasina's room was next to his own.

Thomasina sat on a cushioned wickerwork settee. There was no other seating and, feeling slightly self-conscious, Nat sat down beside her.

'I thought you were feeling tired?' There was an attr ive aroma of cologne about her.

'I am. But whenever I stay with Madame Claris I always come out here for a few minutes before going to bed. I draw much peace and comfort from looking at the sea in the moonlight.'

Beyond the trees the iron-grey sea was crossed by a silver path that led to the low-hanging moon.

'It is beautiful,' Nat agreed, '. . . but, then, so is Insimo.'

Thomasina reached out and touched his arm. 'Give me time, Nat. So much has happened to me since we last met.'

'I'm offering you all the time in the world, Thomasina. A lifetime. *My* lifetime.'

'Please don't say any more, Nat. Not now.'

Her hand was still resting on his arm, but when Nat tried to take it she moved it away. They sat side by side without speaking for perhaps ten minutes, then Thomasina said softly, 'I am going to my room now. Thank you for understanding, Nat.'

Nat rose to his feet and stood facing her in the darkness, awkwardly silent.

Leaning forward, Thomasina kissed him gently on the cheek. 'Good night, Nat.'

Before she could turn away, he reached out and pulled her to him.

'No, Nat . . .'

He kissed her clumsily on the lips and for the briefest of moments it seemed to him she responded. Then she broke free. She looked up at him as though she were about to speak. Instead, she turned and hurried to the open door of her room. Light sliced from the room to the balcony as the curtain was drawn aside. Then the door closed and Thomasina was gone.

Nat sat on the balcony for a long time, gathering his scrambled emotions into some semblance of order, and nursing a childish and forlorn hope that Thomasina might return to him.

CHAPTER THIRTY-THREE

Nat was awoken the next morning by the sound of a light carriage being driven away from the house. Then the deep voice of the grandfather clock in the passageway outside his room informed him that it was eight o'clock. He was accustomed to rising at dawn on the veld, and this was the longest sleep Nat had enjoyed since leaving Insimo. He felt drowsy and heavy-footed as he made his way across the room and drew the curtains.

With sunlight filling the room, Nat looked out on the balcony and beyond it to the sun-painted sea filling the horizon. He winced, partly at the brilliance of the day, but chiefly as he remembered the previous evening out here on the balcony. Thomasina probably despised him for his inexperience and the clumsy attempt at courtship.

The glass door and curtains to Thomasina's room stood wide open, but the room was occupied only by Madame Claris's coloured servant-girl. She was making up the bed.

Downstairs the breakfast table was laid for only one and Madame Claris informed Nat that Thomasina had already left. The carriage that had awoken him had taken her to the docks where the hospital ship was berthed.

'You are not to hurry to the hospital ship,' Madame Claris told him as he began his breakfast. 'Thomasina says Esme will not wake early and the ship will be very busy. There are many operations to be performed, bullets to be removed and limbs needing amputation . . .' The three-hundred-pound body shook in an alarming fashion as Madame Claris shuddered. 'It is tragic that so many young men should be disfigured in such a manner.'

'Thomasina is all right this morning.'

Madame Claris's eyebrows posed their own question long before she spoke. 'There is some reason why she should *not* be all right?'

Doing his best to hide the confusion he felt, Nat said, 'No . . . I thought she looked very tired last night, that's all.'

'Thomasina works too hard. It is as though the memory of her husband demands it of her. You knew him?'

'I was with him when he was wounded.'

'Then you too will know he was a kind man. He would not want her to lose herself in work, but to find a new life.' Madame Claris gave an expansive gesture of helplessness. 'I have told her so, many times. But does she listen to me? No . . . Perhaps she will listen to you?'

'I doubt it, but I'll try again. She could find a new life at Insimo.'

'This Insimo . . .? It is a farm? Thomasina is not a farm girl.'

'It is a farm . . . but no *ordinary* farm.'

'Ah! But then Thomasina is no ordinary woman.'

When Nat set off to visit Esme after breakfast Madame Claris was in the hall waiting. She intended visiting Esme with him. When he asked why, she shrugged the question off.

'Why not? This young girl is alone among people who do not speak her language. I understand better than most how she feels. I also know what it is to be hurt. Come, Dingaan has the carriage waiting at the door.'

Madame Claris's carriage was a heavy, old-fashioned conveyance, of a type that had been fashionable in Europe more than fifty years before. The coachman too had seen better days. Wearing clothes that might have fitted the man he had once been, 'Dingaan' was the aged garden-'boy'. The name of the once-famous Zulu chief fitted him no better than the suit he wore, while his standard of driving provided ample proof that this was a role he seldom filled.

During an incident-filled ride through the heart of Durban, Madame Claris raised her hand in limp-wristed salute to bemused fellow-travellers and pedestrians, at the same time informing Nat that one of the reasons she seldom left her home was because she had become so well known in the town that travelling abroad had become a chore. The next moment she was on her feet berating an innocent fellow-traveller who had the temerity to complain because his pony-trap had been forced off the road by the incompetent driving of Dingaan.

Nat was relieved when they reached the dockside, but there was another hurdle to be overcome before they were able to visit Esme. The gangway between the shore and the hospital ship was too narrow for the Frenchwoman's girth. She eventually made her way on board via the gangway used to load stores.

Once on board the *Maine*, the efficiency of the administering authority showed itself everywhere. According to the orderly who was acting as their guide, this was due to the organising ability of Thomasina.

Nat was disappointed that Thomasina had not come to meet them personally, but the orderly explained that Thomasina Vincent was extremely busy. There were more wounded and sick men on board than had been expected and one of the ship's holds was being fitted out to provide an extra ward.

A white-coated surgeon was leaving Esme's cabin when Nat and Madame Claris arrived. In answer to Nat's question about Esme's condition, the surgeon stepped back inside the cabin ahead of them.

Esme lay on her side in a wooden-sided bunk. She was in a deep sleep. Stepping to a locker at the side of the bunk, the doctor held up a short, slightly misshapen round-nosed bullet.

'Here's the chap that caused all the trouble. I don't often remove one of *these* from my patients. It's a revolver bullet. A *British* bullet. From a Webley pistol, unless I'm mistaken.'

'She was caught in a crossfire. The bullet could have come from either side,' lied Nat.

'To cause the damage inflicted by this bullet it would have had to be fired at point-blank range. I find it difficult to believe that even the most short-sighted soldier could have mistaken this young girl for a *man*!'

'The Boers were trying to break out of the Grandwater basin at night. With small battles going on everywhere it was total confusion.'

'You were there?'

'Yes, scouting for Colonel Hamilton.'

'Carey Hamilton? Thomasina Vincent's brother?'

Nat nodded and the doctor allowed the bullet to drop with a metallic sound into the dish on the locker. 'Well ... you should know what happened, I suppose.'

'Is she going to be all right?'

'Yes. I removed a small chip of bone at the same time. There will be some pain for a day or two, but then she'll be as right as rain. There's not much of her, but I don't doubt she's as tough as leather. Most of these Boer girls are.'

'She's a *beautiful* little thing!' Bending as low over the bunk as her bulk would allow, Madame Claris was gazing down at Esme with a look of utmost tenderness on her face.

'When will she wake?' Nat asked.

'Not for a couple of hours,' replied the surgeon. 'She came round briefly this morning, but I gave her something to deaden the pain and it will make her sleep.'

'You go off and find Thomasina. I'll sit here with the child until she wakes.' The suggestion came from Madame Claris.

'I really should be here,' said Nat. 'Esme doesn't speak English and there might be something she needs.'

'You think you are the only one in Durban who speaks both English and Afrikaans?' Madame Claris asked the question in passable Afrikaans. 'Go and find Thomasina. From all you have told me about Esme it's high time she had a feminine influence in her life.'

Nat left the cabin reluctantly. Asleep in the ship's cabin, Esme looked angelic. Awake, confused and perhaps angry she was quite capable of swearing as coarsely as any *takhaar*.

Thomasina was in the partly converted hold. Work on it was still going on, but already patients were being wheeled in, most having lost shattered limbs in the ship's operating theatre.

Thomasina looked tired, but she showed genuine pleasure when she saw him. 'Nat! How nice to see you here ... but of course, you've come to see your little Afrikaner girl. How is she? I looked in on her when I came on duty, but she was sleeping.'

'The surgeon says she's going to be fine. She's still sleeping but Madame Claris is with her.'

'Really? Then your little friend *is* honoured. Madame Claris rarely leaves her house these days, but I know she was intrigued by what you said about Esme last night.'

Looking at Thomasina, crisp and clean in her own highly individualistic version of a nurse's 'uniform', Nat felt slightly over-awed. 'About what I was saying last night . . .'

'Last night was a delightful reunion.' Thomasina interrupted him before he put his thoughts in order. 'It is a great relief to me to know you are safely away from the fighting. I will be happy when I can say the same about Carey. While you are here I hope to be able to show you something of Durban. It is a very pleasant town. Unfortunately I am going to be extremely busy for some while . . .'

She might have been talking to a casual acquaintance she had not seen for some years.

'Thomasina, last night I asked you to come back to Insimo with me . . .'

'Nat, you and I are both lonely and far from home. You have been fighting in a dreadful war that is not of your making. I see the results of this war every day in the men who come here maimed and badly wounded. The war has taken my husband and I have a constant fear that it will take my brother from me too. Our meeting reminded us both of happier times and of those we love, or have loved. That was all.'

'It was more than that . . .'

'No, Nat.' Thomasina was her most efficient and aloof best. 'Look around you. Do you think I can walk away from this? Go to Insimo and forget the war?'

'Will you come when you are not so busy?'

'Perhaps.'

'Will I see you tonight, at dinner?'

'No. I'll need to stay on board until all the operations come to an end and the casualties are well on the road to recovery.'

'I see.'

Nat fought hard to hide his disappointment. He had thought about their relationship for much of the night. He had never met anyone quite like Thomasina. He doubted whether he ever would. Yet he found it impossible to break through the barrier she had built around herself and find the woman he knew was inside.

Just then a nursing sister with a disapproving expression came to Thomasina complaining that some locally-purchased bed-linen was of poor quality. With a brief apology to Nat, Thomasina went off to inspect it for herself. As he waited for her return a number of noisy soldiers clattered into the hold carrying sections of iron beds between them. It seemed they wanted to put them up everywhere Nat chose to stand.

After shifting his position four times, Nat accepted defeat. Thomasina was still with the stern-faced nursing sister, but now they were surrounded by nurses and auxiliaries.

Nat left the chaos of the ship's hold behind him and went ashore. His low spirits might have received a much-needed boost had he seen the disappointment on Thomasina's face when she finally freed herself from the attentions of the nursing sister and discovered he had gone.

For a few unguarded moments, Thomasina Vincent, the brisk and efficient widow of a senior army officer, was a lonely and vulnerable young woman.

Nat walked about the busy Durban dock area for two hours. The docks were filled with ships of every description. Supply vessels from India and Great Britain; merchantmen bringing horses from South America; and a wide variety of vessels flying the flags of almost every maritime nation of the world.

In spite of his preoccupation with Thomasina, Nat could not fail to be impressed by the staggering quantities of materials and men coming through this port alone, all on its way to the battlefields far to the north. He wished he could bring Adam and some of the Boer leaders here to witness the scale of the British war effort. It might convince them of the folly of prolonging the war. Great Britain's resources were virtually unlimited. In the end they *must* win.

Thinking of Adam brought Nat's thoughts back to his reason for being in Durban. Retracing his steps, he returned to the hospital ship and made his way to Esme's cabin.

To his surprise Esme was awake. Even more surprising her hand was clasped very firmly in Madame Claris's grasp and the Frenchwoman was talking earnestly to her.

When Esme saw Nat her face lit up in a smile that deserved more than Nat's half-hearted response. Madame Claris had her back to him when he entered the sick room, but Esme's sudden smile brought the Frenchwoman's head around. When she saw the reason for Esme's sudden delight Madame Claris looked momentarily concerned. But she recovered quickly. Patting Esme's hand, she spoke accusingly to Nat, in English.

'Why did you not prepare me for such a *delightful* child? After all I had heard I came here expecting someone who would swear like a British soldier and look at least a *little* like President Kruger. Instead I have found a beautiful and gentle child.'

'You should see her on a horse, with a gun in her hands.'

'Such things are in the past.' Gripping Esme's hand tightly, Madame Claris talked in Afrikaans. 'I am going to teach Esme to be a young lady. As soon as she is fit enough to move she will be coming home with me.'

Nat frowned. In English he said, 'You don't know what you're taking on. This is no sick child in need of a mother's love. She's a wild young woman who is used to going her own way.'

'And what do you understand of the need for a mother's love? You have always taken it for granted. Besides, there is nothing wrong with going one's own way – just so long as it is the *right* way. This child has had no one to tell her about this. No mother – and a father who never cared what she did, or where she went. I will teach her that life has its rules, the same as everything else. Whether or not she keeps to them will be up to her. At least she will *know* them.'

Releasing Esme's hand, Madame Claris pushed herself up from the chair with some difficulty. Resting her large hand gently on Esme's head, the Frenchwoman said, 'You must not worry about anything, child. We will have you out of here in no time at all.'

'I hope she doesn't break your heart, Madame Claris.' Nat spoke in English once more.

'I don't doubt she'll break a great many hearts,' snapped the Frenchwoman, '. . . and mine has been broken many times before. Now, where is Thomasina's office? I want Esme off this ship as soon as it can be arranged.'

Madame Claris ducked out through the cabin doorway and lumbered off along the corridor on her quest.

When she had gone, Nat turned to Esme. 'Why have you agreed to stay with Madame Claris? You're not a town girl. You won't be happy in Durban.' He spoke almost angrily and Esme responded accordingly.

'Why should you care what I do? You've just spent the last couple of hours with your fine Thomasina. Madame Claris told me. Go back to her, and leave me alone.' Esme turned her face into the pillow.

'You haven't answered my question,' Nat persisted. 'What do you hope to gain by staying here with Madame Claris?'

'You needn't worry, I won't interfere with *you*, and you won't need to feel any responsibility for me, neither. Anyway, there was nothing else I *could* do. The army won't let me go back to Lichtenburg. If I hadn't agreed to go and live with Madame Claris the *khakis* would have put me into a camp as soon as I was well enough to leave. Made me a prisoner.'

'A prisoner? What are you talking about? I've told no one here you were fighting them.'

'It has nothing to do with fighting. One of the Indian orderlies told me of the new British policy. They're rounding up all the women and children who live on the veld in Transvaal and the Orange Free State and putting them into camps. Then they're burning their farms behind them. That's the side you're fighting for. The *khakis* can't break our people, so they're destroying our country.'

CHAPTER THIRTY-FOUR

In the lonely hill farm in Transvaal the newly wed and recently deserted Margret Retallick almost gave up a number of times during her first few days alone. Once she actually packed her belongings and set off in the direction of the Lichtenburg settlement. Then, when she was a mile from the farmhouse, she stopped and looked back. She saw the farm as Adam must first have seen it. Backed by rising hills and dwarfed by its environment, it echoed the independent character of the man who had carved it from these remote hills. It typified the doggedness of his people. Farms like this were dotted in remote valleys all across southern Africa. Men had trekked hundreds of miles to such places, they and their families suffering and sometimes dying in the seeking. Many more had died – and were still dying in their desperate fight to keep the way of life of their own choosing.

Margret saw the fences re-built by Adam. The new thatch on the farmhouse and his unfinished attempt to clear a paddock from the undergrowth at the side of the house. Suddenly Margret knew she could not go. This was Adam's home. One day he would return. If she were not here he would not come looking for her – and not one of her relatives who had forced Adam into marriage would expect him to. When a man left his farm and went to war it was his wife's *duty* to take care of the property, no matter how remote or ramshackle it might be.

Margret shifted the position of the bundle on her shoulder. It was heavy – but the baby filling her belly was heavier. It was Adam's child, and Margret remembered her earlier determination that it would grow under the eye of both its mother *and* its father.

She retraced her footsteps, slowly at first, but as she drew closer to the house her resolve increased. She *would* remain on the farm. What was more, she would *improve* it. Adam would have no cause for complaint when he returned from the war.

The first task Margret set herself was to complete the clearing and fencing of a paddock. Then she took the old musket from the barn and went into the hills to locate the cows. Adam had said they were here, but it took her three days and two terrifyingly lonely nights to locate them. She was stalked by a leopard and bitten by a snake — which, fortunately, resulted in nothing more than a painful swelling. Then she became hopelessly lost for the whole of one exhausting day, but she located the cattle and returned to the farm driving a cow and its week-old calf before her.

Gradually, over the next couple of months, Margret brought a degree of orderliness to the farm. She collected seed from the vegetables hidden amongst the thick, tough weeds and hacked out a sizeable vegetable garden. She also completed re-building some of the dilapidated outhouses and began to feel a fierce pride in her achievements.

Then one morning Margret heard the terrified bleating of the calf. Snatching the gun from its new place on the shelf above the fireplace, she ran outside. She was horrified to see two natives plunging their spears into the calf as it lay quivering on the hard earth of the paddock.

When she shouted both natives turned in her direction. All they saw was a lone woman standing outside the farmhouse, and, raising his spear, one of the natives ran towards her.

Margret had fired guns before, but never at a human target. She raised the gun and fixed the native in the sights. But she hesitated. The native stopped when he saw her raise the gun; then, encouraged by her obvious reluctance to shoot, he shouted triumphantly and ran forward once more.

When she squeezed the trigger there was a loud report and the gun spewed black powder smoke. When it cleared the native was sprawled on the ground. As she watched he clawed himself to a sitting position and clasped his hands to his stomach. His hands came away glistening in blood. The native stared at the blood in disbelief. Then he began screaming.

Margret ran back into the house for the power-horn and shot. Reloading the gun with shaking hands she returned to the door. The second native must have begun running when he heard the shot. He was almost out of range now, but as Margret aimed she remembered the teachings of her father. Raising the end of the barrel to compensate for distance, she squeezed the trigger.

When the smoke cleared the native was still running, but faster now. The musket ball had passed close enough to put the fear of death into him.

Still clutching his stomach, the first native lay on his side now, his screaming reduced to a dying moan.

Advancing to the paddock, Margret kept well clear of the wounded man. Her concern was for the calf, but it was beyond all help.

That evening Margret brought the cow to the shed alongside the house and dragged the body of the calf to the kitchen. Here she skinned it and cut the carcass into pieces. The hide would provide her with her first carpet, while the meat of the unfortunate animal would be a very welcome addition to her meagre diet.

The native was dead now, his body clearly stiffening, but Margret did not go near him. After eating some of the calf meat and putting what scant furniture there was in the house against the two doors, she sat up all night in the darkness of the kitchen, the loaded musket resting on her lap.

The next day Margret plucked up the courage to approach the dead native. Something had to be done with him, but as she leaned over his body a cloud of flies rose angrily in the air. Margret stumbled a few paces away from the carcass and was painfully sick.

She did not go near the dead man again, but that afternoon unexpected salvation arrived in the person of her sister Gezima, in the company of the Viljoen family.

Cornelius Viljoen had been left with a severe limp as a result of the wound he had received outside Pretoria, but Lucas's arm had healed well, leaving only a barely discernible stiffness. After listening to a brief version of Margret's story, both men hurried to where the dead native lay. Meanwhile, a shocked

Sophia Viljoen ushered Margret, Gezima and Johanna into the house.

It was more than an hour before the Viljoen men returned. During that time they had dragged the body of the dead native well clear of the farm and buried it.

'He was a Bechuana,' Cornelius Viljoen told Margret. 'But you mentioned he had a companion. Which way did he go?'

'Up into the hills to the north.'

The two men exchanged glances and Lucas nodded. 'I'm taking a ride to see what's around.'

When Lucas had left, Cornelius asked, 'How long has Adam been gone?'

'He only stayed one night. Then he went off – to the Brandwater basin, he said.' Pride would not allow Margret to admit that her husband had left in the company of Esme Erasmus.

Tight-lipped and disapproving, Sophia Viljoen nodded at her daughter. 'There, you see. It might have been *you* left behind in this . . . this "place". You've had a lucky escape, my girl. Don't you forget it. To think . . . you might have been living here.'

Cornelius Viljoen had been watching Margret's face as his wife poured scorn on the primitive farmhouse. Hurriedly, he said, 'Yes, it's isolated, but our farm was no better when we first settled there.'

'Perhaps not, but there were neighbours, and you worked day and night for years to make something of the farm. You didn't take off for God-only-knows-where, leaving me with hardly a stick of furniture on which to lay a plate.'

'There wasn't a war being fought in the Transvaal then. These are difficult times.'

'There's not much sense putting work into a place if the *khakis* are going to come and burn it down,' declared Johanna. She averted her glance from Margret and it was left to Gezima to explain.

'They've begun burning farms between us and Lichtenburg – a dozen, at least.'

'Only the farms of those giving active support to the commandos,' corrected Cornelius Viljoen. 'And they've given us fair warning.'

Johanna snorted derisively. 'If you believe that, you'll believe anything. The *khakis* are determined to win this war any way they can. If it means burning farmhouses they'll burn every one in Transvaal — yes, and in the Orange Free State too, if necessary.'

'They won't burn ours,' declared Sophia Viljoen, decisively. 'Lord Roberts himself allowed your father and Lucas to return home. They have the letter to prove it.'

'A piece of paper will burn even quicker than a house,' retorted Johanna. 'I doubt whether a letter will stop the *khakis* burning our house if that's what they want to do.'

'We'll talk no more about it,' said Sophia Viljoen. 'Margret will be safer with us than staying out here on her own. Go and pack your things, my dear. I don't suppose you have much, but however much it is we'll manage it somehow.'

Margret looked at Sophia Viljoen in surprise. 'Pack my things? I'm not going anywhere.'

'Nonsense, child. You can't stay *here*. Not after what's happened. Besides, there's the baby to think of . . . you'll need help at the birth.'

'I'd greatly appreciate your help then. I've worried about it a lot. But it has to be born here, nowhere else. This is Adam's house. His farm. He'd want his child to be born here, especially if it's a son.'

'You surely can't be concerned what Adam thinks of anything. Not after all that he's done?'

'He's my husband, Mrs Viljoen . . . and I did wrong too. I want him to forget that he *had* to marry me. I want to make him a good wife, and give him a good home.'

While his wife stared at Margret, temporarily speechless, Cornelius Viljoen said quietly, 'The girl's right, Sophia, as well you know. Her place is here. I saw this farm when old Theunis had it. A lot of work has been done since then, by both Margret and Adam. When it's closer to her time I'll bring you up here and we'll both stay for a while.'

'Thank you. But where are my manners? You've travelled all this way to see me and I haven't even offered you a cup of coffee. I've got some, you know. I've been saving it for when folk come . . . to see the baby. But it really is wonderful to have visitors. Gezima, I swear you've grown three inches since I last saw you. How . . . how's our ma?'

'She's fine. She says I can marry Lucas as soon as I've turned sixteen. That's in six months' time.'

'Gezima, that's *wonderful*.' Margret's delight was genuine. Before Margret left home her sister had talked of Lucas Viljoen incessantly. 'Will you be coming to live with the Viljoens?'

'No. Ma says it's high time we had a man about our place again. Lucas and I will be living with Ma. Lucas will run things . . .'

While the women chatted, Cornelius Viljoen went outside and limped about the farm, casting a professional eye over the land and the farm buildings. It would never be good land for crops, since the soil was too shallow, but cattle would do well here. He wondered how the cattle brought here by Lucas and the tragically killed Jacob Eloff were faring. The Viljoens had brought six chickens as a present for Margret, and Cornelius released them inside the barn and then set about fashioning a few rough nesting-boxes. As he worked he glanced frequently along the valley in the direction taken by his son.

It was sundown before Lucas returned, a small springbok hanging over the saddle in front of him. As Cornelius limped out to meet him the women crowded the doorway of the house.

'I found the Bechuana.' Lucas Viljoen slipped from his horse. 'He won't attack any more farms.' He handed the springbok to his father. 'I shot this on the way back.'

'Good boy! Come inside now. You've earned a good meal, and Margret says she thinks she knows where Adam hides his brandy . . .'

The Viljoens remained with Margret for four days. When their wagon finally rolled out of sight Margret felt lonelier than before. Sophia Viljoen had brought some cheap linen and a few odds-and-ends with her, and while the women stitched curtains and tablecloths, the men had not wasted their time. Riding into the hills they had returned with four in-calf cows, one cow producing a bull calf that same night. Lucas had also spent time hunting and left Margret with enough meat to provide *biltong* for many weeks to come.

As the days and weeks passed Margret felt the baby grow restless inside her. Each day she hoped Sophia Viljoen would not delay her next visit for too long. It was becoming increasingly evident that the baby's birth was not far away.

Then, in the middle of one morning, Margret heard a sound from outside and went to the door. She saw riders approaching, far down the valley. At first she thought it must be the Viljoen family at last, but as more and more horses came into view she realised there were far too many.

As they drew nearer the sun reflected on the metal of guns being carried by the men and Margret's heart leaped. It must be a commando. Perhaps *Adam's* commando! Running awkwardly to her room, Margret put on her best dress, pulling it over her bulging stomach with great difficulty. Then she quickly brushed her hair, making final adjustments to it in the tiny, stained hand-mirror she had found in the back of a cupboard in the house.

Satisfied she was as neat and tidy as her limited resources would allow, Margret hurried back to the kitchen. Through the window she saw the riders more clearly now – and suddenly Margret's excitement was replaced by stark horror. This was not a Boer commando. The men all wore khaki uniforms and rode in a tight formation that was quite unlike the unmilitary burgher army. These riders were British soldiers. The dreaded *khakis*!

What they would do to her, Margret did not know. She had never met a British soldier. But she had been brought up to believe they were monsters, capable of every kind of atrocity.

The soldiers were approaching the front of the house and Margret left by the back door. There was no time to run to the hills, the soldiers would see her leaving the farm. Instead, she made for the barn. There was a half-width loft there and it was filled with hay, thoughtfully cut for her by Cornelius Viljoen.

Margret could hear voices and the jingling harness and accoutrements of the British soldiers as she climbed the last few rungs of the ladder to the loft. Pulling up the ladder after her, she burrowed deep into the sweet-smelling hay.

Lying here buried in the darkness of the hay gave Margret a comfortable sense of security – until she suddenly felt a strange sensation in her stomach. She gave an involuntary gasp of alarm – her waters had broken! The birth of her baby was imminent.

Within minutes of this frightening realisation Margret felt the first contraction. It was much stronger than she had thought it would be and it took all her self-control to hold back the cry that fought its way to her lips.

The second spasm came as she heard voices in the barn beneath her. This time she needed to push her wrist between her teeth to prevent herself from crying out.

During the brief intervals between her spasms, Margret tried to hear what the men inside the barn were saying, but she could not understand them. They were speaking in neither Afrikaans nor English.

In fact, the men who had ridden up to the lonely farm were mounted infantrymen of the Welsh Regiment. In their native tongue they were discussing what to do with the apparently deserted farm.

'Someone has been here very recently,' said the captain in charge of the troop. 'And there's no shortage of food about the place.'

'Left in a hurry too by the look of it,' said the younger subaltern.

'It has to be Boer rebels. Who else would be in a place as remote as this – and run off before we arrive?'

'We didn't see them go . . .' The subaltern was less certain. 'And there are a woman's things inside the house.'

'It all points to them having posted look-outs who saw us coming. As for a woman . . . It wouldn't be the first commando to have women along. Bad as their menfolk, every one of them.'

'What shall we do, see if we can find them somewhere in the hills?'

'With only forty men and no scout? No, we'll burn the farm and report back to Colonel Plucknett. Let *him* make a decision on pursuing the Boers, if he's a mind to.'

The two officers walked from the barn, but Margret was unaware of their going. Bathed in perspiration, she was trying to control the irresistible force of childbirth without allowing a sound to escape. Her wrist was bloody where her teeth had sunk into the flesh and she could hardly believe that the men in the barn below could not hear her fighting for breath each time a spasm gripped her body.

Before long she heard voices again, followed by another, unidentified sound . . . but then the strong, acrid smell of smoke reached her nostrils. With gathering horror Margret finally realised what was happening. The sound she could hear was the crackle of a fire. The *khakis* were setting fire to the farm!

She started up just as something landed with a thud in the hay, not four feet from her. It was a burning torch, made of thatch torn from the farmhouse roof. Even as Margret lunged for it she knew she was too late. The hay burst into flame with a terrifying roar and Margret screamed, the sound combining both pain and terror.

Her scream was heard by the two soldiers who had been given the task of setting fire to the barn.

'Did you hear that? There's a woman in there!'

One of the soldiers turned back, but his companion gripped his arm. 'It's too late now. Let's go.'

Even as he spoke clumps of burning hay were dropping to the floor, while flames from burning roofing leaped high in the air and burning wood crackled noisily as the dry hayloft floor and the roof supports of the barn caught fire.

'Look. There she is . . . Up there!'

The first soldier pulled away from his companion as Margret emerged from the pyre of hay. Blinded by smoke and consumed by excruciating pain. Margret was enveloped in flames as she staggered about the blazing hayloft and, falling against the ladder, sent it crashing to the floor of the barn below.

Seizing the ladder, the soldier placed it against the loft floor and climbed up, futilely shielding his face with one arm against the heat and flames as he neared the loft.

Somehow the soldier managed to reach Margret. His own clothing was ablaze now, but still he managed to drag her to the edge of the half-width floor.

It was doubtful whether the soldier could have carried Margret down the ladder, but he was not given the opportunity to try. At that moment the blazing hayloft collapsed, sending Margret and the soldier to the ground in a shower of blazing hay and timbers.

In the barn doorway a rescue party of Welsh soldiers had

been brought to the scene by the second soldier's shouts. Heedless of the risk to themselves, four of the men now plunged into the inferno and between them dragged their companion and Margret outside.

The fire victims were hideously burned, and it was immediately evident that both were beyond all aid. The cavalry troop was too small to have a doctor along, but a medical orderly rode with them. He examined both fire victims and after only a cursory examination he stood back, shaking his head, aware of his helplessness. Then suddenly his mouth dropped open in amazement. 'Oh my God! *She's having a baby!*'

Margret lived only until the baby was born. She died without knowing she had given birth to Adam's son. The soldier who had rescued her lingered on for another pain-filled hour before he, too, died.

The soldiers camped on the farm that night with the smell of smoke and the occasional eerie flaring up of a combustible piece of building to remind them of what they had done.

Milk was obtained from the cows and all through the night the men whose profession it was to kill their fellow-men stayed awake in the hope that they might have a brief opportunity to hold the child they were calling 'the miracle baby'.

Margret's baby had survived the fire, a fall, and his mother's death, but he did not live to see the dawn, in spite of all the prayers and attention of his uniformed 'nursemaids'.

As the soldiers rode away the next morning there was not a word spoken and tears glistened unashamedly on more than one cheek. Behind them they left a still smouldering farm — and two graves. Surmounting each mound of earth was a cross, made up from planks salvaged from an old farm wagon.

Carved on one was 'Private Hywell Morgan, Welsh Regiment, died 1 December 1900'.

On the second cross was pencilled, 'Unknown Boer woman, died 1 Dec. 1900'. Scrawled beneath this was, 'Her son, born 1/12/1900. died 2/12/1900 R.I.P.'

CHAPTER THIRTY-FIVE

The presence of a wounded Afrikaner girl on the hospital ship was an embarrassment to the ship's officials. Too many wounded young officers were finding excuses for passing along the corridor outside the room where she lay. If the door happened to be open they would step inside the cabin and talk to her. It did not matter that they spoke a different language. Most managed to bring presents. Biscuits, sweets – even chocolates, packed inside tins that were decorated with a picture of Queen Victoria and inscribed with the sovereign's New Year greetings to her troops engaged in the South African war. The tins were a personal gift from the British monarch and were not intended to be enjoyed by her enemies – not even one as attractive as Esme.

On Esme's fifth day on board the ship it was learned that a delegation from some British women's organisations were on their way from Cape Town. Newly arrived from England, the women were sponsored by anti-war factions. Their intention was to tour army hospitals, many of which had recently come under severe attack from certain civilian surgeons, seconded from their hospitals in England.

It was felt that the presence of a pretty young Afrikaner girl wounded by a British soldier's bullet – however doubtful the circumstances – could provide useful ammunition for critics of the war. Madame Claris was told that she might take her young protégée home forthwith. What was more, the army would be delighted to provide her with transport – immediately.

Word sped around *Maine* that 'their' Boer girl was leaving

the hospital ship, and every man capable of hobbling to the guard rail was there to see her carried to the waiting carriage. Others crowded every porthole and cheered her as she left, and Esme could not help feeling moved by the warmth of their farewell.

Esme's strength returned rapidly in the quiet atmosphere of the Frenchwoman's home, and her presence brought the large house to life. She was given an identical room to Nat's, with a balcony alongside his, but within a week of the bullet being removed from her body she was making brief forays from her room, gazing with undisguised interest at household objects never seen in the hill country where she had been raised.

Thomasina had not returned to her room at the house since the night of Nat's arrival. She was very busy on board the hospital ship, more wounded men having reached Durban from the railway line to the north where a Boer commando had attacked and derailed a military train, causing heavy casualties.

Nat had been to the hospital ship on a number of occasions hoping to see Thomasina, but on the only occasion when he was successful she had been surrounded by members of her staff, each vying for her attention, and it had been impossible to hold a conversation with her. Now Nat spent most evenings sitting with Esme in her room, or on the balcony sharing Esme's company with Madame Claris.

The large Frenchwoman was delighted to have Esme in her home and had already begun to teach her own, highly individualistic English to the Afrikaner girl. She had also brought in a hairdresser to put a little 'style' into Esme's self-cut hair, and she was enjoying discussing plans for her future wardrobe.

Somewhat to Nat's surprise, Esme joined wholeheartedly in both the lessons and Madame Claris's planning. More than once he marvelled at the change in the young girl who only a few weeks before had been dressed as a young man and lying wounded in the cause of the Boer republics.

Esme also proved she lacked none of the intuition of a woman. One evening when Madame Claris had gone downstairs to organise supper for them, Nat and Esme sat on the dark balcony in silence for some minutes before Esme asked mockingly, 'Are you wishing you were sitting here with your Thomasina instead of with me?'

'No, of course not.' They were both aware the denial was a lie.

'She's not for you, Nat. She belongs in another land, with people like herself. Her world would be as strange to you . . . as this is to me.'

It was an argument Nat had put to himself during the many sleepless nights he had had since meeting up with Thomasina again – but he did not want to hear it from Esme.

'I wouldn't say you've found it particularly hard fitting in here,' he retorted.

'How would you know?' She flared back at him. 'You spent a three-day train journey with a half-conscious girl and most of the time since then you've been pining for your fine lady so much you've hardly noticed me. Is that supposed to make you an expert on how I think?'

'I don't need to know how you *think*. On the hospital ship British soldiers were coming to your cabin to enquire after your progress and leave you chocolates. A couple of weeks before you'd have shot them. You have to admit you've changed . . .'

'A few weeks ago *you* would have shot *me* had you met with me out on the veld. Have *you* changed? No, and neither have I. I'm here and I'm making the most of it – but I'm still Esme Erasmus, an Afrikaner girl whose father was killed by the same soldiers who are now out there destroying the Transvaal – *my* Transvaal. Don't tell me I should be grateful to them for digging a bullet out of me. Had they stayed in their own country it wouldn't have been there in the first place. Anyway, I don't suppose they would have been quite so considerate had they known the truth about me.'

Glaring through the darkness towards Nat, Esme shifted her position in order to ease her back and a cushion dropped to the floor between them. Nat picked it up and, as he replaced it on the chair behind her, Esme put a hand up to his arm.

'Don't think I'm not grateful to *you*, Nat. But for you I'd be dead now, I realise that . . .'

'Thank that fool brother of mine – if he's still alive.'

Esme dropped her hand from his arm. 'You needn't concern

yourself for Adam. He's a natural survivor — you're not. Go home, Nat. Go back to Insimo where you belong. If you stay here you'll get badly hurt — and I'm not talking about bullets.'

At that moment Madame Claris could be heard puffing up the stairs, and she arrived bearing a tray with drinks for them. Behind her came the servant-girl carrying a lamp and the conversation between Nat and Esme came to an inconclusive end.

Later that night, alone in his room, Nat went over what Esme had said. She was right, of course. She had merely been voicing the brutal truth he was unwilling to acknowledge. He and Thomasina came from different worlds. His hopes that she might one day marry him and live at Insimo were quite unrealistic. On the journey from Umtali to Fort Victoria, and again at Insimo, he had fooled himself into thinking she and the country were well suited. He had been deluding himself. He must accept this now.

The peace of Madame Claris's household was broken at dawn by a heavy hammering on the front door. The kitchen maid was already up and she opened the door to the noisy caller.

Lying half-awake in his room, Nat heard faint voices in the hall. Then someone ran up the stairs and it was the turn of Nat's bedroom door to take a battering.

As Nat swung his feet to the floor the door opened and a British captain entered the room.

'Mister Retallick?'

'That's me. What's the reason for all the noise? What time is it?'

'Four-thirty, sir. Major General Archer sent me to find you. A large Boer commando has raided Natal. It has blown up the railway line beyond Pietermaritzburg, and derailed a supply train. It is now making off in the direction of the Drakensberg mountains. General Archer is putting together a column to go after the Boers. You're the only scout in Durban and he wants you to go with him.'

The noise in the house had aroused Madame Claris, and she came puffing into the room as Nat pulled on his boots. Taking in the situation immediately, she said, 'You are going back to the war?'

'Yes.'

Nat took two ammunition bandoliers from the wardrobe and slipped them over his head, one across each shoulder.

'You'll be seeing Thomasina before you go?'

'General Archer has already commandeered a train, Mister Retallick,' said the British army captain. 'He's waiting for you at the siding.'

'There's your answer, Madame Claris. Thomasina won't miss me.'

Nat reached down his rifle from the top of the wardrobe.

'You are wrong, Nat. Thomasina is a very lonely woman. The loss of her husband affected her greatly . . .'

'If you'll excuse me, Mister Retallick, I'll get back and tell General Archer you are coming. I had some difficulty finding this house and the general will be wondering why I am taking so long. I would be obliged if you would waste no time . . .' Apologetically, the captain added, 'General Archer is not the most patient of men.'

'I'll be leaving the house in a few minutes – but I came to Durban on a hospital train. I have no horse.'

'My orderly is outside. Use his. We're taking plenty of remounts on the train. There will be one for you.'

Nat nodded and the captain hurried away.

'Nat, please try to see Thomasina, I beg you. She *is* very fond of you. If you do not see her I fear we will both lose her . . .'

'What do you mean?'

Madame Claris was talking in riddles and Nat was trying to hold on to the resolution he had made during the night.

'The hospital ship is sailing for England soon. Thomasina intends to go with it.'

'It will be best for her. She has family there . . . and a familiar way of life. She'll soon get over the loss of Digby . . .' Nat ended abruptly. He was facing up to facts, but he balked at voicing the implication that Thomasina would undoubtedly marry again.

Stuffing the last of his essential belongings into the saddlebags and pulling the last strap tight, Nat said, 'I've left some clothing here. If I don't come back you can give it to Dingaan.'

'If you don't . . .?' Madame Claris shuddered. 'You must not say such things. You *will* return.'

Nat smiled briefly. 'I didn't mean it that way. We might chase this commando across half of Africa. If I'm somewhere near the railway at the end of it I'll probably take a train, heading north.'

'I see.' Madame Claris shrugged disconsolately. 'Will you leave no message for Thomasina?'

'Tell her . . . Tell her only that I wish her happiness and will think of her often.'

'I will tell her, but it would make me so much happier if you would tell her yourself.'

Nat shouldered his saddlebags and followed Madame Claris out of the room to the corridor. The door of Esme's room was open and she was in the doorway, wearing a silk nightdress, bought for her by the Frenchwoman.

'Esme! You should not be out of bed yet. You will catch a chill . . . and put something over that nightdress.'

'I am not Thomasina. *I* have nothing to fear from Nat – but he is not going without saying "goodbye" to *me*.' Esme had learned enough English to have caught the gist of Madame Claris's conversation with Adam and she was unashamed of having been eavesdropping.

Madame Claris threw up her arms in resignation. 'The young girls of today . . . ! But you will have no breakfast, Nat. I will wrap something for you to take . . .' Madame Claris padded away along the corridor, shaking her head.

'Won't you go home to Insimo right away, Nat?' Esme asked the question softly.

'As soon as I know this commando has left Natal.'

'Forget the commando, Nat. Go straight home.'

'I wish your burghers would do the same.'

Esme moved closer to Nat and looked up at him earnestly. 'Nat, I'm not suggesting this because I'm on one side and you're on the other.'

'No?'

'Listen to me. *Adam* is with this commando. It's true. I would have been with them had I not been shot. Before breaking out of the Brandwater basin we arranged to hide in the Drakensbergs, coming out eventually to harass the British in Natal. Adam and the others will be back in the mountains already. It's a waste of time chasing after them. You'll never catch up with them there.'

'You're probably right, but if Adam is with them that's even more reason to go after them and persuade them to lay down their arms. You've sat with me on the balcony and watched the ships loaded with men and supplies lining up to enter harbour. There's just no sense in either side losing any more men in this hopeless cause. It's time for everyone to sit down and *talk* about their problems. Can't I take a message to Adam from you along these lines?'

'You can tell Adam I am *proud* of him. Proud that he and the others have been able to ride into Natal, blow up a train, steal British supplies and have a hundred times their own number of *khakis* chasing their tails wondering where they'll strike next. Tell him *that* – if you ever see him.' Esme spat the words at him scornfully.

Not for the first time Nat wondered if he should have warned Madame Claris about the obsessive hatred for the British that this girl had. But she could do no harm here and, hopefully, the war would soon be over.

He turned to go, but Esme reached out a hand and detained him for a moment. 'I hope you never find the commando – for everyone's sake. If this war *does* end soon . . . come back for me. *Please.*'

CHAPTER THIRTY-SIX

Major General Horatio Archer was a superb cavalry officer, but he was no organiser. Men, horses, guns, ammunition and stores were mixed together at the railway sidings in utter confusion. Most had been loaded and then unloaded again with frustrating frequency.

The problem was that the men with their horses, supplies and equipment could not be placed on a single train. Indeed, it was becoming increasingly apparent that *two* trains were unlikely to prove sufficient.

General Archer was every bit as irascible as the captain had suggested to Nat. Neither was he a young man. In fact, he had requested retirement only weeks before the outbreak of the war. Asked to remain in the army, he had been concerned with training mounted infantry until sent to South Africa. He had reached Durban only a week before, after a rough and uncomfortable voyage from England.

The first train had been half-loaded, then unloaded again on at least three occasions by the time Nat arrived, and General Archer was beside himself with fury. The loading was being undertaken by railway employees, assisted by natives and men of the Army Service Corps, the whole operation supervised by a much-harassed major.

When the captain who had awoken Nat nervously introduced him to General Archer, the angry cavalryman deigned neither to shake hands nor to welcome Nat to his column. After glaring at Nat for a few moments he turned and stalked away, muttering, 'Another damned civilian.'

The captain was quick to apologise, explaining that Major

General Archer had been up most of the night trying to organise this column. He added, 'It hasn't been easy. All the men and most of his officers are new to Africa. There aren't enough mules for the supply wagons, and not enough tents for the men . . .'

'Tents?' Nat looked at the captain incredulously. 'What the hell does he want with *tents*? I've spent a full year out on the veld without ever sleeping in a tent – and so have the Boers. If General Archer intends hunting down Boers he'll need to change his thinking and forget about tents – wagons too. He'll need a fast-moving column if he's serious about beating the Boers at their own game.'

Unnoticed by Nat, the major whose task it was to load the trains had moved into hearing, and he said, 'I wish you would put your views to General Archer. As it is I'm trying to put four train-loads of men and equipment on two trains. It can't be done.'

Nat shrugged. 'What have I to lose? I'd rather go home anyway.'

He found General Archer dictating a message of complaint to General Redvers Buller, commander of the British forces in Natal. It was perfectly obvious that Nat wanted to speak with him, but the general continued his dictation. Eventually Nat became tired of being so pointedly ignored.

'General, I'd like a word with you.'

Waving a hand airily, the general said brusquely, 'Later. I'm busy right now.'

'Carry on the way you're going and you'll still be trying to load trains this time tomorrow. You certainly won't catch up with any Boers – not even in the unlikely event that you get all this lot to where you're going.'

The general's red face turned purple, and for a few moments it seemed he might explode.

'I'm damned if I'll have a pipsqueak of a civilian telling me how to fight a war. Captain Willoughby . . . have this man arrested.'

Nat had not noticed that the British captain had followed him. Now the officer stepped forward. 'Arrested? Yes, sir. On what charge?'

'Charge? Insubordination . . . Or anything else you can think of.'

'Er . . . Mister Retallick is a civilian scout. A volunteer. He's not subject to military discipline.'

'Damn all civilians! There are far too many of 'em mixed up in this war. Get him out of my sight and find me another scout.'

'There isn't another available – and Mister Retallick was personally recommended by Field Marshal Lord Roberts.'

General Archer looked at Nat with renewed suspicion. 'How is it you're known to the commander-in-chief?'

'You meet all kinds of people in a war, General. Now you've heard my credentials – are you ready to hear my views on fighting Boers?'

The veteran army officer glared at Nat, but with an effort he kept his mouth clamped tight shut and nodded stiffly.

'You have far too much equipment and too many wagons. The Boers aren't sitting on some battlefield waiting for you to arrive and deploy your men and set up your guns. They've already lost too many men by doing that. Now they've begun to split into highly mobile commandos, each containing anything from a hundred to fifteen hundred men. These commandos roam the countryside striking at any target that presents itself. Supply depots, convoys, bridges, the railway . . . even small patrols. When they're pursued they split into even smaller bands in order to make their escape and join up again later. They are successful because of their speed and mobility. If you want to catch up with them you'll need to beat them at their own game. Lumber after them with wagons carrying tents and a mountain of stores and you won't even glimpse them – until they are strong enough to attack. When they do they'll hit you so suddenly you'll wonder where they've come from.'

'Dammit . . . that isn't war.'

'Tell that to the families of the men who've already died. The Boers don't look on war as a game. They are fighting for their country – and their freedom. They are fighting to *win* – and they believe they *will* win.'

'I am still going to need stores . . . horses too. My men can't go chasing after Boers with nothing to back them. Pinned down by Boers without stores my men would be forced to surrender. I'm damned if I'm going to allow that to happen.'

'It's part of my job to see you're *not* pinned down by Boers. *We* are chasing *them*. As for horses . . . do you know where they were bought?'

'I understand most are from the Argentine . . . perhaps fifty from Spain. What's that got to do with anything?'

Nat frowned. Argentinian horses were far from ideal for hard work on the veld. They were too large, lacked stamina, and were not the most intelligent of animals. Nevertheless, they were better on the veld than the horses brought out from England by the regular cavalry units. Many of these had never learned to forage for themselves and would starve to death waiting for food to be brought to them.

Ignoring the general's question, Nat asked, 'How many men will make up your column?'

'I hope eventually to have rather more than thirty-five hundred mounted men. There are two thousand here and another fifteen hundred waiting for me at Mooi river.'

Major General Archer was at least discussing the situation now, and Nat did not want to push him too hard, but there was more that needed to be said if the general's force was to operate effectively against the Boers.

'Well, I'm not a general, but if I were in command I'd issue five hundred men with six days' rations and a hundred and fifty rounds of ammunition and then I'd send them and their horses to Mooi river. When I got there I'd pick up five hundred of those waiting for me and set off after the commando, leaving the rest to follow on with the wagons once they arrived. Unless you get on the tail of this particular commando pretty quickly you're not likely to find a sign of them until they strike somewhere else – perhaps a hundred miles away. Now, if you don't mind I'll choose a couple of horses for myself. Whatever *you* decide to do, *I'll* be out on my own with my life dependent on having a good horse beneath me.'

Nat chose two of the Spanish horses. Both black, they had a hint of good breeding – a trait that was patently absent from the rangy, Argentinian-bred animals. After ensuring the animals would be on the first train to leave, Nat returned to the sidings. Here he found a changed scene.

A new train was being put together by the railwaymen. Wagons were being shunted to the main line and added to the long line already there. All the trucks except two were open-topped. Those in front would carry the men in scant comfort, fifty to a truck. Those behind held the horses. In between were two passenger carriages which would carry General Archer and his staff. Ample food and cases of champagne were being placed in the two carriages to ensure the British officers would not find the journey too irksome.

Nat learned he was expected to find a place among the soldiers. Instead, he joined the engineer and the native fireman on the footplate of the lightly armoured locomotive.

The journey to Mooi river took six hours. At times, on a steep gradient, the long train travelled so slowly that Nat was able to drop from the footplate and stretch his legs. The journey was completed without incident, although Nat's vocabulary was extended considerably by the engineer, who cursed his native fireman non-stop for the whole six hours.

General Archer's reinforcements were waiting at Mooi river, a small settlement containing little more than the station, a hotel, and a few indifferent houses. To Nat's delight he discovered the new troops were commanded by Carey Hamilton.

Nat leaped from the footplate of the locomotive before the train screeched to a noisy, juddering stop, and the two friends clasped hands warmly.

'It's good to see a friendly face,' exclaimed Nat. 'When we have time I must give you news of Thomasina. She's at Durban, on the hospital ship.'

'I know.' Carey Hamilton's delight at the reunion matched Nat's own. Fishing in a pocket he pulled out a piece of paper and thrust it at Nat. 'This arrived for you by telegraph not an hour ago . . . but we'll find time to talk later. First I must report to General Archer.'

Carey Hamilton had seen the major general descending the steps from one of the carriages, his usual high colour accentuated by the champagne he had consumed along the way.

Slowly, Nat unfolded the paper. The message was brief, but it gave him a ridiculous sense of pleasure. Addressed to 'Nat Retallick, scout for Major General Archer', it read, *Utterly miserable at not seeing you before your departure. So much needed to be said. Praying for your safe return to Insimo. Fondest regards. Thomasina.*

Nat carefully re-folded the note and placed it inside a buttoned pocket before making his way to where Carey Hamilton stood with General Archer and his staff officers as the train was unloaded.

Aware that Nat had not been included in the party occupying the officers' carriages, Carey Hamilton beamed in Nat's direction as he spoke to General Archer. 'I'm pleased to see you were able to persuade Nat Retallick to act as our scout. You couldn't have made a better choice. He and I have been friends since my sister and I were guests at his magnificent farm. You may have met my sister in Durban – Thomasina Vincent, widow of Colonel Digby Vincent? Yes, Nat has a wonderful place in Matabeleland. It's one of the largest landholdings in southern Africa. He's a law unto himself there. Even Cecil Rhodes is careful not to tread on Nat's toes . . . Isn't this right, Nat?'

'I believe Rhodes and my father crossed swords once or twice,' said Nat drily, amused at General Archer's expression of calculating concern. The commanding officer of the column was wondering whether he might have slighted someone with 'influence' in this part of the world. The war had provided Major General Horatio Archer with a final, unexpected opportunity to bring an honour into the Archer family. He was anxious to offend no one who might be in a position to help him achieve this end.

'I'll go and find my two horses,' said Nat. 'Then I'll set out after the Boers. Do you have any information about them?'

'Very little. All we know is they tore up the railway line and blew a bridge at dusk before heading for the Drakensbergs. They probably didn't expect the damage to be discovered for some time. Unfortunately for them, a small railway pioneer corps team was not a mile to the north. They telegraphed the details immediately and we started things moving. They have no more than an eighteen-hour start.'

'Good. I might catch up with them some time during the night if there's a good moon. I'll take two of *your* men with me. I'll send one back at about four o'clock, the other at dusk. I'll point out a good, safe camp to the second man and find you before dawn to let you know what's happening. Is this all right with you, General Archer?'

'You are the expert out here,' agreed a remarkably subdued

general. 'Do whatever you think is best. I'll follow you as quickly as possible with Colonel Hamilton. He can explain anything I need to know along the way.'

Nat had travelled twenty miles before he sent back the second soldier. He was confident that Carey Hamilton would not be too far behind – and equally certain the Boers were not very far ahead. The train carrying General Archer's advance party had steamed past the scene of the commando raid and dropped the British soldiers much closer to the Drakensbergs than the Boers would have expected. Nat picked up their trail very quickly and it led towards the mountains.

Studying their tracks, it soon became apparent to Nat that the Boers were not riding like men in fear of their lives. They even had a couple of Cape carts with them. The lightweight, two-wheeled carts were favoured by some of the commando leaders. Pulled by two horses, they were able to traverse all but the roughest country.

Once he was alone, Nat proceeded with far more caution than before, even after it became dark. The Boers were notoriously lax about posting sentries, but he was taking no chances.

Nat found the commando sooner than he expected – and he did not have to search hard. The Boers had gone to great lengths to site their camp in a hollow, high on the side of a *kopje*, where their low cooking-fires could not be seen from any distance. But this was Sunday and Nat was guided to the spot by the singing of hymns. Leaving his horses securely tethered, he worked his way so close to the camp that from the shelter of a low clump of bushes he could have thrown a stone in the middle of the men attending the Predikant's service.

The whole of the commando was present and Nat was able to estimate with a fair degree of accuracy that it was comprised of not more than a hundred and fifty men. He peered hard into the darkness trying to distinguish faces. Esme had said Adam would be with this commando and he wanted to know for certain. He had no intention of allowing General Archer to set an ambush if there were a risk of Adam being caught in it. But it was too dark to make out more than one or two of the worshippers.

The service came to an end with the Predikant's blessing on the assembled men and they dispersed quickly. They had evidently already eaten their evening meal because the corporals now went around kicking out the ashes of the low fires as the men spread their blankets and settled down for the night. A Boer commando began its day before dawn and the men rode hard. They did not waste good sleeping time sitting around talking for longer than a pipeful of tobacco took to burn low.

Nat waited for the camp to quieten before making his move. He had just made up his mind it was time to return to his horses when there was a sound only yards in front of him. The next moment a Boer stumbled out of the darkness. Standing not more than six feet from Nat, he relieved himself in the bushes.

The Boer would have returned to the camp unaware of the presence of a British scout had Nat not suddenly stood up in front of him. The light was sufficient for the rifle in Nat's hands to be visible, and the Boer's hands were raised above his head even before Nat's whispered order reached him.

'Just walk forward slowly and keep your arms where they are.' Nat spoke in Afrikaans.

'I have no gun. It's in the camp. I'm unarmed.' The words came in a hoarse whisper.

'Shut up and keep walking.' Nat fell in behind the Boer and led him back to the horses.

'What you going to do with me?' The Boer's voice was husky with fright.

'I'm going to take you with me as my prisoner. There are a few questions I want to ask you.'

'Who are you? Where are you taking me?'

'I'm scouting for a British army column that's not far from here.'

A frightened face was turned towards Nat in the darkness. 'Hell, man . . . you can't do this to me! I'm wearing a *khaki*'s jacket. They'll shoot me. You may be an *uitlander*, but you're not British. You can't let them kill me.'

Nat knew the man was right. The shooting of Jacob Eloff, the Viljoens' hired-hand was only one of many such incidents. There was now an official order that any Boer captured wearing British army uniform was to be summarily executed. The order had been prompted by a number of incidents in which British troops had been annihilated because they had mistaken Boers wearing captured British uniforms for their own troops.

'Take it off and throw it away.'

The Boer, who told Nat his name was Deneys Myburg, gratefully did as he was told. He might shiver on the way to the British camp, but he would live.

With his hands tied securely behind his back, the captured Boer rode Nat's spare horse, and along the way he answered Nat's questions. The first was about Adam.

'Adam Retallick? From Rhodesia? He *was* with us for a while, but about a week ago we met up with another commando, mainly Germans. Adam Retallick rode off with them. They were heading for the Cape, I think. Why, do you know him?'

Nat ignored the question. 'Why didn't he stay with your commando?'

'Agh! We're finished, man. Our field cornet is an old man from the Orange Free State. All he wants is to go home. Half the others feel the same. They've had enough of riding around looking for trouble. If we as much as pull up a piece of railway line we're on the run from *khakis* for weeks. We knew it would happen again this time, but thought we'd be long gone before it was found. Hell! Look at the whole thing logically. It'll take your *khakis* half an hour to put the rail back and two days to mend a bridge. Sometimes we might wreck a train – but who cares any more? You've got plenty more. Is any of it worth the lives of a dozen burghers? I don't think so. The war is over for us. The sooner we realise it the better it will be.'

'If that's the way the other burghers feel, then capturing you may save a great many lives.'

'That's the way *our* commando feels. I can't speak for the others. Some still want to fight – especially the Transvaalers.'

When Nat reached the British camp with his prisoner he was given news that he hoped would help bring the Transvaal commandos in line with the thinking of men like Deneys Myburg. A message had reached General Archer from Field

Marshal Lord Roberts. Pursued by the British army, President Kruger of the Transvaal Republic had fled his country. Crossing the border into Portuguese-ruled Mozambique, he had been taken on board a Dutch warship and carried into exile in Europe. Behind him, two thousand men of his disintegrating army surrendered to the Portuguese authorities.

Field Marshal Roberts's message to General Archer expressed his belief that the war was now in its closing stages. He suggested guide-lines for his commanders to follow. Those burghers who surrendered their arms immediately and gave an oath of allegiance to the Queen of Great Britain would still be allowed to return to their homes. Burghers *not* taking the oath would be treated as prisoners-of-war and sent to overseas camps. Farms and buildings used by enemy forces were to be razed to the ground, as were the crops of any farmer who supplied food to a Boer commando. Any burgher who broke his oath of allegiance would be subject to the death penalty.

Nat thought the news of President *Oom* Paul Kruger's departure from his homeland would send the spirits of his followers plummeting faster than the threats contained in Field Marshal Roberts's message. He suggested to General Archer that he send Deneys Myburg back to his comrades with a suggestion that they lay down their arms, sign the oath of allegiance, and return peaceably to their homes.

General Archer viewed the proposal with a marked lack of enthusiasm, but after a meeting with his staff officers, during the course of which Deneys Myburg was questioned at some length, he agreed to a modified arrangement. Nat would guide the British soldiers to the Boer camp in the darkness and they would take up positions surrounding the commando. At dawn Deneys Myburg would enter the camp, inform the field cornet of the situation and put the British terms to him.

The plan worked perfectly. There was initial consternation in the Boer camp when it was realised there were *khaki* troops all about them. They discussed General Archer's ultimatum for three hours. Meanwhile, the British general fumed, growling that a decision should have been made by the Boer commander without debate.

Eventually Deneys Myburg returned. There were a hundred and twenty-seven men in the commando. A hundred and sixteen had agreed to sign the oath of allegiance and return to their homes. The remaining eleven, whilst fully aware of the futility of further fighting, would not sign an oath of allegiance. They offered their surrender, and General Archer agreed to treat them as prisoners-of-war. The commando was no more – and not a shot had been fired.

The surrender of the commando was a considerable victory for General Archer and it brought a congratulatory signal from the Commander-in-Chief. But the column's work was not yet at an end.

Although President Kruger had left the country and two thousand of his men had surrendered, many more had escaped from the advancing army of Field Marshal Lord Roberts. They scattered across the hills and plains of the African veld like chaff before a windstorm. Many, emulating the *voortrekkers* of old, headed north and westwards to escape the British.

Others drove south-westwards through the Orange Free State, joined along the way by many thousands of burghers whose resistance to British annexation was steadily growing. Together they began making retaliatory raids into the British-administered Cape Colony.

Still more burghers who refused to surrender headed for the mountains of the Drakensbergs, in the area around the tiny Basutoland Protectorate. Here, in the rugged heights, General Archer and his column were sent to hunt them down.

Field Marshal Lord Roberts's war might have been coming to an end, but southern Africa was to be the testing ground for a new, untried concept of warfare. It would call for a different breed of officer. One prepared to try radical new tactics. The war that was beginning was not to be a meeting of armies observing age-old chivalries. This was to be a bitter war of attrition. A *mobile* war. One to push men on both sides to the limit of their endurance. It would be a *hard* war. A *cruel* war, with survival and not victory the sole criterion.

When Lord Roberts bade farewell to South Africa, *his* war *was* over. Handing over his command to the chief of staff, Lord Kitchener, he returned to England to accept an earldom and £100,000 from a grateful country.

Behind him, in South Africa, he left the graves of almost eleven thousand men, only half of whom had died from wounds received in battle. The remainder were killed by disease. Lord Roberts had been preceded to England by another thirty-five thousand soldiers, invalided home. Yet all this would be only half of the final casualty figures.

CHAPTER THIRTY-SEVEN

Deneys Myburg took the oath of allegiance to the British Queen, but he did not return home to his family immediately. General Archer was pleased with the success Myburg had achieved with his own commando, and he asked the Boer to remain with the British column and practise his peacemaking on another commando which was reported to have clashed with a British patrol some miles to the north. When Myburg wavered, Nat reminded him that if he were successful he would be helping to save a great many of his countrymen's lives.

'Hell, man! What sort of a thing is that to say to me, eh? I've been out on commando for more than a year now. I promised myself I'd spend this Christmas home with my boys.'

'You do this and a great many burghers will be able to have Christmas at home with their families.'

'I'll not be thanked for doing it. As far as my friends are concerned I'll be just another "hands-upper".'

'Perhaps. But no matter how many battles are fought the end will be the same. The British are going to win. Those burghers who die now are only taking six feet of land from their country. By staying alive they may one day help negotiate the return of the whole of the republics.'

General Archer's column made contact with the second Boer commando five days after the surrender of Deneys Myburg's comrades. Disregarding Nat's misgivings the general had brought up many of his wagons, declaring he would not take his men among the awesome heights of the Drakensbergs unless he was satisfied they were well supplied. However, he *had* left the men's tents behind in Durban, bringing only a single large tent for his own use, and to act as a headquarters when possible.

The column was close to the Basutoland border, in an area of breathtaking beauty. Towering above the surrounding heights was the peak of the Mont-aux-Sources, rising almost 11,000 feet into the clean, blue sky. Rivers and streams abounded here and the shadowed valleys might have concealed a whole army.

Awed by the sheer majesty of the mountains, Nat thought it sacrilege to desecrate such beauty with sudden death, but the threat of an ambush lurked behind each new ridge, and in the shadow of every broken valley. Scouting such country was impossible for one man, and Nat had enlisted the services of a dozen of Carey Hamilton's best hussars. However, this was home country for some of the Boers they were seeking and they knew every mountain path and escape route.

Time and time again the column was fired upon by a line of snipers concealed high on rugged, rock-strewn ridges and British soldiers killed or wounded. But by the time an artillery piece was brought into play, the Boers had gone.

After many days of this one-sided warfare, Nat found a secure camp for General Archer's weary column in a hollow overlooked by a tall, flat peak. With a strong detachment of soldiers in control of the peak the British soldiers would be able to relax for a day or two.

Nat left the camp before dawn. His intention was to find the main Boer encampment. He believed it lay somewhere nearby to the east. Every attack had come from this direction and the snipers had all escaped the same way. Nat had scouted the countryside well the previous evening and by the time the sun cleared the peaks and poured warm sunlight into the cool valleys he was many miles away.

He proceeded with extreme caution, keeping just below the high ridges whenever possible, using powerful field-glasses to search out the surrounding countryside before moving on.

It was late afternoon before he located the Boer stronghold. Taking a straight line from the British camp it was no more than three miles away, but only an eagle travelled a straight line in these mountains.

Situated in a high, shallow valley, the camp was very much larger than Nat had expected. There must have been upwards of a thousand men here. There was also a field gun, many supply wagons – and a large number of family wagons. It seemed that this commando, at least, had not expected the British to invade its mountain sanctuary.

Nat remained in hiding until the valley was deeply shadowed and the sun dipping beneath the jagged horizon, then he made for the British camp, the journey taking him three hours. He immediately reported to General Archer on his discovery.

'. . . I don't like the thought of so many women and children becoming caught up in a battle.' The British general paced up and down in his tent in front of the officers and Deneys Myburg as he pondered the problem. 'Why the devil can't the Boers leave their women and children at home, like any other civilised people?'

'Because if they do they'll be rounded up and put into camps and their homes fired . . . by civilised people, of course.'

Major General Archer glared in response to Deneys Myburg's quiet sarcasm. When he spoke again it was to put a question to Nat. 'You're the only one to have seen their camp. Have you any ideas?'

'I believe that having so many women and children with them might well work to our advantage. If you can move your troops into position and block off both ends of the valley by dawn, I'll go in with Deneys and suggest they surrender rather than put the lives of their families at risk.'

'You won't be listened to.' The blunt statement came from Deneys Myburg. 'This has to be Commandant Tromp's commando, from the foothills. Man, woman or child . . . it makes no difference to Johannes Tromp. His women are from good *voortrekker* stock. They'll suffer with their menfolk, or die with them, as the Lord wills.'

'Nevertheless, I feel I must give this Commandant Tromp the opportunity to surrender. I'll not have it said I fired upon women and children without any warning. Will you go with Retallick – under the protection of a white flag, of course? Tromp may listen to you.'

Deneys Myburg shrugged. 'If he does it will be the first time

Tromp has accepted advice from anyone. But, yes, I'll go. If enough of Tromp's burghers can be persuaded to surrender they'll out-vote him.'

Nat had taken careful note of the Boer commando camp, and now he drew a map for General Archer and his officers. It was decided that the bulk of the British force would go across the intervening hills to the camp, while the wagons accompanied by a strong escort would take an easier, more circuitous route.

The soldiers broke camp and by the light of a thin sliver of moon made their way to predetermined positions blocking both ends of the valley. Only token forces guarded the hills on either side, General Archer considering it unlikely that the commando would abandon its wagons and flee over the hills.

The British soldiers gained their positions without detection, the Boers being characteristically lax about posting sentries. But the burghers were early risers and they discovered their predicament when the light on the mountains was still awaiting the warmth of the sun. The whole camp was active within minutes of the alarm being raised, and the wagons were quickly man-handled into position to form a defensive *laager* with men, women, children, oxen and horses inside.

'What the devil is their commander doing?' snapped General Archer. 'Does he think we're Zulus armed only with spears? Crowding everyone together like that is unbelievable. A few lyddite shells lobbed among them would cause carnage.'

'Perhaps he hopes the thought of the women and children will stop you from shelling him,' suggested Nat.

'Then he needs to be disillusioned,' retorted the British general.

A few minutes later two shells were fired from the British lines. Aimed one on either side of the Boer camp, they exploded with a ferocious *crack!* that stampeded the Boer animals and set every young child crying.

'Now they know we have a field gun,' said General Archer, pleased with the confusion caused by the two shells. 'Are you ready with that flag, Mister Retallick?'

Nat nodded and, with Deneys Myburg at his side and carrying a long pole from which fluttered a large white flag, he rode from the British lines, heading for the Boer *laager*.

As the two men neared the circle of wagons, Nat was uncomfortably aware that a thousand burghers were watching them over the sights of their Mauser rifles.

The two horsemen approached to within a hundred yards of the *laager* before a shot was fired. Neither horseman was hit, but they brought their mounts to a halt and waited to see if the shot had been a mistake, or a warning.

'That's far enough. We're having no spies coming in here.' The warning came from inside the ring of wagons.

'If I'd wanted to see what's going on inside your *laager* I need only have climbed to the ridge with a pair of field-glasses,' retorted Nat. 'I'm here to parley.'

'Tell Commandant Tromp it's Deneys Myburg of the Frikkiesdorp commando,' called Nat's companion. 'I have something to say to him.'

A great deal of animated talking took place inside the *laager* and it was fifteen minutes before one of the wagons was rolled aside and a voice called, 'Come!'

The two men rode inside the circle of wagons and Nat was immediately aware of the hostility on the faces of those inside.

As the wagon was rolled back into place behind them a tall, thin man with deep-set eyes and a heavy, prematurely greying beard stepped forward.

'Get off your horses.'

It was not an invitation, but an order. When it had been obeyed, the tall Boer said, 'I am Commandant Tromp. You I already know, Deneys Myburg. Who are you?' A long, bony finger was pointed at Nat.

'Nat Retallick, a scout for General Archer.'

'You're from the Cape?'

'No, Matabeleland.'

'Then you're British.' It was a dismissive statement and Commandant Tromp returned his attention to Deneys Myburg.

'Why are you riding with the *khakis*, Myburg?'

'I was captured near the Mooi river with my commando. Most of the burghers signed the oath of allegiance. The rest were taken prisoner.'

'Which are you – prisoner or "hands-upper"?'

After a momentary hesitation, Deneys Myburg said, 'I signed.'

As the angry murmuring of the burghers grew, Nat said quickly, 'Deneys had no choice. His commando was surrounded – just as you are. Besides, the war is almost over. President Kruger has fled to Europe and the British army is swarming over both republics. It's time to call a halt to the killing and to start rebuilding your country. That's why we're here, to ask you to come with us and talk with General Archer.'

'Kruger may have run away, but that's the Transvaal's shame. Mathinus Steyn is *our* president, and Christiaan de Wet is Commandant General of *our* army. We are still fighting – and we'll keep on fighting until we win.'

'Win what, Johannes? Our farms and crops are being burned, our animals slaughtered and women and children either turned out on the veld to fend for themselves, or herded together like cattle in a pen. With each day that passes our fighting men become fewer while more and more *khakis* pour into our country. We *can't* win the war. You know it and I know it. So too does President Steyn. If we don't cease fighting soon there will be no country left to fight for. Then the *uitlanders* will be able to walk in and take what they want. Think about it, man. You know I'm telling the truth. Come and talk to the *khaki* general.'

Deneys Myburg's plea fell upon deaf ears and there was a look of cold anger on Johannes Tromp's face as he said, 'Knowing there are "hands-uppers" living in safety on their farms in my country is a sad fact of life. Having one speak in my presence is an abomination – but when a "hands-upper" tries to persuade his countrymen to lay down their guns and surrender, it becomes treason. I won't have treason preached to the men of my commando.'

'It's not treason but common sense, Johannes, as well you know.'

'We didn't come here to get involved in an argument,' Nat said hurriedly. 'We're here to invite you to talk with General Archer. You've nothing to lose by talking with him. Even if you don't reach agreement, you can arrange for the women and children to be moved out of harm's way.'

'The women and children stay – and I have nothing to say to a British general.'

'Think about it, Commandant. You can't—'

'Enough! Go back to your general and tell him there will be no surrender. We fight. You go, but not him . . .' Commandant Tromp pointed a finger at Deneys Myburg. 'The traitor stays.'

'We both came in under a flag of truce,' Nat protested. 'Deneys Myburg is a prisoner-of-war. I captured him myself.'

'He is a traitor,' Commandant Myburg repeated doggedly. 'And we have procedures for dealing with traitors. I don't think it's any different in the British army?'

'I refuse to leave him behind. I demand that he be allowed to return with me to General Archer . . .'

'You *demand*? Go back to your British masters, Retallick, and tell your general I will be happy to take any more traitors off his hands. Just send them across to me.'

'I am not leaving here without Deneys Myburg.'

'Very well, you may have him . . . soon. Corporal du Toit, you and two of your men stand guard on this man.'

Turning his back on Nat, Commandant Tromp walked to where Deneys Myburg stood. 'Myburg, you are a burgher of the Orange Free State. Your duty in wartime is to serve your country in the commando of your district. Yet you come here today and, acting on the orders of a *khaki* general, try to persuade your countrymen to surrender to the enemy.'

'I came here to plead for you to see sense and so prevent further futile bloodshed.'

'You are admitting that your intention was to persuade your countrymen to lay down their arms?'

'Of course. By carrying on the fight you are destroying all that our fathers fought for.'

'They fought — and they *won*. Deneys Myburg you have convicted yourself by your own words. You will be taken away and shot.'

There was a gasp from some of the listening Boers, but Commandant Tromp did not intend seeking approval for his decision. 'Field Cornet Smit. Choose six men to make up a firing-party, then shoot Myburg.'

Field Cornet Smit was one of the men who had gasped at his commandant's swift verdict and ruthless sentence. 'Johannes . . . are you quite certain this is what must be done?'

'*I'll* do it.' The corporal who was guarding Nat stepped forward. 'I'd shoot *all* "hands-uppers".'

'Very well. Choose your men.'

'You can't do this. It's *murder*!' Nat took a step towards the Boer commandant, but he was immediately grabbed by two of the guards, his arms pinned to his sides.

Deneys Myburg looked frightened, but he could not believe Commandant Tromp would carry out his threat.

'Since when have we begun killing our own people, Johannes?'

'Since some chose to serve the British . . . Take him away, Corporal.'

When Deneys Myburg realised that Commandant Tromp intended to have him shot, he paled and swayed, and the horrified Nat thought he would faint. Then the Boer mediator drew himself up with as much dignity as he could muster.

'I wonder which of us loves his country more, Johannes?'

Commandant Tromp said nothing as the firing squad chosen by the corporal closed in about Deneys Myburg and led him away. One of the men chosen refused to take part in the execution, but another burgher quickly stepped forward to take his place.

Nat was still protesting at the illegality of the Boer commandant's actions, but he was securely pinioned by two burghers and could do nothing.

Deneys Myburg was not taken very far. A space was cleared among the watching Boers, and with his hands secured behind his back he was made to stand in the space between two wagons.

The six-man firing-squad was lined up in front of the condemned man, and now a faint murmur of dissent began in the crowd among burghers who did not agree with the execution of a fellow burgher.

The firing-squad checked their rifles, and then someone suggested that Deneys Myburg should be blindfolded. A man's neckerchief was produced and, as the firing-party came to the ready, the neckerchief was bound around the condemned man's eyes.

The bolts of the rifles were worked, ramming greased cartridges home into grooved barrels, and a hush fell over the watching crowd, broken for an instant by the quickly hushed laugh of a small child.

Deneys Myburg took an unexpected pace forward and,

half-turning, raised his head, as though trying to peer beneath his blindfold to where Nat stood.

The firing-party was called upon to aim, and as the condemned man's head jerked around to face the sound his face contorted in sudden fear. Taking another half-pace forward, uncertainly, as might a drunken man, his mouth suddenly fell open. 'Oh God, *no*! Alice . . . My boys . . .'

Deneys Myburg died thinking of his family. As the corporal of the firing-party dropped his arm, six ·275-inch calibre bullets slammed into his chest, knocking him backwards, his heels scoring the ground. He fell on his back, arms akimbo, his body arching once in an obscene death spasm. Then he lay still, his blood escaping on to the earth of the Drakensbergs.

The silence that followed the shooting ended in a sudden eruption of sound, and Commandant Tromp ordered the men about Nat to release his arms.

'You can return to your general now – and take the body of Myburg with you. That's as much of an answer as I intend to give him. When there is not a single *khaki* left on Orange Free State soil I will be as civil as the next man to the British. Until then I have no time for the niceties of war.'

'I hope every man here agrees with your words, Commandant Tromp. They will have cause to remember them. I came to you under a flag of truce with a man who loved his country as much as any man among you. He came because he wanted to *save* lives. For this you've murdered him.'

'He was executed. The same fate awaits any burgher who follows his example.'

There was a rumble of agreement from the Boers gathered about the two men, but there were also a great many more who preferred to avoid their Commandant's challenging look.

In that moment Nat knew that Commandant Tromp had many waverers in the ranks of his commando. The execution of Deneys Myburg had been a desperate attempt by the Boer commander to stiffen the fighting resolve of his men, using fear of retribution as his weapon. The knowledge made Nat more bitter than before.

Raising his voice, Nat called, 'Does any man here know Deneys Myburg's home? I want to notify his family of what's happened here today.'

'I'll do that.' The reply came from the corporal who had commanded the firing-party. '*And* I'll tell them why he died. It might make the "hands-uppers" and their friends in Frikkiesdorp think again about helping *khakis*.'

'You won't be telling his family anything.' Nat turned a cold anger on the corporal. 'Nor will any other burgher here today. By killing a man who came in under the protection of a flag of truce, Commandant Tromp has sentenced each of you to death as surely as he did Deneys Myburg. You'll be hunted down and killed with no quarter given. The real tragedy is that many of the women and children will die with you. But that's Commandant Tromp's decision – and human life doesn't mean very much to him.'

CHAPTER THIRTY-EIGHT

There was both anger and sorrow in the British camp when Nat returned with the body of Deneys Myburg slung over the saddle of his horse. He was the first Boer many of the inexperienced mounted infantrymen had met. At first the subject of much curiosity, the Afrikaner had become both respected and well-liked by the British soldiers, won over by his friendliness and honest sincerity.

General Archer was furious at the Boer commandant's flagrant disregard for battlefield etiquette and he immediately ordered the British artillery to open fire on the circle of wagons. The barrage quickly became a duel between British and Boer guns, both scoring effectively. The British gun had fired thirty rounds to considerable effect when one of the shells scored a direct hit on a wagon loaded with Boer ammunition. The result was spectacular. The Boer field gun was sent cartwheeling in the air, together with artillerymen and sections of wagons. For many minutes afterwards shells and bullets emerged from a cloud of acrid smoke to pursue zig-zag patterns through the air.

The British artillerymen ceased firing to watch the spectacle – and Commandant Tromp seized the opportunity to prove he was an opponent to be reckoned with.

Smoke from the burning ammunition billowed along the valley, almost reaching the British position held by General Archer and his section of the divided column. As the smoke thinned, a number of Boer horsemen emerged from its cover.

So complete was the surprise that the horsemen were upon the British troops and through their lines before the British officers fully realised what was happening. For a few minutes there was total confusion as the Boers made for the horses, driving a great number before them as they galloped on.

Urged on by their shouting officers, those British soldiers who could seize a horse mounted and gave chase.

Soldiers, Boers and riderless horses were strung out along the valley floor when one of General Archer's staff officers shouted at him, at the same time pointing towards the Boer camp.

Only about a hundred mounted Boers had taken part in the surprise attack on the British lines. Now the remainder could be seen leaving the battered *laager* and streaming away up the steep valley-side. Meanwhile the field gun which had been blown into the air had been brought to bear again and was heavily engaging the remainder of General Archer's force, positioned at the far end of the valley.

The Boer commando was opposed by only a few soldiers posted on the ridge at the side of the valley, and the small British force was quickly overwhelmed.

General Archer fumed impotently as his bugler sounded the recall to the troops pursuing the Boers who had so successfully diverted attention from the escape of the bulk of their comrades.

There were other diversions awaiting the British soldiers. When they advanced upon the Boer *laager* it was discovered that the artillery piece was being manned by wounded men. Around them lay many dead and wounded, including at least a hundred women and children.

Nat had suggested the British commander would have little sympathy for wounded members of the fighting burghers' families, but many of the British soldiers were family-men too. They could not ride off leaving wounded women and children to fend for themselves. The result was that the column wasted a great deal of time tending the Boer wounded and more men than could be spared were detached to escort them to the railway, en route to subsequent internment.

Only when all this had been taken care of did General Archer lead the remainder of his men in pursuit of Commandant Tromp and his commando.

* * *

It was a long and arduous chase. The burghers remained in the Drakensbergs while they could. Doubling back on their tracks on numerous occasions they split into a dozen smaller groups and climbed mountains that no man or beast should have been capable of climbing. But although they kept their freedom the price they were forced to pay was a high one.

Nat followed the trail of the Boer commandant wth relentless tenacity, never once allowing himself to be side-tracked by the many small groups which broke off along the way. He left these to be pursued by the British reinforcements being sent to the mountains in ever-increasing numbers. General Archer and his column remained in close pursuit of Commandant Tromp and his dwindling force.

There were many minor skirmishes, and casualties were sustained by both sides, but only wounded Boers were taken prisoner by the British column. The memory of what had happened to Deneys Myburg remained with the British troops, and flags of truce were ignored on the two occasions they were flown by the Boers.

The dogged pursuit of the elusive Boer commando captured the imagination of the fickle British public, with the result that General Archer, the soldier who had hoped for retirement, became a national hero. Newspaper reports of his exploits were eagerly awaited – and they lost nothing in the telling. The pedantic, stubborn general became one of Great Britain's most unlikely heroes.

For two months Nat led the general and his mounted infantry in pursuit of Commandant Tromp through the mountains to the west and north of Basutoland. The mounted infantry who had begun the campaign as untried recruits became veterans of the new-style war being waged by the Boer 'guerrillas'. They were almost as ragged as the Boer fighters by now. The smart khaki uniforms had long since become tattered, and white skins were burned by the summer sun of the mountains. Many men were on foot too, their horses unable to survive the demands made upon them.

Then, in February 1901, Commandant Tromp broke out of the mountains and led his men back to their homeland veld in the Orange Free State. There were less than a hundred of them.

Ragged and tired, many shared the ignominy of their British pursuers and were horseless.

They headed westward across the veld until they reached the railway line linking Pretoria with the Cape Colony. Here they discovered that the railway line was now guarded by a chain of blockhouses linked together with barbed wire. Built only a few hundred yards apart, they were manned by British soldiers who patrolled the barbed wire along the track at regular intervals. There were armoured trains patrolling the line too, as Commandant Tromp's men learned to their cost.

In a brief but fierce engagement the commando lost twenty-three men, and was forced to double back on its tracks, only narrowly escaping capture by General Archer. Eager for an end to their demanding campaign, the British horsemen turned about and gave chase.

Ten days, and a hundred and sixty miles later, they were back in the Drakensbergs, not far from the Brandwater basin, scene of the mass surrender of so many of the Orange Free State fighting force. Here, Commandant Tromp was finally brought to bay.

Attempting another spectacular escape from his determined pursuers, the Boer commandant successfully scaled a series of mountains where a Basuto native chief had told him only baboons had been before him.

But the British too were fighting a guerrilla-type war now. General Kitchener – the first Baron Kitchener of Khartoum – was a calculating and ruthless bachelor, eighteen years younger than the man he had succeeded. He was also possessed of great energy and a burning ambition. He knew, as did every other professional soldier, that war brought honours and promotion to a soldier – but only to a *victorious* soldier. With the conduct of the war now firmly in his grasp, Kitchener set about winning it as swiftly and decisively as was possible.

The farm-burning policies of Lord Roberts were extended and pursued with a ruthless efficiency that was in itself a reflection of the new commander-in-chief. Blockhouses built along the whole length of a railway line were thrust upon a sceptical army and *made* to work. Lord Roberts had sent soldiers home. Now Kitchener demanded *more*. He not only brought in regular and reserve troops from Great Britain, but also called upon the forces of the British Empire. Australia, Canada, New Zealand – all were represented. He even armed African tribesmen and employed them as guards along his chain of blockhouses, much to the anger of the Boers, who wanted this to remain a 'white man's war'.

Lord Kitchener also recruited a great many 'irregular' soldiers. Companies were formed of men whose particular skill as hunters, scouts and trackers made them invaluable in the new-style war now being fought.

It was Commandant Tromp's misfortune that three such companies had recently been allocated to General Archer. With two companies of Colonel Carey Hamilton's troopers, now among the most experienced 'veld-fighters' in the British army, they formed the spearhead of General Archer's highly mobile force. Hearing that Commandant Tromp had tackled the heights of the Drakensbergs, they decided they would do the same.

Commandant Tromp had succeeded in conquering the mountain barrier – only to be faced with a yawning chasm that sliced through the heart of the mountainous region. A hundred feet wide, its sheer sides dropped to a dark river which flowed over cold rocks that had never felt the warmth of the sun.

There was no way forward, and when Tromp's men tried to turn back they found four hundred advancing British soldiers barring the way.

Out of food, and chilled to the marrow by the cold mountain nights, Commandant Tromp sent out two men carrying a white flag. One was the corporal who had been in command of the firing-party which had executed Deneys Myburg. Even before Nat had time to voice his identification a volley of shots rang out. The corporal and his companion fell riddled with bullets on the rock-strewn mountainside.

The shots had been fired by men of one of the irregular scouting units, comprised of Cape Colony settlers, loyal to the British Crown. When Carey Hamilton remonstrated with them their commander, himself a lieutenant-colonel, dismissed the complaint out of hand. 'You fight the war your way, we'll fight it ours. We've twice been taken-in by Boers who showed a white flag and then opened fire. All right, so they *are* an army of individuals and because one man wants to surrender it might not mean they *all* want to. That's scant comfort to the families of the eleven men we've buried as a result. It's not going to happen a third time – and we're taking no chances with *this* commando. They boast of being "hard" men. Well, now they know they're up against hard men too. Come on, let's see what the rest of them are made of . . .'

It was a fierce battle. Among the rocks around the rim of the deep chasm Commandant Tromp's men fought with hopeless desperation. They could not possibly win, yet neither could they surrender. They were dead men in all but actuality.

The fight moved from boulder to boulder and the end was accomplished by rifle, revolver, and occasionally a razor-sharp skinning-knife. Nat saw Commandant Tromp die. Brought to his knees by numerous bullets, he was struggling to inject a fresh clip of cartridges into the magazine of his Mauser rifle when one of Carey Hamilton's hussars ran up and shot him in the head at point-blank range.

Colonel Carey Hamilton himself led the final assault against the last few Boer survivors. They had made their stand amidst a large pile of crumbling rocks on the very edge of the chasm and the British soldiers were met by a fierce volley that drove them back, leaving six of their number lying on the rocky ground.

Among those who fell was Carey Hamilton. Nat had been fighting alongside the irregular troops and was re-loading his rifle when the cavalry commanding officer was downed. At first he thought Carey had been killed, but then Carey Hamilton raised his head slightly and looked back to where the British soldiers were preparing for a second assault.

The English colonel's plight was a desperate one. If the Boers realised he was still alive they would not hesitate to finish him off.

Calling on the irregulars to give him covering fire, Nat left the shelter of the boulders and headed for Carey Hamilton in a crouching run.

A fusillade of bullets overtook him as he ran and they sang among the boulders concealing the Boers, forcing them to keep their heads down. One or two bullets *were* fired at Nat from the doomed burghers, but they were hastily aimed and went wide.

Nat wasted no time asking Carey Hamilton where he was hit. Grasping the army officer beneath the armpits, he began to drag him back towards the cover of the rocks held by the British soldiers.

When the Boers realised what was happening a few more shots came Nat's way, but then, at a shout from their commanding officer, the British irregulars rose in a body and charged forward *en masse*.

It was the end for the Boers. They stood up to return the fire and died fighting. Two of the hussars helped Nat drag Carey Hamilton the last few yards to safety and Nat examined him to see where he had been shot.

Carey Hamilton had been hit by a bullet which passed through both his legs, breaking a bone in the second. He had also been struck by a bullet which had glanced off a rib. He was suffering a great deal of pain but was in no danger.

Not until a medical orderly arrived to treat the cavalry colonel did Nat realise that he too had been struck by a bullet. Passing between his body and his arm, it had scored a half-inch deep furrow in the flesh of his upper arm. Neither serious nor particularly painful, it was a nuisance only because it was bleeding profusely. Obtaining a bandage from the hardworked medical orderly, Nat had one of the troopers bind it for him.

There were many wounded British soldiers, as well as eleven badly-wounded Boers. Until now no quarter had been given by either side, but the victorious soldiers could not bring themselves to kill wounded men who had fought bravely and well. Commandant Tromp was dead, the battle was over – and with it General Archer's successful campaign.

It was impossible to bury dead men on the rocky mountain top. The bodies of the Boers were simply cast over the edge of the half-mile deep chasm. Dead British soldiers were carried down the mountain until a place was reached where there was enough soil to provide them with a common shallow grave.

Despite the high number of casualties, there was an air of jubilation among the victorious soldiers when they mustered at the foot of the mountain. They had fought a courageous and resourceful enemy in some of the most inhospitable terrain in southern Africa – and they had won.

Later that night, in the camp where they would remain until transport arrived for the wounded, Nat lit a cigarette for Carey Hamilton and offered him a few words of consolation. 'The war is over for you now, Carey. You'll return to England a wounded hero and be given a plum job, somewhere safe and comfortable.'

Carey Hamilton waved away the blue cigarette smoke. 'I'll return to England, certainly – the regiment is due to go anyway – but no desk job for me. I'll be back with the hussars as soon as possible. Hopefully I'll have a brigade in a couple of years.'

Puffing contentedly on his cigarette, Carey Hamilton added, 'I'm the youngest lieutenant-colonel in the regiment and General Archer has told me I'll be a full colonel before I leave South Africa. I can afford to wait out the others now. Unless I do something damned stupid I'll certainly make it to general. With luck I could one day be a field marshal. That should please my grandfather. We haven't had a general in the family since Waterloo.'

'Thomasina will be proud of you – and pleased to have you out of the war.'

'She'll be proud of you too, Nat. Especially when I tell her how you came to my rescue when I lay wounded.'

Carey Hamilton lay back and looked at Nat speculatively. 'You two got on so well in Rhodesia it surprises me that nothing came of your time together in Durban. After all, she's an attractive girl – lonely too, I don't doubt.'

'We hardly saw each other. It wasn't of my making. She was always working so damned hard on board that hospital ship. I tried hard to see more of her . . .' Nat shrugged. 'It's probably for the best. Thomasina belongs in a big city. A place where she can dress up and go out and be seen. There's nothing for her at Insimo.'

'Did you ask her to go back there with you?'

'Yes. She declined.'

'Don't give up, Nat. You have a lot to offer her. You'll be a powerful man in Rhodesia one day. Tell Thomasina so. She's ambitious and you could satisfy all her ambitions. With a woman like Thomasina behind you there'll be no stopping you.'

Nat was not certain he wanted to have to prove his future

prospects in order to interest Thomasina. He had hoped she might love him for what he was, not for what he *might* one day be. ·

Later that night Nat took out the tattered, well-read telegraph message he had received from Thomasina at the beginning of General·Archer's campaign. He knew the message off by heart, but now he tried to read something new into its wording: '*Utterly miserable . . . So much needed to be said . . .*'

Nat folded the message, but instead of replacing it in his pocket he screwed it up and threw it into the fire that burned a few yards away. He should have destroyed it many weeks before. Thomasina would be settled in England now. She had probably already forgotten about him.

As he settled down in his blanket and gazed up at the stars high above him, Nat wondered vaguely whether Esme Erasmus was still in Durban.

CHAPTER THIRTY-NINE

When Adam rode out of the Brandwater basin leaving Esme behind he did not know where he was going. For the moment his only thought was to escape. Following the trail made by the others proved to be easier than he had expected, and within twenty-four hours Adam had linked up with a commando heading for the heights of the Drakensbergs.

For a month he remained with this commando, composed of Orange Free State men. But hiding in the mountains with only an occasional foray to harass a small British patrol, or to tear up a stretch of railway line, became boring. With three other young men he left the Orange Free State men and joined a commando made up of settlers of German descent. Riding south through Natal, they passed no more than ten miles from Durban without encountering any British troops.

The commando eventually reached the Cape Colony. Here they quickly learned it was safe to ride only at night, avoiding roads and railways. Commandos from both Transvaal and the Orange Free State were very active here – and so too was the British army.

There were many Boer sympathisers in this British colony, especially in the predominantly Boer-owned farming areas of the western Cape. It was not particularly difficult to locate one of the major commandos and join forces with them.

But here too Adam quickly learned that the guerrilla tactics of hit-and-run involved a great deal of running but very little hitting.

During the course of two wretched months, when both weather and the enemy combined to oppose them, Adam's commando fought only one major engagement. When he met up with a disillusioned small commando returning north to Transvaal, Adam went with them.

The commando journeyed six hundred miles through British-held territory and along the way took part in enough skirmishes to satisfy Adam's need for action. They also learned – at the cost of five good men – that the British had armed the tribesmen along the Cape Colony's border with the Orange Free State and were offering them a bounty for each Boer guerrilla captured or killed.

As a reprisal, the commando raided a native *kraal* late one night. Riding through the straw-hutted village they threw lighted torches through the doorways of huts and shot the occupants as they ran out. To Adam it was the most satisfying of all the actions in which he had taken part since the war had entered the guerrilla stage.

'Jesus! Look at the land. What do you make of it, Adam?' The speaker reined in his pony at the edge of a highveld farming settlement. Prime Transvaal farming country, it should have been lush with grass and crops and stocked with fat, contented cattle. Instead, the earth was charred black from recent burning for as far as could be seen.

'Who do you think did this? Was it Koos De la Rey, or the *khakis*?'

Adam pointed to where a blackened and roofless farmhouse stood surrounded by demolished outbuildings. 'Koos would burn crops if he thought they might feed the *khakis*. He would never do *that*.'

'Then the *khakis* have been here?'

'Yes. There must have been fighting in this area or they wouldn't have bothered to destroy everything so thoroughly.'

There were eleven survivors of the small party that had left the Cape Colony. Less than a quarter of the original number. Some had died in skirmishes with the British and their tribesmen allies. A few had been wounded and left behind to receive medical attention from their enemies. Others, weary of fighting, had surrendered themselves. The remainder had simply lost the main party, or decided to go their own ways. The survivors were all young men, and by unspoken consent

Adam had assumed leadership of the dwindling commando.

'What can we do now? There's nothing left here.'

'We find Koos De la Rey and join his commando. But first I want to know what's happened to my place and to some of the friends I left behind.'

Waiting until the others had nodded agreement, Adam said, 'Fine. We'll all go our separate ways and find General De la Rey when we can. There must be *someone* left in Transvaal who knows where he is.'

The British army had made a thorough job of destroying farms and crops, thus depriving the essentially nomadic Boer guerrillas of an important source of supply for both horses and men. Nevertheless, total destruction of plant and animal life was not possible and Adam found enough to feed himself and his horse.

He travelled cautiously, but there were no British soldiers here now. Satisfied the country would no longer support a commando of any size, they had moved on. As a result Adam covered thirty-five miles of farmland without meeting another human being.

Adam headed for the Viljoen farm first. After what had occurred when he was last with them he did not expect to be a welcome visitor, but things had been happening in his absence and Cornelius Viljoen was the man most likely to tell him about them.

It did not occur to Adam that the Viljoen farm might also have been destroyed by the British. After all, Nat had obtained letters of safe conduct for Cornelius and Lucas, signed by Lord Roberts himself. Nat had told Adam so during their meeting in the Brandwater basin.

Not until Adam actually rode on to Viljoen land and saw that it too was scorched did he realise that Nat had put too much faith in the signature of the former British commander-in-chief. A few minutes later he knew for certain. The Viljoen farmhouse and outhouses were in the same ruined condition as every other farm in the area. Even the well was contaminated, a number of animals having been killed and their carcasses thrown into the water.

Sitting on the low wall of the well, Adam looked about him in bewilderment. What had happened to all the people? Surely the British soldiers had not killed them all?

Then his gaze turned towards the distant hills where his own farm lay. Would the *khakis* have found their way there too?

Mounting his horse, Adam headed northwards, riding at a canter across the burned landscape, the hooves of his horse kicking up small puffs of grey ash as it went.

It wanted an hour to sunset when Adam turned into the valley where Theunis Erasmus had settled. When he saw the gaping roof and smoke-blackened walls he knew the *khakis* had been here.

Adam had thought very little about Margret. He was reluctant, even now, to regard her as his 'wife'. No doubt she had gone to stay with her relatives as soon as she realised he was not coming back. But what of those relatives now? And the child . . . his child? Perhaps Nat had found them both and taken them to Insimo . . .

As he drew closer to the house Adam was surprised to see that a vegetable plot had been laid out on the slope behind the farm. The paddock too had been cleared and the fencing extended, although much of it was broken down now. He was puzzled, wondering who had carried out the work.

Then Adam saw the graves. He read the inscriptions first, before slipping from his horse. He stood awkwardly looking at the grave containing the bodies of Margret and the child. His *son*. Then he looked at the adjacent grave. Why should a British soldier be buried here too? Had Margret shot him when he and his companions came to burn the farm? Margret and the soldier had died on the same day. The baby the day after . . . What *had* happened? The only certain fact was that Margret had *not* left the farm to stay with her own family. For a brief moment Adam felt a twinge of conscience. This was lonely country for a man. It must have been very much worse for Margret, especially when she reached the later stages of her pregnancy.

Adam looked about him at the ruins of his farm. There was little here worth dying for. Yet Theunis Erasmus had gone to war and died in the belief that he was fighting for the right to live his life here. Now Margret and her child – *his* child. And an unknown British soldier . . .

From the corner of his eye Adam caught a movement farther

along the valley. It was a lone rider. Tying his horse in the deep shadow cast by the burned-out barn, Adam checked his rifle and waited.

Long before the rider reached the house Adam had recognised Lucas Viljoen. The two men greeted each other warmly before Adam asked what had been happening here, and in the Lichtenburg area.

'The *khakis* came. They rounded up all the people they could find and burned our farms and crops. The women, children and some of the men have been put into camps — 'concentration' camps they call them. The rest of the men — those who couldn't prove they'd taken the oath of loyalty to the British — were declared to be prisoners-of-war and shipped off.'

'But *you're* free.'

'So are the rest of the family. With a few others we got out before the *khakis* came. We're camped back in the hills. We keep look-outs posted during the day in case the *khakis* come back to look for us. That's how I saw you.'

Lucas inclined his head towards the graves. 'I'm sorry about Margret and the child. We came here looking for her, but we were too late.'

'Do you know what happened?'

Lucas Viljoen shook his head. 'We found only what you see here. The damned *khakis* have a lot to answer for.'

'Where was Koos De la Rey while all this was going on?'

'He's still fighting, Adam. Winning too, but he's got no more than two hundred men with him. What can they do against thousands of *khakis*? But come. At least there's no shortage of food in the hills. The *khakis* haven't been able to kill off all the game.'

As Adam mounted his horse, Lucas Viljoen looked about him regretfully. 'It's a tragedy, Adam. Margret worked hard up here. Made a garden, brought in a cow, mended fences, and made the house look nice. She even shot a kaffir who killed one of your calves. If Gezima turns out as well she'll make me a good wife one day. She's moved to Johannesburg to stay with an aunt until things change. I'm glad. She's best out of all this.'

'How is Johanna?'

'You'll be able to see for yourself soon enough. Like the rest of the women, she's tired of living in a wagon. But she'll survive.'

The Boer camp had been set up in a beautiful spot, marred only by the circumstances in which those living there found themselves. In a small, blind valley with a waterfall tumbling a hundred feet down a sheer cliff to a stream on the valley floor, it was well concealed amidst trees and thin scrub.

'It's as good a spot as we could hope to find in the circumstances,' explained Lucas. 'There were a few kaffirs around when we first came here, but we chased them out and they've kept their distance ever since.'

It was almost dark now and the flames from the camp-fires cast dancing shadows on the canvas of the wagons. There were ten wagons and probably sixty people living here. Most were women and children.

A mouth-watering smell of roasting meat rose from the cooking-fires and Adam was reminded it had been a very long time since he had tasted any decent cooking.

Johanna was busy at the Viljoens' fire. She was deeply tanned, no doubt as a result of the weeks spent on the sun-soaked veld. She was thinner too, and somehow older looking. as though the hardships suffered by the Viljoen family had matured her.

She gave no indication that she had seen Adam enter the camp, but when he walked to stand behind her at the camp-fire, she said, 'There will be food for you in a minute or two. No doubt you'll be as hungry as De la Rey's men always were when they rode by . . . When we were home on the farm.'

'I'm hungry,' admitted Adam. 'I didn't know you'd seen me arrive.'

'I saw you. I knew it was you the moment word went around that a rider was coming. It's a pity you couldn't have made it a few months earlier. While poor Margret was still alive. You should be ashamed of yourself, riding off and leaving her alone up here.'

'Women are being left alone on farms all over the Transvaal. Besides, I didn't think for one minute she'd stay.' Adam repeated the words he used to allay his own self-guilt. 'I felt sure she'd return home to her family.'

'And admit her husband had left her after no more than

344

twenty-four hours of marriage? You know very little about women, Adam Retallick.'

'I didn't *want* to marry her. You of all people should know that.'

'All I know is that you treated her worse than a kaffir woman. Here . . . take this and get it down you. It's probably your beef anyway. Pa shot a bull yesterday. The vegetables are yours too. I took them from Margret's garden.'

Looking down at the heaped plate, Adam said, 'I had hoped you would be pleased to see me again.'

'Pleased? I'd be pleased if it were Lord Roberts's head sitting on that plate you're holding. But it wouldn't change anything, would it? Nothing can change what's happened . . . to any of us. Go and eat that food before it goes cold. You look as though it's been a long while since you had a good meal in your belly, Adam Retallick.'

Adam carried the plate to the fire where Cornelius Viljoen sat puffing at his pipe. When Adam asked if he might sit at the fire, the head of the Viljoen household nodded gravely and pointed at a spot near him.

Cornelius Viljoen sat watching Adam eat for a while, and then he said, 'You treated Johanna shabbily, Adam, and I can never forgive you for that. But you've suffered a grievous loss and I'll not show malice towards a man who has lost his wife, child and farm to the British. You're welcome to share whatever we have.'

His sentiments were not echoed by *Ouma* Viljoen. When she came from the wagon and found Adam ensconced beside the fire, she pointed a bony finger at him.

'What's he doing here? I thought we'd rid ourselves of him, once and for all.'

'Hush, *Ouma*. The boy's just returned from fighting the British. He's lost everything to them. That was his farm . . . the last one we passed.'

'Lost everything, you say? He's lost *nothing*. Has he seen fifty years of hard work and memories burned? No. Easy come, easy go. That's all it is to *him*.'

'Quiet, *Ouma*.' This time Sophia Viljoen tried to silence the old woman.

'Don't you tell me to be quiet, my girl. That young man is

345

trouble. I knew it the first time I set eyes on him. Not that anyone takes any notice of *me*, these days. I might just as well keep my own counsel. I'm going off to bed – and don't any of you come in the wagon for anything until I'm decently wrapped in my blanket. We may be living in a wagon, but that doesn't mean we have to forget all the decencies of life. We remembered them when we were *voortrekkers*, even when we were fighting off kaffirs. I'll not have Viljoen standards lowered just because we've been run out of our home by the British.'

Glaring about her, *Ouma* Viljoen's belligerent gaze returned to Adam once more. With a final 'Bah!' she turned away and made her way to the wagon.

Later, Adam related his recent experiences to the displaced Boers and told them what he knew of the 'progress' of the war. They in turn gave him details of the British army's clearance of the area.

Nothing that was said gave anyone even a faint glimmer of hope for the future of the South African republics. All agreed that before long those burghers who still fought on would be disputing the ownership of a depopulated and barren land.

At dawn the next morning the refugee Lichtenburg settlers and Adam were captured by the British army. Warning of the presence of the *khakis* was first given by *Ouma* Viljoen. It was the old lady's habit of a lifetime to go to bed and rise with the sun. Having dressed inside her wagon, she climbed out to fetch water for her ablutions and saw the long line of khaki-clad horsemen not twenty yards away, sealing off the valley entrance.

Her loud cries brought women and children peering from inside canvas covers, while beneath the wagons men threw off their blankets. Adam came awake in a hurry and his first thought was to reach for the rifle lying on the ground beside him.

His fingers had just touched the butt when a hoarse voice from no more than three feet away said, 'I wouldn't do that, sonny. Not if you know what's good for you.'

The voice came from the other side of one of the wagon's tall wheels. A rifle was resting on one of the spokes of the wheel, aimed at Adam's head. The soldier was a Scotsman, one of the company of privately recruited scouts who had proved their worth in the Brandwater basin campaign. Adam slowly removed his hand from the butt of his rifle and kept it well clear. The Scots scout had warned Adam. He might as easily have shot him. It would be foolish to stretch his luck too far.

When the wagons had been cleared and the occupants gathered in a tight, sullen group, the mystery of how the soldiers had discovered the whereabouts of the Boer refugees was solved. The soldiers had a local tribesman with them. Dressed self-importantly in a faded khaki topee and a ragged army shirt, he had reported the presence of the refugees to the British army and guided the soldiers to their hiding-place.

There were only seven Boer men in the camp. Five of these were immediately separated from the others. Among them were Adam and Lucas. These five were to be treated as prisoners-of-war. Cornelius Viljoen and another man, both crippled, would be taken with the women and children to a 'concentration' camp near Mafeking. Here, and in many other such camps, were concentrated all those persons, mainly women and children, who had been rendered homeless by the British policy of burning farms and crops.

When those designated as prisoners-of-war were ordered to give their names to a Scouts officer, Adam took the opportunity to object to Lucas's being included among their number.

'Look at him,' he protested. 'His arm is so badly crippled he couldn't manage a rifle, even if he were so inclined.'

Slapping his thigh, the officer retorted, 'I'm carrying an ounce of lead in here. It was put there by a Boer with only *one* arm. A rifle was found in this young man's possession – and one rifle means one prisoner. It was either the boy or his father.'

'But they've both got letters of amnesty, signed personally by Lord Roberts.'

'So? Lord Roberts is in London, telling anyone foolish enough to believe him that the war is over. Lord Kitchener is commander-in-chief here now. It's *his* orders I'm following. If you've got anyone to bid farewell to you'd better do it now. We'll be moving off shortly.'

Johanna had listened to the exchange and now she crossed

to Adam. 'Thank you for trying to help Lucas. You didn't have to do it.'

'You needn't worry about Lucas. I'll look after him — and they haven't got us inside a prisoner-of-war camp yet.'

'Don't do anything foolish, Adam. This war can't go on much longer.'

'It's not over yet, and I have no intention of rotting away in some prison camp while there's still fighting to be done. But what about you? You'll be in a camp too.'

'We'll be all right. If the *khakis* put us in a camp they'll have to feed us. It will be better for *Ouma*, really. She's fond of telling us about her *voortrekker* days, when they lived in a wagon for months at a time, but she was much younger then.'

'I don't suppose she would have liked *me* any better in those days . . .'

'Probably not. But you've hardly behaved in a manner calculated to endear you to *any* of the Viljoen family.'

'I'm sorry for what's happened, Johanna. I really am. Especially for the way I've hurt you. You were the reason I came to fight for Transvaal in the first place.'

Johanna snorted, but Adam took heart from the fact that the sound lacked ferocity.

'It wasn't your *fighting* that landed you in trouble. It was what happened between you and Margret Coetzee.'

The soldiers had begun ordering the refugees to their wagons and Adam said desperately, 'Margret's dead now . . . Will we meet again, Johanna?'

'If it's what you *really* want.'

Adam's delight caused the soldier who was about to order him to join the other prisoners-of-war to hold back for a moment more.

'You mean . . . you'll wait for me?'

'Do you want me to?'

'I *do*. I swear it.'

'Then I'll wait.'

Adam took a step towards Johanna, but an officer was demanding that the soldier guarding him put Adam with the other men.

Prodding Adam with his rifle, the Scots soldier ordered him to move. 'Your time's up, laddie. War calls for sacrifices. This is yours. Over there with the others now.'

'Take care,' Adam called to Johanna in Afrikaans. 'Don't give up hope. I may be seeing you sooner than you expect . . .'

Another prod and Adam was sent on his way. Ten minutes later, their hands tied behind them and with each Boer horse led by a mounted Scots scout, Adam and the four burghers rode into captivity.

CHAPTER FORTY

By the time the train carrying the Boer prisoners-of-war reached Durban, there were a hundred and seventy men from Transvaal on board. The British were enjoying a brief period of rare success against the Boer guerrillas. In a number of minor engagements they had killed and wounded forty-seven fighting-men and captured thirty more. The remainder of the men on the train had ridden into British army camps to give themselves up, dispirited after months of being hounded across the hills and plains of southern Africa.

There was a strong escort waiting for the prisoners-of-war at Durban. The station was crowded too with newly arrived British soldiers, awaiting transportation to the highly fluid 'front'. When the Boer prisoners were allowed to stretch their legs on the heavily guarded platform, British soldiers crowded around for their first glimpse of 'the enemy'.

There were others on the platform. Women volunteers from the town who considered it their duty to perform a daily voluntary service, providing refreshments for the British troops.

When the prisoners-of-war stepped from the train, one of the women volunteers, a colonel's wife, suggested they should extend their charity to include their unfortunate enemies. After all, a number were wounded – and it would doubtless make an interesting article for the bored correspondent of the *Natal Mercury*, who just happened to be on the platform.

Adam was lighting a cigarette for a Boer artillery man who had lost a hand in an accident with a captured field gun, when a voice behind him asked, 'Would you like a tea, or a coffee?'

The question was asked in Afrikaans, which was unusual enough, but it was the voice that caused him to turn around hurriedly, an expression of disbelief on his face.

'Esme!'

'Adam!'

They both spoke in unison, each as amazed as the other. Then the flame of the match he was holding reached Adam's fingers and he shook it free quickly.

Of the two, Adam was the more surprised. He had seen Esme only in the old clothes which were all she possessed when she roamed the hills about her home and, more latterly, dressed as a young burgher. Now she was dressed as befitted a respectable young city girl. Her hair was much shorter than was currently fashionable, but it had been given professional attention to eliminate all traces of the *takhaaren* haircuts she had suffered at Adam's hands.

'What happened? Where were you captured?' Esme was the first to recover.

'In the hills above the farm . . . or what's left of the farm. It's been burned down by the *khakis*. But what about you? What are *you* doing? You'd pass for a *ruineck* anywhere. Is Nat in Durban too?'

'No, he's somewhere in the Transvaal, scouting again. Do you want me to try to contact him? To tell him you're here?'

'God, no! They pulled a couple of Cape rebels off the train at Pietermaritzburg. Talk was that they were going to be tried for treason and then executed because they were born in a British colony. I'd be in a tricky situation if anyone knew I'm from Rhodesia. If Nat knew I was a prisoner he'd try to have me set free – and probably get me shot. Whatever you do, don't tell *him*.'

At that moment a British soldier came along and, using the butt end of his rifle, forced Adam back, away from Esme.

'Is he bothering you, miss? If he is I'll put him back on the train.'

'He's not bothering me.' Esme spoke in English and although her accent was unmistakable it was a considerable achievement for a girl who had spoken nothing but Afrikaans before coming to Durban.

But some of the English women were looking disapprovingly in Esme's direction, and she could see the huge bulk of Madame Claris pushing her way along the crowded platform towards her.

'I have to go now.' The Retallick family likeness was too strong for Adam's capture to remain a secret if the French-woman saw him. 'I'll find out where you're being held and try to visit you.'

Before Adam could reply Esme had gone. Successfully heading off Madame Claris, she served tea to English soldiers for the remainder of the time the Boer prisoners-of-war were on the platform.

Adam and the other prisoners were placed in a hurriedly adapted camp on the dockside, with another hundred prisoners-of-war who had been brought to Durban two days before. The 'prison camp' consisted of a number of single-storey buildings, built to hold freight. Surrounded by two twelve-feet high fences topped with barbed wire, it was to serve as the holding area for five hundred prisoners until a ship arrived from Cape Town to carry the men in captivity to the island of Ceylon. It was such a temporary arrangement that even the camp guard force was provided on a makeshift basis. Some of the guards belonged to the Durban Town Guard force, the remainder were drawn from whichever regiment was staying in Durban long enough to provide armed men for twenty-four hours of guard duty.

Esme's visit to the dockside prison camp caused some consternation. No one knew whether a prisoner-of-war was *entitled* to receive a visitor, but eventually the commander of the guard was located. An officer in a militia unit newly arrived from England, he showed far more interest in Esme than in her mission. When he questioned her about her relationship with Adam, she was able to explain, quite truthfully, that they had met when he took over her father's farm. He was not a *particular* friend, she added, aware of the officer's interest in her, but she *would* like to know about their mutual acquaintances in the area where she had grown up.

After assuring Esme that he was doing her a great favour, the officer granted her written permission to visit Adam and she was escorted inside the double-fenced compound.

It was difficult to find a place to talk where they would not be overheard, but eventually Adam secured a spot close to the wire, looking out to sea beyond the busy Durban docks.

They exchanged details of all that had happened to each other since they parted company and Esme clenched her fists angrily as Adam described the state of the farm. She was equally angry when told it was a native from the hills who had led the British soldiers to the Lichtenburg refugees. The African village headman had always been well disposed towards the local Boer settlers, and many of the natives were known to Esme. It seemed they too had decided the Boers were losing the war and were anxious to ingratiate themselves with the new rulers of Transvaal.

After telling Adam something of her life in Durban since the British surgeon had removed the bullet from her body, Esme asked if there was anything she could do for Adam.

'Yes, you can help me to escape,' replied Adam, promptly.

'Escape from here? The place is swarming with troops and you are miles from Transvaal. It's madness.'

'No. I've raided in Natal. There are plenty of *khakis* here but they are either guarding the railway line or performing garrison duty in one or two of the larger towns. If we keep clear of these we can reach the Drakensbergs and be back in Transvaal without ever seeing a *khaki*.'

'Who do you mean by "we"?'

'Lucas Viljoen, you, and me.'

'You've made your first mistake before setting foot outside the camp. I don't *want* to go back to Transvaal.'

Adam was flabbergasted. 'You can't want to stay here? These are not your people, Esme. Natal is *British*. It was the British who killed your pa.'

'Wrong again. It was the *khakis* who killed him. The British who live in Durban aren't very different from us. Most are descended from settlers who fought kaffirs for the right to live here. They would fight them again, if they had to. But they haven't been content merely to scratch a living from the ground. They've built cities and docks. They have parties and concerts, and they enjoy fine clothes and nice things I didn't know existed.'

'Such things aren't exclusive to the British. There are plenty of places in the Transvaal where they have all these things. Pretoria, Johannesburg . . .'

'I wouldn't know. They certainly haven't come my way before. I was the youngest of eleven girls. I got everyone else's hand-me-downs. I never had a pair of shoes on my feet until a year or so ago because they were always worn out by the time they got to me. The only thing I had of my own was an old musket that no one else wanted. Whenever we had visitors the sole subject of conversation was whether it was going to rain that year, or not. When we girls were on our own my sisters would talk of how best to catch themselves a husband. When I'd had enough of such talk I'd go off on my own, up into the hills. By the time the last of them got herself married they all believed I didn't like being around people. That I *preferred* being on my own. It isn't true, it was just that I didn't want to be around *them*, talking about trapping a man as though he was next day's dinner. People are different here. They talk of what's going on in the *world*. I can *read* now – not much yet, but it's improving. I'm learning about all sorts of exciting things I've never even *heard* of before. I don't want to go back to being the way I was.'

'I feel equally strongly about being shipped to a prisoner-of-war camp in Ceylon. I'm going to get out of here before they put me on that boat.'

'And you want me to help you?'

'You owe it to me, Esme. I risked my life to save yours, in the Brandwater basin. If I hadn't you'd have died, and never known anything about this life you're enjoying so much.'

Adam was speaking the truth, as Esme knew.

'What do you want me to do?'

'Get a gun in to me somehow . . . and arrange to have horses waiting somewhere nearby. Steal them if need be. It will be thought Lucas and I have taken them.'

'That won't be necessary. I can buy them. Nat left me money . . .'

Adam raised his eyebrows. 'Did he now? Tell me, does your reluctance to leave Durban have anything to do with my brother?'

'No!' Esme responded angrily. 'When he was in Durban he spent all his time pining for Thomasina Vincent.'

'Isn't that the woman he escorted from Umtali to Fort Victoria? The sister of the *khaki* officer Nat befriended when we returned from Mafeking? But she's married to some *khaki* colonel.'

'She might have been once. She's a widow now.'

'And here in Durban?'

'Not any more. She went to Cape Town on the hospital ship, *Maine*, while Nat was somewhere on the Drakensbergs chasing Johannes Tromp's commando. But they're saying in Durban that Johannes has been killed with most of his men, so Nat might come back here at any time.'

'Why should he return to Durban?'

'Because he probably believes Thomasina is still here.'

'Then I'll need to make my escape as quickly as possible. When can you have the gun and the horses?'

'I can have the horses by tomorrow. The gun might prove a little more difficult.'

'Do what you can – but do it quickly. My plan depends on the sort of chaos we've got here at the moment. The guards are changing so often that men and officers never get to know each other. If they once set regular guards I'll have no chance at all.'

The next day it seemed Adam's escape plan would suffer a major setback. Nat returned to Durban.

He arrived in the late evening on a special train that carried General Archer and his staff, together with the British soldiers wounded in the final stages of the highly successful campaign against Commandant Tromp.

When the train pulled into the station, Nat enquired hopefully whether the hospital ship *Maine* was in Durban. He was told that the vessel was currently in Cape Town, having made two voyages to Great Britain since Nat was last in Durban. Carey Hamilton and the other wounded men from General Archer's column were to be temporarily accommodated in Durban's hospital.

It was dark when Nat was let into the house of Madame Claris by the servant, but there was no mistaking the bulk of the Frenchwoman as she hurried to the hallway to greet him. In the pale light cast by a lamp on the hall table, Nat did not immediately recognise her companion. Then, as he escaped from Madame Claris's all-enveloping embrace, realisation came to him.

'Esme . . .! Is this really you?' Nat kissed Esme on the cheek, then stood back and regarded her with awe. 'Madame Claris . . . what have you done with the little Afrikaner farm girl I left behind? You've transformed her!'

Pleased with his reaction, Madame Claris smiled. 'No, Nat. Esme is what she has always been, a beautiful young girl. All I have done is to dress her so people *notice* what she is. Now every eligible young man in Durban finds a reason to come calling on Madame Claris. After so many years I am suddenly the most popular lady in town. Such a pity I am too old to enjoy so much attention . . .!'

'Will you be staying for a while, Nat?' The eager question came from Esme. 'Long enough for me to show you something of Durban? It really is a wonderful place.'

Nat smiled and Madame Claris saw he was desperately tired.

'Hush, child. Time enough tomorrow to talk of showing him Durban. You will be hungry, Nat? We were about to eat. There is plenty.'

'I'm starving. Give me a couple of minutes to clean up and I'll join you.' His glance returned to Esme. He was finding it difficult to believe this really was the same girl he had brought to Durban only a few months before.

When he had gone Madame Claris put an arm about Esme's shoulders and squeezed her affectionately. 'Don't try to hurry him, child. You are fond of him but he needs to forget Thomasina first. He realises now that you are a woman and no longer a young girl. Let this be enough for tonight.'

Esme looked up at the large woman anxiously. 'Are my feelings for him so obvious?'

'To me, child, yes . . . but when you are a beautiful woman hiding inside a body like mine you know more about hidden feelings than most.'

Madame Claris thought it would probably take Nat a long time to relax, but plentiful wine and good food had their effect. When the meal had ended he leaned back in his chair and beamed at each of the women in turn. 'I haven't tasted food like that since I was last here – and there have been times in recent weeks when I thought I never *would* again.'

'It has been a hard campaign?' The question came from Madame Claris.

'The hardest I've known . . .' Nat was silent for a while, then he said, 'I heard at the station that some Boer prisoners have been brought in. I thought I might go down to speak to them tomorrow. See if they've heard anything of Adam.'

'I've already spoken to them. They know nothing of him.' Esme's reply was hurried . . . *too* hurried. Madame Claris was looking at her strangely. 'I was at the station serving tea to British troops when the prisoners arrived. A couple were Lichtenburg men I'd met once or twice at home. I took some things to them in their camp. They know Adam and say he's safe, but they don't know where.'

'Oh well, it's enough for the moment to know he's well. I keep hoping he'll see sense and return to Insimo, where he belongs.'

'Perhaps he thinks the same about you,' said Esme quietly.

'Um . . . perhaps he does.' Nat stifled the fourth yawn in as many minutes. Turning to Madame Claris, he said, 'That was a wonderful meal, but I really am very tired. If you don't mind, I'll go to my room now.'

'Of course. I am happy to know you are safely back in Durban.'

Rising to his feet, Nat smiled at Esme. 'We'll talk again in the morning . . . Perhaps while you're showing me something of Durban.'

Esme's delight was so evident that Madame Claris felt pain on her behalf. The Frenchwoman was both shrewd and imaginative. From a number of things Esme had let slip she guessed more of the truth behind Esme's wounding than the young Afrikaner girl would ever know. Madame Claris also knew that, in spite of her background, Esme was extremely vulnerable, especially where Nat Retallick was concerned.

The large Frenchwoman was an incurable romantic. When Thomasina had been under her roof and so unhappy after the loss of her husband, Madame Claris had hoped Nat might prove to be her salvation. Now her affection was for Esme – and the young girl was far more vulnerable than Thomasina Vincent. She also cared far more for Nat Retallick. Madame Claris prayed hard that he would not hurt her too badly.

Esme went to her room soon after Nat. He had almost

357

completed his packing when he heard a sound on the balcony outside. Parting the curtains he saw a woman silhouetted against the sky and his heart began racing excitedly. Hurriedly opening the french windows, he almost fell on to the balcony in his eagerness.

'Thomasina . . .?'

The silhouetted figure turned towards him and he saw it was *not* Thomasina Vincent.

'I'm sorry to disappoint you, Nat. Madame Claris gave me Thomasina's room. It was so lovely it seemed a shame to leave it empty.'

'I . . . I only wanted to tell her about her brother,' Nat lied. '. . . He's one of the wounded men we brought back to Durban.'

'Oh!' Esme desperately wanted to believe him. 'Is he badly hurt?'

'It's serious enough to have him sent back to England. But he's luckier than many others.'

'Was it really bad out there this time?'

'Worse than before . . . but, then, it always is. All this killing is so utterly senseless. The Boers can't possibly win, you know.'

Esme nodded. 'I realise that now. Since I began helping the women at the station and the docks I've seen British troops arriving by the boatload, day after day. It's said there are more British troops in Transvaal now than there are Afrikaners.'

'I wouldn't be surprised – but I don't know what they're doing. We saw few of them when we were chasing Commandant Tromp.'

'No doubt they were busy burning the farms. Pa's farm . . . *Adam's* farm, was one of them – one of the prisoners told me,' she added hastily.

'What of Adam's wife? She was expecting a child.'

'Dead. The child too . . .'

Esme realised she had already said more than she had intended. 'One of the men I spoke to said he had seen their grave at the farm. He . . . he didn't know how it had happened.'

'God! What a mess this war is making of everyone's life. I hope Adam doesn't learn of it just yet. It might provoke him

358

into doing something reckless. I think I'll go and see those prisoners myself and see what I can find out . . .'

'Not tomorrow, you won't. You're escorting me about Durban.'

Esme knew she had to keep Nat away from the prisoner-of-war camp while Adam was there. She could do little else to further Adam's escape for the moment.

'I've got a souvenir for you. It's more than that, really. With the state of things in Transvaal you might find it useful if ever you return.'

Going inside his room, Nat returned carrying a leather belt and holster. Inside the holster the light gleamed on the dark metal of a revolver. 'Here, it belonged to Johannes Tromp.'

'Thank you, Nat.'

Esme knew she held the key to Adam's escape in her hands. The one thing she had believed would be almost impossible to obtain. She wished she could tell him of the use to which it would be put. Instead, she stepped forward and kissed him.

'What was that for?' Nat put a finger to the corner of his mouth where her lips had touched him.

'Isn't that what English girls always do when they are given a present?' Esme put the gun down on the table. 'Perhaps it's different when a girl is given a *revolver*?'

'I wouldn't know. I can't ever remember giving a present to a girl before – English *or* Afrikaner.'

Nat was standing close to Esme and he could smell her newly washed hair. It was a freshness that reminded him of Insimo and a world far removed from war.

'I'm glad,' said Esme. 'It's the first present I've ever been given by a man.'

She was looking up at him and suddenly it seemed the most natural thing in the world to bring his face down to hers and kiss her. The kiss began softly, tentatively, their lips hardly touching. Then it was as though he had applied a match to kindling. He felt her body tremble against his, and then she was pressed so tightly to him that all the trembling stopped.

Suddenly there was a loud knocking at Nat's bedroom door and Madame Claris called, 'Nat, are you there? I have something for you . . .'

Breaking free of Nat's embrace, Esme backed away from

him. She looked up at him for a moment, as though waiting for him to say something, but then the knocking on Nat's door was repeated.

Snatching the gun from the table, Esme fled to her own room as Nat went to answer Madame Claris.

When he opened the door Madame Claris walked past him into the room. In her hand she held a number of letters.

'These came while you were away. I should have given them to you earlier.'

Walking to the open french windows, she peered out to the balcony before closing the windows and drawing the curtains. 'The nights are cooler now, but we are still troubled by mosquitoes. It is better to have your windows closed. The light attracts them.'

Nat made no reply. Most of the envelopes he had been given were in the free-flowing handwriting of his mother. Two more were the laborious work of his youngest brother. The remaining letter bore a Cape Town postmark and the handwriting was unfamiliar to him.

Tearing open the envelope Nat read the letter quickly and his expression changed from puzzlement to delight. When he had finished he read through again before looking up at Madame Claris.

'It's from Thomasina. She's in Cape Town – something to do with a "Ladies' Committee". She wants me to go there and travel with her up-country as her guide and interpreter.'

Outside Nat's room Madame Claris closed the door behind her, then shook her head.

'Poor Esme,' she whispered to herself. 'Poor, dear Esme.'

CHAPTER FORTY-ONE

Two days later Esme paid another visit to the Boer prisoner-of-war camp. There was a new officer and guard on duty but the pass issued on her first visit proved sufficient and she was allowed inside after an apologetic but thorough search of the basket in which she carried a variety of foodstuffs.

'Where have you been?' Adam greeted her ungraciously. 'I thought you'd changed your mind about helping me.'

'Your brother returned from the wars. He intended coming here to ask about you. Fortunately . . .' her voice belied the expressed sentiment '. . . fortunately a letter from his Thomasina sent him scuttling off to Cape Town to see her. He took passage on a ship last night.'

'So brother Nat has rushed off to his rich widow. It sounds serious – although I can't imagine someone like her wanting to live the simple life at Insimo. Perhaps he'll go to England with her and *I'll* get to run Insimo after all.'

'I thought your main concern at the moment was getting out of here?'

'It is, but first I need a gun.'

'I've got one. A revolver. It's strapped around my body, beneath this dress – but I'm not going to lift my skirt and unhitch it out here.'

'Well done, Esme! I knew you wouldn't let me down. Come into the hut.'

Inside the one-time store room the burghers greeted Esme respectfully, and it was apparent they were aware something was afoot. At a word from Adam, four men who were playing cards left their seats at the table, each going to a different window.

When a burgher stood at each door and window, Adam said, 'There's no chance of a *khaki* walking in on us now. You can give me the gun.'

Turning her back on Adam, Esme reached under her skirts. As she fumbled with the buckle of the gun belt she hissed, 'How many men are involved in this escape?'

'Lucas and me are the only ones breaking out. Any more and we'd have every *khaki* in Natal on our tails. We'd be lucky if we got five miles. As it is, the two of us have a good chance of making it all the way home to Transvaal.'

'*Three* of us,' corrected Esme as she turned around and handed the revolver and holster to Adam.

'You're coming? But I thought . . .'

'I've changed my mind.'

Adam gave Esme a perceptive look. 'There must be more to my brother than I realised. I believe he has something to answer for.'

'More than he knows. He provided me with the gun you're holding. It came from Commandant Johannes Tromp.'

Even as they spoke Adam was checking the gun. It was fully loaded, and there were more cartridges in a pouch on the belt.

'How are you going to escape – and when?'

'Leave the details to me. Do you have horses?'

Esme nodded. She had bought three good horses from a dealer who specialised in supplying mounts for senior British army officers. 'I've also obtained decent clothes for you and Lucas. Some I've bought, the remainder were left behind by Nat. You wouldn't get far in Natal looking as though you've just ridden in off commando.'

'Good girl. Can you have everything ready tonight? We'll be breaking out soon after dusk.'

Esme gasped. 'So soon?'

'It has to be. We've heard that more prisoners will be arriving tomorrow, transferred from a camp inland. Experienced camp guards are coming with them to take over here. Once that happens escape will be well-nigh impossible.'

One of the men at a window called a warning. Hurriedly pulling out a loose plank from the wooden wall Adam stuffed the revolver in the space and put the plank back into place. He was just in time. The door opened and two British soldiers entered the hut. They found the occupants lounging about in a relaxed manner, and at the table the four burghers had resumed their game of cards.

By the time Esme left the compound she knew exactly what she had to do. She would be required to wait with the horses not far from the camp until Adam and Lucas joined her. Then Esme and the two escapees would ride north, away from the guarded railway, following the coast towards Zululand until dawn. Then they would head inland, riding through sparsely populated country, making for the Transvaal border.

But first Adam and Lucas Viljoen had to make their escape.

The young militia captain in charge of the prisoner-of-war compound was in the habit of walking around the camp on an informal inspection each evening, at a time when the camp guards were being relieved by the night-duty shift. The soldiers employed on guard duty were from a different regiment each day and changeover time was a period of maximum confusion and uncertainty. This was the time Adam had chosen for the escape bid.

When the captain walked into the hut on this night Adam was waiting for him. Stepping from the shadows beside the door he put the revolver to the officer's temple.

'Don't make a sound or I'll kill you.'

The unfortunate officer stopped as though he had been turned to stone. Minutes later, gagged, stripped and bound, he was bundled beneath a bed in a dark corner of the room and Adam was pulling on his uniform. It was a reasonable fit and when Adam stepped through the doorway and called to a passing guard the soldier had no hesitation in obeying his order.

Once inside the hut the soldier was subjected to the same treatment as his commanding officer, and this time it was Lucas who emerged as a British soldier.

Adam and Lucas reached the gate and passed through just as the incoming guard force entered, the sergeant in charge calling for a smart 'Eyes right!' by way of a salute to the 'officer'.

Adam and Lucas quickly disappeared into the darkness,

leaving increasing confusion behind them. When the outgoing guard mustered they learned they were a man short. Then the soldier who had been guarding the gate reported that a soldier had left the camp in company with an officer. It was immediately presumed it had been the missing guard accompanied by the camp commander.

Not until the early hours of the morning did a fellow officer come to the camp to inquire after the missing captain. When he had not returned to his tent after completing his duty it had been assumed he had gone to the Durban hotel used as an officers' club. However, the club was now closed and the captain had not returned.

Because it had been reported that the officer and one of the guards had been seen *leaving*, it did not occur to the British authorities to search the camp until the morning roll call revealed that two of the Boer prisoners were also missing.

By the time the unfortunate British soldiers were discovered trussed and gagged beneath beds in the hut, Adam and Lucas were many miles away, riding with Esme through the rolling hills of inland Natal.

Something happened on the outskirts of Durban that marred the exhilaration Esme felt at being actively engaged in Transvaal's cause once more.

As they rode their horses along the sand, within earshot of the waves crashing on the long beaches, they saw a fire near the sea's edge and heard the sound of singing and laughter, accompanied by occasional raucous shouting. It seemed there was a happy party in progress.

Suddenly a figure appeared from behind a group of rocks, swinging an oil-lit 'bull's-eye' lantern.

'Hey! You on the horses. Just a minute.'

Behind Esme there was a soft click of the hammer of a revolver being cocked. Then the beam of the lantern swung in her direction and settled on her face, dazzling her.

'Why, it's Esme! Hello, old girl. What are you doing out here at this time of night? Come to join my party . . .? Yes, of course you have. Jolly decent of you . . . But it *is* my birthday, after all.'

From the erratic weaving of the lamp's beam and the slurred

speech of the man holding it, Esme realised he had been celebrating his birthday well.

'Thank you, Justin, but I must be getting along. I hope you have a lovely party.'

'Who is it?' The whispered question came from Adam.

'A young English officer. I've met him once or twice at the station. You and Lucas go on. I'll keep him talking for a while.'

'*Come* on, old girl . . . Come to my party. Bring your friends with you . . . Pleased to have 'em.'

Moving closer the drunken officer looked up at Esme and overbalanced, falling backwards on the sand.

'I say . . . sorry about this. I've had a skinful . . . My birthday, you see. Oh, that's jolly decent of you . . .'

Adam had slipped from his horse and appeared to be helping the officer to his feet. But even as he was thanking Adam there was the crack of a revolver shot, muffled by the fact that the end of the barrel was being pressed against the young officer's jacket.

The soldier's mouth dropped open and he slumped to his knees before pitching forward on his face.

'Adam! You didn't *have* to do that,' Esme cried out in distress. 'He was no danger to us. He was far too drunk.'

For a moment Adam said nothing. His head cocked to one side, he was listening to the sounds from the party. They were as happy as before. It seemed no one had heard anything.

'He was a British officer – and we're at war. Lucas, give me a hand. There's a pool over by those rocks. We'll pitch him in with his pockets filled with stones. He won't be found until tomorrow, and we'll be miles away by then. Esme, douse the lamp – but bring it with you. I've always wanted one of those.'

CHAPTER FORTY-TWO

Nat arrived in Cape Town on board the ship bringing Carey Hamilton and other wounded British officers from Durban.

Thomasina was at the dockside to meet the ship, but she greeted Nat with none of the enthusiasm he had anticipated. He told himself it was because she was upset at the sight of her wounded brother being carried from the ship, unable to walk. Nevertheless, had he not been carrying her letter in his pocket he might have been forgiven for thinking she was not pleased to see him. Her smile might have fooled others, but it contained none of the honest delight he had seen on other occasions.

'It's great to see you again,' he said hesitantly. 'I came as soon as I received your letter.'

'Letter?' Nat was not sure whether her puzzlement was genuine or feigned. Then her frown vanished. 'Oh! The letter asking you to act as a guide for the Women's Committee on Refugee Camps? Why? I sent that *ages* ago. You remember, Henry?'

She addressed the question to a tall, dark-haired man who was standing on the dockside behind her, then turned back to Nat again. 'I'm sorry, I haven't introduced you. Nat, this is Henry Dudley, *Lord* Henry Dudley. He is on the High Commissioner's staff. Henry, this is Nat, the young man from Matabeleland of whom I have spoken so often. He does terribly dangerous work scouting for the army against the Boers. It was he who telegraphed to me about poor Carey. Tell me, how serious *is* his wound, Nat?'

Nat released Lord Henry Dudley's hand. He had never

before seen Thomasina in such a brittle mood. It was as though he was meeting a complete stranger. 'Carey has a nasty leg wound, but he'll walk again.'

'Thank God for that!' Thomasina's emotion was genuine now, at least.

Stretcher bearers were placing the wounded on specially fitted-out wagons as Thomasina walked across the quayside to stand beside her brother's stretcher, leaving the two men behind. Lord Dudley broke the silence that stood between the two men. 'Thomasina is very fond of her brother.'

'And he of her. It's the way brothers and sisters should be.'

'Quite so. You have brothers and sisters, Mister Retallick?'

'Two brothers now. A third was killed by the Matabele, together with my father.'

'How tragic.' Lord Dudley gave the faintest of shudders. 'But one hears of so many tragedies occurring in Africa. Small wonder it is known as the "Dark Continent".'

'You wouldn't say that if you saw Insimo, our farm. I doubt if there's a more attractive place on earth.'

'Really? Of course, you come from Rhodesia. I've often heard Rhodes speak of it as a very beautiful country. You know Cecil Rhodes, of course?'

'We've met, once or twice. My father knew him well, even though they never agreed about what was best for Matabeleland.'

'I think Rhodes has mellowed somewhat since those early days. If you are in Cape Town for a while I will arrange for you to meet him.'

'I hope to be leaving soon . . . although it depends very much on Thomasina and her committee.'

'I see. Well, that's a matter for you to discuss with Thomasina. I *do* know she has already visited a number of camps here, in the Cape Colony.'

It was becoming increasingly apparent to Nat that his presence in Cape Town was something of an embarrassment for Thomasina. The letter she had written, inviting him to Cape Town, must have been at least a couple of months old by the time it was received by him. Such a possibility had simply not occurred to him.

It was equally clear there was a close relationship between

Thomasina and Lord Henry Dudley. It seemed Nat had arrived in Cape Town too late – and for a great many reasons.

Conversation between Nat and the polite English peer was beginning to falter when Thomasina returned to them. For some reason she now seemed more kindly disposed towards Nat, even suggesting that the three of them should lunch together. Lord Dudley excused himself from the arrangement, explaining that he was having lunch with Lord Milner, the British High Commissioner, to discuss the Commissioner's impending visit to London.

'Then *I* shall take Nat to lunch and let him tell me how this war is *really* progressing.'

The coach on the quayside belonged to the High Commission, but after letting Lord Dudley off at the High Commissioner's impressive home, the driver took Thomasina and Nat on to a nearby hotel. Here Nat booked a room for the duration of his stay in the busy sea port and afterwards he and Thomasina took lunch at a balcony table with views across the bay and its famous flat-topped, purple-hued mountain to one side.

Nat was aware of the curious stares coming his way as he escorted Thomasina between the tables of the dining-room. The stout serge suit he wore was both practical and sensible wear for Durban, but it was all wrong for the fashion-conscious community in Cape Town.

When Nat self-consciously voiced his thoughts, Thomasina reached across the table and squeezed his hand reassuringly.

'My dear, when handsome young men come *here* for lunch dressed in such clothes, everyone knows they must have come from "up-country". From the *war*. The very fact that you are not in uniform positively intrigues them and I am the envy of every woman in the place. We'll find you some good clothes to show you off to everyone when the occasion arises, but it is not important for the moment.'

Thomasina removed her hand from his and picked up a menu. While pretending to scan the many dishes on offer, she said, 'Carey told me what happened when he was shot. He said he would have been killed had you not rescued him. He also told me *you* were wounded when you pulled him to safety.'

Nat still had a dressing on his wounded arm, but it was

almost healed now and he rarely remembered it.

'Carey is a brave officer, and a good man. Too good to be left to die on a rocky hillside in the Drakensbergs.'

'You're a good man too, Nat. I owe you an explanation . . . and an apology.'

The head waiter came to the table to take their order and further conversation was suspended while they chose their meal.

When drinks had been brought to the table, Thomasina looked out over the bay, and began to speak.

'I shouldn't have written to you, Nat. I know that. I think I knew it then. When I wrote to you I was feeling very, very lonely, and most unhappy. I had been working hard on the hospital ship – and then suddenly there was no more to be done. On the voyage from Durban to Cape Town I found I was a passenger. The only passenger on a ship where everyone else had far too much to do. I had time to think and I realised that all I really cared about was here, in Africa. Carey . . . and you too – and I *am* fond of you, Nat. Then, when I arrived here I heard there was some scandal about the state of the refugee camps – "concentration camps" they are being called now. Henry asked me if I would remain in South Africa and prepare a preliminary report for a Women's Committee that was being sent from England. I agreed, of course. It gave me a reason to remain in South Africa. That was when I wrote to you.'

'I received the letter only a few days ago, when I returned from General Archer's campaign. I came as soon as I could.'

'I realise that now.' Thomasina nodded unhappily. 'I feel dreadfully guilty. Things have changed since I wrote that letter.'

'*I* haven't changed. Neither has the way I feel.'

'Nat, please don't make it more difficult for me.'

'Does Lord Henry Dudley have anything to do with the way you're feeling now?'

Thomasina leaned back as an African waiter slid a bowl of soup into place on the table before her. 'Henry has asked me to marry him.'

'Have you said "yes"?'

'Not yet.'

'In my thoughts I've asked you the same question a hundred times.'

'I think I have known this for a very long time, Nat. I am both honoured and flattered. When I sent that letter to you I almost believed I felt the same way about you.'

'You could, Thomasina. You *still* could. Come back to Insimo with me. Stay there for a while and I'll prove it to you . . .'

'*No*, Nat. It was thinking of Insimo that finally convinced me it would not work for us. Insimo means *everything* to you. I doubt whether a day passes when you don't think of the farm. You talk about it with such pride whenever the opportunity arises. And why shouldn't you? It is a wonderful place and its history must be a constant source of pride for you and your family. I shall never forget the happy time I spent there. But I could not live at Insimo, Nat, any more than I could contemplate spending the rest of my life *anywhere* in Africa.'

'I could leave Ben to run Insimo. Sell it even . . .'

'No, Nat. I would never allow you to make such a sacrifice for my sake.'

Nat was convinced that the food on his plate would choke him if he tried to eat any more, and he dropped his fork to the plate with a clatter that turned the heads of diners about them.

'Are you going to marry Lord Dudley?'

'Probably. He will probably be returning to England very soon. His father, the Earl of Asthall, is a sick man. Henry is an only son and will need to put the family affairs in order. Carey too will be returning on the next hospital ship. I have been asked to submit one final report – and then there will be nothing to keep me here any longer.'

Thomasina looked at Nat sympathetically. 'You and I met in exciting circumstances, Nat. We travelled together in your wonderful country – and you saved my life. Mine, Carey's . . . and I know you did your best for poor Digby too. I feel so *dreadful* about all this . . . But it *wouldn't* work out for us. Really it wouldn't. I must have been one of the first women to come into your life, but there will be others. There *are* others, right here. Before I leave I will introduce you to some of the most eligible young ladies in Cape Town . . .'

'Don't patronise me, Thomasina.' Nat spoke fiercely. 'I've made a fool of myself – all right, I can live with that, but not with your pity.'

'I swear it isn't pity I feel for you, Nat. You will never know how close I came to being everything you could possibly have wanted me to be. There was a time when I wanted you every bit as much as you think you want me now. But it involved a commitment on my part . . . and it was a commitment I could not make.'

Nat and Thomasina were occupying a table in an alcove draped with bougainvillaea, their table some distance from its nearest neighbour. But although their low-voiced conversation could not be overheard, it was evident to the diners in the hotel that they were having a serious and animated discussion.

Looking up, Thomasina saw that she and Nat were attracting a great deal of interest.

'Shall we finish this conversation elsewhere, Nat? Cape Town is a very small community. If we remain here tongues will be running wild tomorrow.'

'What more is there to say? Anyway, it's time I returned to Insimo. In Ma's last letter she said they're coping well enough, but they need me to make some decisions about the future. I'll catch the next train north.'

'I won't try to stop you, Nat. I have work to do and you could be of great help to me, but I have no right to ask anything more of you. Not now. However, you'll be here for another three days, at least. There won't be another train to Rhodesia before then. All available rolling stock is being used on the Pretoria line.'

Thomasina pushed her plate away from her. 'I don't think either of us feels like eating. I'll leave you now, but I'll be in touch with you again later today. I am desperately sorry things have turned out this way. The last thing in the world I wanted was to hurt you . . . but I think I had better go now, or I will make an absolute fool of myself in front of everyone . . .'

CHAPTER FORTY-THREE

The hotel where Nat had taken a room was one of Cape Town's best. Built in the Dutch colonial style, the rooms were high-ceilinged and airy, with many open, rounded arches to welcome the slightest breeze coming off the sea.

Sitting alone in his room after Thomasina had gone, Nat felt that an important period of his life had turned full circle. Soon after Thomasina had come into his life he had ridden away from Insimo to go to war. Now she was going out of his life for ever — and he was returning to Insimo.

But Thomasina was not allowing Nat to slip away just yet. That evening she and Lord Henry Dudley called at the hotel to take him to a party being held at Groote Schuur, the home of Cecil Rhodes. There was no time to have clothes specially made for the occasion, and once more Nat found himself the object of many curious glances — until another man entered the room wearing clothes of a similar, hard-wearing material, albeit with an expensive cut. The man was Cecil Rhodes.

When he saw Nat, Cecil Rhodes frowned. He was used to having his guests dress for a special occasion when they were invited to Groote Schuur. He said something to a young man who had entered the room with him and the young man shook his head. His frown deepening, the most powerful man in southern Africa strode purposefully across the floor, heading in Nat's direction, but before Rhodes reached Nat the great man was adroitly intercepted by Henry Dudley.

Lord Dudley accompanied Cecil Rhodes across the room, talking all the while. When the two men reached Nat, who was standing with Thomasina, he said, 'Cecil, you have met

Thomasina before, of course . . .' Rhodes took Thomasina's hand and bowed, but his gaze was still on Nat. '. . . Now this is a young man I *know* you will find interesting. Nat Retallick. His heart, like your own, is in the country north of the Limpopo river. He's scouting with the British army. Arrived here only today, as a matter of fact, after guiding General Archer's column on a most successful campaign.'

Cecil Rhodes' scowl disappeared immediately. He could forgive men of action for most things. Gripping Nat's hand, he said, 'Retallick? Not Daniel Retallick's son . . . from Matabeleland?

Nat nodded and Cecil Rhodes beamed. 'Now *there* was a man to be reckoned with. He and I didn't always see eye to eye on things, but I admired him greatly. Not many men stood up to me and won – but Daniel Retallick did. Cost me the best piece of land in Matabeleland too.'

Cecil Rhodes drooped an arm about Nat's shoulders and in a high-pitched voice that carried to every corner of the room, he said, 'This is an occasion to remember. The two greatest land-owners in Rhodesia together under the same roof.'

Always one to gain maximum effect from any situation, Cecil Rhodes shook hands with Nat again as his guests applauded. Rhodes stayed chatting to Nat for some minutes. Then, after suggesting that Nat should accept a senior administrative post with the Chartered Company in Rhodesia, the richest man in South Africa strolled away to receive the adulation of his other guests.

Nat remembered his mother's bitterness whenever she spoke about this man. It was her belief that, had he wished, Rhodes could have prevented the Matabele uprising in which Nat's father and brother died. The reason he did not do so, she said, was because when the brief but bloody war between the Matabele and their arrogant white neighbours came to an end, Rhodes had expanded his own empire to include all the land between the Limpopo and Zambezi rivers – with the exception of the Insimo valley.

As soon as Cecil Rhodes had moved on, Nat found himself the centre of interest for the other guests. Soon he was being introduced to the eligible young ladies Thomasina had mentioned. Thomasina herself remained with him for a while, skilfully warding off the attentions of those she did not think 'suitable' for him.

Eventually Nat was left alone to enjoy the company of a girl who had only recently arrived from England. She was the daughter of a senior officer on Lord Kitchener's staff – 'An officer destined for the highest rank,' Thomasina whispered as she suggested he escort the girl to another room where Rhodes's guests were about to be entertained to a piano recital.

The English girl was pleasant and attractive enough for Nat to receive many envious glances from the young men in the room. However, unfairly perhaps, Nat found her dull when compared with the few girls of his acquaintance. Esme, Johanna Viljoen – and Thomasina, of course. He wondered why this should be, and then he realised that life had not yet touched the young English girl.

Nat felt a pang of jealousy when he saw Thomasina leaning close to Henry Dudley, smiling at something he was saying to her. She was undoubtedly the most attractive woman in the room, as well as the most expensively dressed. Nat knew he was a fool ever to think he had a chance with her, but it did not help.

'She's a very lovely woman.'

'Who?' Nat asked guiltily.

His companion smiled and ignored the question. 'Have you known her long?'

'Thomasina and her late husband visited me at Insimo – that's my farm in Matabeleland.'

'Tell me about Insimo.'

The girl was a good listener, and Nat found himself telling her of all the things he was longing to see again. His eulogising was brought to a close only when an outbreak of polite hand-clapping greeted the arrival of the piano soloist.

Despite Nat's earlier reluctance to attend the social function, he was actually enjoying himself when a young British police captain brought Nat's evening to a sour close.

Introduced to Nat after the recital, he frowned. 'Retallick? I've heard that name earlier today.'

Nat smiled good-naturedly. The young policeman had spent much of the evening drinking with his companions in a

374

separate room. 'I doubt it. Retallick isn't a common name in this part of the world.'

'That's why I remember it ...' The policeman's brow cleared. 'Got it! We had a telegraph from Durban today. Someone named Adam Retallick escaped from a prisoner-of-war camp with another Boer. A gun was taken to the camp by some girl who visited him. She's gone missing too ...'

Nat thought about the escape for the umpteenth time as he dressed and breakfasted in his room the next morning. He was emotionally very confused about Adam's escape. Although he did not want to think of his brother confined to a prison camp for the remainder of the war, Adam would at least have been safe there. But Nat also nursed a secret admiration for his brother's initiative in escaping. Esme's too – because Nat had no doubt she was the girl involved. Probably she had used the revolver *he* had given to her ...!

Nat's first impulse had been to return to Durban and learn exactly what had taken place, but he realised this would serve no useful purpose. Adam and Esme would have been well on their way to Transvaal within hours of escaping. Adam must have been in the prisoner-of-war camp when Nat was in Durban, which meant that Esme had deliberately lied to him, the escape planned at the very time Esme claimed to have no knowledge of Adam's whereabouts. He remembered holding Esme in his arms on the balcony of Madame Claris's house ... and his question about her relationship with Adam ... but Nat was to be given little time to ponder the matter this morning.

He had hardly finished his breakfast when there was a heavy knocking on his hotel-room door. As he went to open it he could hear voices raised in argument outside.

There were three people in the corridor. One was a terrified African in hotel porter's uniform. Another was a formally dressed European whom Nat recognised as the hotel manager. The third was a middle-aged woman, plainly dressed, who had her back to the door and faced her two companions defensively.

'What's going on ...?'

Hearing his voice, the woman turned to face Nat and the

manager spoke hurriedly. 'I'm sorry, Mister Retallick. My porter stupidly gave this lady your room number and she insisted on coming up . . .'

'I am quite capable of speaking for myself, thank you.' The woman, in her mid-forties, spoke English with a soft accent that belied the determination of her strong features. 'Mister Retallick, you have a Cornish name, but you neither look nor speak like a Cornishman.'

'My father was born in Cornwall. My mother is Portuguese.'

'That would explain it. Mister Retallick, I wish to speak with you. My name is Emily Hobhouse. I *too* am from Cornwall.'

When the hotel manager began to protest once more, Nat silenced him. 'It's all right. I'll speak to Mrs Hobhouse.'

'*Miss* Hobhouse.'

It was evident the woman had never doubted Nat *would* see her. Not waiting for an invitation, she pushed past him and entered the room. Wrinkling her nose, she said, 'It's stuffy in here.'

Striding to the window she threw it open and drew in a couple of deep breaths before turning back to Nat. 'I am surprised that a man so used to the open air can breathe with all the windows in his room closed.'

'Do you mind telling me what you're doing here, Miss Hobhouse? I don't think we've met before.'

'We haven't, Mister Retallick, but I have heard that you have been asked to take Mrs Vincent to Transvaal, and have refused.'

'Thomasina didn't specify where she wanted me to go. But, yes, I am returning home to Matabeleland – although I really don't know what it has to do with you . . .'

'She *needs* a guide, Mister Retallick. An honest, *reliable* guide.'

'I'm sorry, Miss Hobhouse. I've been an army guide – a scout – for too long. I am going home now.'

'You're lucky to have a home to go to, Mister Retallick. The women and children packed into concentration camps on the veld have lost *their* homes. Burned by British soldiers. *Sixty thousand* of them, Mister Retallick. Think about it – and their numbers are increasing every day.'

'Miss Hobhouse, I've seen a great many things in eighteen months of war. I've had enough.'

'Oh? Do you hate the Boers so much?'

Nat was startled. 'Hate them? I *like* them. They're a good people.'

'Yet you would fight their men for eighteen months and not give a couple of weeks of your time to help save their women and children? You have a strange way of showing your "liking", Mister Retallick.'

Now Nat recognised the trap into which he had fallen, but still he was puzzled. 'I know nothing of these camps, or where they are. The army . . .'

Emily Hobhouse's snort of derision had silenced more experienced speakers than Nat. 'The army, you say? Young man, the army show only camps they don't mind people seeing – and the Lord knows *they* are bad enough. I want you to find the others and take Mrs Vincent to see *them*.'

'I still don't understand *your* interest in this. You are English . . .'

'So? Does being English absolve me from all responsibility for what my countrymen are doing in the guise of war? I am a Christian, Mister Retallick. A *practising* Christian. I came here to distribute a few luxuries collected in England for the families of our enemies. To tell them we were praying for them.'

Emily Hobhouse smiled, but there was only sadness in the expression. 'I brought *luxuries*. Do you now how it feels to be able to offer nothing but a pair of new, shiny shoes to a young child dying of malnutrition? Or a school book to another who is dying of typhoid? The Boer women and their children are on near-starvation rations in these camps, especially those with husbands and fathers on commando. Oh yes! The families of Boer fighting men are actually on *reduced* rations. They have no soap, most have precious little decent water, and the sanitary facilities would cause the most wretched native to shudder in disgust. It is hardly surprising they are dying in ever-increasing numbers. When I lived in a parish of some two thousand inhabitants in Cornwall a funeral was an event that brought people from their cottages to watch it pass by. Here, in one of Kitchener's concentration camps of a similar size, twenty-five women and children are being buried *every day*. Death hovers over each camp like an ominous black cloud. Every woman and child is aware of its presence, and the realisation of their plight gives them no hope for a new tomorrow. I have seen all this, Mister Retallick. I have *wept* for them and *with* them until there are no more tears left in me.'

'Why don't *you* go out looking for these other camps? You obviously know more about them than anyone else.'

Emily Hobhouse shook her head. 'I could find them, Mister Retallick. But I wouldn't be allowed to enter any one of them. Lord Kitchener doesn't like women busying themselves in the army's business – especially if it is likely to bring about a major change in his strategy. Besides, it is time for me to return to London and tell the British public what is happening here.'

Nat had a sudden thought. 'Does Thomasina ... Mrs Vincent, share your views on conditions inside the camps?'

'Not entirely. She has only visited what I call the "show" camps, here in the Cape Colony. But I believe her to be a compassionate and honest young woman. Find the camps in the Transvaal, Mister Retallick – I *know* they are there. If you can persuade Mrs Vincent to look at them you might be able to achieve more in a few days than I have in many heartbreaking months of crusading.'

Emily Hobhouse's voice was vibrant with emotion. Suddenly she walked to the window and stood for several minutes with her back to Nat.

When she turned around again she had regained full control of herself once more, 'I am not a humble woman, Mister Retallick. Begging does not come easily to me – *but I am begging you now*! Go out and find these camps. Make certain Mrs Vincent sees them too. Unless you do, more people will die in these terrible camps than have perished on all the battlefields of South Africa.'

When Thomasina and Nat arrived in Mafeking, Lord Henry Dudley was with them. He had assumed responsibility for the concentration camps before they left Cape Town, more than two months before. Nat suspected that Lord Dudley would not have chosen to visit those camps outside the Cape Colony had *he* not changed his mind and agreed to accompany Thomasina on her tour of inspection.

On the way north they had made many stops to check on the camps in the Orange Free State. Standards here varied enormously. Some were reasonably well run – others less so. All were depressing.

The last call had been on the camp at Kimberley. It was a large camp and the inmates had a number of minor complaints, but it was a well-run camp. It might have been even better had the inmates been willing to carry out some work for themselves. There were men in this camp, but they refused to do anything, even when payment was offered to them for their services. Neither would they attempt to grow their own food.

Such unwillingness to help themselves puzzled Thomasina and Lord Henry, until Nat questioned some of the Boers in the camp. He learned that the majority were farmers with homes on the veld. They had been turned off their land and forced to watch the destruction of homes, crops and livestock. Many were 'hands-uppers', men who had taken the oath of loyalty to the Queen – but all now nursed a bitter hatred towards the men who had destroyed everything in the world they owned.

On the way north Nat had seen some of the results of the latest British policy. The veld was dotted with roofless farmhouses and it was uncannily devoid of livestock. It was a depressing picture, but Lord Henry Dudley declared airily that the British government was merely pursuing a policy dictated by the burghers themselves. He pointed out that it was the men of the commandos who first began burning the farms of the 'hands-uppers'. He also claimed that many of the women and children in the camps had been accompanying the commandos until food ran short, or until their British pursuers drew near. Then they had been abandoned to their fate, in the certain knowledge that the British soldiers would not leave them to die on the veld.

Thomasina carefully noted all Lord Henry's comments, but his smug justification of Kitchener's policy suffered a rude setback at the Mafeking camp. Here almost all the inmates were interned as the direct result of the army's systematic burning of homes, and the conditions under which they existed were appalling.

The camp was filthy, lacking all facilities to keep it clean. Water was in short supply and that provided for drinking proved to be brackish and discoloured. There were no beds in the camp, the occupants being forced to sleep on the ground. When Nat questioned the residents they complained of a shortage of food and all the other necessities of life. Crowded more than eight to a tent, the inmates were all in generally poor health and there was currently a diphtheria epidemic sweeping through the camp. On the day the inspecting party arrived six children died from the disease. Their bodies were laid on the damp ground inside a shabby tent, awaiting burial.

Making his own shocked tour of inspection, Nat entered the makeshift mortuary and saw a kneeling woman dressed in the sober fashion of a *trek-vrou* doing her best to tidy the shabby clothing covering the emaciated body of a small boy.

Nat stood back respectfully until the Afrikaner woman stood up. Then, when she turned around, they both stared at each other in amazement. It was Esme!

But this was not the healthy, happy girl who had welcomed Nat on his return to Durban. Esme had lost a great deal of weight and looked thin and ill. For one brief moment she looked overjoyed to see him, but the expression was short-lived.

Gripping Esme by the arms, Nat asked, 'Esme, what are you doing *here*? Where is Adam?'

'Adam is where he's happiest. On commando. As for me . . . I can't talk about it just now, Nat. So much has happened. I feel as though I'm walking in a nightmare . . .!'

Breaking free, Esme turned and fled.

CHAPTER FORTY-FOUR

After the shooting of the young British army officer on the beach north of Durban, Adam led his two companions towards Zululand, following the coast until dawn brushed colours on the sky far out over the sea. Then the three riders turned inland, making for the empty hills that rose steadily to the Drakensbergs and the highveld of the Boer republics.

They rode in silence for much of the time until eventually Adam drew in his horse beside Esme.

'Are you still sulking about that *khaki* officer I killed?'

'It wasn't necessary to shoot him. He was just a happy, drunken, normal young man celebrating his birthday. I *knew* him. He had talked to me, at the railway station.'

'He was a British officer – and we're fighting a war. Living in Durban has made you soft, Esme. Don't worry, a few weeks on commando and you'll be your old self again.'

'I've no intention of going out on commando – and if you've any sense, neither will you. I couldn't remain in Durban after helping you to escape. They'd have realised immediately who gave you the gun — and that might have got Nat into trouble too, for giving it to me – but I'm not riding around the veld with a rifle slung over my shoulder again. My days of pretending to be a man are over for good.'

'Well, well, well! So Theunis Erasmus's little girl has finally become a lady! I wonder whether that's due to Durban society – or whether brother Nat has something to do with it?'

'Neither. I've seen the soldiers and equipment the British are bringing into South Africa. You must have seen it too, from the camp. We can't win this war, Adam. Not by fighting.'

'She's right.' Lucas broke one of his long silences to agree with Esme. 'If we carry on fighting the *khakis* will destroy our country. You've seen what they've already done to our farms. If the war goes on much longer we'll be left with nothing. The Transvaal will look just as it did when the *voortrekkers* first got there.'

'What they did once can be done again. This time without fear of British interference. We can beat the *khakis*. We *will* beat them. The country is on our side, not theirs. I escaped from a prisoner-of-war camp to fight, and that's what I intend doing. *You* can both please yourselves.'

Nat dug his heels into his horse and rode off ahead of the others.

'Adam isn't one to give up easily,' said Lucas. 'But he'll come to see sense eventually.'

Esme shook her head. 'He enjoys killing too much. What will you do, Lucas?'

'What *can* I do? There's nothing left of the farm and I can't give myself up at one of the *khaki* concentration camps. I'll have to go along with Adam and join a commando. The *khakis* have left me no alternative. How about you?'

'I've got ten sisters scattered around the countryside. Three of them live in Pretoria. Unless the *khakis* have burned the cities too, I'll stay with one of them.'

The overland journey to Pretoria was fraught with dangers and difficulties. On the third day they strayed into Zululand and were surprised by a party of tribesmen, two of whom carried British-supplied rifles. Armed only with the revolvers supplied by Nat and the unfortunate prison-camp commander, Adam and Lucas killed four of the Zulus and captured both rifles. Then they rode hard for the remainder of that day, fearing retribution from the tribesmen and their British allies.

Soon after this incident they reached the mountains on the Orange Free State border, and a dangerous cat-and-mouse game began with British patrols. One night they managed to steal three British horses and a quantity of food, but they paid for their daring with two days of close pursuit.

The fugitives managed to escape by doubling back on their tracks, returning to the mountains and travelling northwards for three days and nights until they reached country that Adam recognised. They were in the Transvaal, but a long way off course.

Heading in the general direction of Pretoria, carefully avoiding roads and towns where they might encounter British soldiers, they rode through a desolate, dead land. The effect of the brutal British policy of destruction was appalling.

From skyline to skyline there was not an unburned building, while the whole veld was totally devoid of livestock. In places it seemed the land itself had given up hope, the breeze chiselling desert patterns in the dust of burned and parched fields.

Forty miles from the British-occupied capital of the Transvaal, the fugitives met up with a Boer commando. It was an offshoot of a much larger Boer force currently roaming the western Transvaal, scoring many minor victories and keeping a great many British soldiers fully committed.

Koos De la Rey had achieved a reputation among British and Afrikaners alike as a brilliant commander and a chivalrous fighting man, but the men who served him did not always share this latter trait, some regarding chivalry as a weakness.

The commando encountered by Adam and his companions came from the Zoutpansberg, the wild Transvaal country bordering on Matabeleland. The majority of the burghers in the commando were *takhaaren*, men as wild and untamed as the land whence they came. They had come south seeking action.

The *takhaaren* commando surrounded the three riders and demanded to know where they had come from, Esme attracting particular attention.

'We're heading for western Transvaal to join up with Koos De la Rey,' explained Adam briefly.

'With a girl?' The Afrikaans spoken by the black-bearded *takhaar* who pushed his horse to the front of the commando was barely intelligible. With a start, Adam recognised the Boer he had knocked from his horse when he crossed the Limpopo river from Matabeleland early in the war.

'She's with us. That's all you need to know.'

The *takhaar* turned bloodshot eyes in Adam's direction, but there was no recognition in them. They were the eyes of a man whose brains were addled through imbibing far too much of the porridge-like native beer.

'Had I wanted to listen to braying I'd have kicked the crutch of Uiys Groebler's mule. I was talking to the *vrou*.'

Adam had knocked this *takhaar* from his horse at their previous meeting. He did not doubt he could do it again, but while the attention of the commando was focused on Adam, he saw Esme slip the revolver from the holster she had worn at her waist since the two men had acquired rifles.

'The answer you'll get from the *vrou* will be no different.' Esme held the revolver loosely in one hand, using the other to pull up the head of her travel-weary horse. 'Who I am and where I'm going is of no concern to any *takhaar*.'

Angrily, the bearded man drove his horse towards Esme. 'I've beaten the Devil out of three wives and thirteen children. I'll not let him speak through the dirty mouth of a shameless young *vrou*. Give that toy gun here . . .'

As the *takhaar* reached out to take the revolver from Esme, she thumbed back the hammer and pulled the trigger.

It was the scream of the wounded *takhaar* as much as the report of the gun that made the Boer's horse rear away from Esme. But its rider was not to be unseated twice in Adam's presence and he brought the animal under control with one hand as the other spilled blood in a circle about him.

When the horse stopped dancing, the *takhaar* held up his bloodied hand before him and stared at it in disbelief.

'She's shot off two of my fingers. Look . . .!'

An unsympathetic laugh escaped from one of the wounded man's companions. Seizing the opportunity, Adam said, 'He's lucky it's *all* she shot off. She used that revolver to help me escape from a prisoner-of-war camp in Durban. Before that she was wounded during the fighting in the Brandwater basin.'

Adam's words provoked a mixture of amusement and admiration. The burgher in charge of the commando grinned. 'You hear that, Arni? If you stick your finger in a *meerkat*'s mouth you got to expect to have it bitten off, eh, man?'

'Damn your talk! I'll deal with *her* later. Help me stop this bleeding before I bleed to death. You hear? Help me, will you?'

Still grinning, the leader of the *takhaaren* commando turned his attention to Esme. 'I'm Uiys Groebler. If you shoot a Mauser as well as you handle that revolver you're welcome to join my commando – and I promise you no man here will lay a hand on you again.'

'Since when has one *takhaar* been able to speak for another? If you don't find *khakis* to fight with you'll fight each other. No, this war is over for me. I'm going to find my sisters in Pretoria. If you've got any sense you'll go home too. The war on the veld has already been lost. Our future will be decided in an office in London, or Cape Town. Not here.'

The good humour of the men of the *takhaaren* commando vanished as swiftly as it had appeared. A woman who showed enough spirit to handle a gun and fight alongside her menfolk was one thing. A woman who tried to dictate to men was another.

Hurriedly, Adam said, 'I'd like to join up with you – especially if you intend meeting up with Koos De la Rey.'

The *takhaaren* leader nodded and looked at Lucas, who had been sitting his horse saying nothing. 'How about you?'

'I'll stay with you if you don't mind this.' He held up his partially crippled arm. 'I got it after Pretoria.'

'Can you still use a gun?'

'As well as any man here.'

'Then you're welcome.'

Ignoring Esme, the commando leader said, 'If you want to say any "goodbyes" make them quick. We're moving off.'

He wheeled his horse and the men of his commando followed, leaving Adam, Lucas and Esme together.

'You won't change your mind?' Adam put the question to Esme.

'Will you?'

Adam shook his head and Esme turned to Lucas. 'How about you? No one will say anything if you refuse to fight again. You've been wounded once already.'

'What would I do? Where is there for me to go? If you can get word to my family of what I'm doing I'd be obliged.'

Without another word, Esme pulled the head of her horse around and rode away, heading for Pretoria.

CHAPTER FORTY-FIVE

It was Esme's first visit to the Transvaal capital. She was impressed by its size – and by the large number of trees lining its broad avenues. Riding down the side of a *kopje* to the town the red and blue roofs of the houses reminded her of a giant patchwork blanket spread out on the veld.

As Esme drew nearer the size of Pretoria began to awe her and she realised she had no addresses for any of the sisters she believed were living here.

The town was teeming with British soldiers. They were everywhere. Marching along the streets, strolling along the footways, and living in the tented camps that surrounded the railroad lines to the north, south and east of the capital. Many buildings were flying the British flag – so many it seemed the British were determined not to allow the residents of Pretoria to forget they were a subjugated people.

By the time she reached the centre of the city Esme was more confused than ever. Then she saw the tall, thin spire of a church rising above the rooftops.

The Predikant was kindly, but the names of Esme's sisters meant nothing to him. He shook his head as he stood in the doorway of his church. 'I'm sorry . . . try Predikant Maritz. He knows most of the families in Pretoria.' He pointed to another spire, some distance away. 'That's his church. You'll find him there, or at his house beside the church.'

Esme found Predikant Maritz in his small house in the shadow of the church and repeated her enquiry.

Looking at her intently as she spoke, the Predikant suddenly asked, 'What's your name?'

'Esme. Esme Erasmus.'

'Ah! I thought so. You're the youngest daughter of Theunis Erasmus, corporal of the Lichtenburg commando.'

'You knew him?' Esme's childish delight brought a sad smile to Predikant Maritz's face.

'I knew him well, child. I was with him when he died. It was my hand that wrote his will, leaving the farm to Adam Retallick and not to you. You've met Adam, of course? His wife too, perhaps?'

Esme hesitated, wondering how much she could trust the preacher. Her hesitation was enough for the shrewd Predikant.

'You need say nothing. I see you *have* met our fierce young champion from Matabeleland.'

'His wife is dead. The farm destroyed by the *khakis*. I left Adam only this morning. He has joined up with a *takhaaren* commando.'

'I am sorry about your farm. Even more sorry about Adam's young wife. I fear she knew little happiness in this life. As for Adam . . . Well, he and the *takhaaren* should make a fearsome combination. I sometimes feel our God might be happier if both were fighting for the British, instead of for us. But come, let me tell you what I know of your sisters . . .'

Seated in the lounge of the Predikant's neat little house, Esme learned that two of her sisters had gone from Pretoria. One was in Johannesburg with her husband. The second had gone north with her husband and family, making for the wild, inhospitable Zoutpansberg region to escape from the British.

'What of Kristine?'

Esme asked the Predikant about the third of her sisters. Kristine was five years older than Esme and the most attractive of all the Erasmus girls. She had been married at the age of fifteen to a man twenty years her senior who worked for a Pretoria bank. They had met when he visited a neighbouring farm to foreclose on a loan made by his bank. Kristine had been the envy of every one of her sisters when she set off for Pretoria with her husband, in a carriage hired in the capital.

'Ah yes . . . Kristine Zeederburg!' There was a strange look on the Predikant's face. 'I'll take you to her house.'

'That won't be necessary. Just tell me how to get there.'

Predikant Maritz's hand on her arm brought her back to her seat.

'Put your horse in the stable at the rear of the church. It will be better if I take you to your sister's house. It is getting dark. With so many foreign troops here, Pretoria is no place for a young girl to be walking alone.'

Esme said nothing. Beneath her dress she still wore the holstered revolver that had once belonged to Commandant Tromp, but the fewer people who knew about it the better.

It was quite dark by the time they reached the house where Predikant Maritz said Kristine lived. Esme would have hurried to the door had the preacher not said firmly, 'It might be better if I go first.'

Puzzled, Esme followed Predikant Maritz up the pathway to the house. He knocked loudly three times before there was any sound of movement from inside. Then the door was opened and in the dim light from a lamp somewhere in the passageway Esme made out the outline of a woman. It was not light enough to see her properly, but Esme could see the woman was wearing a dressing-gown made of a very shiny material.

'Freddie . . . I've told you before about being early. You're not due here for another half-hour . . . Oh!' She stopped chattering when she saw it was not 'Freddie'.

'Good evening, Kristine. I have someone who has come a long way to see you.'

Predikant Maritz stood to one side and Esme walked uncertainly up the three steps to the door.

'Hello Kristine.'

'Oh, my God!' Kristine Zeederburg's hands flew to her face. 'Oh, my God!' she repeated. Suddenly taking a grip on herself, she said, 'Wait here.'

The next moment the door was slammed shut in Esme's face.

'I don't understand . . .' Bewildered, Esme turned back to the preacher.

'No, child . . . neither do I.'

They could hear raised voices inside the house. One was Kristine's, the other belonged to a man. Then there was the sound of a door being slammed shut at the back of the house. Minutes later the front door opened once again.

'You'd better come in.' It was hardly the welcome for which Esme had been hoping, but at least she had found *one* of her sisters.

'I'll wait here.' The Predikant stepped back into the shadows as Esme walked past her sister into the house and the door closed behind her.

'Kristine . . . What's going on? Where's Piet . . . and little Pieter?'

Piet Zeederburg was Kristine's husband, Pieter their five year old son.

'Predikant Maritz has spared you all the sordid details of my life?' Kristine Zeederburg's laugh sounded more a cry of despair. 'Perhaps he couldn't bring himself to tell you. Piet threw up his position in the bank. Gave up everything to join the Pretoria commando. Then he let himself be captured, leaving me here with *nothing* . . . except debts.'

'What of Pieter?'

Kristine Zeederburg's head turned this way and that, as though seeking a means of escape from the room. When she spoke again her voice had dropped to a whisper. 'Pieter is dead. There was an accident in the street outside the house. Pieter's little dog ran out of the garden . . . he ran after it. Our brave burghers were getting out of Pretoria as fast as they could go. One of their artillery guns ran over Pieter. They hardly stopped to see what they'd done.'

'Oh, Kristine . . .! What can I say? I'm so sorry.' Esme held out her arms to her sister.

'Kristine Zeederburg stood motionless in front of her. 'Don't expect tears from me, Esme. There are no tears left. None.'

'It will be all right. The war will soon be over. When Piet comes back . . .'

'Piet is *never* coming back. I will never have him back again. I'll kill him if he tries to enter this house. If he hadn't gone away none of this would have happened.'

'Kristine, can I help you?'

'I don't want your help. Nor any help from that Predikant who is hiding outside to see who comes calling. It's not the first time. You can tell him I've seen him skulking out there before tonight . . .'

'What do you mean? Why should he hide to see who comes here?'

Walking to a table in a corner of the room, Kristine Zeederburg poured a large drink from a brandy bottle. Esme observed that her hands shook alarmingly.

'Don't pretend innocence to me, little sister. I was there when Zipporah found a man for *you*, remember? He'd have taught you a thing or two about life, even if you hadn't learned it already from running wild for so many years. I hear you spend a lot of your time in the kaffir *kraal* up in the hills. Didn't you ever see those farmers' sons come riding in with newly shot game slung across their shoulders? Or did you think they were gifts brought out of brotherly love for the poor kaffirs? Of course not. You knew damn well they were paying to learn how to be men with the little kaffir girls. Well, the British soldiers are no different – but they pay with money. *Good* money. It's their money that keeps me alive, not some Predikant on his knees in church.'

Looking defiantly at her shocked sister, Kristine Zeederburg said, 'Well, how do you *expect* I should stay alive? Go out on the veld and let the British put me in a camp to die ... like Helena?'

'Helena's in a camp? Where?'

For a moment Esme pushed Kristine's disclosures aside. Helena was the oldest of the Erasmus girls, the one who had worked hardest for the family after their mother died. Even when she married an impoverished young farmer and had a family of her own Helena still did what she could for her orphaned sisters.

Three years before, when the thin soil of her husband's farm failed to produce a crop and there was not enough grass to feed their livestock, Helena's husband had given up and trekked northwards with his family in search of a new life.

Helena's departure had brought about the final break-up of the Erasmus family. That had been when Esme began to find increasing solace in the wild hill country beyond their farm.

'She's in a place called Piendorp, somewhere on the Elands river. It can't be too far from where we used to live because it seems many of the Lichtenburg women are being held there too.'

Esme knew Piendorp. When the war started it had been no more than a single, mud-walled farmstead in one of the loneliest valleys and abandoned by its farmer-owner many years before.

'When did you hear about this?'

For the first time since Esme had arrived at the house, her sister showed signs of unease. 'A soldier brought me a message a month or two ago. He'd been on guard duty there. Helena wanted me to help her . . . But how could I? You've seen what I have to do to keep *myself* alive. That reminds me . . . I've got a "friend" due any minute now. I don't want that Predikant frightening him away . . .'

Walking back through the darkened streets of Pretoria, Esme was silent for a long time. Eventually, Predikant Maritz said gently, 'You mustn't take your sister's shame to heart. This war has brought vicissitude to a great many of our people. Some cope with it better than others. I'll go and see her again. If I choose my time carefully I might be able to appeal to her sense of decency.'

'Kristine will do whatever is best for Kristine. She always has, and somehow manages to come through with just a little more than anyone else. I'm more concerned for another of my sisters . . . Helena. Kristine says she's in a concentration camp at Piendorp.'

Esme heard Predikant Maritz's sharp intake of breath.

'You've heard of it?'

'Only rumours, but none of them good.'

'That settles it. I'm going to Piendorp. There's nothing to keep me here in Pretoria any more.'

'The veld is no place for a young girl to ride alone in these unhappy times.'

'Predikant Maritz, people have been saying that to me since I was old enough to sit a horse. Don't worry, Piendorp is no more than a day or two's hard ride away.'

'If you're determined to make this journey I'll come with you. No, please don't argue with me, girl. A preacher is one of the few men able to ride about the Transvaal without fear of arrest – and it's time I saw one of these concentration camps for myself. In the meantime you'll spend the night at my sister's house. She lives just around this next corner.'

Esme and Predikant Maritz reached the Piendorp camp in the afternoon of the second day after leaving Pretoria. They had spent the intervening night with a preacher friend of Predikant Maritz, at Rustenburg. The small town was overflowing with British troops engaged in a new drive to destroy farms and crops.

On their ride from Rustenburg, Esme and Predikant Maritz saw much evidence of the success of the drive ordered by Lord Kitchener. Here, on the winter-dry veld, the British soldiers had set fire to enormous tracts of grassland, ensuring that Boer horses as well as Boer men would go hungry.

The two riders smelled the concentration camp long before it could be seen. The foul aroma was borne on a light breeze as they rode along a shallow valley dissected by the Elands river.

'What is it?' Esme wrinkled her nose in disgust as the odour became worse.

'I fear it's a smell you'll never be able to forget,' declared Predikant Maritz grimly. 'I smelled it at Paardeberg, after Piet Cronje had been surrounded by the British army for ten days. It's the smell of uncleanliness and dirt; of death and disease. Above all it's the smell of despair. I fear we've found our concentration camp.'

The Piendorp concentration camp was around the next turn in the valley. It was every bit as bad as Predikant Maritz and the foul smell had suggested. About a hundred tents of various sizes were pitched on a slight incline, close to the river. The tents were of various shapes and sizes, uniform only in their shabbiness. The camp occupied an area of about a quarter of a mile square, with the recently re-roofed old farmhouse at its centre. That the tents were not adequate for the population of the camp was immediately apparent, the accommodation being supplemented by a great many grass and wood shelters. There were wagons here too, placed about the camp to form a loose-knit *laager*.

A few British soldiers were in evidence, but they probably numbered no more than fifty. Most were gathered about a number of camp-fires set apart from the tents of the Boer women.

The arrival of Esme and Predikant Maritz caused a stir in the soldiers' camp and an officer rose from a fireside and hurried towards them, buttoning his tunic as he neared.

'Who are you? What are you doing here?' The officer addressed the Predikant, although his eyes kept straying to Esme.

'I am Predikant Maritz, from Pretoria. This is Esme Erasmus. We've come hoping to find her sister. You are the superintendent of the camp?'

'The superintendent died yesterday. I'm in charge of the guard . . . I suppose of the camp too now. There's no one else.'

'Can we look for this girl's sister?'

'If you wish . . .' The officer was a lieutenant, very young and uncertain of himself. Suddenly he blurted out, 'You'd do better to go back to Pretoria without going near the camp. We have both enteric fever and measles here.'

'How bad are things?' Predikant Maritz asked sharply.

'Very bad. We're losing between thirty and forty people each week now. Mostly children.'

'Do you have a doctor?'

'We had. He was one of the first to die, together with the woman who helped him.'

Predikant Maritz's face was grim as he asked, 'How many people in the camp?'

'Seven hundred . . . Perhaps eight.'

'Then at the present mortality rate there will be no one here in six months. They will all be dead!'

'I doubt it; more are being brought in all the time.'

'To a camp where there is not one epidemic, but *two*?'

'I only obey orders.'

'I wonder how many men will use that excuse to the Lord on Judgement Day? Where is the hospital?'

'We're using the farmhouse. There's nowhere else.'

Slipping from his horse, Predikant Maritz handed the reins to Esme. 'Find somewhere for the horses. I'll see you at the hospital.'

After picketing the horses with those of the soldiers, Esme picked her way cautiously between the tents. There had been little regard to sanitation or basic hygiene when the camp was set up. The space between the tents was filled with every imaginable kind of filth.

Esme found Predikant Maritz giving the last rites to a woman who lay on a disgustingly filthy blanket on the floor. Even so, the woman was more fortunate than many. At least half the occupants of the primitive 'hospital' lay on the mud floor. Most were children, some with mothers squatting beside them, others alone.

One of the children tossing in the throes of feverish delirium called for water, and Esme looked about her. There was a metal bowl and jug at one end of the room, but the bowl was filthy, while the jug contained no more than a half-inch of brackish water.

Esme asked one of the squatting mothers where she could obtain water. The woman looked up from her patently dying daughter blankly. When Esme repeated the question the woman replied, 'The river.'

Predikant Maritz had completed his spiritual duty now. The woman had died. After folding the dead woman's hands across her chest, the preacher took the jug from Esme. 'I'll fetch the water. I want to speak to that *khaki* officer. You go and look for your sister. There's nothing any one person can do in here. Go!'

Paul Maritz left the makeshift hospital with an anger in him that boded ill for the young British army lieutenant. Before today the preacher had heard only rumours of the British 'concentration' camps. Vague, disquieting rumours that no one had quite taken seriously. The British were the enemies of the Afrikaner people, to be sure, but they were *civilised* enemies, probably the most civilised people in the world. It was unthinkable that they would subject women and children to suffering on such a scale as was suggested.

Now the Predikant was witnessing this unthinkable tragedy for himself – and he was angrier than he had ever been in his life.

Esme found her sister Helena sharing a tent with eight others. Three were children – two of them Helena's own. Helena was kneeling on the ground cradling a baby in her arms when Esme entered the tent.

Esme watched in silence for a while, shocked by the dreadful change in her sister. When they last met Helena had been a cheerful, hard-working woman with a great pride in her appearance. Now she kneeled on the filthy ground, wearing a dress made from an old blanket, her hair greying prematurely and her face as lined as an old woman's. It shocked Esme to remember that Helena was no more than twenty-nine years old.

Just then Helena looked up and saw Esme. For a few moments her expression alternated between bewilderment and disbelief – then suddenly she burst into tears.

Dropping to the ground beside her older sister, Esme put her arms about both woman and child.

'Hush, Helena, don't cry. It will be all right. Don't cry.'

'Let her weep. It's the only luxury left to us in here.'

The face of the girl who spoke was vaguely familiar. Then Esme remembered a rare photograph Lucas Viljoen had showed her with some pride. This girl was one of the family group. She was Johanna Viljoen, Lucas's sister.

Esme returned her attention to Helena, doing her best to comfort her. Suddenly the baby in Helena's arms went into some kind of a fit. One minute it was rigid, the next it trembled as though stricken with malaria. Then, after a dreadful spasm that curved the baby's thin body backwards in the shape of a Bushman's bow, its body relaxed slowly, all torment gone, and Esme knew it had died.

Helena knew too and she began to wail noisily. Quickly Johanna crossed to her and gently prised the child away, saying, 'Poor woman . . . that's the third she's lost. One out on the veld, and two in here.'

Seeing Esme's shocked expression, Johanna said, 'It's not exceptional. A woman in the next tent has lost all seven of hers. At least Helena has two left . . . at the moment. Get her out of here, if you can. I'll deal with the baby. Take her to her daughter in the hospital.'

Predikant Maritz was in the makeshift hospital with the young army lieutenant and two British soldiers who glanced apprehensively about them. The Boer preacher was pointing out the shortcomings of the facilities in no uncertain terms, while the army officer listened apologetically.

'It's absolutely *disgusting*! I wouldn't shut a kaffir's dog in such a place – yet you have more than *eighty* sick women and children in here!'

'The women themselves are responsible for the state of the place. According to the camp superintendent they are *trekboers*. They don't know how to behave inside four walls.'

'My mother was a *trekboer* for half her life, but there wasn't a cleaner house than ours in the whole Transvaal. The superintendent is dead and can't be taken to task for such misguided notions. But *you* can. These people have to be moved. The whole camp needs to be shifted – and quickly.'

The lieutenant paled at the suggestion. 'I can't do that. These are sick people. Besides, my orders are merely to guard them.'

'These women and children are in your care, whether you want them or not – and they're dying. It's impossible to clean up the mess that's accumulated here, so I'm moving the camp a mile along the valley and closer to the river. You can guard them just as well there as here. Now, are you and your soldiers going to help me?'

With the aid of the British army, Predikant Maritz had the move completed by the time darkness fell. There were no more facilities here than before, and they would be forced to manage without the hospital building, but it was clean. Calling the women together, the Predikant impressed upon them the importance of observing strict hygiene. River water for drinking had to be drawn up-stream of the camp. The middle section of the river was reserved for washing – a near-impossible task without soap – while camp waste would be disposed of down-stream. It was simple hygiene, but even this had been totally lacking until now.

The move had proved hardest for the occupants of the hospital, but Predikant Maritz had bullied the army into using their wagons to convey the more seriously ill. One of these was Mary Botha, the four year old daughter of Helena, and her mother travelled in the wagon with her.

Esme carried Helena's sole surviving son, Tobias, to the camp. An underweight little boy, he looked up at Esme from dark eyes that seemed vastly oversized in his pinched, undernourished face. Esme carried him in a shawl donated by one of the Boer women. In spite of the coolness of a highveld winter evening, Esme could feel the heat of the fever-ridden body burning through the woollen wrap.

'It's all right, Tobias. We'll soon have you in a nice clean place, and then you'll get better in no time.'

For a moment more the small boy stared up at Esme uncertainly – and then he smiled. In that brief moment Esme's heart went out to her sick young nephew. Hugging him to her, she made a silent promise to move heaven and earth if it would help his recovery.

The hospital at Predikant Maritz's new camp was housed in the best of the tents. There were blankets for less than half the patients, but at least they were clean. The Boer preacher had begged them from the British soldiers, convincing them they were more able to withstand the cold of the night than the sick and weakened patients of the concentration camp's hospital.

Tomorrow, the Predikant promised, he would have more blankets to distribute, when those used in the old camp had been washed.

That night there was a faint glimmer of hope in the Piendorp concentration camp for the first time since disease had begun to strike down its unfortunate inmates. Now there was someone on hand who cared whether they lived or died. Furthermore, it was one of their own people. A Predikant.

In the hospital tent, as Esme and her sister toiled to clean the sick children and make them comfortable, Esme heard her sister's story.

Three years before, Helena and her husband had trekked northwards as far as the edge of the Zoutpansberg – *takhaaren* country. Here they began farming once again. But this venture proved no more successful than anything else Helena's husband had ever attempted, and so they began trekking once more.

Then the war began and Helena's husband joined a commando with all the other men in his vast, sparsely populated area. For a while the women and their wagons had accompanied the men wherever they rode, but as the tide of war turned against them it became necessary for the commandos to range farther afield. Mobility was of paramount importance and soon the families were left far behind, camping in women's *laagers* on the veld.

It was a difficult life for the women, hardy though they undoubtedly were. Raising a family without a man in such wild and inhospitable country posed many new problems. Not least of them were the tribes who roamed the veld. They were quick to learn of the presence of unprotected Boer women and their attacks became frequent in the remoteness of the highveld.

For some women it came almost as a relief when they were rounded up by British soldiers and brought to the Piendorp camp. Helena was one of these. She had lost her eleven month old son only three weeks before, after he had suffered from under-nourishment for too long. Now she believed there was hope for her four surviving children.

Disillusion came tragically quickly. A measles epidemic was raging when they arrived at Piendorp. Helena's oldest daughter was one of many deaths. Then, as Esme had witnessed, a second son had succumbed.

There were four other deaths in the camp that day. One was *Ouma* Viljoen, the indomitable matriarch of Johanna's family. After a lifetime spent defeating one hardship after another, she lost her last battle to enteric fever.

Those who had the strength tramped up the hill to witness the burials in the well-filled camp cemetery, and on the way back Esme told Johanna brief details of the escape of Adam and Lucas from the prisoner-of-war camp in Durban.

Johanna had once expressed to Nat Retallick her dislike of the war and her hope that the fighting would soon cease, but now her face lit up with a fierce delight at Esme's news. 'If only poor *Ouma* had known this before she died. Pa should be told about Lucas too, but we don't know where he is. He was taken to another camp, somewhere near Pretoria, I believe.'

'Predikant Maritz will find him when he returns to Pretoria . . .' Esme hesitated. 'Are you pleased for Lucas . . . or for Adam?'

'Why?' Johanna looked at Esme suspiciously. 'Is my answer important to you?'

Esme shook her head. 'It doesn't matter to me how you feel about Adam. But he'll not settle down, Johanna. Not even when the war is over. He *enjoys* fighting too much.'

'That's *my* business,' replied Johanna, fiercely.

'Of course.' Esme shrugged her shoulders. Adam was not her problem.

Baby Tobias did not improve with the change of location. In fact he developed a chest infection that made breathing very difficult for him, and Esme listened with great concern to his rasping breath for long, sleepless nights.

Esme had no experience with children. She had always convinced herself she did not like them, and carefully avoided coming into close contact with them. Tobias was the only child she had ever held in her arms — and yet now Esme loved him with all the love that was in her. With typical determination, Esme decided that she was not going to stand helplessly by and watch Tobias die.

Predikant Maritz sympathised with her, but pointed out that there was little hope of a doctor arriving in time to help any of those who were currently in the camp hospital.

The British army lieutenant had sent off two urgent requests for medical assistance, but in a reply the commanding officer of the area in which Piendorp was situated pointed out that British soldiers were being wounded every day by the husbands and fathers of the women and children now in Piendorp. British army doctors were needed to treat *them*. He suggested that if the commandos could be persuaded to surrender, there would be doctors enough for everyone.

'That settles it,' declared Esme when Predikant Maritz broke the news to her. 'If a doctor won't come here, then I'll take Tobias to them.'

'Pretoria is two days' ride away, Esme. More if you're travelling with a sick child. I doubt if Tobias would survive such a journey.'

'Will he live if he stays here?'

Predikant Maritz opened his mouth to give her a reassuring reply, but his eyes met Esme's direct look and the confidence he tried to show to the inmates of the concentration camp left him. He shook his head. 'No, Esme. If the child remains here he will die, as surely as all the other sick children are going to die. Take him. At least give him a chance to die in freedom. I despair, Esme. Truly I do. What have our people done that our children should suffer so? Is our freedom worth the shedding of so much innocent blood? Will there be anyone left to inherit this "freedom" even if we win?'

For the first time since Esme had known him, Predikant Maritz spoke like a dispirited and defeated man . . . but Esme was already planning ahead for Tobias.

'I'd like to leave immediately if Helena agrees. She's not fit enough to come with us herself, and she can't leave Tobias's sister. Do you think the lieutenant will let me go?'

'You and I are not prisoners, Esme. As for Tobias . . . What does it matter to a *khaki* officer how he loses another Afrikaner child? Take Tobias and go – but first borrow some old clothes. Dress like a *trekboer vrou*. I'll speak to the lieutenant. When you reach Pretoria . . .'

'I'm not going to Pretoria. You said yourself it's a two or three day journey. I'll head west, towards Mafeking. There's good road once I reach Zeerust, and I know the country. I should make it by tomorrow night . . .'

Esme did not reach Mafeking the next day, as she hoped. At Zeerust she was stopped by a British army patrol. Fortunately, the officer in charge was himself the father of a child of Tobias's age. Esme and Tobias were given food such as the two year old boy had never known, and a messenger sent to a nearby army camp returned accompanied by an army surgeon.

For six days Esme and Tobias remained at the British camp. During this time the small boy's health improved greatly. Then orders were received from the area commander that Esme and her young charge were to be escorted to the concentration camp at Mafeking and detained there.

It was useless Esme protesting that she was not a prisoner. Besides, she could not have abandoned Tobias. The small boy had become very dependent upon Esme and secure in their new relationship, Esme agreed to take Tobias to the Mafeking concentration camp.

Along the way they were joined by another hundred and fifty women and children who had been rounded up after evading the British army for many months on the open veld. The newcomers carried heart-rending stories of suffering and privation with them into the Mafeking concentration camp.

They also carried with them the deadly germs of diphtheria. When the still weak Tobias Botha caught the disease he never stood a chance of surviving.

CHAPTER FORTY-SIX

Nat and Thomasina located Esme that evening when the other camp inmates were queing for their daily ration of food. Lord Henry Dudley had gone to Mafeking with the camp superintendent to requisition the stores Lord Henry considered essential for the well-being of the inmates of the concentration camp.

When Nat pushed back the flap of the tent, he saw Esme hunched in a corner, beside a sagging tea-chest that served as both cupboard and table. She had her arms about her drawn-up legs and her head was resting on her knees.

When she did not move immediately, Nat thought she must be asleep, but as he walked across the ground towards her, she looked up. Her reddened eyes showed she had been crying for some time and it came as a shock to Nat. Esme had fought British soldiers, had been wounded and operated upon, yet he had never seen a tear. Now she sat on the ground inside the tent, looking totally defeated.

He dropped to his knees beside her and put an arm about her shoulders. 'Esme, what's been happening to you? Please . . . I want to help.'

Esme leaned towards him . . . but then she saw Thomasina. She pulled back, her expression hardening.

'Just for a moment I thought you might have come here looking for *me*. I should have known better. I should have realised "her ladyship" wouldn't be far away.'

Rising stiffly to her feet, Esme gave Thomasina a look that expressed all the hatred of her people for the British. 'Tell me, is it right you've sent all the strongest Boer women and children to prison camps in India and left the rest here to die? That's what the women in this camp are saying.'

'Coming from a Boer girl whose life was saved by a British surgeon, such a ridiculous statement hardly calls for a reply,' snapped Thomasina. 'We're here to compile a report for the British government on conditions in the camps. Where facilities are poor — and I don't deny there is much room for improvement here — action will be taken to improve matters. As a matter of fact, a senior member of the British High Commission is in Mafeking at this very moment, ordering beds, mattresses and all the other things that are lacking.'

Thomasina did not add that part of the reason Lord Henry had gone to Mafeking was because he had no stomach for what he had found in the camp. Instead, she saw the tiredness in every line of Esme's body and her attitude softened. 'What are you doing here, Esme? I thought you had found a new way of life with Madame Claris. What happened, did you become unhappy there?'

Nat held his breath, hoping Esme would not mention her part in the escape of Adam and Lucas Viljoen.

Esme shrugged. 'I'm very fond of Madame Claris . . .' She gave Thomasina a direct look. 'I suppose I'm really a *trekboer* at heart — and we must all eventually return to where we belong.'

Thomasina was a shrewd woman. She understood the implication of Esme's words. A quick glance at Nat was enough to assure her that he knew too.

'There's a flaw in your argument, my dear. If it were true there would be no such thing as progress. However, I do agree we should all choose the place where we are happiest — but there can be little happiness for anyone in a dreadful place like this.'

'No one has *chosen* to be here,' corrected Esme bitterly. 'It's the *khakis* — the British soldiers who bring everyone here after burning their houses, belongings and crops.'

'Regrettable things happen in a war.' Thomasina was tight-lipped once more. 'Soldiers are called upon to make some very difficult decisions.'

'At least Mafeking camp is better than the one at Piendorp . . . But I must go back there to tell my sister about . . . about Tobias. Nat, can you arrange anything for me?'

Thomasina was thumbing through the book in which she made her notes. She came to the official list of concentration camps and ran her finger down the page.

'Did you say "Piendorp"? I have no camp of that name here.'

'Perhaps the Cape government wants to forget it too. Everybody else has – except for those who have been taken there to die . . .' Suddenly tears welled up in Esme's eyes again. 'I brought Tobias from there to *save* him. I might as well have let him die with his mother, just as his brothers and sisters did.'

Nat and Thomasina exchanged a brief, concerned glance.

'Where is this camp?' Nat asked the question.

'Fifty miles north-west of Rustenburg. On the Elands river.'

'How bad *are* conditions there?'

'Far worse than here, even though they've moved to a clean site. There are not enough tents or blankets and no doctors or medicines to cope with epidemics of typhoid and measles. They have no soap, are on low rations – and no camp superintendent since the last one died. When I arrived there with Predikant Maritz we could smell the camp from two miles away. The Predikant is doing his best, but he can't work miracles. There's a family there you know, Nat. The Viljoens from the Lichtenburg district. Old *Ouma* Viljoen died on the day we arrived. Tobias's brother died on the same day . . .' Suddenly Esme's voice broke.

Nat felt an urge to put his arms about Esme and comfort her. He had never seen her so vulnerable. The death of her small nephew had affected her far more than he would have believed possible. Instead, he put his hand on her shoulder and squeezed it in a clumsy gesture of sympathetic reassurance.

Esme moved away from him. She was not able to cope with sympathy. Certainly not from Nat.

'Will you take us to this camp, Esme? I, Nat and Lord Henry Dudley . . . he's the representative of the British High Commission.'

Only a slight lift of Esme's eyebrows gave away her thoughts. Nat was travelling in exalted company, but it was something he would become used to if he planned a future with Thomasina Vincent.

'I'll take you, but you'll need a strong stomach.'

'I was a soldier's wife in India, Esme. It would take a great deal to shock me.'

Lord Henry Dudley's stomach was less hardy than that of his intended bride. When the general in charge of the Mafeking area suggested it might be 'unwise' for such an important member of the British High Commission to make such a journey, Lord Henry telegraphed to Lord Milner, the British High Commissioner in Cape Town, asking his advice.

Lord Milner's reply was prompt and unequivocal. Thomasina might make the journey, accompanied by a suitable escort, of course. Lord Henry was *not* to make the journey under any circumstances. Furthermore, Lord Henry was required to assume additional responsibilities in Cape Town. He was ordered to return forthwith.

Lord Henry's relief at not having to journey to yet another concentration camp outweighed his reluctance to leave Thomasina with Nat. He departed on a train the next morning after personally signing documents releasing Esme from the Mafeking concentration camp, and authorising Esme and Nat to accompany Thomasina wherever her inquiries might take them.

The party set off with only a handful of soldiers for an escort. The general had wanted to send two full companies, about two hundred and fifty men, but Nat had been able to persuade the British officer that such a party would only invite trouble. A strong Boer commando would not hesitate to attack two hundred and fifty British soldiers, or even a thousand. Such an escort would either have to put Thomasina at risk by fighting, or be forced to show a white flag and state their business – thus acknowledging Boer domination of the district.

A small party on a mission to aid Boer women and children would prove far less provocative.

As it happened they met with no commandos, but they found plenty of evidence of their presence on the veld.

When they were twenty miles from Piendorp Nat noticed an unusual number of vultures circling in the sky away to the right of the small party. Telling the sergeant in charge of the escort to keep the party heading towards the concentration camp, Nat set off to investigate. He returned with a grim story. A British supply column had been attacked whilst encamped beside a small stream. There were many bodies at the site, and signs that the survivors had retired to the south, leaving their dead behind.

'They were probably attacked by *takhaaren*,' suggested Nat. 'They had plenty of time to loot and burn the wagons. Had it been any other commando they would have buried the bodies.'

'When do you think the column might have been attacked?' asked the sergeant nervously.

'At dawn this morning . . . So now we'll travel fast and hope the commando has gone home.'

Esme was dismayed to find the Piendorp camp in as bad a state as it had been when she and Predikant Maritz had first arrived there, and there appeared to be more inmates than before.

Esme hurried away to locate her sister, leaving Nat and Thomasina to look at each other in horror. Piendorp was *far* worse than they had expected. Just then the young British lieutenant arrived looking very flustered.

'I'm sorry, Mrs Vincent. I never saw you arrive. We've had an altercation at the far end of the camp. One of the women who was brought in was allowed to bring a cow with her. We wanted to kill the animal for food, but somehow the woman stole a soldier's rifle and is threatening to shoot anyone who comes near the animal.'

'Is it really necessary to kill her cow? Does it give milk?'

'It did, but now we desperately need the meat. I've got children actually *starving* to death. The situation is desperate. The major who brought in the last arrivals promised to send supplies within a day or two, but they haven't reached us yet.'

Nat remembered the bodies he had seen earlier that day. 'Your supplies won't be arriving. The Boers got to them first.'

The British lieutenant looked at Nat in horror. 'We *must* have supplies. There are almost a thousand women and children here now. I have no meat and very little of anything else. I've already given up my own soldiers' rations because they refuse to eat while children starve. What else can I do?'

'Is the Predikant still here? The one who came with Esme Erasmus?'

'He's with the owner of the cow, trying to take the rifle from her.'

'I'd like to talk with him,' said Nat.

'While you are doing that I'll be taking a walk around the camp,' said Thomasina. 'But I dread what I might find . . .'

'One of my soldiers will come with you, Mrs Vincent. The women in the camp hate the British. Any one of them would murder you if they thought your coat would keep her child alive for one more night . . . and who can blame them? God knows, we've murdered enough of *them* in this camp.'

Thomasina looked at the tired young man sharply. 'I am here to ascertain facts, Lieutenant, not to listen to dramatic utterances. If you will arrange for someone to accompany me we can both go about our respective duties.'

Esme found Helena in one of the hospital tents, lying beside her sole surviving daughter. Both were suffering from enteric fever.

Helena recognised Esme, but she spoke with great difficulty. 'Tobias . . . where's Tobias? You got him there safely? He's all right . . .?' The questions came out in a painful whisper.

Esme's eyes burned and she would not trust her voice. She nodded.

A look of pure joy came to Helena's face. 'Thank you. Thank you, Esme . . . You're a . . . good girl. Christiaan will have someone waiting for him now . . .'

She turned her head in an attempt to look at the child lying in the crook of her arm. 'Will you see if Mary needs anything? She's so cold . . . If only we had a fire . . .'

Esme leaned over the small girl. When she had entered the tent she had thought the child was sleeping. Now she saw she was dead.

Esme had brought her own blanket in with her. She unrolled it and laid the blanket over mother and child. 'There. That will warm you both.'

'You're a good sister, Esme . . . The best of the lot.'

Esme stumbled from the tent blinded by tears and ran into Nat and Predikant Maritz.

'Esme! What's the matter, child. Is something wrong with your sister . . .?'

Esme nodded and turned away, but Nat put out his arm to stop her running away. The next moment she was sobbing in his arms.

Momentarily resting a hand on her head, the Predikant said softly to Nat, 'I'm glad she's found someone at last . . .' Then he ducked inside the hospital tent.

Nat held Esme for a long time, occasionally smoothing her hair, or talking softly to her until the sobs began to subside.

Predikant Maritz had just called to Esme as Thomasina and her escort came towards the tent. Thomasina saw Esme free herself from Nat's arms, and when she reached him she asked, 'Have I interrupted something?' Her manner was decidedly chilly. 'I would hardly have thought this was either the time or the place . . .'

'Esme's found her sister. She's either dead or dying.'

'Oh!' Thomasina put a hand on Nat's arm. 'I'm sorry. It's this camp. I've never known such unmitigated horror. What can we do?'

Predikant Maritz emerged from the tent. Behind him, before the flap fell back into place, Nat could see Esme kneeling beside two still forms covered by a blanket.

'First we must get some food. Predikant, there is a *takhaaren* commando operating somewhere in this area. Do you have any idea where it might be?'

'I've no doubt I can find it if it's essential. Why?'

Predikant Maritz knew of Nat's reputation as a British army scout. He would give no information away.

'They are the only men I know who can kill enough game to feed everyone here – but we need to have it quickly.'

'Bring it here? It's only a small commando and you have fifty British troops guarding the camp. We're at war . . .'

'Leave that to me. You ride off and find the *takhaaren*. Tell them to shoot anything that's edible and bring it here quickly. If its safe for them to come in I'll have white flags flying over the camp.'

'It's a short-term solution only. Tomorrow they will be hungry again, what then? We can't maintain an unofficial truce permanently. Keeping it would prove too much of a strain for both sides.'

'Thomasina can solve that problem. If she will write a telegraph message to Lord Dudley asking him to close the camp and transfer the women and children to Mafeking, one of the troops can ride to Rustenburg and wait for a reply.'

'I have already made up my mind to demand the closure of this camp,' declared Thomasina. 'It's a shameful affront to human dignity.'

'Then we're agreed. Let's go and find that lieutenant.'

The British officer was reluctant to sanction a truce without approval from higher authority, but Nat and the Predikant argued that any delay would mean more deaths from starvation and ultimately prove more embarrassing to the British than a truce. Eventually it was Thomasina's telegraph message that won the day.

In her bold, clear handwriting, she wrote, *'To Lord Henry Dudley British High Commission Cape Town stop necessary to close Piendorp Camp immediately to safeguard lives and reputation of British government stop Request urgent repeat urgent transfer of inmates to Mafeking be authorised stop awaiting your reply stop Thomasina Vincent.'*

Within an hour a soldier was galloping towards Rustenburg and Predikant Paul Maritz was riding north into the hills. Meanwhile, at the camp two wagons were broken up to provide fuel for the cooking-fires for the game it was hoped the commando would bring in.

While all this was going on Helena and Mary Botha were lowered into a shroudless grave, someone having stolen the blanket with which Esme had covered them.

CHAPTER FORTY-SEVEN

The *takhaaren* commando rode up to the concentration camp cautiously, in spite of the conspicuous white cloth flags flying above the camp and the welcoming cheers of those children not yet afflicted by the dual onslaught of typhoid and measles. Rifles were very much in evidence. Even those burghers with dead animals slung across the saddle in front of them carried a gun at the ready. In the van was Predikant Maritz.

His revolver holster removed from his belt, the British lieutenant walked self-consciously from the camp beside Nat when the Boer horses were pulled up a hundred yards short of the camp.

'There are no armed men in the camp.' Nat spoke in Afrikaans. 'This is the officer in charge of the camp guard.'

'Where are his soldiers?' one of the *takhaaren* asked suspiciously.

'Half are unarmed in the camp to help distribute food. The remainder will remain in their own camp with their guns.'

The Boers murmured angrily at this news and Nat added hurriedly, 'Just keep your men away from them and they'll stay in their own camp. You have my word for it.'

This had been the lieutenant's sole condition for agreeing to the unorthodox cease-fire. It ensured that he had armed men near at hand should the Boers break the truce. It also safeguarded his weapons.

'I'll vouch for his word.' Predikant Maritz rode forward and shook Nat's hand in a gesture of friendship, made for the sake of the nervous *takhaaren*.

'I'll second that, Uiys. My brother is nothing if not truthful.

In fact, he's everything that I'm not.'

'Adam!' Nat strode past the Boer leader and reached up to clasp his brother's hand. 'Esme told me you'd joined up with a *takhaaren* commando. I'd no idea it was this one.'

'You're here with Esme?' Adam grinned. 'That's cosy for you both.'

'Spare her your humour, Adam. She's lost her sister and the whole of the sister's family. But there are others you'll want to see here . . . and Lucas too.' Nat shook hands with Lucas, who sat his horse beside Adam. 'Johanna's here, and her mother.'

'Johanna . . .? Where?'

'You'll find her soon enough. Let Lucas see them first. You help me get these carcasses in here. There are people in this camp who haven't eaten for days.'

The reunion of the two brothers allayed the suspicions of the wary *takhaaren* and they rode up to the camp where the animals they had killed were slung to the ground and seized upon eagerly by the women.

Soon the wagon-wood fires were roaring and the unfamiliar aroma of roasting meat rose in the air. By dusk the first of the meat was being served and rich meat stew was being taken off to feed women and children too weak to join the fireside revelry.

Drinks were going the rounds too. Good Cape brandy was taken from the saddlebags of the *takhaaren* commando, filched, Nat suspected, from the supply convoy waylaid on the road from Rustenburg.

Everywhere he looked, Nat saw *takhaaren* and British soldiers eating and talking together, sharing the brandy bottles and toasting each other in mutually unintelligible good humour.

Thomasina was not in the camp. She accepted that the *takhaaren* commando could save the women and children but she did not approve of the fraternisation between British soldier and Boer. She had removed herself to the nearby army camp where the British lieutenant had placed a wagon at her disposal.

It was not only the soldiers who were fraternising with the *takhaaren*. Nat saw more than one young fighting-man wander off into the darkness with his arm about the waist of an Afrikaner girl. No doubt Paul Maritz saw it too, but tonight the Predikant was allowing the lusts of the flesh to pass unchallenged. Many Boer women and children would survive a few days longer, thanks to these tough, coarse and unsophisticated men from the Zoutpansberg. A little 'gratitude' was in order – in whatever form it might take.

One of the couples who slipped away from the fireside, believing themselves to be unobserved, was Adam and Johanna. Nat wondered whether *Ouma* Viljoen would have been as understanding as the Predikant had she been alive.

After a while, Nat realised he had not seen Esme for some time. She had left the fireside with a bowl of soup for one of the sick orphans who still occupied the tent where Helena had died. She should have returned by now.

Nat made his way to the hospital tent. It was illuminated inside by a single candle and as he approached he was startled to see an indistinct shadow thrown on to the canvas wall. Suddenly the shadow split and became two and Nat realised a struggle was going on inside the tent. He threw back the flap in time to see a heavily-bearded *takhaar* strike Esme with the back of his hand and knock her to the ground. On the floor to one side of them two terrified young children lay watching the drama.

As the *takhaar* made for Esme again, Nat shouted and stepped inside the tent.

'Go away, *ruineck*. This is none of your business.'

Instead of replying, Nat hit the *takhaar*. The man's beard absorbed much of the force of the punch, but it forced him to take a couple of backward paces. He was not hurt, however, and came back at Nat with a rush. Nat's answer was to hit him twice this time, once in the face, the second time a glancing blow that landed behind the other man's ear and sent him stumbling to one knee.

When the *takhaar* rose to his feet the candlelight glinted on the blade of a knife held in the man's hand.

Esme saw it too and, as Nat took a cautious step backwards, she shouted, 'Out of my way, Nat. Let me get a shot at him.'

She shouted the order in Afrikaans and the *takhaar* did not wait for Nat to obey her. Turning quickly he fled from the tent.

'Damn!' Esme reached beneath her skirts and the revolver

disappeared from view. 'I should have shot him. That man's trouble.'

'You know him?'

Esme was on her knees beside the children, assuring them that all was well. Looking over her shoulder at Nat, she said, 'We met once before. I shot off two of his fingers on that occasion.'

'I'll go and find him . . .'

As he turned to go, Esme rose to her feet and caught his arm. 'No, it's over now. Leave it. But . . . thank you, Nat. Thank you for helping – and thank you especially for caring . . .'

Nat turned back to her, but as they looked at each other a woman came into the tent with a tin mug filled with soup. Like Esme she had remembered the orphans with no mother to attend to their needs.

Joking that if everyone did the same the children would soon be better fed than anyone else in the camp, the woman propped up one of the children and began spooning soup into its mouth.

Outside, Nat paused and wiped a fleck of blood from the corner of Esme's mouth, his finger lingering for a moment on her lips.

'Stay in the firelight, Esme. I smelled drink on the *takhaar*'s breath. With luck he'll drink himself unconscious before the evening's done, but I'd rather you took no chances.'

'Thank you, Nat . . . But you'd better go now. Before your fine lady sees us together again and gets the wrong idea.'

Esme's words took Nat by surprise. Before he could make a suitable reply she had slipped away into the darkness, leaving him alone with his thoughts.

The next morning, when the camaraderie of Boer and British soldier had been replaced by thick heads and voices, more than one young girl was regretting the passion of the previous night. But Johanna had no regrets as she and Adam approached Predikant Maritz and asked him to marry them.

After a serious discussion with the young couple, to which both Nat and Sophia Viljoen were called, the Predikant assented. He was not a man to waste time. With the assembled inmates of the Piendorp concentration camp and the hungover

412

takhaaren commando for his congregation, Predikant Maritz performed one of the most unusual marriage ceremonies of his career.

Despite the surroundings, it was a moving ceremony for all who witnessed it. At the end, Predikant Maritz put a hand on the head of each newly-wed, saying, 'Obey the words of the Lord. Go forth and do his bidding. It is young people like you who hold the future of our country in your hands. Cherish it, even as you cherish one another – and may the Lord be with you both.'

While the camp was still bubbling with excitement over the unexpected wedding, a shout went up that a horseman was approaching. It was the soldier who had been sent to telegraph to Cape Town. In his pocket he carried Lord Henry Dudley's reply, and Thomasina handed it to the British lieutenant to read aloud.

'*Close down Piendorp camp upon receipt stop Refugees to be conveyed to Mafeking stop Proceed via Rustenburg stop Wagons and escort will be sent to meet you stop Dudley.*'

The lieutenant's cheer was as loud as anyone else's. His unexpected term of duty in charge of a concentration camp had been a nightmare, one that would recur in the night hours for many years to come.

The army officer gave orders for the camp to be broken immediately. The sick were to be carried on the wagons, together with the pregnant and old women. The remainder would walk, or be carried on the horses of the soldiers.

The *takhaaren* commando prepared to move off too, and as they saddled their horses Nat suggested that Adam should return with Johanna to Insimo. As Nat had anticipated, Adam refused.

'No, brother. There's still a war to be won here. *You* go home. Tell Ma that I'm a twice-married man now, but that she won't be seeing Johanna until the war is over. You must keep the fatted calf for me until then.'

'Johanna, can't you talk some sense into your new husband? If not, then *you* come back to Insimo. Your mother can come too. Wait the war out there. Thomasina will arrange for your release.'

Johanna shook her head. 'No, Nat. This is our country.

413

Adam and Lucas are fighting for us and Pa is in a prison camp in Pretoria. We'll stay until it's over. One day we'll be proud of our part in all this.'

'It looks as though you'll be travelling alone, brother . . . Although I somehow doubt that.' With this enigmatic remark, Adam shook his brother's hand before going off to say his farewells to Johanna's mother.

Nat was talking to the Predikant when a shadow fell over them. Looking up he saw a *takhaar* sitting his horse and looking down at him. It was the man who had attacked Esme the night before.

'Now I remember where I've seen you before.' The *takhaar*'s voice carried a ring of triumph. 'You were a scout for the *khakis*. You led them after us when we raided Matabeleland. More than half of us were killed because of you . . . my two brothers among them.'

His words brought an angry murmur from the mounted men behind him. Men who scouted for the British army were hated even more than the soldiers who followed after them.

'I came after you because you'd attacked and burned my home, killing my stock and my herdsmen. If it hadn't been for you I would never have become involved in this war. I'd have stayed in Matabeleland, minding my own business.'

'You killed my brothers. In the Zoutpansberg we have our own law. *Voortrekker* law. It means we take care of our own, the way the Bible tells it. "An eye for an eye. Tooth for a tooth".' There was a click from the *takhaar*'s rifle as it came down and lined up on Nat from the Boer's hip.

The gunshot made many of the children in the camp jump. An expression of surprise crossed the mounted *takhaar*'s face before the rifle slipped from his grasp and he pitched forward from the saddle.

Ramming another cartridge home in the magazine of his rifle, Adam strode forward and stood before Uiys Groebler, leader of the *takhaaren* commando. 'You heard it from his own lips, Uiys. *Voortrekker* law comes from the Bible – but there's more than one saying there. Mine is that "I am my brother's keeper". Should I have stood back and watched him killed?'

The *takhaaren* leader looked down at his dead comrade in

silence for some minutes. Then he said, 'He never did have room for more than one thought at a time in his head.'

To Nat, the *takhaaren* leader said, 'I will be obliged if you will bury him.' Then the *takhaaren* leader turned away and waved for his men to follow him.

Adam grinned down at Nat. 'Go home, brother. You're a babe out here on the veld. Go back to Insimo where you belong – and tell Ma I still remember my Bible. It will please her.'

CHAPTER FORTY-EIGHT

When they reached Rustenburg Esme announced she would be returning to Pretoria with Predikant Maritz. The announcement took Nat by surprise.

'Why? You ask me why?'

Esme bristled indignantly when Nat asked her the reason for her decision. She looked tired, as though she had not slept well during the two nights they had spent on the road from Piendorp. 'Do you think I should spend the remainder of the war in a concentration camp?'

'No . . .' Nat grappled with the thoughts that were only half-formed in his mind. 'I . . . I was hoping you might like to come to Insimo, with me.'

Now it was Esme's turn to be surprised. 'It's a kind thought, Nat . . . and I'm grateful . . .' Esme's glance strayed to where Thomasina was saying goodbye to the British lieutenant. Another officer, a colonel, had been detailed to take the refugees on to Mafeking. 'But I don't think it would work.'

'I would like you to come, Esme.'

Her face showed her indecision for some moments, then she leaned forward and kissed him quickly. 'Goodbye, Nat.'

Turning away, Esme hurried to where Predikant Maritz stood with their two horses.

While Thomasina was talking to the lieutenant she had been watching the scene between Nat and Esme. Now she walked quickly to where Nat stood gazing after Esme.

'Did I hear Esme saying goodbye to you?'

'Yes. She's going to Pretoria with Predikant Maritz.'

'Really? How fortuitous. I intend going that way and

travelling on the Pretoria line to Cape Town. The lieutenant has just been telling me it's a much safer journey than travelling on the line from Mafeking. It seems we are all saying farewell to you, Nat. I am afraid it is something I have never been very good at doing. Goodbye, my dear. When one day you come to England you must stay with Henry and me.'

She kissed Nat with considerably more warmth than Esme had displayed, then she walked to where Predikant Maritz was helping Esme to the saddle of her horse.

'Predikant Maritz, I am so sorry to trouble you, but do you think you could wait until I obtain a horse and a Cape cart? I would like to accompany you to Pretoria.'

Esme had turned away when Thomasina approached. Now she swung around again. 'Pretoria? I thought you were going to Mafeking?'

'No, my dear. One visit to Mafeking in a lifetime is quite sufficient.'.

'But what about Nat . . . and Insimo?'

'Nat and Insimo? I don't doubt they will prosper together. Personally, I can't wait to return to England with Lord Henry Dudley. Did you know Lord Dudley and I are to be married? The wedding may possibly take place in Cape Town, although I hope to persuade him to wait until we reach England . . .'

Esme was not listening. She was looking to where Nat was disconsolately walking his horse towards the wagons containing the Boer women and children.

Esme left the Predikant and Thomasina without saying a word. Her eyes were on Nat. As she rode towards him her thoughts were of Insimo . . . and a new future.

EPILOGUE

The war between Great Britain and the two Boer republics of Transvaal and Orange Free State came to an end shortly before midnight on Saturday, 31st May, 1902.

Both Nat and Adam Retallick survived the war, Adam and Johanna settling on the Viljoen farm in the Lichtenburg district, whilst Nat guided Insimo to increasing prosperity.

Others were less fortunate. Lucas Viljoen was shot from his saddle and killed only two days after his sister's wedding. His father, Cornelius Viljoen, lived only long enough to hear that his country had surrendered. He died, apparently of a heart attack, the next day.

Gezima Coetzee, sister of the unfortunate Margret, met and married a Scots soldier in Johannesburg, returning to Scotland with him when the war came to an end.

Measured against modern warfare, the Anglo-Boer war was small. Yet during the course of the conflict more than 400,000 British and colonial troops passed through the ports of South Africa. Of these, some 22,000 found a lasting resting place in the soil of this beautiful but turbulent land, two-thirds of them dying from disease.

The Boers lost about 4,000 men in the field. Those who were maimed, and those who died of their wounds later, went uncounted, as did the many men, women and children whose bleached bones became one with the veld.

The concentration camps killed many more. It is estimated that 20,000 women and children failed to survive the rigours of internment. The spectre of these camps generated a bitterness that lingers in southern Africa to this day.

South Africa regained self-government within only a few years of the hard-fought Anglo-Boer war, but the final link with Great Britain was not broken until South Africa left the British Commonwealth in 1961. It is a young country. A raw country. A country where the bitter harvest of history still ripens.